"WHAT'S YOUR CHRISTMAS WISH?"

"This," Nate whispered, slowly bringing his mouth to Kara's. His kiss was light, gentle, and heat pooled deep between her thighs as his mouth opened to hers. His tongue laced with hers, exploring her, bringing her deeper, as he pulled her tight. Kara reached up and wrapped her arms around his neck, letting their bodies fuse together, pressing the length of herself against the hard plane of his chest.

He pulled back slowly, looking into her eyes as a lopsided smile tugged at his mouth.

"And we didn't even need the mistletoe," she whispered.

"What can I say?" Nate said. "This is shaping up to be the best Christmas yet."

"I couldn't agree more," Kara said through a smile, as her lips found his once more.

A Match Made on Main Street

Mistletoe on Main Street

Also by Olivia Miles:

Mistletoe on Main Street
A Match Made on Main Street
Hope Springs on Main Street
Love Blooms on Main Street

~CHRISTMAS~ COMES TO MAIN STREET

Book 5
in the Briar Creek Series

OLIVIA MILES

FOREVER

NEW YORK   BOSTON

Copyright © 2016 by Megan Leavell
Excerpt from *One Week to the Wedding* copyright © 2016 by Megan Leavell

Cover images © Shutterstock
Cover design by Elizabeth Turner
Cover copyright © 2016 by Hachette Book Group, Inc.

Forever
Hachette Book Group
1290 Avenue of the Americas
New York, NY 10104
forever-romance.com
twitter.com/foreverromance

First Edition: September 2016

Forever is an imprint of Grand Central Publishing.
The Forever name and logo are trademarks of Hachette Book Group, Inc.

The publisher is not responsible for websites (or their content) that are not owned by the publisher.

The Hachette Speakers Bureau provides a wide range of authors for speaking events. To find out more, go to www.hachettespeakersbureau.com or call (866) 376-6591.

ISBNs: 978-1-4555-6718-8 (mass market), 978-1-4555-6719-5 (ebook)

Printed in the United States of America

OPM

10 9 8 7 6 5 4 3 2 1

To Avery

Acknowledgments

I'd like to thank my editor, Michele Bidelspach, for her insight and enthusiasm, and for helping me to make this book the best it could be. No one understands my characters or this series better, and I'm forever grateful to have her dependable ear when I need it. I'd also like to thank my agent, Paige Wheeler, for her support and perseverance and for helping to make this book possible.

Thank you to my copyeditor, Lori Paximadis; my production editor, Carolyn Kurek; and everyone at Grand Central who had a part in bringing this story to life.

Special thanks as always to my friends and family who continue to cheer me on. And of course, thank you to my readers for welcoming my characters and for spending a little time in a fictional town that has started to feel like home to me.

CHRISTMAS
COMES TO
MAIN STREET

CHAPTER 1

The wind whipped down Main Street, stirring up gusts of snow that swirled and danced in the glow of the lamplights and landed on the fresh spruce wreaths secured to each post by a red velvet ribbon. Inside Sugar and Spice, the air was warm and fragrant, the music low but festive, and the mood positively cheerful.

Well, mostly cheerful.

Each morning, when Kara Hastings tied on her crisp cotton apron and started her first batch of cookies for the day, she felt energized and excited, but by the time dusk fell, she struggled to remember what she had been thinking, starting her own bakery right before the holiday rush.

Nonsense. This is what she had wanted! A cookie business all her own. Days spent in the kitchen, creating new flavors and taste-testing samples. But hours upon hours on her feet were taking a toll and oh, how she longed to snuggle under her warm duvet, pop in a Christmas movie, maybe pour a little eggnog, and—

Nope. No time for that. Not when she planned to get a head start on her gingerbread house kits tonight. Her sister-in-law Grace had offered to sell some at Main Street Books, and Briar Creek's first annual Holiday Bazaar was just days away. Kara had envisioned dozens of gingerbread kits, all wrapped and ready for sale, tied with a big satin bow, and trays upon trays of cookies in every shape and flavor.

Kara eyed her display case with a critical eye. She'd nearly sold out again, and she'd box up the rest for a late-night snack, if she didn't collapse into bed before she had a chance to pop the top. She frowned, thinking of the nightmare she'd had last night where she spilled the flour canister and couldn't find any more to replace it, and then she'd mixed the sugar with the salt... And then people stopped coming by and she had to close the business.

It was just what they all assumed would happen, Kara thought as she bit into a chewy oatmeal cookie. It tasted sweet and buttery with hints of cinnamon and spice. Her father's favorite, she recalled, conjuring up a murky memory of mixing dough with him in the kitchen. He didn't cook, and he was lousy at cleaning up, but he loved making cookies with his three children, especially at Christmas.

Kara smiled sadly to herself when she thought of her dad. It was because of him that she had this place and because of him that she worked as hard as she did to make it a success.

She swallowed the last bite of cookie, wiped her hands on her apron, and looked up at the ceiling. "Oatmeal spice. Just for you, Dad."

She turned the sign on the front door to CLOSED and marched back to the kitchen, just in time for the oven buzzer to alert her that the latest batch of gingerbread was ready. Sliding on her red ticking stripe oven mitts, she pulled the tray from the oven and began carefully transferring each piece of gingerbread to the cooling rack.

One down... four to go, she calculated as she popped the

next sheet into the oven and set the timer, stifling a yawn with the back of her hand. Even with the multiple ovens, she'd be here for another couple of hours. She made a mug of peppermint hot chocolate and took a seat at one of the small tables in the storefront to work on the decoration part of her kits: clear plastic tubes filled with colorful sprinkles, packets of glistening gumdrops and other candies, and an instruction sheet she'd designed herself, complete with stamps of little gingerbread men dancing their way down the paper.

A knock on the door startled her and caused her to spill some candies on the floor. It wasn't the first time she'd had to shoo away a last-minute customer hoping to pick up a quick item for a holiday party or school event. Flustered, she looked up to see her sister Molly waving through the glass, her hand covered in a thick red mitten that was nearly the same color as her nose. Kara hurried to unlock the door and let her in.

"I didn't think you were coming back until tomorrow!" she said excitedly. She could still feel the chill on her sister's wool coat when they hugged.

"I decided to come back a day early." Molly grinned at her as she pulled back. Her blue eyes lit up as she looked around the room. "Wow, you've done a lot with this place since the last time I saw it."

It was true. In the three months since she'd signed the lease, Kara had gradually added to the shop, slowly bringing it to life. For the holiday season, she'd decorated with a candy cane theme, focusing on glittering red and pink ornaments that went nicely with her pink and white logo. Most customers picked up cookies to take home, but a few liked to stay and enjoy them. This made her nervous at first, but she was yet to hear a complaint, and now she looked forward to the company.

Someday she'd like to hire an assistant, someone to manage the storefront while she did the baking in the kitchen. But for now, until she could afford it, she was on her own.

In every possible way, she thought a bit sadly. One by one her friends and family members were pairing off, getting married, and she...well, she was still waiting for Mr. Right, even if she'd long ago stopped looking.

She shook away the thought. She was getting sentimental. The holidays were good for doing that. It was too easy to notice all the couples cozily holding hands as they walked down Main Street or shared a cookie in her shop, arguing over which one to try. Too easy to then notice how quiet her apartment was, night after night.

She supposed she should be grateful she was so busy. She was almost too busy to notice. Almost.

"I guess that's what I get for not coming home for Thanksgiving." Molly flashed a rueful smile and brushed past Kara to the glass display case, which was mostly cleared out by this hour. Snow still rested on her red knit hat as she shook her head and bent down to admire one of Kara's newest Christmas offerings. "These gingerbread houses are too cute. Such detail!"

Kara grinned. She took special care in making sure each one was unique. It kept things interesting, and also helped her to challenge herself. She was learning as she went, experimenting, really, and she had a long road in front of her. Hopefully.

"Will you make me one?" Molly asked, turning to give her a hope-filled smile, and Kara burst out laughing. The youngest of the three siblings, Molly had never been shy to ask for what she wanted. But this was one time Kara was putting her foot down. Time was getting away from her, and the holiday demands were more stressful than she'd prepared herself for. Even if some of it, like the gingerbread houses, was of her own doing.

"If I have any left over after Christmas, then yes, you can have one." The chances of it weren't likely, though. She'd originally made this one for her counter, just for decoration, but the reaction she'd had from the customers had opened up a new possibility, and a whole lot of work to boot. She was now selling at least a few a day, in addition to her kits and cookie sales.

"Maybe you can set one aside for me," Molly suggested.

Again, Kara laughed, though this time, she was less amused. "Nice try. Come on back to the kitchen. You can help me roll out dough."

"Okay, but I can't stay for long. Mom is expecting me in time for dinner."

"So you told her you were coming in a day early and not me?" Kara stopped at the marble counter and stared at her sister, who stood in the doorway to the kitchen, still wrapped up in her scarf.

"I tried calling you." Molly plucked a cookie from a tray but hesitated as she brought it to her mouth. "Can I?"

Kara waved her hand through the air. The shop was closed now; no use letting things go to waste, and that one was a little burned around the edges, which was why it hadn't gone out with the rest. "Yes, go ahead." She pulled a plastic-wrapped ball of dough from the fridge and brought it over to the center island, sighing when she thought of the work ahead.

"Didn't you get my messages?" Molly asked, licking the crumbs from her fingers.

Kara coated the counter surface with flour and did the same with her rolling pin. "I saw you called, but no, I'm sorry, I didn't have time to listen to the messages." She hadn't even had time to eat lunch, unless you counted nine cookies around three o'clock to be a square meal.

"Well, can you take off early to come to dinner? Luke and Grace will be there, too," Molly said, referring to their brother and his wife.

Kara sighed. She hated letting the people in her family down, but lately, she didn't seem to have much choice. "Can I take a rain check?"

Molly's face fell and for a moment Kara saw a flash of that five-year-old girl who had a way of getting the last piece of cake, even though it was left over from Kara's birthday. She quickly did the math, estimating the number of hours she had left tonight. She supposed she could slip out to dinner, then come back, work until about two-thirty, then get a few hours of sleep before being back at six tomorrow...She blinked. What was she thinking?

"I'm sorry, Molly, but I didn't know you were coming back early, and I have about four more hours of work here before I'm done for the night."

"Can't it wait?" Molly pressed. "I just got home!"

Kara felt her shoulders sag. She only saw her sister a few times a year, and she would love nothing more than to lock up and reconnect over a glass of wine. "I'm sorry, but no."

"Oh, fine."

From the corner of her eye, Kara could see Molly's exaggerated pout. *Don't give in. If you give in, you'll be here all night.* Besides, even if she did slip out for a bit, she'd hardly be able to enjoy herself, worrying about all the work she still had to do.

"I just couldn't wait to see everyone and share my news," Molly said casually, playing with the fringe on her scarf.

Kara stopped rolling the dough. It was another well-practiced tactic of her sister's, and this time it worked.

"What's the news?" she asked, wiping a loose strand of hair from her forehead with the back of her hand.

Molly's smile turned sly as her blue eyes began to gleam. "I'm engaged!" she squealed, jumping up and down. Stepping toward Kara, she plucked her other mitten free and fluttered her fingers in front of Kara's face, showing off a huge diamond ring.

Kara stared in stunned silence, trying to take in the overwhelming amount of information coming at her all at once. She knew her sister was looking for a reaction, for Kara to be jumping up and down with her, squealing right along, but her mind was spinning, and the ring was flashing, catching the bright overhead lights, and all she could manage was, "To *who*?"

Molly's eyes widened. "To my boyfriend, of course." She took a step back, her shoulders slumping. "Todd."

"Todd." Kara nodded slowly. "I thought you two broke up last year."

Molly dismissed this statement with a wave of her hand. "Oh, I wouldn't say we broke up. We were just taking a break."

Given the tear-filled midnight phone calls, the chocolate Kara sent via overnight post when Molly insisted it would make her feel better, the trip Kara had taken to Boston to wallow with her pale sister in a bed that hadn't been made in weeks, Kara would stand to disagree with Molly's hindsight view of that time in her life, but she said nothing, because what could she say?

"Congratulations," she said, shaking away her confusion. She smiled a little wider. "Congratulations, honey!"

"Hopefully the rest of the family will be more excited for me than you are," Molly said, quickly shoving her hands back into her mittens.

Kara took a step toward her sister and set her hand on her shoulder. "You caught me by surprise, that's all. I had no idea you two were even back together. But I'm happy for you, Molly. Honestly I am."

Molly smiled. "I knew I could count on you. And that's why I want you to be my maid of honor."

"Me?" It was the obvious choice, given that they were sisters, but Kara was still trying to process the fact that her sister was getting married at all. Her younger sister. Married. Deep down she'd always thought she'd be next in line, even though she hadn't dated in... forever. Who was there to date in Briar Creek? Childhood friends? That didn't sit right somehow. And the handful of dating experiences she'd had over the years with men from neighboring towns hadn't lasted more than a matter of months, and none had made her heart soar the way she thought it should.

"I'm thinking winter. Valentine's Day. Won't that be romantic?"

That was two months away. "So soon?"

"Why wait?" Molly looked at her quizzically. "Anyway, we'll have lots to go over while I'm in town. Guest lists. Wedding dress shopping. Flowers... I'm depending on you, Kara. Please say you'll help me!"

"Considering you write for a bridal magazine, I doubt I can be much help," Kara began.

"But it wouldn't be any fun without you," Molly replied, wiggling her eyebrows playfully.

Kara looked into her sister's pleading gaze and tried to ignore the knot of panic that had formed deep in her gut and the sirens that were going off in her head reminding her of everything she had to do and how little time she had to do it.

The oven. That wasn't a siren. That sound was the buzzer going off.

Kara hurried to grab her oven mitts, but by the time she had flung open the door, she could see she was just a minute too late. The edges of the gingerbread were dark, and nothing could be done to salvage them. She'd have to redo the batch.

Kara dropped the tray onto the counter and willed herself not to cry. It was just exhaustion taking over, making her emotional. Making her think about throwing in not just the towel but the oven mitts, too.

Beside her, Molly was still waiting for a response, her eyes wide and earnest, her smile so bright that Kara felt ashamed of herself for even feeding into her own problems. Her sister was getting married. Her only sister. If the roles were reversed, wouldn't she be shouting it from the rooftops, wanting Molly to match her enthusiasm?

"I can't think of a better way to spend the holidays," Kara said through a desperate smile, and she was immediately rewarded with a whoop of delight and a long, hard hug.

"Thank you, thank you!" Molly cried. She pulled her hat back on her head, talking quickly. "I'll call you tomorrow. Or stop by. Or maybe I'll stop by tonight. If I'm not too tired. Oh, this is going to be so much fun!" She clapped her hands, the sound muted through the thick wool, and then shook two clenched fists in front of her to underscore her joy before turning and disappearing through the kitchen door, leaving Kara alone once more.

Kara stared at the ball of gingerbread dough, still waiting to be rolled out, and sighed. Christmas had just become a little crazier.

It was past ten by the time Nate Griffin pulled to a stop in front of the white mansion across from a snow-covered town square. He sat in his car, tense from the drive, and took a few minutes to decompress before he dared to knock on those front doors. Or did one just let themselves into a B&B? Not one to patronize small-town inns, he wasn't sure of proper etiquette. He'd knock, he decided, though no doubt his aunt was already staring out the window, tapping her foot, wondering what was taking him so long.

No good deed, he thought, dragging out a sigh. He'd thought he was off the hook for the holidays this year. And yet here he was. In Briar Creek. For the next two weeks.

And Briar Creek loved Christmas. At least, that's what his aunt had told him when he announced his visit. The poor woman probably thought she was selling him on something, when all she was doing was making him wonder again why he'd sent his parents on that Mediterranean cruise, so carefully planned, booked specifically for the season as a Christmas gift—to both his parents and himself. It was the perfect coup, until his father had to go and suggest he spend the holiday with Aunt Maggie, because they couldn't bear the thought of either of them being alone...

He'd tried to point out that Maggie never spent Christmas with them anyway. Christmases were spent as just the three of them, year after year after year. But then his mother had pointed out that this year they had intended to spend it at her inn in Briar Creek, and oh, she'd be so disappointed. And she had that hernia after all. And she really was looking forward to it. And oh, Briar Creek was such a charming town...

Charming indeed. Dead was more like it. On his drive through town—if you could even call it that—the lights were out in every storefront he passed, even the few restaurants. Only one light glowed in the otherwise empty stretch—from a bakery.

He had half a mind to stop in, bring his aunt a gift. Then he remembered how picky she was about her food and decided against it.

No good deed, he thought again.

He roved his gaze over to the town square, illuminated by the twinkling white lights wrapped around the center gazebo. Fresh snow glistened, conjuring up every travel-book image he'd formed of Briar Creek at Christmastime, and he felt his spirits lift a bit.

He was just grouchy and tired from the drive from Boston. It had been a long week. Hell, it had been a long year. The break would do him good, and so would a change of scenery. He'd kick back in an armchair, catch up on emails, and prep for the big meeting he had next month. The time would fly by...

Nate killed the ignition, and there was an almost immediate hint of chill in the car. Grabbing his duffel bag from the passenger seat and deciding to come back for the rest tomorrow, he pushed out of the car and walked up the salt-sprinkled cobblestone path to the inn. Two identical wreaths made from red berries hung on the black-painted double doors, and from the windows that framed them, he saw a shadow cut through the golden light. Before he could even reach for the door handle, the door swung open, and there stood his aunt Maggie, looking even more festive than the Christmas tree in his office lobby.

"Ho, ho, ho!" she sang, grinning so wide, Nate felt an immediate pang of guilt for the less-than-generous thoughts that had plagued him for the duration of his two-hundred-mile drive.

"Aunt Maggie." He smiled warmly, taking in the familiar lines of her face, which had grown deeper since the last time he'd seen her. He was suddenly aware of how much time he'd let pass, and seeing how much his visit meant to her, he felt a wave of shame he couldn't put in check.

"Come here and give your old aunt a hug," she ordered,

and pulled him in. One of her dangling, glittery, reindeer-shaped earrings caught his scarf, and Nate wrestled with Rudolph's flashing nose as Maggie giggled, her head bent as she waited to be freed.

"I see you have a matching sweater," he said once he had untangled himself.

Maggie patted the reindeer on her stomach and adjusted her flashing earrings. "Women like to accessorize. You'd have known that already if you'd settle down and find a nice girl."

And so it began...

"I made you dinner," his aunt said as she ushered him into the sitting area of a lobby. Sure enough, there was a steaming pot pie on a plate and a glass of milk. His favorite meal as a kid. He was touched that she remembered, even though he'd kill for a beer.

He didn't bother to mention that he'd already eaten after work. She'd gone to great effort, and he was never one to turn down a home-cooked meal. They didn't come often. Though perhaps if he visited his parents a little more often, they might.

Guilt churned in his gut, but there wasn't any time to dwell on it, not when his aunt was looking at him so pertly, her hands folded patiently in front of her, her green eyes wide, waiting for a reaction.

"This looks delicious," he said honestly. "Thank you."

He shrugged out of his coat, eager to relax and settle in, even if he still felt a little uneasy about being here at all. The flames flickered in the hearth and the lobby was quiet. He didn't know what he'd been expecting. More guests perhaps? A bar? But then this was an inn, not a hotel, and above all, it was his aunt's home.

Maggie brushed the snow from the shoulders of the thick

wool before hanging it on a rack near the front vestibule. Nate took the time to look around. He had only visited the inn a few times, and he'd been too young then to form a clear image. Now he was impressed with what he saw. The lobby was tastefully furnished in a traditional but lived-in style, impeccably clean and modestly decorated for the holidays. Fresh garland was wrapped around the banister of the winding stairs, and an arrangement of red, white, and green flowers was set on the polished cherrywood check-in desk. It was clear that his aunt took pride in the place, and no doubt people paid a pretty penny to stay the weekend. The ski resorts weren't far, he knew, though he'd only picked up skiing in recent years and didn't get to the mountains much. But people liked country getaways. Some people.

"You're looking a bit thin," Maggie said as she came to sit across from him near the crackling fire. "Tell me. What do you normally cook?"

He was hardly thin, but Maggie liked to fret, and he decided to humor her. She eyed the fork, and so he picked it up, happy he'd done so when he brought the bite of pie to his mouth. Rich, buttery, and creamy. Just like he remembered.

"I don't cook, Aunt Maggie," he said, grinning. He didn't need to meet her eye to sense the disapproving pinch of her lips. "That's what microwaves are for."

"Microwaves!" She tossed her hands in the air and shook her head. "Well, good thing I've got you for a couple weeks. You'll be fattened up by the new year."

Nate paused as he brought another forkful of pot pie to his mouth, recalling the six o'clock trip to the gym he'd put in that morning. There was no telling how much butter and cream had gone into this thing—enough to undo forty-five minutes on the treadmill, that much was for sure.

He opened his mouth, savoring every bite. This was a

vacation—sort of—and people were supposed to indulge a bit on vacations. He eyed the milk, wondering if he could ask for a glass of wine at least.

"Drink up," Maggie said, noticing.

Nate grimaced. "I think I'll pass," he said.

"I understand." His aunt winked. "It's late. You don't want to have an accident in the middle of the night."

Nate choked on the last bite of his pie. "What? Aunt Maggie, I'm thirty-two years old."

But she just gave an innocent shrug. "So? Why don't I show you to your room? I'd love nothing more than to sit and chat with you all night, but it's late and I have to be up at four to start breakfast."

Nate frowned as he pushed himself off the couch. His aunt was in her early seventies, older than his parents by a handful of years. She'd never had any children, and her husband—his father's brother—had died years back, leaving her alone to run this inn. He thought of what his parents had told him, the concerns they'd had for Maggie's health, and hesitated.

"Why don't I make breakfast tomorrow and give you a chance to sleep in?"

She stared at him blankly before bursting into a roar of laughter. "My dear boy, I appreciate the gesture, but it's the one meal I offer here, and, if I do say, I'm known for my breakfasts, and I wouldn't want to let my guests down…" She patted his arm and gave a little smile.

Nate opened his mouth to protest but then decided to drop it. He'd already admitted he couldn't cook, at least not from scratch, and the last thing he wanted to do was cause trouble for his aunt by upsetting the guests … and something told him they wouldn't appreciate his scrambled eggs with buttered toast, which was about as far as things went with his culinary skills.

"But I'd like to help while I'm here," he pressed.

A look of interest passed over her face. "I'll remember that," she said mysteriously.

Nate picked up his duffel bag and flung it over his shoulder. From the gleam in his aunt's eye, he had the unnerving suspicion she had plans for him while he was in town, and he couldn't begin to imagine what they entailed.

CHAPTER 2

Good morning, sleepyhead. Rise and shine!"

Nate frowned as the soft voice lulled him from his sleep, and he resisted the urge to pull the duvet over his head and roll over. He became all at once aware of a strange bed, a firm mattress, flannel sheets, and a warm pillow.

And someone in his room.

He popped his eyes open to see Maggie sitting cozily on the edge of his bed, smiling serenely down at him. "You looked so peaceful," she whispered loudly. "I almost didn't have the heart to wake you."

Yet she had. Nate blinked away the fogginess of a good night's sleep, trying to orient himself with his surroundings. The room was dim, and just a bit of early light poked through the edge of the curtains that were tightly drawn across each of the four windows. His aunt had put him in a corner room—"best in the house!"—but he hadn't properly looked at it until now. He ran a hand through his hair and started to sit up, until he remembered he wasn't wearing a shirt. "What time is it?" he asked, pulling the blankets a little closer.

"Six forty-five," Maggie said matter-of-factly. She gave his leg a little pat over the comforter. "Up and at 'em. You don't want to miss breakfast."

"Six-forty—" He blinked and dropped back onto the pillow, staring at the ceiling. Yep. No good deed. He was used to getting up early, hitting the gym before work, but the drive last night through heavy snow had left him tired, and though he was loath to admit it, the bed was ridiculously comfortable. He certainly couldn't complain about the accommodations. The wake-up call, however . . .

"I made peppermint scones this morning. Always popular with the guests," his aunt continued as she walked to each window and pulled open the long curtains. Sunlight hit him square between the eyes and he squinted, holding up a hand. "The croissants tend to go quickly. I set one aside for you, just in case you didn't make it down in time."

"Thank you," Nate managed, even as it occurred to him that he had most definitely locked his guest room door last night and that his aunt had taken the liberty of letting herself in with one of the keys that hung from a ring hooked to her apron belt. He'd have to set some ground rules with her— later, once he was properly attired.

"Breakfast starts at seven, runs until nine, but I figured you'd want to get an early start on the day. There's so much to see and do in Briar Creek, after all!"

From his drive through town last night, Nate highly doubted that but managed a polite smile while he waited for her to finally leave his room. Briar Creek was his aunt's home after all, and she was clearly very proud of that fact.

"Well, I'll leave you to it," Maggie said as she walked to the door. She paused as she set a hand on the knob. "Still hard to believe my little Nate has chest hair! Where does the time go?" She shook her head in disbelief and let herself out, seemingly unaware of the groan Nate emitted as he sunk fully under the weight of the covers.

He counted to ten and then flung off the blankets, hoping she wouldn't surprise him with another visit while he was in the shower. Unsettled, he ran the taps and jumped in, eyes darting while he washed his hair at record speed, and he sighed with relief when he finally wrapped a towel around his waist.

Still, he took far less time than usual in selecting his clothes for the day, not that he'd bothered to bring much with him from Boston. There were no meetings to go to. No suits required. It felt odd, and empty, as if he was forgetting something, when in fact he was just living like so many others did at this time of year. Taking a step back. Enjoying the holidays.

He resisted the urge to check his email before heading down to breakfast and, after careful deliberation, left his phone on the nightstand, telling himself that nothing was so urgent it couldn't wait and that this was his vacation, technically.

His aunt was settled in the big dining room, chatting with guests, when Nate came downstairs at twenty past seven. Over her green sweater and black pants, she wore an apron covered with a holly and ivy print. The plates anchoring the buffet table donned a painted picture of a Christmas tree, and carols played from somewhere in the distance. Even though breakfast had just started, he was surprised to notice that the basket of croissants was indeed picked over, and several tables were already filled.

"Most of the guests are heading up to the mountain shortly," his aunt said as he helped himself to a cup of coffee from the carafe. "The bus arrives at quarter to eight to shuttle them. I don't mind if you want to go skiing with them."

"Maybe another time," Nate said. "Today I thought I'd hang out with you. Maybe walk around town a bit." Maybe buy a padlock for his guest room...

His aunt's face lit up. "Oh, you should definitely get out and explore, especially with the fresh snowfall we had last night! Why it's simply a winter wonderland out there! Certainly nothing like you have in Boston," she was sure to add, pinching her lips.

"We have snow in Boston," he assured her, taking a sip of his coffee. It was smooth and rich and exactly what he needed at this hour. He was still groggy, still in a state of disbelief that he was here at all. He should be en route to the office right now.

He couldn't shake the feeling that he was playing hooky.

"Yes, but *dirty* snow! City snow is always so *messy*. It's the soot and the smog and..." She shuddered. "Once you've been to Briar Creek, you start seeing things a little differently."

Unlike himself, who had been born and raised in Boston, his aunt was a Briar Creek native. This inn was her family's house, and when his uncle married her, he settled into it with her. Nate and his parents had visited a few times but not regularly. There wasn't much opportunity for a vacation growing up, even if the accommodations were free of charge. "It's good to know you're so happy here," he said diplomatically, taking a croissant from the basket.

"I think you will be, too. If you just give it a chance." His aunt winked and then, turning to another guest, began chatting enthusiastically about the condition of the ski slopes thanks to all the fresh powder.

Nate took the opportunity to grab a muffin and hurry back to his room, where he worked for the next few hours preparing for a big meeting he had scheduled for the first week of January. At the management consultant firm where he worked, his colleagues were always taking advantage of their allotted time off, coming back with tans and stories of trips abroad. It didn't bother Nate. He'd been working for so long and so hard that he didn't know how to stop. Didn't want to stop. Didn't want to think of what would happen if he took a step back. Not a day went by that he didn't feel lucky for what he had, and the thought of losing it felt all too real.

By midmorning, he'd cleared out his inbox and decided to get some air. The Main Street B&B was technically just off Main, but the north end of its grounds extended to the corner of Briar Creek's downtown—*If you could call it that*, Nate thought. Nate tucked his hands into his pockets, happy he'd managed to slip away before Maggie noticed he was missing gloves, and quickened his pace through the biting wind. In the light of day, the town did seem more alive, and shoppers filled the sidewalks, ducking in and out of shops that were outfitted for the season with more than just a wreath on the door. His aunt was certainly correct that Briar Creek was a winter wonderland. Every lamppost was wrapped in garland or ribbon, and even the fire hydrants were capped with Santa hats. It was almost enough to get him into the Christmas spirit. Almost.

A crowd was gathered around the shop window at the next corner, and Nate paused to see what the hype was about. Of course, he realized, scowling to himself. A toy store, decked out for the season with strands of lights, tinsel, and enough toys to make dozens of children *ooh* and *aah*. He'd been one of those kids. Once. Until he'd learned that Christmas wasn't the same for everyone and that Santa didn't always visit, no matter how nice you'd been.

Turning from the window before his mood completely plummeted, he felt the impact of a soft wool coat, felt a whip of silky hair in his face, and heard a woman's dismayed cry as several packages fell to the ground.

Startling, Nate blinked, trying to digest what had just happened. A woman was already bent over reaching for the boxes, and Nate stooped to help, reaching for a white cardboard box tied with red ribbon that had landed facedown on the snowy sidewalk.

"I'm sorry, I—" He hesitated, distracted for a moment by the flash of bright blue eyes that snapped to his, contrasted against dark hair that fell at the woman's shoulders. She couldn't have been much younger than him, and the distress in her gaze told him that no further apology would help matters. Nate held out the white box he'd picked up from the salted sidewalk and brushed off the snow. The contents of the box rattled ominously. "I'm sorry, I didn't see you there. Is it—broken?" But the answer was obvious.

Still, the girl opened the box, her shoulders dropping as she inspected the contents. "Oh my God!" she groaned, and, to his horror, tears filled her eyes as she looked back at him.

Quickly, he reached into his back pocket for his wallet and began fumbling through the bills. "Here, let me reimburse you."

But the girl just waved his money away. "No, it won't help." She stared despondently at the box, her nose turning pink.

"But you just bought it," he insisted, holding out what he hoped was enough money.

"It can't be replaced. Not easily, at least." She pinched her pretty red lips as a flush spread over her cheeks. "It's something I—Oh, never mind."

Frustration coursed through him, and, finally, he shoved the cash back into his wallet. No doubt a special order, and probably a Christmas gift. "I didn't mean to crash into you. I'm genuinely sorry."

The girl nodded miserably, staring down at the box, her lashes fluttering as she blinked away the tears. Nate sighed and shoved his hands into his pockets, his mind racing.

"Let me make it up to you," he tried again, and she slid her eyes slowly up to his, shaking her head.

"Next time watch where you're going," she said suddenly. "You could have knocked me over. Or one of these kids." She motioned to the group of youngsters near the toy store window who had barely noticed the exchange; they were too busy mentally adding to their lists for Santa.

Nate took a step back, surprised at her sudden burst of anger. She was clearly upset by whatever was broken, and maybe he was to blame. "Tell me what I can do to fix this."

The girl pinched her lips and, to his surprise, dropped the white box into the nearest trash can. "You've done enough," she said, and, swooping up her remaining shopping bags, hurried away, her red knit scarf trailing behind her.

Nate watched her for a few blocks and then turned, shaking his head. And people wondered why he hated Christmas.

Kara knew that crying over broken cookies was right up there with crying over spilled milk, but she couldn't help it. She was *exhausted*, and the thought of making another three dozen snowflake cookies for the inn—before tea time!— was enough to make her march back to the bakery and hang the CLOSED sign on the door. For good.

Bells jingled as she pushed open the door of Main Street Books. She stomped the snow off her boots on the mat as her sister-in-law finished ringing up a customer. Sweet cinnamon bread and fresh coffee wafted from the adjacent café, but it did little to lift her spirits.

"Why so glum?" Grace asked as she came around the counter.

"Some tourist just crashed into me on my way here and he...he broke my cookies." *Not just some tourist, though*, she thought. *More like a really hot tourist*. A face she'd certainly never seen before. Her heart sped up when she thought of that square jaw, the crinkle of concern at the corners of his deep-set eyes. That mouth.

Then she thought of the cookies. Crumbled and cracked, after she'd worked so hard on making them just so. God knew Mrs. Griffin inspected each and every one. Fresh tears sprung to her eyes, but any concern she had that she was being wholly ridiculous vanished when Grace's expression crumbled and she pulled Kara in for a much needed hug.

"Were they for a delivery?" Grace asked when she let her go.

Kara nodded slowly. "For Main Street Bed and Breakfast. Mrs. Griffin is going to kill me!"

Grace didn't argue with that. Mrs. Griffin was a strong-minded businesswoman and a difficult person to please. She had high standards, ones Kara clearly wasn't going to live up to today. She could just imagine the passing comment to her mother...

"Have you told her yet?"

"No." Kara sighed and set the bag of—fortunately undamaged—gingerbread house kits on the counter. "But I have to tell her. She expected those for tea today."

"You go call her while I set up these adorable kits. I've decided to place them on some of the higher shelves in the children's corner, lest little hands get curious." She winked, and taking the bag, she disappeared to the back of the store.

Kara pulled her phone from her pocket and stared at the screen, thinking of the way she'd behaved on the sidewalk. Normally around a guy who looked like that she'd be all flush-faced and flustered. Instead, she'd been so upset that she could only react to her disappointment, not to that smooth voice or the tingle that she felt when his coat brushed her arm.

She'd been hard on that guy. Rude, really, and that wasn't like her. Neither was skipping out on her own sister's engagement announcement dinner. The stress was getting to her, bringing out a side of her that she didn't like and making her feel even more unsettled than usual. It was Christmastime, after all. It was supposed to be a season of happiness and cheer. Here she was, making Christmas treats night and day and not enjoying the season at all.

Today that would change. And if she saw the man again, she'd apologize. Chances were, though, he was already on his way to the slopes for a day of skiing. The fresh snowfall last night no doubt made for excellent powder on what could be a very icy terrain. But in a town as small as Briar Creek, she'd be bound to see him again eventually. The thought of it was a little bit thrilling, even if he had broken her cookies.

Leaning against the counter, Kara punched in the number for the inn and held her breath, waiting for Mrs. Griffin's familiar singsong voice.

"What do you mean the cookies are gone?" she exclaimed when Kara told her what had happened in one long burst of information. "But my guests! They'll be wanting Christmas cookies with their hot chocolate and Earl Grey!"

Kara winced. "I understand, and I'm so sorry. I had them all ready," she added. They'd been perfect, each cream cheese sugar cookie cut and baked into a snowflake shape and then decorated with royal icing and sanding sugar until it sparkled. She prided herself on each one being slightly different from the next, since no two snowflakes were alike. "I'm afraid there's going to be a delay."

"Well, I'd like them within the hour," Mrs. Griffin said, as if that was that.

"An hour?" Kara blinked, happy that her regular client wasn't there to see her distress. Mrs. Griffin loved to bake, and she wasn't shy about boasting about it, either. Kara had appreciated the business the innkeeper had given her, knowing that Mrs. Griffin could just as easily have made her own cookies for her daily holiday tea. Now she realized that perhaps the woman hadn't done it out of pure charity or simple support, but because she actually needed Kara's input. Three dozen cookies wouldn't take long to bake, but decorating them took time. "No problem," Kara sighed, and ended the call.

"I have to get back to the bakery," she told Grace as her sister-in-law came back to the front of the store.

"Already? I was hoping we could have a cup of coffee. Molly told us the good news last night. At least, I *think* it's good news." The women exchanged a glance.

"I know," Kara said, frowning. "I was a little confused by it myself. Last I heard, Todd had broken things off last year and started dating someone else."

"Well, it seems like he's had a change of heart." Grace shrugged, but the raise of her eyebrows told Kara she was equally unconvinced. "You sure you can't stay for a coffee?"

"I wish." Kara tightened her scarf around her neck. "But I have to redo the cookies for Mrs. Griffin and get them over to her before tea. That sounds nice, doesn't it? High tea? A carefree afternoon with a tray of finger foods and a hot toddy . . ." She smiled wistfully.

"You deserve a break," Grace said warmly.

"After the holidays," Kara said. The familiar twinge of worry tightened her stomach as she pulled her hat down a little tighter. After the holidays there was bound to be a downturn in activity. She wouldn't need to worry about the daily Christmas cookies for the inn anymore, and her gym was offering a New Year's discount for new members. People indulged during the holidays. After...Well, she'd cross that bridge when she came to it. For now it just cemented the fact that she'd better make the most of this busy time instead of complaining about it.

"I'll see you at the Christmas Bazaar then?" Grace held open the door as Kara stepped out onto the icy front step. It had started to snow again, and the wind was picking up. The cold air helped to clear her head and push back the panic she felt at the mere mention of the bazaar. She'd been looking so forward to it, and it would be her own fault if she wasn't able to enjoy it.

"If not before," Kara said, and turned to hurry back up Main Street to her bakery, scanning the streets and shop windows for any sign of the man who had crashed into her earlier. She'd been so surprised, and so upset, that most of it had passed in a blur, but now she seemed to recall a wide grin that crinkled clear hazel eyes, a strong square jaw, and a straight nose.

She'd know him if she saw him again, and suddenly she was rather hoping she would. So that she could apologize...and maybe see if he was sticking around town for the holidays.

CHAPTER
3

The Main Street Bed and Breakfast was one of the most beautiful buildings in all of Briar Creek. Ever since she was a little girl, Kara had admired it, especially at Christmastime, when Mr. Griffin hung a pine wreath from each window and door and set candles on each sill. It was classic New England in architecture, a large white Colonial with black shutters and a double door with brass hardware, and the Griffins had been meticulous about its upkeep, adhering to its historical registry status and making it one of the most attractive country inns in the entire state of Vermont.

Clutching the box of cookies to her chest, Kara stomped her boots on the rug inside the inn's warm vestibule and looked around the lobby, cozily outfitted for the holiday with a tree, garland, and a crackling fireplace. A few guests lingered in armchairs, reading books and sipping mugs of steaming hot cocoa, but Mrs. Griffin was obviously busy elsewhere in the inn.

Kara poked her head into the dining room, where sure enough, Mrs. Griffin was assembling tiered trays for the afternoon Christmas tea she offered each December. Kara had enjoyed it a few times over the years with her mother, sister, and aunt Sharon, and she'd been honored to be an integral part of it this year. Not only was it sentimental, but also several guests took her card or placed an order before they left town.

"There you are!" Mrs. Griffin turned and wiped her hands on her red and white apron. "Just in time."

Relief caused Kara to breathe a little easier as she stepped deeper into the room. "Three dozen snowflakes." She smiled as she handed over the box. As she did every day, Mrs. Griffin popped the lid and inspected the contents. It never stopped being a bit unnerving.

"These look perfect," Mrs. Griffin said, but before Kara could celebrate that small victory, she remarked, "But I hope I don't have to wait until five minutes before tea to have them next time."

Knowing it was no use to explain the accident again, Kara just nodded. "It won't happen again."

"Good. I know you're still new to this, but part of making a business a success is keeping your word and delivering the highest-quality product at all times. If you're going to continue running the business—"

Kara stepped back at the blow. "Of course I'm going to continue running the bakery. It's my business. I've signed a lease. Why wouldn't I?" But she knew why. Because she'd quit everything else before it, and everyone knew. She bit back on her teeth, willing herself not to get too fired up or defensive. After all, there was truth in the woman's words, even if the truth hurt.

Mrs. Griffin just gave her a placating look. "Well, it's important to keep the customer satisfied. That's my advice."

Kara continued to nod, more wearily, and considered that she had made a perfect product the first time around and that it wasn't really her fault that her efforts had been crushed, literally. "It's just that—"

Mrs. Griffin held up a hand. "Customers don't want to hear the excuses, my dear. They just want to be satisfied. And they don't want to hear what it took to get to that point. The work goes on behind the scenes. The outcome is for the public."

Kara sighed. "I had them ready but—"

"It was my fault," a deep voice behind her cut in.

Kara turned in surprise, coming face-to-face with the stranger from the sidewalk. He gave her a sheepish grin, but his hazel eyes were sharp, if not a bit hard, and Kara felt her cheeks heat with more than just embarrassment. She shifted the weight on her feet and stood a little straighter, trying to redeem her first impression but knowing it was probably no use.

She should have considered he'd be a guest at the inn. She opened her mouth to apologize for her earlier outburst, suddenly a little nervous to talk to this handsome stranger, but Mrs. Griffin interrupted. "What do you mean, your fault? You've met?"

The man slid a glance to her, cocking an eyebrow in a devilish way that felt intimate and personal, as if they were in on a secret together, and Kara felt her insides do a little dance. He was taller than she remembered, with broad shoulders and nut-brown hair and a smile that probably made many women stop to take a second look.

"I wouldn't exactly say we've met. I bumped into her on the street, and I'm afraid I crushed the cookies." He turned to look at her full-on, and Kara dropped her gaze to his full lips as his mouth curved into a hint of a smile. He was probably a very good kisser, she realized with a start. "Cookies, eh?"

"That's right," Kara said a little defensively. Okay, she had better lose the edge, unless she wanted to turn off the cutest thing that had hit Briar Creek since her mother's next-door neighbor got a puppy last summer.

His eyes roamed over her lazily before he glanced at the innkeeper once more. "It was my fault, Aunt Maggie."

Aunt Maggie? Kara frowned, recalling at once the endless comments Mrs. Griffin was always making about her elusive nephew, often resulting in subtle eye rolls between the single women of Briar Creek. She never tired of boasting about his successes. The good college. The good job. The new car. The good looks. Kara had just assumed, as they all had, that Mrs. Griffin was exaggerating the thick brown hair, the piercing deep-set gaze, the hundred-watt grin. If anything, she hadn't done the man justice.

Kara blinked at him, trying to remember all the stories she'd drowned out over time. Baltimore, was it? No, Boston. Something with business—Mrs. Griffin had been sure to mention his MBA a few times.

She licked her lips and reached up to pull off her thick knit hat with the oversized pom-pom. She could only hope her hair wasn't standing on end from static. "So...you're the nephew."

"You say it like you know something I don't," the man remarked in amusement. "I'm Nate," he said, outstretching his hand as his grin turned a little friendlier.

"Kara," she muttered in return, trying to unlock herself from those golden eyes. His hand was warm and smooth and his grip was firm and not exactly fleeting. She waited for him to drop his arm and then pushed the smile from her lips as she grazed her thumb over her fingers, still feeling the tingle from his touch. She forced her attention to Mrs. Griffin, who was watching the exchange with unabashed interest.

"Well, how nice that you two already met," Mrs. Griffin said coyly, all mention of the reason for it now forgotten. "Nate's in town for the holidays."

"From Boston?" Kara asked. When his gaze narrowed in suspicion, she added, "Your aunt is very proud of you."

Nate gave a grin to cover his overt embarrassment, but Mrs. Griffin just stepped forward and proclaimed, "And why shouldn't I be proud of my handsome nephew?" She waggled her eyebrows at Kara. "He has an MBA, you know."

Kara glanced at Nate, who was shaking his head, looking mortified. She resisted the urge to point out that, yes, she did know, suspecting it would only make things worse for Nate. "Impressive."

"Indeed!" Maggie declared.

"Aunt Maggie," Nate groaned. "I don't think Kara needs to hear my résumé. She probably has work to do, and aren't your guests eager for their tea?"

Mrs. Griffin waved a hand through the air. "Oh, they can wait a minute…"

"I should really get back to work, too," Kara said reluctantly. It wasn't often that handsome nephews rolled through town, and it had been too long since her body had responded the way it did to Nate's charm. She thought of how nice it would be to stay and chat, to get to know this new face a little better. But then she felt the familiar weight on her shoulders and the ticking of the clock that made her pulse kick with each passing second. She had many more cookies to bake if she had any hope of leaving at a decent hour tonight. Besides, Nate was unfortunately right—Mrs. Griffin had guests to attend to. "My sister's in town, too, actually," she said to Mrs. Griffin as she slowly made her way to the door, stealing another glance in Nate's direction, her heart speeding up when she caught his eye.

"Staying with your mother?" Mrs. Griffin inquired smoothly, but there was a sudden light in her eyes that made Kara pause. "Is your mother, um..." The innkeeper stopped to fiddle with a napkin on a nearby table before slanting Kara a glance. "Is she entering the contest this year?"

For a moment, Kara frowned, and then she remembered. Briar Creek's annual event, the Holiday House contest. Wow, the holidays really were under way, and she was holed up in her kitchen while it almost passed her by.

"I suppose," she admitted, feeling again like a bad daughter. She hadn't been to her mother's house since Thanksgiving, hadn't even driven that way, but now with Molly in town, she would have to carve out more time. Or manage her time better. Something. The familiar knot of panic tightened her abdomen.

At least, she thought brightly, her mother couldn't remark that she wasn't working hard enough.

"Mmm." Mrs. Griffin just nodded, but it seemed she had much more to say. "Did she decide on a theme?" Quickly she added, "She always has such creative ideas."

Kara shrugged. Again, she didn't know for sure, but now she seemed to recall her mother mentioning on the phone one night that this year she was going with *The Nutcracker*, as if she wasn't already surrounded by the ballet at her dance studio.

"I think she's doing a *Nutcracker* theme, but don't take my word for it." Kara grinned.

"The Nutcracker!" Mrs. Griffin looked a little pale. "My, that is ambitious. It makes sense, of course, but my... She'll go head-to-head with Kathleen Madison this year, no doubt!"

Grace's mother had won the Holiday House contest for twelve years in a row before she stepped down to become a judge, but she started competing again two Christmases ago, and Mrs. Griffin was correct in her assessment. If you were going to compete with Briar Creek's best interior designer, you had to bring out the big ideas. Perhaps her mother was hoping to win this year…Guess she'd find out next time she visited. *Tonight*, Kara promised to herself. Tonight she would stop by her mother's house, see Molly, and have a proper family dinner like the one she'd missed last night.

"Well, I'll let you get on your way," Mrs. Griffin said almost eagerly as she took Kara by the arm and helped move her toward the lobby.

Confused, Kara glanced back over her shoulder to see an equally bewildered Nate watching her go. He nodded in acknowledgment but didn't offer much of a smile. No doubt he was still upset by how she'd treated him earlier, and she couldn't blame him for that. So much for apologizing to him right now, not with Mrs. Griffin standing guard, soaking in every ounce of their exchange.

She'd just have to wait until tomorrow, when she delivered the next batch of cookies. Suddenly, she was rather looking forward to it.

"Such a pretty girl," Aunt Maggie remarked as she came back into the dining room. She gave Nate a knowing smile. "Single, too."

Nate sighed. Yes, Kara was pretty. Quite pretty. But that wasn't the point. It was as good a time as any to set some boundaries in his personal life. "Aunt Maggie, we need to talk—"

But his aunt just put a hand on his arm and urgently said, "We do."

She settled herself onto a dining chair and pulled one out for Nate. She patted its seat and tipped her head in expectation.

Nate glanced anxiously at the clock on the wall. "Isn't it time for tea?"

"I have more important matters to discuss," his aunt said gravely, and Nate felt the blood fade from his face. Oh my God, she was dying. She was sick, or something. This was why his parents had insisted he come up here for the holidays.

"What's going on?" He swallowed hard as he took the seat next to her. He studied her face as she bit at her lip, her eyes darting back and forth, her brow knit with a frown. He braced himself for the worst. For what she would say. What he would do. He'd have to call the cruise ship, find a way to bring his parents back.

"It's just..." She wrung her hands together fitfully. "It's just that darn Holiday House contest!" she cried.

Nate felt the last of his air escape him in a rush. He stared at his aunt, who appeared on the verge of tears and finally, after what felt like minutes, blinked. "The *what*?"

She looked at him imploringly. "The Holiday House contest! It's Briar Creek's annual event, and this year marks the twenty-fifth celebration! It's a *huge* honor to win. You get a front-page picture in the newspaper." She gave him a look that told him this should summarize the importance, but he just stared at her. "Every year that Kathleen Madison whips up something over-the-top and takes home the grand prize. And it's not just for Christmas, I tell you. You should see her in the fall. The second a leaf starts to turn, she's out there, fiddling with cabbage and kale and mums. Oh, I've tried to start earlier and earlier, but there is no way I am going to put out gourds in August, and so sure enough, every year her house transforms, as if overnight, first for fall, then...for the holidays." She eyed Nate heavily.

This was a lot to take in. Gourds. Kale. Weren't those

things you ate? Nate ran a hand over his face, hedging his response. "So...you want to enter the Holiday House contest?"

His aunt slapped her hands on her knees with such force that Nate jumped. "No, I want to *win* the Holiday House contest! This year marks the first time there will be a grand prize other than the newspaper feature. It's because of the twenty-fifth anniversary, you see. If there is a year to win, this is it!"

Nate glanced into the lobby, where a crowd of guests had now gathered, no doubt wanting their tea. Maggie was oblivious to them as she shook her head miserably, burying her forehead in her hand.

"First prize this year gets a front-page picture in the paper, ten thousand dollars, and—"

"Wow." Nate pulled back against his chair. "Ten thousand dollars? Really?"

His aunt's expression turned triumphant. "And a write-up in a travel magazine. Henry Birch runs the paper now, but he used to write for the magazine. He's arranged it all. Can you imagine what that would do for my business?"

Nate could. He could also see just how much this meant to his aunt. "Why don't you enter then?"

"Oh, but I couldn't do it all on my own." She studied him under the hood of her lids.

Nate shrugged and thought, *What the hell.* What else did he have to do with himself for the next two weeks? "I could help." How hard could it be to add a bit more garland to the front steps or add another Christmas tree in one of the other rooms in the house?

"Oh, you will? But of course you will!" His aunt leaned forward and gave him a good hard squeeze, and Nate sputtered against the force of her arms. "Oh my," she said standing, suddenly noticing her audience. "It's time for tea! Come in, everyone, come in!"

She set two firm hands on Nate's wrist as he pushed in his chair. "We'll talk about this later."

Nate laughed under his breath as he left the room. Crisis averted. His aunt was healthy, and all that silly drama was over a few decorations.

Tea wasn't really his thing, but a cup of coffee right now sounded delicious. He wondered if the bakery where Kara worked served it. Quickly shrugging into his coat, he hurried out the door to find out.

The bakery was farther up Main Street than he recalled from his drive into town. Nate recognized the pink and white striped awning up ahead and lengthened his stride on the icy sidewalk. The lights were on inside, illuminating a glass display case and peppermint-themed decorations, but the sign on the door read CLOSED, and the door, when he tried it, was locked.

Nate stepped back, lingering for a moment to see if Kara appeared from the back door to what he assumed was the kitchen. He glanced down Main Street, but there was no sign of the red winter coat or the glossy dark hair. Disappointed, he stepped back and walked a block until he came to a diner on the corner. It was cold, and the wind was picking up. Deciding it was here or tea at the inn, which was way too hoity-toity for his comfort level, he pushed through the door, immediately rewarded with the sounds of upbeat holiday tunes and chatter from the crowded room. He followed the smell of coffee, feeling a little out of his element in a room full of people who all seemed to know each other so well, but then he perked up when he recognized the girl standing near the counter.

His heart sped up a notch as he moved quicker to the end of the room, noticing the long legs in black pants, the boots that hit just below her knees.

"We meet again," he said, coming up to stand next to Kara.

She turned to him, her blue eyes bright with surprise. Her cheeks were pink from the cold, a stark contrast to her porcelain skin, and it heightened the rosy color of her full lips, which parted into a smile. *Slow down there*, he warned himself. So she was pretty. Wholesome and fresh-faced in a way that made her seem approachable, friendly. Unlike most of the girls he met at bars or through friends or work. It was the small-town thing, he considered. The country air. But there was something else, something different about her than the women he'd met lately. He couldn't help it. He was curious.

"I'm happy to run into you, actually. I owe you an apology for how I behaved earlier."

Nate held up a hand. "Consider us even. You did have to face the wrath of Maggie Griffin on account of me."

Kara smiled. "Oh, she's not so bad."

No, she wasn't. Intense, yes. A little nutty, sure. But she'd been good to him all his life, even though he didn't see her much. Good to his parents, too. Even though Maggie wasn't a blood relative, she was his family. He liked that Kara didn't misunderstand her more difficult side.

He leaned in, close enough to catch a hint of her sweet scent. Vanilla and sugar and something he couldn't quite put his finger on. "So, uh, now that she's out of earshot, level with me. What has she said?"

"About you?" Kara's blue eyes twinkled. "You mean other than your MBA?" She laughed, and he joined her. "Oh, all good things, Nate. All good things."

He liked the way she said his name, casually, as if they

were old friends. He didn't have many of those. Growing up, he didn't have the time. And now he had even less of it.

"Here you go, hon," a woman said as she slid a paper cup to Kara. "And what'll it be?" the woman asked Nate.

"Just a coffee," he said, turning over a mug.

"Aunt Sharon, this is Nate Griffin," Kara began to explain.

"Maggie's nephew!" the woman behind the counter exclaimed. Her eyes roamed his face in wonder as she held out her hand. "Pleasure to finally meet this man we've heard so much about."

"All good things, Kara has assured me," he muttered, internally rolling his eyes at whatever perfect and probably half-false image of himself his aunt had given over the years.

"Oh, of course." Sharon grinned. "Well, except…" Seeing the horror that flashed across his face, she leaned over the counter and patted his arm. "Just joking with you. Coffee it is. On the house."

"Thanks," Nate said, feeling a little humbled. So many people knew about him, and he couldn't say the same. He didn't keep in touch with his aunt, at least not directly. His parents called her and relayed information to him, but that was it. He glanced over his shoulder at the groups of people who seemed to know each other so well, and for a moment he started to realize why his aunt loved this town so much. It was a community. Something he'd never had, or at least not something he'd ever been embraced by. "So, do you know everyone who works here?" he asked Kara when Sharon had moved on to the next customer.

"Well, Sharon's my aunt. And she owns the place. And I tend to come in here about four times a day for a refill. And some company," she added, her cheeks pinking a bit more.

"But don't you own a bakery?" Nate asked.

Kara ripped open the tops of two sweetener packets and stirred their contents into her cup. "Yep."

He frowned, confused at her simple response. "And you don't sell coffee there?"

She blinked a few times, seeming taken aback by the question. "Well, it's a cookie bakery, really. I just make cookies."

Nate shrugged. "So?"

She pressed the lid onto her cup and turned to him, clutching her coffee with two hands. "So, I make cookies. People come in for cookies."

Nate stared at her, confused. "Yes, but don't people want something to drink with their cookies? Coffee seems like the natural choice. Or tea." Hot chocolate. Something. He tipped his head. "If you serve coffee, they may stay and linger, have an extra cookie. It might seem like small change, but the orders can add up, and so could the revenue."

Now her face was as red as her coat. Her chin was lifted, her arms crossed, and her gaze hard. "I'm doing just fine, thank you."

"Yes, but one small change could make a big difference."

Kara began gathering her handbag. "Perhaps. Now if you'll excuse me, I have to get back to work."

"I didn't mean to offend you," Nate said, reaching out a hand to stop her. "I was just trying to help. It seemed like the obvious combination. Cookies and coffee. Cookies and tea…" He grinned, but she didn't even meet him halfway.

"Well, we can't all have MBAs, can we?" Kara asked brusquely. She waved to her aunt as the woman poured his coffee, and before he could register what had just happened, she was walking through the door.

"Cream and sugar?" Sharon asked as Nate dropped onto a stool.

"Sure," he said absentmindedly.

Sharon slid him the bowl. "You should check out the bakery on your way back to the inn. Best cookies in town!"

Nate grunted a response and brought the mug to his lips. Something told him stopping by the bakery wasn't such a good idea today, but he'd find out what time Kara planned to bring over the inn's delivery tomorrow. And he'd be waiting.

CHAPTER 4

Molly flicked through a tabloid she'd bought at the bus station yesterday afternoon and tossed it to the side. She'd hoped the glossy cover with the promise of celebrity gossip would distract her from this growing knot in her stomach, but all it had done was make her restless and agitated.

She should have known there would be questions last night when she'd made the big announcement, hoping she sounded more convinced than she felt. But of course everyone wanted to know where Todd was, would he be joining them for the holidays? And she had to go and lie and tell them he was working over the holidays—a big case and all—and chivalrous guy that he was, he'd told her to go ahead and enjoy a few weeks in her hometown.

The truth was that Todd was enjoying a few weeks of his own, on a ski trip in the Alps with his buddies. A trip she'd encouraged him to take. A trip she'd pushed for, even when he'd suggested joining her in Briar Creek instead. She'd told him he deserved a little fun, that absence would make the heart grow fonder. But so far, their time apart was only making her second-guess her future more than ever before.

Molly tossed the magazine across the bed and frowned. Honestly, this was crazy talk! Todd was everything she'd dreamed of when she was a little girl. Everything she pictured when she wrote her monthly article for the bridal magazine. Tall, dark, dashing...He was perfect, really.

Just as perfect as the three-carat brilliant-cut stone on a platinum band she now wore on her left hand ever since the day she'd picked it out, with his input of course, even if his contribution had been more of the reaching for the credit card variety.

Molly twisted the engagement ring on her finger. She had to admit, it was pretty, and she did like wearing it, but when she looked at it, all she saw was a nice piece of jewelry, hardly the sentiment she should be feeling right now. Hardly the sentiment of a blushing bride-to-be.

She pulled another magazine from the stack, hoping this would do the trick, trying to visualize herself walking down the aisle, committing to Todd forever.

She closed her eyes, but the image did not come, at least not easily. And her stomach started that twisting, queasy, nauseous churn it did every time she thought about what she was doing. Was she really going to go through with this?

She shook her head. Of course she was. So they'd had problems. So he hadn't been the most faithful early in their relationship. Yes, he'd taken a year away. But then he'd realized he missed her. Decided that she was the one. That he couldn't live without her. Those were his words! He couldn't live without her.

Once she had thought she couldn't live without him. But now...

She closed her eyes and replayed his words from the day he came back to her, proposed to her...It was so unexpected. So shocking. She'd dreamed of that moment, never thinking it would happen, and then there he was. Apologizing. Promising. It *was* really romantic when she stopped to think about it...

She hurried through the last few pages of the magazine. She just had cold feet. A common problem with their readers...One she could recognize and expertly handle.

Molly shut the magazines into a drawer and threw herself back down against the pillows, staring up at the ceiling. It was only late afternoon, but it was already dark. She hated this time of year. It made her tired long before it should, and she still had things to do before her mother got home from the dance studio. She'd promised to get the giant nutcrackers set up in the front hall, anchoring the front door, and then one character per stair, all the way up to the landing, so the judges would have a "feast for the eyes" when they entered the house. Where her mother had found those dolls, Molly would never know, but they sort of creeped her out, not that she'd tell her mother that. Rosemary Hastings had a vision, and just like with her dance studio, Molly knew better than to argue. Besides, it would keep her busy.

Really, did she not want to marry Todd? Did she want to throw away a candlelit Valentine's Day wedding and all the roses that would go along with it? She'd written on the subject enough times to know that you did not walk away from a handsome man with a summer house and a damn good job, all because your tummy hurt at night when you started thinking about the future and all its unknowns.

She'd have to be a fool to turn down a proposal laced with all those possibilities.

Molly hauled herself out of her bedroom and went down to the front hall, where boxes of decorations were just waiting to be cracked open. Most her mother would want to do herself, to be sure it was done right, but a few things Molly could handle. She started with the creepy dolls, drawing special fascination from the Mouse King, with its beady eyes and scratchy whiskers.

Soon, the toys were arranged as instructed. *Well, that took all of ten minutes,* Molly thought with a frustrated sigh. She peeked into another box, knowing better than to get a start— her mother had very particular ideas, and apparently this year's contest was more important than previous ones. Honestly, Molly wasn't even sure why her mother was bothering. Everyone knew Kathleen Madison was going to win, as she did every year she entered. But who was she to argue...

Besides, if her mother let her help, it would give her something else to focus on. Something other than the fact that Todd, her fiancé, had called twice that morning and she had yet to call him back. He didn't even know that she'd set a date.

A date that was close. A date that didn't allow for doubt.

A date she wasn't sure she could stick to.

The arrogance of that man! Kara was still reeling from her conversation with Nate Griffin—who clearly liked to boast about his MBA as much as his aunt did—when Molly pushed through the bakery doors.

The storefront was quiet. Only a group of mothers and toddlers sat near the corner, and they'd be leaving soon. The youngest boy had already dropped his sugar cookie to the floor and then stomped all over it during a tantrum. Kara was eager to sweep up the mess and get back to the kitchen. She had four gingerbread kits to finish before she could go home, and she also needed to work on the finished houses she'd be selling at the Holiday Bazaar.

"I was going to stop by the house for dinner tonight," Kara said. "Unless you'd rather grab a bite together."

Molly rolled her eyes. "Mom needs my help for the Holiday House contest. Fair warning, if you come by, she'll put you to work."

The thought of doing more work on her night off made her almost want to come up with an excuse, but Kara just shrugged her shoulders. It would be fun to help decorate the house. It might help put her in the Christmas spirit, and she did want to spend more time with her sister before she went back to Boston.

Boston. Just thinking about the city made her think of Nate. Nate with his big degree and his even bigger opinions.

She'd switched majors four times. She'd switched jobs plenty more times than that.

She lowered her voice and leaned across the counter to Molly. "Do you think I should be selling coffee?"

Molly looked confused. "You mean you don't?"

"I guess I just assumed everyone in town got their coffee at the Annex. I mean, I do." Kara sighed, thinking of Main Street Books' café. They sold coffee. And tea. And all sorts of food items. Okay, so she was messing up. Just as she had feared. She'd been open for over a month and she was selling cookies and milk and nothing else to drink. And she made a mean hot chocolate. What had she been thinking?

It was an oversight. A big one. She'd been so focused on her cookies and the decorations, she'd overlooked the obvious.

Dread coated her chest like an icy bath. She could picture the shop, boarded up, the awning faded, the sign taken down, the FOR LEASE sign in the window right where her candy cane decorations now hung, sparkling against the setting sun. She could picture her mother, Mrs. Griffin, even Nate, that know-it-all, walking by, shaking their heads, saying yep, they knew it, no surprise there. It was just a matter of time, after all.

Well, that cemented it. Tomorrow morning she'd be offering coffee. And tea. And hot chocolate. With a candy cane tucked to the side for good measure.

She'd get mugs made up with her logo, too. For now, she'd have to borrow some from her mother's house. And hope they didn't break. And hope her mother didn't ask questions, like why she didn't have her own mugs yet and why, so long after opening, had she only just begun to offer beverages?

The group in the corner finally left, and Kara picked up her broom and dustpan and walked over to the table. "Mind turning the sign on the door?" she asked her sister as she began cleaning the mess. "I doubt anyone else will be stopping in before I officially close in five minutes."

She needed some time to think, to focus on her baking, doing what she loved. She needed to get Mrs. Griffin's arrogant nephew out of her head...every last bit of him, down to that cocky grin and those perfect teeth. He'd probably be Molly's type—she loved the preppy, well-bred look—if she wasn't already engaged to Todd. Molly liked the city guys, but then Molly had always been more confident. Maybe it was because she was the baby, always doted on and told she was cute, whereas Kara had always floated, a little unsure, wary of her role as eldest daughter under their mother's somewhat critical eye. Rosemary Hastings had a strong personality, and she wasn't shy with her opinions.

Not unlike someone else Kara knew...Oh, how she dreaded the thought of delivering those cookies to the inn tomorrow. She bent to pick up the crumbs with the dustpan, trying to recall how long Mr. MBA planned to stick around town.

"Hey, you busy tomorrow?" Kara asked Molly.

Molly shrugged. "Not especially. But please don't tell Mom that. She'll put me to work on the decorations again, and you know I won't do it right."

Kara gave a little smile. "She obviously has a vision."

"You should have seen her trying to pry the information out of Grace last night, to see what her mother is planning. We all know Kathleen will win. I'm not sure why Mom is even trying."

"Because it's fun for her. And because she loves it." Kara knew their mother could be competitive, but the ballet studio's performance of *The Nutcracker* was far more important to her than the version she had going on at the house. "It's a way to get into the spirit of the season."

"I suppose." Molly didn't look convinced. "Anyway, what did you have in mind?"

"I was wondering if you could do some deliveries for me tomorrow. I'll pay you."

Molly's blue eyes softened. "No payment required. That's what sisters are for. Besides, I owe you a bit of my time if you're going to be helping me so much."

Kara led them into the kitchen and deposited the crumbs in the trash bin. "You sure you won't be busy with wedding planning?"

"Oh." Molly turned away, falling silent for a moment. "You know me...I've had my wedding planned for years. I was just waiting for the right guy to come along and fulfill the fantasy." Her laugh seemed a little hollow.

Considering that Molly was in the wedding industry, it made sense, Kara thought as she washed her hands and dried them on a towel, but Molly seemed distracted, distant almost. "Are you sure everything is okay?" she ventured, giving her sister a hesitant smile as she leaned against the counter. "I don't mind taking a break if you'd like to talk. We could have some tea? Or hot chocolate? We can even splurge and go for extra whipped cream."

Immediately, Molly smiled, but it didn't seem to quite

meet her eyes. "Of course everything is okay. Why wouldn't it be? I'm engaged. I have a gorgeous ring, a gorgeous fiancé, and I'm going to have a gorgeous wedding. And it's Christmas. What's not to be happy about? Besides, look at how busy you are! I'm here to help *you*, remember?"

Kara tried not to frown as she pulled some dough from the refrigerator and reached for her rolling pin. If Molly said everything was okay, she'd go along with it for now. "So, when is Todd arriving?"

"Oh." Molly looked a little pale. "He's not coming for Christmas. I thought I told you that."

Kara did her best to keep her expression neutral, even though warning bells were going off in her mind. Her sister was uneasy, that much was clear, and Todd wasn't coming for Christmas. There were many things wrong with this picture.

"No, you didn't mention it."

Molly wandered around the kitchen and stopped to pick up a few cookie cutters. "Oh, I thought I did. He's tied up with work. A big case. He has a really important job."

Kara nodded politely, telling herself to stay out of it. If Molly was happy, then she would be happy for her, especially if her decision was already made. And who knew, maybe Todd really was busy with a big case. Maybe he had altruistically insisted that Molly go back to Briar Creek on her own.

Kara highly doubted this.

"You didn't want to stay in the city with him?" she asked.

Molly seemed momentarily stricken. She studied the cookie cutters, then set them down. "Oh, no...He'd be busy at the office the whole time anyway. Besides, we'll have lots of Christmases together. In the future..." She seemed to gulp.

"Well," Kara said, deciding not to press, "Ivy makes the best bouquets. We can go over to Petals on Main together while you're in town."

"Perfect." Molly grinned. "So what about you . . . any men in your life? You know you're welcome to bring a date to my wedding."

Kara gave her sister a long look, but she couldn't deny the pang in her chest when she considered a date on her arm. For some reason she envisioned Nate Griffin. Nonsense!

"Oh, no, I don't have time to date," she said, brushing away the twinge of hurt she felt. She'd never had a serious boyfriend, and the men she'd gone out with off and on over the years never really made her feel that spark. She cut herself some slack; after all, who could really feel something all that magical with the man she'd watched pick his nose all through English class from first through fourth grade, for example?

Kara sighed. There were certainly some limitations to small-town life. Not that she would trade it for the world.

"I just haven't found that spark yet," she clarified, and Molly nodded sagely. Perhaps that was what Molly and Todd had; perhaps it explained everything. They had a spark. She'd heard it was a powerful thing.

"Besides, where would I meet anyone?" *Wasn't that the truth*, Kara thought to herself. Briar Creek was hardly a viable dating pool, and the one man she'd found interesting in years was just passing through town.

She frowned and tried not to let that thought depress her too much. Her friends insisted she should try online dating, and maybe she would. Once she had the business under control. And Nate's all too handsome face out of her head.

"Okay, I won't push it," Molly said, holding up two hands in defense. "But I do think that when Mr. Right comes along, he'll have been worth your wait. Let's just hope that he doesn't take too long." She winked. "Now, where do you need me to deliver these cookies tomorrow?"

"To the inn," Kara said, happy to have dodged that visit for at least one day. But Briar Creek was small, and chances were she'd be running into Nate again before he left town.

This time, she wasn't looking forward to it. Well, not completely...

Maggie was waiting for him in the lobby when Nate returned a few hours after tea had finished. He stomped the snow off his boots and hung his coat on the rack near the door.

"I made dinner for us," Maggie said, taking him by the arm and leading him to the back of the inn, where an addition housed her private quarters. Like the inn itself, it was decorated with traditional furnishings, only unlike the inn, there were no decorations in sight. No tree, he noticed as he entered the small sitting room. No stockings, either. Frowning, he followed her into the kitchen, where, as promised, a roast and potatoes were waiting on the stove.

"I thought we could talk about the Holiday House contest," Maggie said as she plated the food.

"Sure," Nate agreed, taking a seat opposite the head of the small rectangular table. Did his aunt eat here alone night after night, while her guests went to restaurants? The thought of it saddened him. But then, maybe she liked solitude. Maybe, like him, she was too busy to notice or feel the emptiness. "So, what were you thinking? A little tinsel? A tree near the mantel? Some stockings? Maybe some colored lights on the bay window over there?" He gestured to the sitting room, just beyond the kitchen.

Maggie looked at him in overt shock. "Tinsel? *Colored*

lights?" she almost screeched. She began muttering to herself as she crossed the kitchen and took a three-ring binder from a shelf. Instead of bringing him his plate, she set the binder on his place mat with purpose.

Nate stared at the object. "What is this?"

Maggie quietly brought the plates to the table and took her seat. She took her time opening her cloth napkin and setting it in her lap. She took a sip of her wine. "First of all, we'll need a theme. I've envisioned...the twelve days of Christmas."

Nate slid the binder to the side under his aunt's disapproving pinch of the lips. He took a bite of creamy potatoes, all at once recalling her promise to fatten him up for the holidays, and then thought, to hell with it, and took another. She also seemed determined to give him some work to do, so he didn't need to feel guilty about not hitting the gym.

"Are you familiar with the song?" she asked.

"Um. Vaguely," Nate replied. He took another bite of his dinner. It was warm and buttery and delicious. But instead of feeling happy, it brought out a sense of sadness in him, a loss that he didn't like to think about. There weren't enough dinners like this growing up, and the few times there were, they were too cherished to even be fully enjoyed. So rare it was almost impossible not to think of how special they were.

He forced another piece of roast into his mouth. No use going down that path. He ate in the best restaurants now. Could afford the best wine, even if he didn't buy it. And his parents...He'd sent his parents on a cruise.

He couldn't undo the pain of their past. But he could sure as hell make up for it now. And he did. And he would. Forever.

"I seem to recall something about a partridge in a pear tree," he said to his aunt, steering himself back to the present. It was better to stay there, in the current moment, than to dwell on the dark days.

"Well, why don't I remind you?" His aunt set down her fork and began quietly humming before breaking out into song.

Nate felt his jaw slack as her voice croaked on the last line of the first verse, hoping that would be enough, but no, she was going for another round, grinning away, undeterred by an audience. He laughed under his breath for a moment, wondering if this was some sort of joke, his aunt's coy way of getting him into the spirit, but she just narrowed her eyes on him without missing a beat and continued along with the carol.

He tried to keep his expression neutral, but as her voice carried out the long notes, quivering at times the way one might hear in the opera, it took everything in him to force back his smile.

By the fifth verse, he had to bring his fist to his mouth, sinking his teeth into his hand, biting hard enough that he feared he might break the skin, his eyes stinging as his shoulders shook, as his aunt went through all twelve versus.

He could have stopped her at the first—she'd jogged his memory by then, even if she was painfully out of tune—but she seemed to be enjoying herself so much, her voice growing louder and more confident, that he didn't have the heart to hold up a hand.

"Oh, I've brought tears to your eyes." Maggie gave him an indulgent smile as she picked up her fork and knife, her Christmas carol now finished. "You were always such a sensitive boy. It was a shame that you never had any brothers or sisters, but then…"

She trailed off, and Nate was happy she did. He never knew the reason why his parents never had more children, but it was the practical choice, even if not the emotional one. Both of his parents had worked around the clock to keep a roof over their heads. Another child would have been another expense.

God knew what a burden he was at times.

He reached for his tall glass of milk, again wishing it was something stronger. He'd go down to the pub tonight. The walk would clear his head. The drink...perhaps it might lift his spirits. And maybe Kara would be there...Now there was a thought. From what he'd seen, there was only one bar in town. Although, if last night was any indication, she worked well into the night. He liked a strong work ethic. It made her even more appealing.

Deciding to risk exciting his aunt, he took a sip of milk and set the glass down. "So, Kara...does she come by the inn every day?"

As expected, Maggie's green eyes widened and a knowing smirk curved her mouth. "She supplies the cookies for my holiday tea, so yes, she drops by every day in December. She usually comes by in the late morning, in case you're interested."

"I didn't say I was interested," Nate replied. Only he was interested. Very interested. Not just in her pretty face, but in her determination. She stuck up for herself, and he admired that. God knew he could relate to it. Life was tough enough when you backed down, and he'd never been one to do that.

"Pretty girl," his aunt mused, bringing her glass to her lips.

"Hmm." Nate pushed the food around on his plate. "She runs the bakery all on her own, then?"

It was hard to fathom, knowing what he did of the food industry. He'd been asked to consult on a few restaurants, and a strong team was crucial for success and profitability.

A one-woman shop was far from efficient. But then, employ-ees were expensive, and they needed to be properly man-aged, too.

Across the table, his aunt nodded. "She opened it at the beginning of October. Dumped everything she had into the place, too."

Nate raised his eyebrows. A dangerous move, and not one he'd have advised. She looked to be in her late twenties. "She must have scrimped and saved everything she'd ever made then," he remarked.

"Oh no." Maggie shook her head. "Inheritance."

Nate felt his shoulders deflate a little. Of course. He picked up his fork and resumed eating. There was no point discussing Kara or her bakery again. He knew the type of girl she was. Opportunities were handed over, not earned. She didn't know how the other half lived.

Too bad. She was really pretty. But she clearly wasn't the one for him.

CHAPTER 5

Kara stared wearily across the town square to the Main Street Bed and Breakfast, a box of three dozen snowflake cookies clutched in her hands. She cursed under her breath and resumed her walk, saying a silent prayer as she crunched through the snow that she could get in and out without so much as a glimpse of Nate or his cocky grin.

If only Molly had been able to help out, but she'd ended up getting a last-minute appointment at a bridal shop half an hour away, and because Kara felt guilty enough for not being able to break away from the shop to go with her, she'd seen no choice but to tell her sister that of course it was fine, she'd deliver the cookies herself, that it was no big deal, obviously.

Except that it was. And with each step she took that brought her closer to the inn, her heart pounded just a little faster; she was already having internal arguments with Mrs. Griffin's nephew in her head, her defense detailed on a mental list she'd added to as she'd iced each individual cookie.

She hurried past the pond, where skaters were laughing on the ice, and crossed the street to the big white inn, her eyes darting. No sign of him yet, but the lobby would be the true test. Head bent, she jogged up the stairs, almost falling a few times, and, with one last breath for courage, pushed through the front door.

Inside, the air was warm and fragrant and a fire crackled in the hearth. Guests milled about, talking in low voices, but from the swift sweep of her gaze, Nate was not to be seen. Kara slipped into the dining room, which was mercifully empty, and set the box of cookies on the buffet table against the far wall. Mrs. Griffin was often busy with housekeeping or other guest duties when Kara stopped by. No need to linger. Especially not with that smug nephew possibly under the roof.

She hurried back into the lobby and out the front door, gulping the cold air as she giggled to herself. She'd done it. In and out, without an altercation. Now, to just repeat the scenario until Nate went back to Boston, his fancy job, his fancy apartment, and his fancy car...all the results of his fancy degree.

"Careful of the ice!" a voice called out as she ran down the front steps.

Kara felt her stomach drop as she came to a halt, gripping the iron railing. She looked over her shoulder to see Nate coming around the side of the inn, looking even more handsome than she remembered. And it was an image she'd tried to forget. He wore a forest-green sweater under an open charcoal-gray wool jacket, jeans, and boots that must have belonged to Mrs. Griffin's late husband. His hair was tousled, his hazel eyes impossible to read under the hood of his brow, his grin friendly.

Well. Okay, so that was unexpected. And she didn't quite know what to do with it. She could smile back, or she could just wave to acknowledge him and be on her way. But he was cute. And there wasn't anyone else around. It would be rude to just run off...

"Cookies made it all in one piece today?" he asked, grinning a little wider.

Kara narrowed her eyes but then decided to make light of their awkward first encounter. "Since I was able to walk over without being body-slammed, yes." She grinned as she motioned to the pile of logs he carried, wondering why she didn't just turn on her heel and leave then and there, get back to the bakery. God knew she had work to do if she was going to be ready for the bazaar tonight. She told herself it had nothing to do with the fact that he was the sexiest guy to cross the Briar Creek border since... well, ever. She could look. But she couldn't touch. The guy was arrogant. A city boy who thought he was better than them all, more sophisticated, more knowledgeable. "Your aunt put you to work, I see."

He softened a bit, but there was a new edge to his voice when he said, "I don't mind hard work."

Kara held his sharp gaze, wondering why he had grown so defensive. "That makes two of us, then."

"Everyone needs a hobby," he said, shrugging.

Kara tipped her head. "Excuse me?"

"I just meant I admire your efforts," Nate said simply. He wasn't smiling anymore, and she didn't like the way his eyes lazily roamed over her face.

"It's not an effort," she corrected him. "It's a business. And one I need to get back to, if you'll excuse me. Please tell your aunt the cookies are on the console in the dining room."

Honestly! This man may have an MBA and, according to his doting aunt, a Lexus and some fantastic apartment with sweeping skyline views, but one thing he certainly didn't have was any charm. Clearly, Mrs. Griffin's opinion of him was even more biased than she'd always thought. He was handsome; she'd give the innkeeper some credit there. But that's where it stopped.

"Be careful of the ice," Nate cautioned again as she hoisted her tote higher on her shoulder.

She said nothing but kept walking down the brick path, eager to be on her way, anger heating the blood in her veins, making her forget the snow and the wind and the fact that it was winter at all. From the looks of it, the gossip mill had already gotten around to him, regaling him with all her previous failures: the stint at the stationery shop, the week or two at the pub, the whopping six months at the insurance office. He clearly looked down on her. Successful businessman and small-town shopgirl. He didn't need to be such an ass about it.

She lifted her chin, reminding herself he'd be gone soon and that her life in Briar Creek would continue as it always had and that when he came back to visit—if he ever came back to visit—he'd be surprised to see that her bakery doors were still open, her cookies still fresh, and her spirit far from crushed.

He wanted to call her bakery a hobby? She suddenly had an urge to turn Sugar and Spice into a national chain and open one on the corner of the street where he lived.

She smiled at the thought, and she was just getting to the part of imagining his expression when he saw her face on the cover of some national business magazine, when her boots hit something slippery, she felt her legs come out from under her, and the world went into slow motion as she dropped onto her butt, her eyes now level with the boxwood hedges that lined the inn's front path.

Under any other circumstance, she would have yelped. Loudly. But given the knowledge of Nate standing behind her, no doubt watching the entire thing, she'd managed to keep her lips pressed tightly even though pain shot through her tailbone, hot as fire.

"Told you to be careful," he said, approaching, but there was a hint of concern in his voice.

Gritting her teeth against a comeback, Kara struggled to pick herself up, already feeling the sting of a bruise on her left hip. Her cheeks flared with heat and she was aware of a soggy mark on her butt and thighs. She brushed at her backside quickly, letting her hair fall over her face as she struggled against the slick pavement.

A hand appeared in front of her. She hesitated and then, cursing silently, set her hand in it. She'd forgotten her gloves at the bakery, and she was surprised by the warmth of his skin, despite the cold temperature. His palm was smooth, his grip firm, and she was so busy anticipating the awkward moment when she released his hand, and the gratitude she would have to project, that she didn't even notice the patch of ice near her left heel. No sooner was she halfway up than she was going down again. And this time, she was taking Nate with her.

She caught the surprise in his eye as he tipped to the side, struggled with his footing, and landed with a heavy thud beside her.

Horror washed over her body as she lay next to him outside the Main Street B&B, staring up at the gray sky. Somewhere in the distance, she could hear children squealing as they played in the snow on the town square, but otherwise, the street was quiet, the world still, punctured all at once by a rumble of laughter.

Nate's chest rose and fell as his amusement cut through the wind, and Kara joined in, too, though a little less enthusiastically.

"Good thing you didn't have any cookies on you this time, or I never would have heard the end of it." Nate's grin seemed a little easier as he picked himself up and then, more carefully this time, helped Kara to her feet.

"Consider us even," she said, still hot with embarrassment. She motioned to the birch logs that had spilled into the snow, no doubt now wet. "I hope there's more dry wood in the pile."

Nate glanced at the logs and gave a good-natured shrug. His eyes crinkled at the corners when he met her gaze. "Gives me something to do. I'm not really used to keeping idle."

"Well, there's lots to do in Briar Creek," Kara said. "And I'm sure your aunt would be thrilled to have you spare her an insurance claim and salt the walkway. I know I'd be grateful..." She looked up at him, grinning slowly.

What was she doing? If she didn't know better, she'd say she was flirting with the man! But no, no, she was just giving him the benefit of the doubt. She couldn't punish him forever, after all. And he had helped her up. And she had pulled him down... And he was a visitor. She should show him a little hospitality, at least.

Nate barked out a laugh. "Good point. But that will take all of five minutes. What else do people do around here?"

"Oh..." Kara shrugged. She'd been locked in her kitchen for so many hours these days that she almost couldn't remember what she used to do for fun. "There's a gym. And a few restaurants on Main Street. Some shops. There's always a lot going on in town during the holidays."

Nate's lip curled a bit. "So I've heard. My aunt is very passionate about this town."

Now it was Kara's turn to laugh. "That she is. But we all are, I suppose."

"You've lived here all your life then?" Nate asked as he bent down to pick up some logs.

Kara reached for one that had rolled near her foot, careful not to slip again. "Born and raised. I left for college, though." She took satisfaction in saying that. Even if she hadn't figured out her life until recent months, she had earned a degree. She wondered if that surprised him.

"And now you run the bakery."

"Now I *own* the bakery," she said proudly.

"Hmm." Nate took the last log from her and turned slightly back to the house. "Well, good luck with it."

"What's that supposed to mean?" she asked sharply. Maybe she was being sensitive, but his attitude bothered her, and she didn't appreciate it.

"I just mean that most new businesses don't make it past the first year. You could love what you're doing or selling, but if you don't know how to properly manage your business or balance the budget, you could get yourself into trouble. A good product isn't enough."

"And you know this because . . ."

"Because it's what I do for a living," Nate said simply. "I go in, analyze practices and procedures, and put together an action plan to keep a business going."

"People pay you for your opinions?" She supposed she should be happy to have gotten free advice, but she couldn't bring herself to feel grateful. She just felt ticked. This was her business, and if she needed help, she'd ask for it.

"Quite a bit, actually." He tipped his head, his mouth slipping into a crooked grin.

"Well, I'm doing just fine," she said briskly.

He had the nerve to look amused. "If you say so."

Her heart skipped a beat. Was there something he knew that she didn't? Something beyond her glaring oversight not to offer any coffee or tea? "I do. I've put everything I have into that bakery, and I believe in it."

"Everything you have, huh?" He let out a low whistle.

"Well, it wasn't that much to begin with!" Kara was blinking rapidly, feeling a sudden urgency to get back to her bakery, to bake, to make hot chocolate, to add to her plans for tonight's bazaar. Was there time to toss in a few dozen snowflake cookies, individually packaged? Her heart was racing. There would be. If she hurried. She could put them in the oven while she finished up the gingerbread houses, decorate them right before she left. Since she'd taken the apartment above the bakery with the lease, she wouldn't need to worry about finding time to freshen up. Not that she needed to primp for anyone.

All she needed was to make this business work. Not just for herself, but for her father…She'd spent every dime of her inheritance on this endeavor. It was the last gift he'd ever given her, and she'd wanted to make it grow, to turn it into something that could last, that would remind her of him. The thought of losing it would be like losing a bit of her dad all over again.

She blinked back the tears that suddenly stung her eyes.

Nate was just a jerk. He was under her skin. He knew how to rile her up. How to press every button.

"I should go," she said, and this time she managed to get off the property without falling on her bottom.

Or falling too hard for Nate.

The Holiday Bazaar was held in a large meeting hall in the town's library, made almost unrecognizable by the decorations and lights and holiday music that streamed from speakers. Briar Creek's decorating committee had really outdone themselves this year by creating a village feel in the room, with winding paths allowing a flow of people to peruse the stalls, hot chocolate stands, and popcorn vendors, and beautifully decorated Christmas trees spread throughout.

Kara's booth was ideally located in the center of the room, with other edible gifts. She glanced around at the competition, even though most were hobbyists, as Nate would say, women who liked to bake at home and sell their goods at school bake sales and community events. Someone sold fudge, another pies, and another beautiful ribbon candy in glistening holiday colors. But no other cookies. Or gingerbread.

Kara eyed the room carefully, looking for her mother, who said she'd be here tonight. Sure enough, there, one aisle away, was Rosemary, talking animatedly with one of the dancer's moms, no doubt about the upcoming show.

Catching Kara's eye, Rosemary held up a finger and quickly ended the conversation before making a beeline for Kara's stand. Kara blew out a breath. Oh, boy.

"You haven't set up yet?" her mother remarked, staring quizzically at the table.

"I just got here," Kara said. She checked her watch. She wasn't even late.

"But most of the other stands are already set up. Why didn't you come earlier?" Rosemary's ruby-painted lips were pinched, her blue eyes bright with expectation.

Kara counted to three. There was no use losing her temper. She'd just make a scene. Besides, this was nothing new.

"I had to work." Kara sighed. "A few customers lingered." *And I'm not even late*, she said firmly to herself. *I have plenty of time to set up.*

Rosemary just shrugged, her eyes widening slightly. "Well, what are you offering?"

At this, Kara perked up. She popped the lid on a few boxes, feeling proud as she did so. Rosemary leaned forward with interest and then, pulling back, said, "That's all? I would have thought you'd be offering twice as much. If not more!"

Kara swallowed back her anger, but she could feel a heat rising in her cheeks. "I didn't want to let anything go to waste. Besides, it's my first time selling anything here. I don't know what to expect."

"Well, hopefully you'll do well." Rosemary gave her a reassuring pat on the shoulder, and with a tight smile, she was off.

"*Hopefully* I'll do well?" Kara repeated once she was out of earshot. She turned to inspect her cookies, wondering what her mother saw that she did not. They were all perfectly baked and decorated. Each uniform in size.

"You know what she meant," Molly said, coming to stand close. "She doesn't like that phrase 'break a leg,' so she comes up with alternatives."

Kara slanted her sister a glance that showed she didn't agree. "More like she's being cautiously optimistic about my potential." *More like she doesn't believe I can be successful.*

"She's just concerned," Molly said, setting a gentle hand on Kara's back.

"Maybe," Kara said, biting her lip. She couldn't even look at her sister, or she feared she would burst into tears. She felt rattled and out of sorts. She'd been so confident about her selection tonight, and now...

Kara let out a shaky breath as she began setting up her table. Molly had offered to help, and Kara now wasn't sure how she'd ever thought she could have transported the items herself. While her kits were carefully packaged, her constructed gingerbread houses needed special care. She tentatively lifted her favorite from its box and examined it from all sides, making sure none of her decorations had fallen off.

Satisfied that everything was intact, she set it at the front of the table. "We'll put the cookies on this tiered tray," she instructed Molly. "The rest can stay in the boxes until I need to restock." *If* she needed to restock. The bazaar was busy—busier than she'd even thought it would be—but that didn't mean people would be running over to buy up her goods. The gingerbread houses were really for decoration, but as for the cookies—whatever she didn't sell tonight would be donated to the Forest Ridge Hope Center, where she and her family helped organize a food drive each holiday season. At least then she would know her efforts had not been in vain.

"Did you say Ivy has a stand here tonight?" Molly set the individually wrapped snowflake cookies on the top tier of the tray. With their glistening sugar and festive shape, they certainly were the prettiest of the offerings.

Kara nodded. "I saw her when we came in. She's near the front of the room, near the big Christmas tree."

"I've been meaning to congratulate her on her engagement to Brett," Molly said, referring to their cousin. "Everyone's getting married it seems!"

Kara looked up from unpacking a box and stared at Molly until her sister's smile slipped a bit. "Not everyone," she grumbled, reaching for another handful of wrapped cookies.

"Oh. I'm sorry. I didn't mean it like that. It's just, well . . . Your time will come!" Molly's grin was as enthusiastic as her tone, but her words were empty. It was the condolence she'd heard too often these days when friend after friend, or now, sister, announced their upcoming nuptials, and Kara didn't even have a boyfriend in sight. Heck, she didn't even have a date for New Year's Eve.

"Will it?" She wasn't so sure. The local dating pool was limited, and it had been ages since she'd even had a dinner invitation. She'd spent years waiting for that spark, and no one had ever come along and made her feel it. Except Nate. Nate with his glossy good looks and shiny degree and endless unsolicited advice. No use falling for him in the romantic sense, despite that perfect grin and those classic good looks.

"Sure it will. Look at me and Todd. A year ago I thought I'd never see him again, and now we're engaged." Molly blinked rapidly, then let her eyes fall to her ring finger. That thing really was blinding.

"Imagine that." Kara pressed her lips together. Still, her sister's situation was proof that anything was possible. She'd remember that on the days she felt pessimistic about the future of her love life. "For now, though, I'm too busy for a boyfriend. The bakery takes up enough of my time. I don't see how I could juggle a relationship and a new business." But it would be nice to have someone special in her life, like the men all her friends had found. Especially during the holidays. It seemed like everyone was walking hand in hand now or shopping for something for their special someone.

She pushed away the pang of self-pity. She was getting sentimental when what she really needed to get was focused.

"Tell Ivy I said hello," she said to Molly as she set the last gingerbread kit on the table. "And while you're walking around, see if you come up with any good ideas for what we should buy Mom for Christmas."

Molly's face blanched. "Do I have to?"

Kara had to laugh. It was a running joke in the family that their mother had returned nearly every gift she'd ever been given. Notoriously difficult to shop for, she'd returned clothes and jewelry, let gift cards go unused, and claimed to have everything she really needed while sitting on the edge of the love seat in high expectation as her adult children handed over their gifts, the store receipts always slyly tucked under the tissue paper.

"It was much easier when we were younger. She was perfectly happy with a homemade ornament or card." Kara smiled wistfully.

"That's because Dad took over the real gift giving," Molly said, her mouth pulling into a frown. "She even returned the candle I got her last year. Who doesn't like a candle? I guess it wasn't her favorite scent." Molly leaned forward, lowering her voice. "And in my bedroom closet I found a stash of bracelets Luke and Grace got her for Mother's Day last year. Knowing Luke, he hadn't included the receipt."

"She doesn't like bracelets," Kara said knowingly. Rosemary had slipped and announced that over Thanksgiving. Grace had looked a little startled at that fact.

"Are you really going to make me be the one to pick something out?" Molly tipped her head, frowning. "Why don't we just offer to give her ... a hug?"

Kara burst out laughing. "Now that's a gift she would have to keep. Why don't you get her an ornament? Something *Nutcracker* themed. She'd have to love that."

Molly lifted one eyebrow. "Would she?"

Kara waved her sister off. "Go. Have fun."

She watched as her sister disappeared into the gathering crowd and folded her hands in her lap. And waited. Her heart was beating a little faster, and even her posture felt more stiff and alert than usual. A woman holding a toddler was walking toward the stand. Her eyes caught Kara's briefly, and Kara gave a small smile, waiting in growing anticipation for the woman to come over and ask about the items. Instead, she just walked by, stopping to look at the fudge instead.

Kara felt her cheeks heat with embarrassment. She tried to look busy by rearranging the wrapped cookies on the tiered tray, even though Molly had already done a perfect job of displaying them.

Finally, after what felt like hours but had probably been only a few minutes, one of the women in her mother's book club stopped in front of the table. "Look at these gingerbread houses! And these cookies!" Mrs. Nealon picked up one of the plastic-wrapped snowflake cookies and admired it. "I'll take six of these if you have enough."

Kara beamed but adjusted her expression to not reflect

her overt joy. "Absolutely." She took six from the tray and placed them in one of the small shopping bags she'd ordered especially for the holiday season, with her logo printed against a peppermint-striped background.

Mrs. Nealon handed over the money. "It's so good to see you're still making cookies."

Kara tried her best to keep her expression neutral as she made the change and handed it over. Covering her hurt with a laugh, she said casually, "Oh, but I just opened the bakery, Mrs. Nealon."

"Yes, but…" Mrs. Nealon raised her eyebrows, giving Kara a knowing look. She accepted her bag and gave Kara's hand a little pat. "Well, keep up the good work, honey. I'll be sure to send all my friends over to your stand."

"Thanks," Kara said weakly. She fell back against her chair and stared at her cookies. She'd sell every last one of them tonight. She'd make sure of it.

Nate knew he was in trouble the second his aunt mentioned the words *Holiday Bazaar*. But even hours of dread couldn't have prepared him for Briar Creek's annual event. Everyone in town must have gathered in the large meeting room in the basement of the town's library, which was covered from floor to ceiling with decorations, giving it the feel of an old-fashioned market, complete with vendors.

Nate stopped at the hot chocolate stand and pulled out his wallet. He handed a steaming mug to Maggie, who was almost too distracted to accept it.

"Now remember, the good stuff goes fast, and Kathleen and Rosemary will no doubt be on the prowl. I don't want them knowing my theme, not yet anyway."

"Aunt Maggie, I thought these women were your friends." Nate took a sip of his drink, already feeling the itch to leave.

There were too many people crowded into one place, and while he was used to sharing space, having grown up in the city, the underlying theme of the event bothered him. Holiday music blared from speakers, and everyone was wearing red and gold and green. The air even smelled like cinnamon.

"Well, of course they're my friends. My *dear* friends!" his aunt huffed, and her flashing earrings seemed to blink in double time. Tonight's pair were in the shape of Christmas lights. One red. The other green. Nate wasn't sure if they'd each been part of a set or if this was intentional. He wasn't going to ask.

"Then why the secrets? It's all in good fun, right?"

Maggie's nostrils seemed to flare slightly as she inched toward him, lowering her voice. "It is most certainly not all in good fun. Not when cold hard cash is on the line, not to mention that write-up in the travel magazine. Do you realize what that could do for my business?"

"Seems to me that regardless of who wins, you win. The article will ultimately feature Briar Creek, and if it draws tourists, they'll have to stay at the inn."

This was little consolation to his aunt. "The bottom line is that I want to give it my all. Now, do you have the list?"

Nate reached into his coat pocket and took out the folded sheet of paper. "It's all right here." All twelve items.

"Good, then you'll know what to look for. Let's tackle the drummers drumming first. That is, if Rosemary hasn't already bought up all the nutcrackers," she added. Some, she'd been sure to tell Nate on their hasty walk to the library, carried drums. They'd do. In a pinch.

"Tell you what," Nate said, tearing the list in half. "Let's tag team. That way we don't risk everything being bought before we get to it."

His aunt's eyes gleamed. "Good thinking. I'll start at

the back of the room; you take the front." She snatched the ripped paper from his hand and hurried away, her stride sharp with purpose.

Nate tossed his hot chocolate cup in a nearby trash can and skimmed his list with a groan. When she'd said she wanted to enter the decorating contest, he'd assumed she'd meant some lights, not a bona fide production. And here he'd been worried about being bored...

He could almost smile at the thought, but the holiday smells and cheerful banter that melted into the sounds of the carols set him on edge. He felt out of place, not just because he was surrounded by couples and groups of people who knew each other well but because they were all here for one collective reason. Because they loved Christmas.

And he just wanted to avoid it.

Nate ground down on his teeth and studied the list again. It was different now, he reminded himself. At this very moment, his parents were on a cruise, probably enjoying some moonlit stroll along the deck, the sea air in their face, while he... he was stuck in Christmas land.

The first item on his list were turtle doves. Should be easy enough, he thought as he joined the crowd. He walked past quilts and knitted stockings until he came to the ornament section. His aunt had it in her mind that the tree in the lobby should be decorated with an item for each day of the song. He found his half—or close enough. The French hens were more like chickens, but he was pretty certain he wouldn't do better.

He was just getting ready to find his aunt, show her what he'd found, and with any luck, get the hell out of here, when he spotted Kara one row back, sitting behind a stand, her chin cupped in her hand. There was a sadness in her face that troubled him, reminding him of all those days he'd spent in the school cafeteria alone, unhappy, hoping someone would come along. He shifted to the left, vying for a better look as a family crossed in front of his view.

Her dark hair was swept up in a ponytail, revealing the delicate sweep of her neck. She blinked up at the people as they walked by, giving a small smile. He watched as she sighed, the way it rolled through her slim shoulders, and then dropped her hand to straighten some items that already looked straight.

That did it. Gripping his bag of ornaments, he wove his way through the crowds to her stand, stopping right in front of it. She startled when she saw him, blinking rapidly as her mouth dropped in surprise.

"Oh. Hello." Her smile was hesitant as she looked up at him. He grinned back warmly, realizing this was the first time he'd had a proper look at her when she wasn't bundled up in a down parka. She wore a soft gray sweater that dipped in the front, revealing her collarbone and a hint of cleavage. He pulled his eyes upward, catching her wide blue eyes, clear and bright and contrasted with her dark hair and creamy complexion. She was a beautiful girl, but then wasn't that how it usually went in wealthy circles? He could still remember the scent of his mother's employer's perfume the time he'd had to come with her to work one day, under strict instruction to stay in the kitchen and read, not disrupt the family. But boredom and curiosity had gotten the better of him, and he'd gone exploring, ended up hiding under the bed in the fanciest bedroom he'd ever seen, easily bigger than the entire apartment where he'd lived, listening to the woman hum under her breath while she adjusted her earrings in the mirror. She was a beautiful woman; even at eight he could tell. And she lived in a beautiful house. And her life was so carefree, she walked around humming.

He started wishing his mother would hum. That the little pinch between her brow would go away.

The first gift he'd bought his mother when he could afford it was a bottle of perfume. She only wore it on special occasions. She cherished it. Whereas her employer had simply taken it for granted.

Nate tipped his head, studying the display Kara had set up. He had to admit she was at least trying. Some girls like her might have spent their inheritance shopping or traveling through Europe. He should cut her some slack.

The gingerbread house in the center of the table caught his eye, and he crouched to give it a better look. The decorations were simple but neat, with icing piped around each doorway and window frame, and little green wreaths placed on the front door.

"This looks a lot like my aunt's inn," he observed, standing up again.

Kara looked at him. "I'm surprised you noticed. It was inspired by the Main Street B&B, actually. It's always been one of my favorite buildings in all of Briar Creek."

It was impressive, though no doubt she was used to those types of things. "You made this?"

Kara nodded. "I made everything you see here."

He rolled back on his heels. There was no disguising the fact that he was impressed. "Are they for sale?" He had an idea for the inn; one he hoped his aunt would forgive him for. He chewed his lip, deciding it was worth the risk.

"They sure are!" Kara motioned to the tag that was peeking out from under the house.

Nate did a double take, then counted to three before he got in another fiery argument with Kara. No good would come from telling her she was undercharging... by a landslide. In his neighborhood in Boston, people would pay two to three times what she was asking for, and he'd put money on the fact that folks around here would, too. She was selling herself short. But why?

He glanced around the room, even though he hadn't met either Kathleen or Rosemary and would have no idea if they were in fact standing right next to him at this very moment. He spotted his aunt at the back of the room, stuffing something into her bag as she cast a suspicious eye to the right and then to the left. Oh, Maggie. It meant so much to her. And he had to admit, the more he got into it, it was sort of fun. Sort of.

He leaned down so he could speak softly and be heard over the din. His blood stilled as her face grew close, and his groin tightened as his eyes roved over the slight pink in her cheeks, the little upturn of her nose, and the pert little set of her full, red lips. His mouth felt dry as he tried to remember what he'd even been about to say. She blinked at him expectantly.

He shook off the attraction. So she was a pretty girl. He knew lots of pretty girls. Girls who were a much better fit for him than Kara ever could be, and not just because she lived in Briar Creek. He just hadn't met one in a while; he'd been too busy working to focus on a love life. He'd change that when he got back home. Slow his pace a bit. But not too much.

He could never do that.

"Do you do custom orders?" he asked.

She considered this for a moment. "Yes and no. I make the houses to order, but I tend to go off the same general design."

"I was wondering if you could add a few things to this house." He pointed to the one that resembled the inn. "Do you know that song 'The Twelve Days of Christmas'?"

Kara laughed softly. It was a pretty, light sound. One he wouldn't mind hearing again. "Sure. Who doesn't?"

Of course. Like so many others around here, she couldn't get enough of the Christmas spirit. And why shouldn't she? Santa had probably brought her everything on her wish list growing up. And then some.

He doubted she'd ever seen the pain in her father's eyes when he handed over a single gift and watched his child's face fall.

"Would you be able to add the items from that song to the house? However you think is best."

"I could do that," she said after a brief hesitation. "Do you want me to bring it by the inn tomorrow?"

Nate shook his head. "I'll pick it up. It's sort of a surprise, for my aunt. So if you don't mind, I'd like to keep this between the two of us."

It was hard to fathom that her mother, or this Kathleen Madison woman, would be as competitive over this contest as his aunt, but just in case, he'd cover his bases.

"It's our little secret then." She smiled at him as she reached for a pen and scribbled "sold" on the tag.

Even the ink was sparkly. This entire damn town sparkled.

But it was the light in her eyes that seemed to sparkle the most in that moment. Gone was the frown he'd noticed earlier. The look of defeat he'd found so troublesome. There was a lift in her shoulders now, an energy that was almost contagious, and quite adorable really.

"Our little secret," he repeated as he stepped back.

He resisted the urge to turn around, steal another glance at the pretty girl with the dark hair and the electric-blue eyes.

He'd known lots of girls like Kara over the years. They might seem fine on the surface, but deep down . . . it was best to steer clear.

CHAPTER 6

Nate spent the next morning chopping more wood for his aunt and stacking it in the pile behind the back wing of the house, where Maggie's personal quarters were. The snow was practically knee-deep by now, and the patio furniture was tarped, creating peaks of snow that rose like small mountains against the back of the house. Several of the guests had chosen to take advantage of the fresh powder and hit the slopes, but Nate suspected if he tried to join them, his aunt would have something to say, now that she was so focused on not just entering but winning the Holiday House contest. He could have chopped down half the trees in the woods behind the house to avoid going back in there and seeing the fire in her eyes. He was happy to help, but when she'd not so casually suggested an evening drive-by of the competition so she could have a peek in the windows of this woman Kathleen Madison, he had put his foot down.

"You still haven't changed your mind about tonight, then?" she asked hopefully when he came into the back of the house carrying an armful of logs.

"If they're your friends, you should just stop over. I don't understand all the secrecy."

"Oh." Maggie tossed her hands in the air and reached for a few logs on top of the pile. "You wouldn't understand. It's all about the reveal. The unveiling. Making your big debut."

"Like a bride on her wedding day?" It was the best analogy he could come up with, but his aunt seemed to like it.

"Exactly! Not that you would know. Tell me, do you have any girlfriends back in Boston?"

Nate walked into the lobby and fed a log into the fire. "No one special."

"I've seen you talking with Kara Hastings," his aunt said pointedly. "You two seemed pretty cozy lying in the snow outside my front door yesterday. For a moment I thought you were making snow angels, and then I thought perhaps you were just doing something naughty." Her smile was laced with suggestion.

Nate sighed and watched the flames grow and dance as he crouched to stoke them. Falling back on his heels, he set the iron poker in its stand and turned to his aunt. "If you must know, she fell. And I fell with her. You really should be more careful about the front walkway. I don't think you want a guest breaking their neck and suing you for damages."

The glint in his aunt's eye vanished as her face paled. "God help me, I forgot to salt it. I usually do it every morning after I've gotten the breakfast ready."

Realizing he'd upset her, Nate set a gentle hand on her arm. "It's okay, Aunt Maggie. I'll do it while I'm here. Maybe it would help to leave a note to yourself near the breakfast dishes or something. It helps me to cross things off." It wasn't true, but she didn't need to know that. His aunt was energetic and spirited, but she wasn't as young as she used to be, and it saddened him to see that change in her. Again the guilt crept in that he hadn't visited over the years. All the more reason to make the most of these few weeks together. There was no telling when he would get back.

"That's a good idea," Maggie said, nodding. She looked around the room, seeming a little lost. "I have some rooms to clean. Kara should be by soon with the cookies. Will you look for them?"

Nate's pulse sped up at the thought of seeing her again. "I'm heading into town soon. Why don't I just pick them up on my way? Save her the trouble."

Maggie paused at the base of the stairs. "She's a nice girl. It would be good for you to have a friend in town. Might give you a reason to come visit me a little more often." She winked before she hurried up the flight.

Nate frowned, thinking of that hernia his parents had mentioned . . . He'd have to remind her to take it easy when he got back from the bakery.

The cookie shop seemed farther up Main Street than he remembered, and Saturday traffic was busy. He had to bustle his way through the crowds that flowed in and out of the shops, his eye trained on the pink striped awning.

Strands of white lights framed the window of Sugar and Spice and caused the decorations to glisten. As he pushed through the door, he noticed that most of the tables were full and that there were several customers in line at the counter. He pushed back his disappointment that they wouldn't be alone and instead took the opportunity to stand back for a minute and observe.

Kara noticed him as he came in. He caught her eye as she glanced up from helping a mother and child select a cookie, and he matched her small smile with a wave. Deciding to let her tend to the customers in line, he took a seat at one of the few open tables. He had to admit the store itself was impressive—a reflection of what money could buy. It appeared to be a full build-out, cleanly designed with modern touches mixed with traditional charm that blended easily into the small town's landscape. The first impression was a good one. Everything else, though...

He sucked in a breath when he saw the customers at the table next to him tie their scarves and zip their coats and leave their dirty plates on a crumb-covered table. He glanced at Kara to see if she noticed or planned to do anything about it, as another customer searched for an open table, her plate balanced in her hand.

He stood, offering his table to the woman and child Kara had just helped. Kara was too busy ringing up the next order to notice, and still, the other table went unswept.

Little things like this could make or break a business. And he hadn't even seen her books yet. From his time consulting on restaurants, he knew how costly some ordering issues could be. It was his job to step in, spot the problems, and suggest a plan of attack for running a more efficient business and setting everyone up on a path to success. He might be on vacation right now, but he couldn't turn off the part of him that was always noticing areas for improvement, especially in a new business.

There was only one more person in front of him in line now, and Nate studied the cookies behind the spotless glass partition, his mouth admittedly salivating. She kept things simple, a strategy he agreed with: Some small business owners like her might tend to go overboard, offer everything and anything, and then end up with waste and a confused clientele. But Kara seemed to be clear in her brand. She sold cookies. Nothing else.

Except...Nate's eyebrows rose as Kara handed a steaming mug of coffee to the woman in front of him. Catching his eye, her cheeks turned the same shade of pink as her soft sweater, and she looked away, focusing instead on making change for the woman.

"So, you decided to take my advice after all, I see." He

grinned, even when he saw a wave of fury pass through her eyes. He couldn't help himself. She'd been so damn stubborn the other day at the diner. So determined to refuse his friendly suggestion. Now it would seem she'd had a change of heart.

"I'd been thinking about offering coffee for a while," she replied briskly. "I just wanted to wait and see if there was any demand for it."

He nodded slowly. "And is there?" Of course there was.

Kara just shrugged. "It would seem so, yes."

He bit back a smile. Something told him Kara wouldn't appreciate it, and he didn't feel like getting on her bad side again. "Good." He rolled back on his heels and looked around the room. "You have quite a bit of traffic in here. Are you running everything on your own?"

"Saturdays are always like this, especially during the holidays since everyone's out shopping. Can I interest you in a peppermint white hot chocolate?"

So she'd taken his idea for coffee and taken it one step further. While hot cocoa might be a good idea from a sales standpoint during the Christmas season, he had to question if the amount of time it took to prepare each cup offset the profit.

"Tell me, is peppermint used in everything in this town? My aunt made peppermint scones for breakfast the other morning."

Kara grinned. "'Tis the season."

"Hmm." His lips thinned. That was probably why he'd never liked the taste. Bad associations.

"I get the impression you're not quite as into the holiday spirit as most folks around here."

Ah. Caught. "What gave it away?" he asked.

Kara studied him for a moment, and he felt his stomach churn with unease as he stared at her pretty face, watching her clear blue eyes roam over him. Her lips were soft and supple and parted just enough to make him wonder what it might be like to kiss her.

He stiffened. No good thinking that way.

"Well, for starters, you don't have that sort of drunk-on-Christmas look that everyone else around here gets this time of year. And you didn't jump at the chance for peppermint hot chocolate, either."

"I don't like peppermint," he replied.

She pointed a finger in the air, her lips curving. "Aha. Suspicion confirmed, then."

He shrugged. "Christmas was never that big of a deal in my house. Most years I'm too busy working to pay much attention to it anyway." More like he worked hard to avoid it... This year's gift to his parents was supposed to eliminate that gut-churning feeling every time they gathered for the holiday, and the memories that haunted him, shadowing what should be a festive event. Instead, he was now caught up in the spirit of the season at every turn. And, if his aunt had any say in it, from every angle.

"Well, Christmas is a very big deal in Briar Creek. And in case you haven't noticed, your aunt takes it very seriously."

"Oh, I've noticed." He laughed, thinking of the bags of decorations she'd triumphantly found at the Holiday Bazaar. Tonight they'd continue their efforts of transforming the house. With any luck, they could knock it out in a few hours and be done with it.

"Let me just wipe down a few tables and then I'll show you the gingerbread house. I didn't want to box it up in case you had any changes."

"Sounds good." He watched as she came around the corner, the pull of her gray wool skirt accentuating her subtle curves. Her long legs were covered in black tights, and for a moment he could almost imagine peeling them off, running his hands over her smooth, creamy legs, his gaze latching with those electric blue eyes.

He swallowed hard against the desire that built as she bent over a table to wipe it with a rag, giving him a full view of her perfect backside. He could have stared at her all day, if he wasn't suddenly distracted by the jingling of bells over the door as a new round of customers came in.

"I'll be right with you," Kara said pleasantly as she walked over to clean another table.

Nate frowned, resisting the urge to check his watch to see how long it would take her to attend to the people who stood slightly impatiently at the counter beside him. Finally, Kara came back around the corner, a stack of dishes in her hand, her smile broad but her cheeks flushed. She was flustered, and why shouldn't she be? She was doing too much, managing it all. She'd be better off paying someone to help out, relinquish some control. Because that was what it was about, he gathered. If she'd had the cash to create this place, then she had the cash to pay for some assistance.

Nate turned to the group of women beside him. "Ladies first." He grinned and stepped back, letting Kara tend to them so she wouldn't feel rushed when she was showing him the gingerbread house. He wanted to make sure it was what he'd envisioned. And, truth be told, he didn't feel the need to hurry back to the inn. For a variety of reasons.

"If you won't take a hot chocolate, then how about a cup of coffee?" Kara asked when she finished ringing up the other customers.

"Coffee sounds great," he admitted.

She handed him a mug. "Cream or sugar?"

He took a long sip of his coffee. It was smooth and dark, and better than the offerings at the diner. "Black is fine."

Kara scanned the room, then tipped her head toward the kitchen. "Follow me, then."

Nate glanced over his shoulder at the door, deducing that she could probably afford to leave the counter unattended for a few minutes, and followed her through the swinging door into the kitchen, which could have been a scene straight from the North Pole, if one existed. The snowflake cookies he'd come to associate with her were lined by the dozens, some iced, some already sugared, the rest plain and waiting. The far counter was covered with gingerbread houses in various forms of completion, and the air smelled of vanilla and molasses and, of course, peppermint.

He fought the urge to pick up a candy cane–shaped cookie made from twisted white and red dough. Kara noticed and said, "These are today's special. I stick with a standard menu and offer something new each day, in addition to seasonal favorites, of course. Try one."

He took her up on the offer and bit into the cookie. He'd assumed it would be your run-of-the-mill sugar cookie, but this was something much different—and better. Cream cheese and something like chocolate coated his mouth. Not too sweet, the texture perfect.

"These are my red velvet cream cheese candy canes. I've already sold three dozen since I opened this morning," Kara said proudly before glancing shyly away.

"You have a good business model," he said after finishing the cookie.

Kara perked with interest. "Well, that must be good news. Here I thought you'd be full of more ideas for improvement."

"Well…" Nate regretted the word as soon as he saw her expression fold. He lowered his coffee mug before he'd had a chance to take a sip and set it down on the nearest counter.

"Well what?" Kara leaned a hip against the center island and folded her arms across her chest, accentuating the curve of her breasts through her pale pink sweater. Her lips were pinched, her nose pert, and he didn't think he'd seen her look cuter.

He held up a hand. "Look, I'm a management consultant. I tend to spot opportunities for improvement everywhere I go." Other than the inn, he had to admit. His aunt ran that place with the expertise of a veteran, and it showed. She was a perfectionist, like Kara. The difference was that Kara was new to this and, possibly, in over her head. "I didn't come here to insult you, I promise. You have a beautiful shop, you make damn good cookies, and you probably have a concrete business plan in place."

Kara blinked. "What do you mean by a business plan?"

Nate stifled a groan. Of course. She hadn't taken out a loan, hadn't needed one. No one was backing this place. She'd sunk her own money into it. She hadn't needed to pitch her idea to anyone, hadn't needed to prove that she could make it a success.

He gritted his teeth. Reminded himself for the umpteenth time, *Say nothing*.

"I can tell you want to say something," Kara cut in. She lifted her chin, her gaze steady. "Go on."

Nate pulled in a breath. Since she'd asked for it…"I think…I think you might serve yourself better by hiring some part-time help."

She snorted. "That's all you've got?" She shook her head, laughing to herself as she walked over to the back of the room, where the rows of gingerbread houses were kept. "Of course I need part-time help. The only problem is that help doesn't come free."

"Yes, but…" He frowned, suddenly wondering if he'd misread the situation. But no. His aunt had specifically said that Kara had used her inheritance to start this business, and she'd as good as admitted it herself when she admitted to not having a business plan.

Kara turned. "Believe me, I'd love nothing more than to hire someone to help me out. Especially around the holidays. But for now, that's not in the cards."

He wanted to tell her it would never be in the cards if she drove away business by trying to juggle too many parts of the business. She should focus on what she did best: baking. She was one hell of a baker.

He couldn't resist. He reached for another cookie, cocking his eyebrow when she caught him. "May I? I'll pay."

Her expression softened. "You may. And it's on the house. Now, speaking of houses..."

She carried the gingerbread house from last night's bazaar to the center island and carefully set it down. It was even more charming than he remembered it, made even better by the thoughtful additions she'd made to the decorations. She'd even placed a pear tree in the front yard, complete with a little partridge.

"How did you make this?" he marveled, bending for a closer look. He was astounded to realize that if you looked through the windows, she'd actually decorated the inside of the house as well. The walls were painted, some to even look like wallpaper, and there was a hearth and Christmas tree in the main room. Even a staircase draped in garland.

This thing could sell for three times what she was asking, if not more. And Kara was basically giving it away for free. He couldn't imagine how much time this took. Had she calculated her hourly breakdown after the cost of supplies?

He scowled to himself. He doubted it.

"Everything is edible, well, technically. I use different ingredients: icing, sugar, marshmallow, marzipan paste, gummy candies, pretty much anything I can think of. I have an entire candy closet back there." She laughed and came to stand next to him, bending so she could point out the details. "Here are the two turtle doves," she said, gesturing to the little birds that sat atop the chimney. "And here are the twelve drummers drumming."

Nate followed her hand to the perfectly formed and painted miniature drums, complete with gold batons, that were tucked around the back of the house, near the pond where seven swans were swimming, but he struggled to concentrate on the gingerbread house, no matter how exquisite. Her hair brushed his arm, and her face, this close up, was smooth and creamy, her nose slightly upturned, her lips full and pink. He stiffened at the surge of heat that fired in his blood.

"Oh, and here are the lords a-leaping. I have to admit, I struggled with this one." She laughed as she reached out her arm to point out her handiwork, her body grazing his in the process. Nate felt something in his groin tighten as the soft material of her sweater skimmed his hand. She seemed smaller this close to him, and more animated, too. Her blue eyes danced as she walked him through the changes, and her smile never left her face. He liked being close to her like this. Liked the femininity of her energy, the little gestures she made with her fingers, the sweet smell of vanilla that seemed to float off her body.

"So, what do you think?" she asked as she righted herself to a standing position. She was staring at him expectantly, her eyes somewhat hopeful, and there was no way he couldn't be dead honest with her.

"I think you are doing yourself a major disservice," he said.

Her smile dropped at once. "Excuse me?"

"This gingerbread house. How long did it take you from start to finish, including the custom changes I asked for?"

Kara shrugged and looked at the house in dismay. "I don't know. I didn't really calculate it. I time how long I bake everything, but the rest ... I just work until it's finished."

Meaning she started early and finished late. If she ever finished at all.

"This gingerbread house is worth four times what you're charging."

"Four times!" Kara scoffed and looked at him like he was half crazy. He refused to feed into it. "Please. Maybe in the big city, but not in Briar Creek."

"The supplies alone cost money. Then you have to factor in your time. This is a work of art, Kara. You have a real gift," he added softly.

She stared at him for a moment, then dismissed his words again with a wave of her hand. "I don't want to take advantage of anyone. I think this is a fair price and clearly my customers do, too. I've limited myself to three completed houses a day, and I always sell out."

No surprise there. Deciding to let the matter rest, he reached into his back pocket and pulled out his wallet. He had twice what she'd asked for on him in cash. He handed it all to her.

Kara glanced at the money and back to him, her cheeks reddening. "I can't accept that."

"Take it." He thrust his hand forward. "You did extra work on it. You've earned it."

A small smile teased the corners of her mouth. "Wow. Well, thank you. It wasn't necessary, but thank you." She took the money and slipped it into her apron pocket. Composing herself, she joked, "Just think, at this rate, I might be able to get some part-time help after all."

She'd be able to get some part-time help by tomorrow if she'd listen to some of his suggestions. Then she'd be able to spend more time making the gingerbread houses and cookies she sold, too.

He'd let his advice sink in, like his suggestion for coffee. And he hoped she'd listen to him, too. Something told him she didn't just want to make this business a success. Something told him she needed to.

Four hours after Nate left with the gingerbread house and the cookies for tea, Kara was still struggling to wipe the grin off her face. He'd liked her cookies. A lot. And he'd loved her gingerbread house.

Oh, she knew that folks in town thought they were cute. And she really did love coming up with new ideas for each one. But a compliment from Nate meant a little more, given the fact that he assessed businesses for a living. And whether she wanted to admit it to herself or not, he did seem to know what he was saying.

"Well, aren't you chipper this afternoon," Molly said when she came into the shop.

It was true that her good mood had carried her all through the afternoon, and she'd accomplished a record amount in the short period of time. "Ready to meet Ivy?" she asked as she untied her apron strings from her waist.

Before Kara started the bakery, she used to see her friend Ivy almost every day. These days she was lucky to see Ivy once a week, even though they both worked on Main Street. Come the start of the year, she vowed once again, she'd get a better balance on things. She'd take advantage of the holiday demand, get through this crazy time, and then hopefully grow her business in a new and better way in the new year. And after Nate's words, she felt downright optimistic that this could happen.

"Sure." Molly didn't seem quite as enthusiastic as Kara would expect a bride to be. After all, didn't most girls dream of the day they would pick out the flowers for their bouquet? Kara knew she had, and she remembered Molly doing the same. Molly loved weddings, always had—ever since she'd been chosen to be a flower girl in a distant cousin's wedding at the tender age of four—and it was one of the reasons she'd been so determined to get a job at the bridal magazine.

Her sister seemed quiet as they walked toward Petals on Main, and Kara filled the gaps with stories from the bazaar, where she had sold all but five cookies by the end of the night. It had been a success, even if they still didn't have a Christmas present for their mother...

Ivy was finishing up a beautiful holiday arrangement when the sisters entered the shop, full of red and creamy ivory blooms. Molly perused the shop while Kara chatted with her friend, eager to catch up on the latest details of her upcoming wedding.

"When I see flowers like this, I start to wish I'd gone with a Christmas wedding." Ivy sighed and blew an auburn strand of hair from her forehead. "But I always knew when I got married I'd have peonies, and so...spring it is!"

"Peonies are very popular with our readers," Molly agreed sagely.

"It will be worth waiting for," Kara said, even though she couldn't exactly relate. Still, it was what she told herself when she started to get a little lonely or wonder when her turn would come, as her sister said. She liked to think that by the time the right guy came along, she'd look back on her life and know that he was worth it. Still, despite how much she tried to convince herself she was fine just having her bakery, it would be nice if he'd come along soon...

And she wouldn't mind if he looked sort of like Nate.

"So you're getting married in Briar Creek?" Ivy remarked. "Here I thought you'd want something big and splashy in Boston."

"Oh." Molly shrugged. "There's nothing unique about that. A country wedding, though...you can really build on that theme."

"Are you still planning on Valentine's Day?" Ivy asked Molly.

Molly looked up from the red roses she was inspecting. "Yep. Valentine's Day. The most romantic day of the year!"

Kara decided to keep her feelings to herself, even if she did worry Molly was hurrying things a bit. She had a bad feeling that Molly was rushing the wedding out of fear that Todd would break things off again, and if that was the case, she probably shouldn't be marrying him at all. But was that really for her to say? She wasn't sure. She'd talk to her mother about it first.

Ivy considered this. "Red would be the obvious palette then, but pink or purple would work just as well. I've always been partial to lilac, personally."

Molly scrunched up her nose. "I know my mother would love nothing more than for me to go with pink, but it's really not me at all. I'll let you have pink, Kara," she teased.

"Gee, thanks." But Kara didn't mind. Neither girl may have followed in their mother's love for ballet, but Kara had always been partial to pink—it was one of the reasons why she'd chosen to make it the color scheme of her shop. Of course, she couldn't deny that she got a little thrill from seeing her mother's expression at the first walk-through. She couldn't help it; even now, at her age, she longed for her mother's approval, no matter how difficult it was to come by.

Molly related, but it wasn't the same for her. She was the youngest and in many ways could do no wrong. And now she lived in Boston, and when she visited, her mother rolled out the red carpet.

All the more reason for Kara to make her mark in town and prove to her mother, and to all the doubters, that she could stick with something and succeed at it. She hoped to prove it to herself, too.

"What about a mixed bouquet in shades of red, white, and purple?" Ivy suggested. She pulled a binder from under her workstation and began thumbing through pages of past events, each picture almost prettier than the one before it. Stopping halfway through, she turned the binder and slid it to Molly. "I may tuck in a few pink flowers just for variety, but I promise it will be subtle."

"I trust you," Molly said. She reached into her tote and pulled out some examples of pages she'd ripped from past issues of the magazine she worked for. "I like this kind of vase. It really creates a sense of height. It makes a statement." She shuffled through the cutouts. "So long as it looks just like this, it will be perfect."

"Then you're the easiest bride I've had all year, and that's counting myself." Ivy laughed. "I know I gave Grace a hard time when she couldn't commit to a dress, but I'm still undecided."

"We'll go together then. I know all the latest trends, and I might even be able to get you a good deal," Molly said, and the girls began chatting excitedly about lace and satin and taffeta and veils. Kara felt her smile slowly begin to fade as the tug in her chest grew a little tighter. She was happy for her sister and friend—how could she not be—but she couldn't help but feel a little left out.

She waited politely until the conversation had ended before changing the topic. "Mark's party is tonight. Are you both going?" She hadn't been sure she would make it, but she'd been so productive this afternoon that she could stand to take a night off to enjoy herself. And if she got twitchy, as she sometimes did, she might pop into the bakery to get a start on tomorrow afterward.

"Wouldn't miss it," Ivy said, nodding. "Brett made sure to swap shifts for the night, so he's not on call. What about Todd, Molly? Is your fiancé going to be joining us?"

Molly reddened as she flipped through her magazine pages. "Oh. No...No, he has to work, so...He's still in Boston." Her smile was bright, but if Kara didn't know better, she'd say it was masking something.

"Oh, too bad." Ivy shrugged. "Well, you girls will have each other then. And you never know, Kara. A cute guy might be there."

Kara highly doubted that. She'd long ago given up on finding a man around here. She'd dated several, and that hadn't panned out, and the other eligible bachelors weren't her type. She'd known them all her life, and they were officially friend material only.

She thought of Nate, wondering if he might have liked to have gone to the party. *Ridiculous*, she thought, brushing away the thought. He was visiting his aunt, and even if he was around Kara's age, he probably wanted to focus on time with his family, not go to a party with a group of strangers. It wasn't like he'd be sticking around after Christmas anyway. No one had even met him up to this point. But oh, had they heard about him...

"I'm fine just spending the evening with all of you," Kara said, meaning it. "I need the break."

"It's tough work starting a new business." Ivy gave her a look of understanding. "Scary, too. Heck, I'm still always a little worried about losing this place or not being able to meet my loan payments."

Kara laughed uneasily, knowing her friend was only half joking. Petals on Main had been open for years and its business was steady. Kara knew she was fortunate not to have to lose sleep wondering if the bank would come after her if she failed, but that didn't mean the fear was any less.

If she lost the business, then what would she have for herself? It was all she had. And all she had left of her father, too.

CHAPTER 7

Mark and his fiancée, Anna, lived with their dog, Scout, in a restored log cabin near the edge of Briar Creek. The party was already under way by the time Kara pulled to a stop on the snow-covered gravel driveway. She'd dressed for the occasion, to help get into the spirit of things more than anything else, but she couldn't deny the flutter of hope that maybe Ivy was right, that there might be a handsome someone behind the door.

Knowing she was just setting herself up for disappointment by thinking this way, she grabbed the bottle of wine and box of the candy cane–shaped cookies that Nate had praised earlier from the passenger seat and pushed open the car door. Her heeled dress shoes were all wrong for the wet and heavy snow, which was still falling steadily, and she hurried up the stairs to the front porch, letting herself into her cousin's house, where she was greeted by the friendly golden retriever who wore a red plaid ascot.

"I can't believe Mark let you dress up Scout." Kara laughed as she greeted her friend Anna Madison, soon to be her cousin-in-law, if she and Mark ever took enough time away from their restaurant to set a date.

She still felt a little guilty that by giving her notice last summer at Rosemary and Thyme she'd somehow set back their plans, but Anna had quickly found a replacement to take over her position in the back office, and she and Mark both understood and supported her desire to start a bakery and have something of her own. It was Anna who had taught her to bake, after all. Still, Kara would sleep a little better when they finally tied the knot…and took a much-needed honeymoon.

"I slipped it on right before the party started," Anna confessed, laughing. "To be honest, I'm not sure he's even noticed yet. He was too busy prepping the appetizers when people started arriving, and now he's on his second beer with his brother." She rolled her eyes, but Kara knew Anna was only pretending to be annoyed. She and Mark went far back. They'd drifted apart and come back together. It did happen sometimes. However, in the case of her sister and Todd, she wasn't so sure.

"Is Molly here yet?" Kara looked around the room, already crowded and buzzing with guests she recognized, to search for her sister.

Anna nodded as she took Kara's coat. "She's over near the tree with Ivy and Grace."

Already Kara felt more alive. The music was playing Christmas carols, strands of white lights gave the entire house a festive glow, and Anna was mentioning some special drink they'd concocted just for the evening. It couldn't get better than this.

Except…maybe it could.

Kara turned with interest to see Nate Griffin walking through the door, eyes wide, hands tucked into his pockets, smile a little unsure. He was dressed up more than usual, in black pants and a charcoal-gray cashmere sweater. She could just picture him in Boston, with his sleek city cloth-ing, slipping into a trendy and lively restaurant or hitting a bar after a long business meeting. It was a reminder of how different their worlds were—and despite all the nice things he'd said about her cookies today at the shop, she couldn't help but feel a little nervous around him. No doubt the other girls he spent time with had big corporate jobs and weren't covered in flour and sugar for half the day.

"Nate?" She smiled as her heart sped up a little, wonder-ing how this came to be.

His expression visibly relaxed when he saw her. "Kara. This is a surprise."

"A pleasant one, I hope." She smiled pertly and then felt a wave of heat rush over her skin. Oh my God, was she flirting with him? She was; she most definitely was. But then, why shouldn't she? He was cute. Damn cute. And he was single. Mrs. Griffin had been sure to point that out a good hundred times, leading them all to secretly assume something might be wrong with him or that he wasn't quite everything his aunt had hyped him up to be. But no, nothing was wrong with Nate Griffin, at least not in this moment, and not when he smiled at her like that, causing his hazel eyes to crinkle around the corners.

"My mother said you were going to be stopping by," Anna cut in as she extended her hand. "I'm Anna Madison. My fiancé Mark Hastings is just over there." She gestured vaguely to the kitchen.

"Hastings? Any relation?" Nate asked Kara.

"My cousin. You'll probably meet a few of my family members tonight," Kara said. She smoothed her black sequin skirt over her hips, and when she looked up, she noticed that he'd followed her hands, tracing the movement with his eyes, his smile suddenly replaced by something unreadable.

Something that sent a little tingle down her spine. She waited until Anna had moved on to greet another guest to say, "I used to work with Mark and Anna at Rosemary and Thyme. You might have noticed it on one of your trips down Main Street. The restaurant on the corner with the tall windows?"

He looked impressed. "I did. Looks like a nice place. How long were you there for?"

"Oh..." Kara hoped to gloss over the details of her work history. It didn't exactly shed her in the best light to admit she'd changed jobs sometimes twice yearly since she'd finished college how many years back. "A while. Anna ran a bakery before they teamed up and opened the restaurant. She taught me most of what I know."

"Well, she did a good job then." Nate grinned, and Kara felt her stomach roll over.

She lifted a drink off a tray that Anna carried back to them, and Nate did the same. She did her best to ignore the subtle wink her friend shot her before she moved on to the next group, happy to proffer her culinary efforts. Taking a long sip for courage, Kara turned back to Nate. "So, what brings you by tonight?"

"It was my aunt's idea. She wanted me to get out of the house." He leaned down to speak into her ear, his voice low and husky, his breath tickling her neck and sending a quiver through her insides. "Between you and me, I think she's trying to sell me on this town."

"Oh?" Well, this was an interesting turn of events. "Any chance of you moving here?"

He held her gaze for a beat. His face was so close, she could see the faint shadow of the bump on his nose, the full mouth framed by that square jaw. *Oh, Lordy.* He certainly was handsome.

"Nope."

Kara blinked. "Oh," she said again, at a loss for anything else to say. She hadn't expected him to be so blunt, or so certain. She pushed back the swell of disappointment. She was being ridiculous. There was nothing to be disappointed about. He was a good-looking man, passing through town like so many of the other tourists who came and went this time of year.

"I like city life," Nate mused. "I grew up in Boston. It's all I know."

"It would be difficult to leave home," Kara agreed. Briar Creek had its drawbacks, as small-town life sometimes did, but she couldn't imagine leaving it. She'd rather invest in it. And that's exactly what she was doing, wasn't it?

She blinked back the tears that stung her eyes, as they did every time she thought of her dad. The holidays were always more difficult. He should have been here with them. But so long as she had her bakery, perhaps a part of him was.

She took another sip of her drink, this time properly tasting it. It was cranberry flavored, with a peel of orange draped artfully on the rim. There was no use getting sentimental now. Now, when she was at one of the best parties of the year, with her best friends, and there was a sprig of mistletoe just an arm's length away. And one of the cutest guys she'd seen in a while was standing at her side. And he liked her cookies.

This was certainly not a time for tears. In fact, things had never looked brighter.

Nate had to admit he was having fun. When his aunt had broached him with the strong suggestion of coming to the party, he'd immediately refused on account of not having been invited or knowing the hosts, but then she'd pulled out her guilt card and insisted that she needed him there to scope out the competition. Kathleen Madison's daughters would be in attendance, she'd said, and after a glass or two of Champagne he might be able to get them to reveal something about their mother's plans for the Holiday House contest. He'd squawked at that, but then his aunt had gotten all teary eyed and tried the reverse psychology angle instead, opting to sit in a chair by the fireplace and admit defeat, right down to suggesting she might return all the items she'd purchased at the bazaar.

It wasn't until he was out of the house, directions to this cabin in the woods in hand, and on his way to all but crash a party that he realized he'd been played. Maggie couldn't have returned those gifts if she'd tried—they were crafts from a fair, for God's sake—but nevertheless, she'd gotten her way, and, standing close to Kara, he was happy she had.

She looked particularly pretty tonight in a black sleeveless top and sparkly skirt. Her dark hair was swept back, and she wore a touch of red lipstick that dramatically contrasted with her bright blue eyes. Her top was cut low, revealing a hint of cleavage tucked behind a chunky necklace. She sipped her drink slowly, as if pacing herself, and Nate did the same. He'd originally planned on getting in and getting out, but now he wouldn't mind if the evening lasted a while.

"You know," Kara said, a slow smile curving her mouth, "I was thinking of inviting you to the party tonight." Her lashes fluttered as she lowered her eyes, and she took a sip of her drink as a faint blush traced her cheeks.

Nate's pulse skipped with interest. So she'd been thinking of asking him out, huh? And what would he have said? Yes, he realized with a jolt. He'd have said yes. Because she was pretty and sweet and interesting...even if she was all wrong for him. She was just like the girls he'd known growing up, and he knew that in time a different side of her would shine through. Once she learned where he'd come from, what his background was, that his blood didn't run blue, she'd give him the boot.

He took a sip of his drink. Some festive libation that tasted slightly like cranberry juice, but fortunately, better. "And why didn't you?"

"I wasn't sure it would be your type of thing." Kara shrugged, her cheeks positively flaming now, and he decided to cut her a break. If it wasn't for her overt embarrassment, he'd have assumed she'd meant this wasn't his scene, that he might not fit in. Wasn't good enough. But there was nothing in her expression that said any such thing.

"Truth be told, it's not," he admitted. "I tend to avoid Christmas parties."

"Ah, so you really are a Scrooge." She laughed and took a sip of her drink.

"Not a Scrooge," he corrected. "More like . . . a realist."

She tipped her head quizzically. "But Christmas is the time to suspend reality and get caught up in the magic of possibilities. Anything can happen at Christmas."

He stared at her, realizing by the earnest way she blinked up at him that she honestly believed this. And God, if he didn't like her a little more for it. She took another sip of her drink and licked her bottom lip slowly, completely unaware that he was watching it all with a growing ache.

He ran a hand through his hair and coughed into his hand. He was at a party, not out on a date. And, according to his aunt Maggie, he will still on a mission. Kara was right about one thing: Anything was proving possible. A few days ago he never would have thought he'd be roped into decorating an inn for this ridiculous competition. He had half a mind to just write his aunt a check for the prize money and be done with it. But he supposed that magazine article couldn't be bought. Shame.

"Come on," Kara cajoled, elbowing him gently. He nuzzled closer to her, liking her nearness. Maybe it was because he was in a room full of strangers, or maybe it was because she was so easy on the eyes, but he felt oddly familiar with her now, cozy even. He liked having her around. "Can you honestly tell me you don't feel a little more vested in the spirit of the holidays since arriving in Briar Creek?"

He stared at her, fighting against the truth he was trying to deny. "I can honestly tell you that I still have no holiday spirit."

She laughed and playfully swatted his arm. Sobering a bit, she lifted her chin, glancing at him sidelong. "I don't believe you. No one who hates Christmas would be so interested in one of my gingerbread houses."

"I told you," Nate explained. "That's a gift for my aunt."

"Well, I hope she liked it," Kara said.

"Oh, she did." After he'd explained for thirty-five minutes straight that Kara had no idea it was intended for the Holiday House contest, that she wouldn't feed the secret to her mother, and that no one knew they were even entering the contest, much less what their theme would be. He trusted Kara; why, he didn't know, but he did. And he'd learned over the years to have a good read on people. Which was why he felt so conflicted about where he stood with her. A part of him wanted to put his arms out, keep her there, at a safe distance. A pretty girl from the other side of the tracks who would scoff at a boy like him. But the other part couldn't help exploring, wondering if there was something more.

His aunt certainly seemed to like her. And she wasn't the easiest person to impress.

But then, his aunt wasn't like him. His aunt had grown up in Briar Creek, in the big white house across from the town square. She'd known hardship—everyone had—but she hadn't known poverty. And she'd certainly never felt the isolation that came with it.

"If I know Maggie, she'll wear you down before Christmas Eve," Kara continued. "Christmas is a big deal to her."

"So I've noticed," Nate agreed. "She's roped me into helping her with this Holiday House contest." He was allowed to reveal that much, his aunt had insisted on his way out the door this evening. Just enough to broach the topic...

Kara lifted an eyebrow, seeming amused. "Oh, really? So the man who hates Christmas is going to decorate the house for the holidays?"

"I can climb a ladder and hang tinsel."

Kara laughed. "I don't imagine that tinsel is what Maggie had in mind."

Nate tensed. "You think you can do better?" His tone was sharper than he'd intended, and he cursed himself for the slip. She'd hit a nerve, even though she probably hadn't intended to—reminding him of all the kids he'd gone to school with, who seemed to make it their daily mission to make him feel different and unworthy.

Kara looked up at him, startled, her smile shadowed by confusion that knitted her forehead. "I'm just saying..."

"I know what you're saying," Nate said, setting his drink down on a nearby end table. She was saying what they'd all said, that he wasn't good enough, that he wasn't one of them, that they could do better. That they were better. "So what about you? Are you entering the Holiday House contest?"

"Oh, my mother is, of course."

"What about you?"

"What about me?" Kara shook her head. "I have an apartment, so..."

But he wasn't going to let her off the hook that easily.

"So? You make one hell of a gingerbread house. Why not enter one in the contest?"

Kara stared at him like he was half crazy, but he saw the interest that sparked in her eyes. "The gingerbread house is not a real house."

"It's still a house. I've read the rules." He'd been sure to, just to make sure he adhered to them correctly and didn't do anything to mess with his aunt's chances of winning. "You think you can beat me with holiday decorations. Prove it."

Her lips pinched as her little nose wiggled and then lifted ever so slightly. "That's the most ridiculous thing I've ever heard."

"Why? Seems to me that a gingerbread house is about the most quintessential Christmas house that can be entered." He locked the defiance in her gaze. "Oh, I see, you don't think you can win."

"I know I can win," Kara said with a lift of her chin.

"Okay, then, a hundred bucks says the inn places higher than your gingerbread house in the contest."

She hesitated, folded her arms across her chest, stared at him with fire in her eyes. "That sure of yourself, are you?"

"I'm a hard worker," Nate said bluntly. "And as you said, it's Christmas. Anything is possible."

"I don't want your money," Kara said.

"I get it. You're worried you won't win." He shrugged, grinning as her nostrils flared. "Tell you what? We'll keep it friendly. The inn places higher, you owe me dinner. You win, I treat you."

The motive was ulterior, but he couldn't resist the thought of an evening alone with her. There was something interesting at play here, something he couldn't quite put his finger on. Maybe it was the challenge of redemption, even if Kara wasn't one of the bullies at his school. Or maybe it was just the promise of a dinner with a pretty girl. He couldn't be sure.

"Mr. Griffin, you have a deal," she said, extending her hand. He took it, surprised at the firmness of her grip, the confidence in her single shake, but he lingered for a moment, savoring the warmth of her palm, which felt so small in his own hand. A rush zipped down his spine at the softness of her skin and pleasure of her touch, and he lingered before finally releasing her hand from his grip.

"A gambling woman," he remarked, studying her over the rim of his glass as he took a long sip.

Kara shrugged. "Only when the odds are in my favor."

He cocked an eyebrow, but a smile was pulling at his mouth. Win or lose, he stood to win something here, but from the little pinch of a frown between Kara's brows, he reckoned she was going to be a formidable opponent.

"To the best Holiday House," he declared, raising his glass to hers. "Good luck."

Her lips curved into a smile, and there was a spark in her eyes when she met his gaze. "Oh, I won't be needing any luck. But something tells me you will." She winked, clinked his glass before he knew what had hit him, and with a quick sip, turned to meet her friends, leaving him standing in the middle of a party he hadn't been invited to, with the sinking suspicion that her parting words were right on the mark.

Maggie was waiting up for him when Nate came home that night. She'd been busy, he noticed. Nearly all of the decorations they'd purchased were on the tree, with the much-celebrated partridge in a pear tree ornament near the very top.

"The guests joined in the fun," she announced as she

adjusted a string of garland. "I'm getting too old to do the heavy lifting."

"I would have stayed back and helped," he reminded her pointedly.

"Nonsense," she said, beckoning him to sit with her near the fireplace. "It was important for you to go to that party. But I have to tell you, Nate. We have a situation on our hands."

"Oh?"

"Kathleen Madison is going all out this year. She'll be impossible to beat. Impossible, I tell you."

Oh, right. He was supposed to have found out information on her entry—it was the purpose of him going to the party. Something he hadn't managed to do once he'd gotten sidetracked by long legs in black lace tights and sharp blue eyes that pulled him in, mesmerized him, made him doubt himself and where he'd come from.

"I had to call Kathleen, obviously, to tell her to let Anna know that you'd be stopping by the party. It was the perfect excuse, actually. *And*, with a bit of gentle persuasion, I was able to get her to spill. She's going with the theme of white Christmas." Aunt Maggie stared at him with wide eyes, as if he should understand the implicit enormity of this fact. "She's even had the walls in her home repainted!"

"Well, that's going a bit far, don't you think?" Nate shook his head. He still didn't see what was wrong with some colored lights and good old-fashioned tinsel. A couple stockings, and there. Done.

"She's an interior designer," Maggie stressed. "She's won every year she's entered. I thought maybe she'd take a break and judge this year, as she's done before, but it seems that once she saw the prize, she decided to pull her best tricks out of her hat! She downplayed it, but she did let it slip that a write-up in that magazine could expand her clientele. And it would, of course. A designer's showcase. Oh, I may as well just forget the whole thing. You can't beat Kathleen Madison. And you can't beat white Christmas."

This was a lot of information to take in at once, and Nate had a feeling that once Maggie recovered from her shock, she'd end up more determined than ever. It was a setback, but she'd been assuming Kathleen's entry would be unbeatable anyway.

"So, is that what has you so upset then? Nothing else...?" He leaned forward to rest his elbows on his knees, watching his aunt carefully. He still worried about her health. Her age. How hard she worked to keep this old house running.

"What else could there be? This is the worst news, I tell you. The worst!" Maggie shook her head, lost for a moment in the dancing flames in the hearth. "She's repainting walls. White. Or, no, off-white. The shade will be perfect, of course."

Nate murmured something he hoped sounded sympathetic.

"When Kathleen started going on and on and on about her hopes of winning, it was all I could do not to burst. I finally just couldn't take it anymore."

"So she knows you're entering then?"

"She knows I'm stiff competition." His aunt sniffed.

Nate smothered a grin. "So you're not going to quit then?"

"Well, how can I now?" She smiled. "So...did you see anyone familiar at the party?"

Nate shrugged and leaned back in his chair. He was tired, even though it wasn't very late. In Boston, he'd still be awake, working at his computer, probably at it for another few hours before calling it a night. Here, though, he felt almost lulled by the flames, by the quiet. It was so quiet. "Oh, the girl who drops off the cookies," he said, purposefully leaving off her name lest it looked like he cared. Even though he did.

"I thought you might run into her tonight."

Nate looked sharply at his aunt. "I thought you sent me over to that party to get the goods on Kathleen."

"Oh, in a way." His aunt fiddled with the fringe on the bottom of her Christmas sweater. "It was just the excuse I needed to call Kathleen."

"That's not very nice," Nate said firmly, but his aunt's face remained the picture of innocence. "I didn't even know anyone there."

"You knew Kara," she said simply.

He had to laugh. Yes, he knew Kara. But what did he really know of her? That she was a rich girl who ran a bakery that would be lucky to last for another year? That she was as stubborn as she was beautiful and that maybe the two went hand in hand? She was intriguing; he'd have to give her that much. And sweet in some ways. But he'd be smart to keep his distance from her, even if his aunt had other plans.

"If you think you can play matchmaker while I'm in town, you may as well save your energy for the decorations. I'm going back to Boston in two weeks," he reminded her.

"So?" Again, the innocent shrug.

"So," he said, pushing himself out of his chair. "Kara and I are from two different worlds."

And he'd be best to remember that.

CHAPTER
8

What had she been thinking, agreeing to enter this contest? She hadn't been thinking; that was just the problem. She'd been too busy staring into those mysterious, deep-set eyes. Too busy feeling the heat of desire replaced by something even more fiery as he dared to call her bluff. Too busy thinking of all the people who'd made their little comments over the past few months. The nonbelievers. She'd been thinking with her heart, not her head, and now...Well, now she'd have to just find a worthwhile excuse and learn to ignore the inevitable jabs Nate would no doubt toss her way when he discovered she wasn't going to compete against him.

She'd say she was too busy, and wasn't that the truth! She was already struggling to make time to have brunch with her family this morning, even though she opened later on Sundays and Mondays were her day off. Christmas was just around the corner now. She wasn't so sure whether that was a good thing or a bad thing anymore.

Kara felt her shoulders relax as she rounded the corner and her childhood home came into view at the end of the street. The large dormer Cape was set far back from the road, off a winding driveway that Kara and Molly used to roller-skate on when they were younger. Now it was plowed and salted, and mounds of fresh snow were piled high at each side. Kara followed the brick-paved path up to the navy blue front door, where a simple magnolia wreath was hung from a brass hanger, and pressed the doorbell before poking her nose up against one of the long glass panes that framed the door. Inside she could see boxes of ornaments, some already open, the contents spilling, gathered in the hall. Molly came scurrying from the kitchen, Rosemary calling something after her.

"Good thing you're here," Molly said as she pulled open the door and Kara stepped inside.

The air was warm and smelled of fresh yeast and cinnamon—a telltale sign that her favorite holiday bread was in the oven. She unwrapped her scarf and set it on the bench near the front door, then dropped onto it to remove her boots. "Let me guess," she said, smiling. "*The Nutcracker*?"

"This time of year…" Molly clucked her tongue and shook her head. "I should have stayed in Boston."

"You don't mean that." Kara set her boots on the mat to dry. Christmas was a big deal in their family, and they'd always found a way to all be together for it, regardless of their busy schedules. Kara paused, remembering Todd. He was in Boston, so perhaps Molly would have preferred to spend the holidays with him. It was certainly unusual.

Molly gave a rueful smile. "No, I suppose I don't mean it. I'm happy I'm here but, well…you know how it is. Last night Mom was calling out orders in her sleep, reprimanding the soldiers to stand in a straighter line. Nearly gave me a heart attack, I tell you!"

Kara laughed. *The Nutcracker* had been an annual tradition for the Hastings family for as long as she could remember. People from all over the county came to see the show, which was held the week of Christmas. Kara and Molly had performed in it as children, never earning the coveted role of Clara, though, as neither of them had inherited their mother's natural grace.

Kara thought back to her slip on the ice outside the inn and winced. She'd always had two left feet, probably a little to her mother's disappointment.

The girls wound their way through boxes of decorations on their way to the back of the house, where their mother was assembling a fruit salad at the center kitchen island.

"The house looks beautiful, Mom," Kara said, admiring the garland that had been swagged from the big bay window near the eat-in table. In the adjacent family room, the hearth was flanked by oversized nutcrackers, and a garland of sugarplums covered the mantel.

"I was thinking that your father always loved seeing the house decked out for the holidays. I wonder what he might have thought of this year's efforts..." Rosemary gave a strained smile, and her eyes misted before she quickly blinked the tears back.

Kara's eyes fell to the armchair in the corner, where her father would sit and read the paper or watch them open gifts on Christmas morning. The armrests were tattered, and she could remember her mother tutting that it needed new upholstery, but after he was gone, that subject was closed. No one really sat there now. But it was hardly empty. Each time Kara stared at that spot, she could almost see him.

A hard lump had formed in her throat. She looked away, blinking quickly.

"It will look even better once I'm through with it. Molly's been a real help," her mother added, giving her younger daughter a grateful smile. "And speaking of help, I was hoping I might have a word with you about your cookies."

Kara counted out plates in the cabinet and carried the stack over to the table, trying to keep her hands from shaking. It was no use. Her heart was speeding up and her mouth had gone dry. Mrs. Griffin had probably mentioned something about the cookies being late the other day. Now her mother would worry, want to see if things were all right or if she was in over her head.

"Yes?" she asked, but her voice was nothing but a breathless gasp.

"Would you be interested in making some cookies to sell during intermission at the show?" The show was, of course, *The Nutcracker.* "I usually offer soda and bags of popcorn, but your cookies would be so much more festive."

Kara finished setting the last plate on the red woven place mat and turned to face her mother. "Would I be interested? I'd love to!" She could barely contain her smile when she considered the possibilities, but it was something far deeper that made her heart soar. *The Nutcracker* was the highlight of her mother's year. She oversaw every aspect of the show, down to the smallest detail. Including Kara's cookies wasn't just a thoughtful gesture. It meant she believed in her ability, saw it as more than a passing hobby.

"Excellent!" Her mother set the wooden spoon down as Kara's brother called out from the front hall.

Luke and Grace were barely in the kitchen before Rosemary asked him, "Anything new?"

Grace and Kara exchanged a knowing look. It was no mystery that Rosemary was itching for a grandbaby, even though Grace and Luke were happy to take their time with the next phase of their relationship.

"Nope, nothing new, Mom." Luke grinned and rolled his eyes slightly at Kara. "Molly's engagement was the big news for the year."

Molly looked flustered as she set a plate of hash browns on the table. "Oh, well, and Kara's new shop, of course. Let's not forget that."

"Well, Christmas is still a bit more than a week away," Rosemary said as she finished setting the table. "Perhaps I'll wake up to a surprise that morning."

Kara shook her head at Grace, for once happy to be the single girl in the room. Now that Molly was engaged and their mother had a wedding to plan, Kara didn't have to worry about hurrying up and finding someone or answering these types of questions. Still, a little part of her wouldn't mind, she supposed.

Crazy talk, she told herself. For years she'd tolerated her mother's less-than-subtle hints, the little suggestions she made about various eligible men who were never her type. It wasn't until Kara announced her plan to open the bakery that her mother finally settled down and started looking at her a little differently, too. It felt good to know her mother was proud of her, and even better to know she believed in her, Kara thought, thinking of the cookies she would make for the ballet performance.

"So, Grace," Rosemary said as they all sat down to eat at the rectangular table centered near the kitchen's large bay window. The backyard was covered in snow, and Kara took a moment to sip her coffee and enjoy the view of the flocked branches and the bright cardinals that nested in the pine trees, their color a stark contrast against the glistening white. "I suppose your mother is busy as a beaver with her decorations."

Grace nodded sagely. "Oh, yes. She's going all-out this year, given the prize."

"What prize?" Kara asked, her attention immediately pulled from the winter scene. There had never been a monetary prize for winning the Holiday House contest. There was a front-page photo in the town's newspaper and, of course, some bragging rights that lasted through about mid-January—hardly an incentive to spend her precious time this way, even if it would wipe that smirk off Nate's handsome face when she beat him fair and square.

"This year marks the twenty-fifth anniversary of Briar Creek's Holiday House contest," Grace said. "Henry pulled some strings at the travel magazine where he used to work, and they're going to run a full article on the winner. My mother is already dreaming of what that could do for her design business," Grace added with a little shake of her head.

"But that's not all," Rosemary said. "This year, the winner gets a ten-thousand-dollar prize, too."

Kara knew her jaw had slacked. She tried to wrap her head around such a thing. "Paid by who?"

"The tourist bureau!" Luke chimed in. He glanced around at the women, grinning proudly at being able to participate in the conversation.

"It's a big driver for the town," Grace agreed. "It's fun for everyone, but ultimately, we all benefit, regardless of the winner."

"Still. To win…" Kara took a sip of her coffee, her mind racing. She'd spent every last dime of her inheritance between the build-out of the shop and initial supplies. She'd had nothing to her name by way of savings before she opened—a string of minimum-wage jobs over of the years hadn't amounted to much. The pressure to turn a profit was huge, and a cushion like this would be…very helpful, to say the least.

"To win would be fun." Grace laughed. "I suppose I should just come out and admit that I managed to convince Luke to enter."

Rosemary gave her son a stern look. "And I thought there were no announcements today?"

He cocked an eyebrow. "I think there's only one announcement you're waiting for, and you're just going to have to keep waiting."

"Oh, you know I'm just teasing. Though I suppose if you hold out much longer, I may just have to ask Brett about volunteering to hold babies in the hospital nursery..." Rosemary pressed her ruby-painted lips together and stirred some milk into her coffee.

Kara blinked down at her plate of food, remembering the glint in Nate's eyes, the way his banter turned edgy, from defensive to offensive, almost. Imagine, a holiday house made out of gingerbread! It was preposterous, it was ridiculous. It was...genius. After all, what said Christmas better than a gingerbread house? And what said Christmas better than...home?

Kara eyed her father's armchair, contemplating her decision. She'd have to get started soon if she intended to enter. Because one thing was more certain than ever: If she was going to enter, she was in it to win it. Not just because of the money, but because she'd love to see the look on Nate's face when she showed him what she was made of.

Besides, in her book, the man always treated on the first date.

A date. That was what he'd implied, hadn't he? He'd been caught up in the moment, in the heat of her body, so close to his, in the soft melody of her laugh and the proximity of those soft ruby lips. Win or lose, they'd agreed to it, but he intended to win. There was no chance in hell he was going to let this contest go to anyone other than his aunt.

Nate glanced out the window of the library, which was

positioned at the far end of the house, its side windows looking out onto Main Street. If he craned his neck, he could
almost see Sugar and Spice's awning blowing in the wind.
He peered through the falling snow, looking for a glimpse
of her. She'd be dropping off the cookies for tea soon. He
supposed he could keep himself useful, continue with the
decorations for this room, which he hoped to finish today,
but he couldn't resist the opportunity to see her again. It was
quickly becoming a highlight of his visit, and one, he realized with a jolt, he would miss when he went back to Boston.

He checked his watch and decided to risk it. As he'd
suspected, his aunt had woken with a new vengeance this
morning, handing over a detailed list she called her "action
plan," and it started with this library. He'd already wrapped
each window in pine garland, but he had a box of knickknacks
to get through before it would pass her inspection, and he didn't
dare disappoint.

He picked another ornament from the box and set it on a
side table. It had been years since he'd decorated a tree—he
didn't bother with one in his apartment, and his parents set
theirs up on their own. When he was a kid, he loved getting out the dusty box and combing through its contents,
content to spend an afternoon hanging each hook on just the
right branch, hoping that Santa would reward the effort with
a new bike or skateboard. But the bike never came. Or the
skateboard. And eventually, Nate had come to associate a
feeling of dread when he saw that box come out of the closet.
For some, it was a season of cheer. For others . . . stress.

But for Maggie it was a season of cheer, and for that reason, Nate told himself firmly, he'd put his head down and
push through. He was a grown man, after all, and Christmas
had long since stopped having so much meaning pinned to it.

He took care with each task, finding a strange sense of

enjoyment in it. He'd always enjoyed working with his hands as a kid, finding it therapeutic, even finding some success with it. He frowned for a minute when he thought of those paintings his mother still kept throughout the apartment, long after he'd told her to take them down. They were from another place and another time. But she loved them, and he never could deprive her of something that made her smile.

It was almost noon by the time he'd finished in the library. Guests were gathered in the lobby, bundled warm for snowshoeing, some returning with shopping bags. Many were getting ready to check out, their weekend getaway over, the drive home looming before them along with the start of the workweek. Normally he looked forward to Monday, even though Sundays were hardly a day of rest. Hard work suited him, gave him a purpose, something to strive for. Made him feel in control.

He realized with a start that he hadn't bothered to charge his cell phone since it had run out of juice last night. No doubt emails were pouring in—work didn't stop for him on weekends or days off. He supposed he'd have to check in eventually. But today, he had to admit he was looking forward to the promise of a quiet week in Briar Creek, without the rush of energy he felt back in the city. Each day that he was away from it, his anxiety lessened, as did the fear that it would all go away if he took a step back.

His life would never be like the one he'd come from. He'd made damn sure of that.

Casually, he walked to the front window just in time to see Kara coming down the sidewalk, holding a white box no doubt filled with those delicious snowflake cookies, the pom-pom on her hat wiggling in the wind. Her eyes darted to the house and she stopped at the base of the front path, pulling in a sigh that rolled through her shoulders, before finally approaching.

Nate pulled back from the window. His aunt was busy prepping croissant dough for tomorrow morning's breakfast. Kara could just put the cookies on the dining room console as she'd done before, but what fun would that be?

He wanted to see her, he realized. He wanted to talk with her. Wanted to know her. Wanted to believe she was different than all the others he'd known like her before.

He tensed, as he always did when he thought of his past. She was an attractive girl, and he felt a spark between them, but he needed to be wary around her, just in case.

"Hello," he said, grinning, when she pushed through the door. She looked especially pretty today, with cheeks pink from the cold.

Kara's eyes widened a notch as she began stomping the snow off her boots. "Here are your cookies," she said, handing him the box. Her gaze trailed over the big tree in the corner. "I can see you've been busy," she observed.

"That's just a preview of what's to come." Nate resisted the urge to pop the lid on the box and take a taste of one of her creations. He hadn't yet joined his aunt for the holiday tea, but this afternoon he just might. Roving his gaze over Kara, he said, "Feeling the heat of competition?"

"If I know your aunt, she's not going to make this easy for me." Kara shook her head as her eyes darted around the lobby. "I suppose I'd better get back to the bakery and roll up my sleeves."

Nate's pulse skipped a beat, and before he could process what he was doing, he reached out and set a hand on her arm. She turned to him, brow knit, mouth lightly parted in question, her lips so plump and her cheeks so pink from being outside, he couldn't stop staring at her. "Don't go yet." He swallowed hard, wondering if he'd overstepped, and realizing he was still holding on to her arm, finally dropped it.

"I mean, stay and warm up by the fire for a few minutes at least. You look so cold." Her blue eyes were bright and clear as they locked with his, and the flush in her cheeks darkened a shade.

She hesitated before her mouth curved slowly. "I guess it wouldn't hurt to stay for a few minutes. It's one of the coldest days we've had so far this year."

"Just don't let me catch you scoping out the competition," Nate joked, feeling his shoulders relax.

Her smile came a little easier. "It wouldn't change my vision. I know exactly what I have planned."

"Already?" Nate couldn't help but admire her tenacity. He settled into an armchair near the fire, just opposite Kara, but still, they were hardly alone. A few guests sat together on the love seat and others at a small table near the front window.

It was better that way, he told himself. There were many reasons not to fall for Kara, the least of which being that he was just passing through town.

"Christmas is only ten days away," she pointed out. "And the judging is held on Christmas Eve."

Ten days. And then he'd be back in Boston. On his way into Briar Creek, he was already counting down the hours, but now, the time seemed fleeting and all too brief.

"So it is," he said. "You like a little healthy competition then?"

"More like I like the sound of the grand prize," she said, raising an eyebrow. "That's what made me decide to enter."

"And here I thought it was my wager," he said.

"Oh, your wager is still on," she said. She held his gaze, her cheeks blushing.

Nate smiled. "Good. I could use a home-cooked meal. And trust me, you don't want anything I'd whip up."

Kara laughed. "Oh, so now I'll be cooking the dinner?"

"Why not? You clearly know your way around a kitchen. I can handle the buttons on the microwave. It stops there."

"Well, there happen to be a few excellent restaurants in town," she replied. "I'll make the reservation in your name this afternoon."

"That confident, are you?" Nate asked evenly.

Kara's brow pinched slightly and the tone suddenly shifted. He'd hit a nerve, drawing on his earlier suspicions that she might not just be as sure of herself as he'd first thought.

"I'll do my best," she said through a smile. "That's all any of us can do. Still, it would be nice to win. I suppose you've heard about the prize money?"

Nate narrowed his eyes. This was a strange comment, coming from her. Still, he shrugged. "I have. My aunt was sure to mention it."

"Well, it's exciting. And I'm hoping it will help me get into the Christmas spirit, too."

"And here I thought you were just bursting with good tidings already," Nate replied. He eyed her lazily. She was still tucked into her puffy red coat, her hat still resting on her head, but her mittens sat on her lap as she held her hands out toward the fire. They were pink and cold looking, and he had an urge to lean forward and knead each digit through his hands, warm her from the outside in.

"I suppose I haven't had as much time to enjoy the holidays as I'd like this year." She glanced wistfully into the dining room. "The holiday tea is always such a treat. I'll be sad to miss out this year. If only I wasn't so busy."

With a resigned smile, she began pulling on her mittens and stood. A knot of disappointment landed square in his gut. She was here and gone all too soon. And all he had to look forward to for the rest of the day was decorating this old house.

"I guess I'll see you tomorrow then," she said, edging toward the door.

Tomorrow. He liked the sound of that.

CHAPTER 9

Even though the bakery was officially closed on Mondays, Kara had gone in just before sunrise to get an early start on her gingerbread house entry for the Holiday House contest. She'd decided to make the house in the shape of her own childhood home, the one where she'd shared so many wonderful Christmas memories with her family, capturing a moment in time when she was the happiest. After closing the shop the day before, she'd drawn the pattern out on parchment paper, and by early morning all the pieces of gingerbread had been baked and cooled. The designs would take the longest, but if she worked steadily on them each day, she was sure she could accomplish what she'd set out to do.

Kara looked at the drawing she'd made and sighed. If only she could go in back time, even just for a day. She'd do anything to wake up on Christmas again with that unmatchable sense of possibility and run into her parents' bedroom. What wouldn't she give to sit around the breakfast table in her flannel pajamas, sipping hot cocoa while her father poured coffee and flipped pages in his newspaper? It was so long ago, but somehow, at this time of year, it still felt like yesterday.

Christmas had never been the same since her dad had died. The first few years were the worst, even though their mother tried to make it special for them and not show her sadness. She had *The Nutcracker* to keep her busy, and now, as an adult, Kara understood why it meant so much to her. It wasn't just the perfectionist in her, or the proud business-woman; it was that her annual show was the perfect distraction, the best way to fill a part of her heart that was missing.

Kara smiled at the drawing, knowing she had to capture that moment of pure joy. Children running down the stairs, a tree surrounded by glittering presents, Dad at the table, sipping coffee.

Deciding she could take a break for a few hours, Kara put on her coat, hat, and boots and grabbed her skates from the closet in the small office off the back of the kitchen. The walk to the town square was short, and the sun was shining, casting long shadows on the roof of the white gazebo at its center. Main Street B&B stood proudly at the far end, look-ing even more stately than usual in its Christmas décor. Kara couldn't help but look for some subtle changes, something new that might have been added since her visit yesterday, but it would seem all the magic was happening inside, not out... at least so far.

She craned her neck to get a better view of the side of the house when she spotted him, her heart giving a little jump at the image. Nate came around the path, sprinkling salt on the bricks with a large shovel. She hesitated when she saw him, wondering if she should keep going, get to the rink before it filled up, but as she watched him push his shovel into the bag of salt again and continue his work, she had to grin. He was a nice guy, really. And a handsome one, too. That much was undeniable. He had a hard shell, one that wasn't common in these parts, but under it, she suspected, was a good heart.

Not every nephew would give up his Christmas vacation to cater to an eccentric aunt—it was no wonder Mrs. Griffin sang his praises far and wide.

She walked a little closer, cutting to the edge of the green instead of winding left as she would have to get to the skating rink, and waited for a moment to see if he would look up. He seemed to be grumbling something under his breath with each scoop, something about "no good deed," and Kara couldn't help but laugh to herself. Mrs. Griffin certainly was putting the poor guy to work.

Looking up, he grinned at her before she'd even had the chance to lift her mittened hand into a wave. "How long have you been standing there?" he asked, resting his hands on the handle of the shovel. It was a small gesture, but the moment he was taking to give her his full attention sent a little flutter through her stomach. It had been a long time since a man had paid such notice, and even longer since one this handsome had done so.

Men like Nate didn't pop up in life. At least, not often enough.

"Long enough to see that you're earning your keep." Kara laughed. "Tell me, do you ever get a break?"

"I'm used to working all day," Nate said. "I'm not sure if I'd know how to sit back and relax, to be honest. But to answer your question, no, I haven't taken a break since arriving here. It would seem my aunt had plans for me from the moment she knew I was coming."

"You're good to her," Kara said gently.

Nate gave a modest shrug. "Not good enough. I feel bad that I haven't visited before. Life gets busy."

Kara nodded. He could say that again. Soon, Molly would be back in Boston, and Kara knew she'd be kicking herself for not having been able to properly enjoy this visit more. This afternoon they were going to look at invitations together—that was something—and after, they'd have dinner while their mother was at dance rehearsals. Still, the passing of time was always on her mind at this time of year. And by next year, who knew...maybe Molly would be spending the time with her new husband's family.

"I'm headed over to the pond," Kara said, gesturing to the end of the town square where the seasonal rink had been constructed. "You're welcome to join me if you want."

Her heart sped up as she waited for him to consider her offer. It wasn't like her to be so forward with men, but Nate wasn't like any other men. He was a friend, sort of, and he wasn't a potential boyfriend or anything. He was a visitor, who would be gone all too soon.

She told herself she was just being friendly. After all, the poor guy needed a little fun, and he didn't know anyone else...

Still, she couldn't deny the bubble that swelled in her belly when he grinned a little wider and said, "Sure."

"Great," she said, managing to keep her tone casual. "They rent skates if you don't have any."

"Let me just tell my aunt where I'm going so she doesn't call the police and report me missing or anything." Nate appeared to be only half joking. "Sometimes she forgets I'm not ten years old anymore," he explained ruefully before disappearing through the front door.

Kara took a quick minute to pull her lip gloss from her pocket and swipe it over her lips. She smoothed her ponytail and readjusted her hat and told herself that she was being wholly ridiculous. So he was cute. So he was very cute. Lots of men were cute. It was just that none of them had made her feel that spark before.

A few moments later, Nate appeared at the door again,

clutching something thick and wooly in his hands. "She insisted I'd need this," Nate said, crossing the street to meet her. In the winter sunlight, his eyes appeared lighter than usual, a pale gold, set behind thick brows. She took in that wide grin and the square jaw, and okay, she swooned a little.

Kara inspected the red and white wooly item in his hands. She could have sworn it was made of angora. "Is that a... woman's hat?" she asked, clasping her hand to her mouth to stifle her laughter.

Nate glanced back at the house and then shoved it onto his head. Santa's jolly face smiled back at her, almost more distracting than Nate's wicked grin. "Come on," he said, taking her by the arm. "I'll take it off once I'm out of sight."

The red yarn was woven with tinsel that reflected off the sunlight as they crunched through the snow, forgetting the shoveled path in their quest. Nate waited until he was safely beyond the gazebo to pull it off. "Here," he said, handing it to her. "I think this would look better on you."

"Oh, but I already have my hat," she demurred, patting her pom-pom.

"That you do," he said, his eyes roving her face, spreading a tingle of warmth all down her belly. "But something tells me you could wear this hat and somehow still look cute."

Kara blushed and looked down at the snow, blinking away the compliment as she stared at her boots, the tips of which were cozily close to his. He was a smooth talker, maybe even a little bit of a flirt. Better not to read too much into these things...

"The skate rental stand is just over there," Kara said, pointing to the wooden shed used for storing boots. She settled herself onto a bench while Nate went to get skates, watching the skaters as she slid off her boots. In the center of the ice, a teenage girl was showing off a camel spin, finishing with a grand flourish that no doubt grabbed the attention of the hockey players down at the end of the rink, trying their best to look like they hadn't been watching. Kara shook her head, grinning, and began tightening her skate laces.

"Nice skates." Nate's slow, deep voice spread a tingle over her as he came to sit beside her. "Do you come here much?"

"Not as often as I'd like," Kara admitted. "When I was younger, I came every weekend. More on school breaks."

"Then you must be good," Nate said, grinning.

"Good enough," Kara said. She looked at him warily. "Why? You're not going to challenge me to something again, are you?"

He laughed, a rich, booming sound that echoed through the brittle winter air. "No. I'll be lucky to stand up without falling on my face," he said.

"That won't be anything new for us, will it?" Kara grinned as she stood. She held out her hand. "Come on, last one on the ice buys hot chocolate afterward."

Nate hadn't been planning on holding Kara's hand, no matter how good it felt in his own, despite the layers of gloves he wished he could peel away. His feet wobbled as he hit the ice, and he felt the slip on his blades before he'd even taken his first stroke, but Kara was patient, walking him through it, no hint of amusement noticeable in those piercing blue eyes.

"I didn't do this much as a kid," he said after they'd successfully made the first lap.

"Growing up here, it's what we all did," Kara said. "Well, except my mom. She runs the dance studio, and she was always too afraid of breaking a limb." She laughed, but her eyes went flat as a man and little girl passed them.

Her mouth turned downward as she watched them skate, her eyes never leaving the little girl, who giggled and squealed as her father picked her up and twirled her around.

"My dad was the skater in the family. Hockey," she explained, slanting him a glance. "But he loved the ice. I did, too. Still do."

"Does he still get out here much?"

Kara looked momentarily startled. She paused before saying, "Oh, no. My dad died when I was ten."

Nate stopped skating, nearly tripping over his toe pick. He hadn't expected that one. His aunt Maggie wasn't shy when it came to the local gossip mill, and this was one thing she hadn't mentioned. He was suddenly filled with a deep shame for assuming Kara had always had it easy in life. He looked at her, frowning. "I'm sorry to hear that."

Kara shrugged, but he could see the pain in her eyes as she looked far out to the sledding hill, where kids were propelling themselves down the steep slope on inner tubes. "It's been a long time. When I come here, though...it's like he's with me, you know? Like he's sitting over there on the bench, watching me skate. Like he's holding my hand."

Nate glanced down at the hand that still held his and gave it a little squeeze. "Life is unfair," he said, shaking his head.

"It is," Kara agreed, "but I've learned to live in the moment. Focus on what I have. Enjoy it while I can."

Nate thought of the time he was spending with his aunt and nodded. "It's easy to get tripped up by things that don't really matter."

"Like the Holiday House contest?" Kara gave him a knowing smile. "Although I enjoy our town's traditions. It's part of our culture, part of our community. It's tight-knit here. I like that."

Nate didn't say anything. Tight-knit was something he was all too familiar with, but no matter how close a community, there was always an outsider, always someone left out or cast aside. Someone different from the others.

Something a girl like Kara could never understand.

"Come on," she said, releasing his hand and skating quickly away from him. He watched her long legs, covered in skintight black leggings, move and sway with each graceful glide, the way her thighs extended, the muscles taut as she expertly maneuvered herself over the mirror-like surface. She stopped and turned, her smile contagious as she waved him toward her. "Five laps. Ready? Go."

She was off like a shot before he'd even had a chance to process what she was saying, and he shuffled his feet beneath him, knowing it was probably a losing fight, but one he was willing to try for, because there was something about Kara he just couldn't resist.

Kara accepted her hot chocolate with a smile and took a seat at a table under a heat lamp, choosing a chair that gave her a view of the skaters on the rink. "I think I'll make a weekly habit of coming here," she announced, smiling serenely at the view. "It's important to give yourself a little downtime every once in a while. It helps to keep things in balance."

Not that he would know. For as long as Nate could remember, he'd had his nose to the books or a computer, or he'd holed himself in the school art studio, creating alternate realities through a brush and canvas. He'd barely looked up, afraid of what would happen when he did. But now that he'd risked it, he had to admit he was enjoying himself. More than he'd ever thought possible.

"How's the hot chocolate?" he asked as he unzipped his

coat. It was surprisingly warm under the heat of the lamp, and both of them had worked up a sweat on the ice, even if Nate's excursion had been in trying to keep himself from falling rather than getting around.

"Almost as good as the one I make," Kara said. She set her mug down and glanced at him from under her lashes. "I've been meaning to thank you...for suggesting that I include coffee on my menu. I don't know how I could have missed that."

"It's easy," Nate said, shrugging. "You're too close to the business to see what areas need improvement. And you were probably so focused on making sure your cookies were just right that you overlooked the drinks. It happens."

"Well, I'm just glad I've rectified it. I'm new at all of this, and it's important to me that I get it right. There are a lot of people in town who think I'll fail."

"Don't listen to other people or what they say. They can only knock you down if you let them. If you want something badly enough, you'll find a way to make it work. But don't do it in spite of them. Do it for yourself." His face flushed with anger and he reached for his mug, trying to hide it.

Kara was watching him with surprise in her eyes. "You sound like you're speaking from experience."

More than she would ever know. He squinted into the sun, waiting for the air to cool the temper from his skin. He didn't feel the need to elaborate or dwell on his past. Not when he was having such a nice day. She'd hit a nerve, reminding him of a time in his life he'd rather forget. Especially today.

Pulling himself from darkening thoughts, he looked over at her, grinning when he noticed the whipped cream that clung to the corner of her pretty mouth. He waited for her to notice, but she was looking out onto the rink, watching the skaters go past.

He knew he could say something, gesture with a napkin, but instead he reached over, his smile broadening as she blinked at him in startled surprise, and wiped the cream from her mouth with the back of his thumb.

"Whipped cream," he explained. He felt the pull of her smile under his finger before he brought his hand away.

Kara wiped quickly at her mouth. "Ah, see, a true competitor wouldn't have lent a hand," she remarked.

"I hardly think I've given you an advantage." Nate smiled easily, leaning back into his chair, watching as Kara swiped a napkin over her mouth. "Besides, I've started to realize you're a formidable opponent. I'm not so sure how my aunt will feel about that."

"Oh, none of us stand much of a chance with Kathleen Madison in the mix," Kara replied. She sighed as she wrapped her hands around the mug. "But it sure would be nice to win."

"This bakery means a lot to you," he commented. "When something means that much, you find a way to make it work."

"I hope so," Kara sighed. "But it's not just the fear of hearing people say they told me so that worries me." Kara stirred the marshmallows into her hot chocolate, watching them melt. "When my dad died, each of us got a bit of inheritance. I saved mine all these years. I...I couldn't bring myself to spend it, you see. I felt like once it was gone, it was gone, and that last little part of him would be, too. When I started to realize what I wanted to do with my life, that I was good at baking and that I wanted something to call my own, I thought this was a chance to use the money for something good. Every day when I walk into that bakery, I feel like a part of him is there with me. Like he helped me build it."

Shame nipped at him, sharper than the December breeze, and Nate swallowed hard against his growing guilt. He'd misjudged her. Done exactly what the kids at school had done to him. Labeled her.

"He did help you build it," he said, leaning forward to touch her wrist.

She smiled sadly at him, the sweet sight tearing at his chest. "I just couldn't bear it if anything happened to that bakery. I know people think I'll get bored and quit one day. But I won't. It's hard work, I won't deny that, but I can do it." She grinned as she locked his eyes. "And winning the Holiday House contest will certainly help."

He lifted an eyebrow, deciding to follow her change of tone. "Hey, I've got a few surprises up my sleeve, I'll have you know. Don't count me out just yet."

"As do I," she said, pursing her lips. "And as for counting you out...I don't see that happening." She held his gaze for a beat, until her cheeks turned a bright pink, and then hastily brought her mug to her lips.

Nate drained the rest of his own beverage, eyeing her carefully. Something was shifting between them. Something he enjoyed.

"You'd better put that Santa cap back on before your aunt catches you without it," Kara warned, flashing him a mischievous grin. "You know, everything she ever said about you was true, by the way."

"You mean the stuff about my fancy car and my fancy degree?" Nate shook his head. He only had the car because it was necessary for client meetings—because there was a certain image he needed to portray in his position.

"That, and the other stuff, too. She said you were smart and kind. And quiet. She adores you, Nate. I can see why."

His brow shot up in surprise. A pretty girl was paying him a compliment, and maybe one he didn't completely deserve.

He should have trusted his gut, ignored the surface-level information.

Kara was sweet, and pretty, and entirely unlike any other woman he'd met in a while. He certainly hadn't expected to meet someone like her when he'd agreed to come to Briar Creek for the holidays. But then, he hadn't known what to expect then.

One thing was becoming certain: This was one Christmas he was never going to forget.

CHAPTER 10

Molly was waiting on a bench outside the Paper Pixie when Kara called her name from across the street. Molly bounced up and waved back, watching as her sister scurried across the slushy street.

"I hope you weren't sitting out there for long," Kara said, alarm flashing in her bright blue eyes. "It's freezing out here. I went skating this morning, but I think the temperature has actually dropped since then."

Molly just shrugged. The cold air never bothered her, and besides, she needed it to clear her mind today. She'd hoped that planning this wedding would make her feel excited about the prospect of marrying Todd, but all it did was fill her with more doubts.

"Shall we?" Molly wrapped her hand around the big brass handle and pulled the door open, momentarily disarmed by the beautiful holiday display that centered the room. She reached out and touched one of the homemade paper wreaths, feeling the creaminess of the paper in her hand. For a long as she could remember, she'd loved paper—collecting and storing it, often afraid of writing on it for fear of ruining it—and pens. Colored pens. Sparkly ink. One year she'd received a calligraphy set for Christmas. She wondered if her mother had kept it... She'd look when she went back to the house. Maybe she would do her own lettering for the menus or something. As they liked to suggest at the magazine, a personal touch was always important at a wedding.

"You always did love paper." Kara laughed under her breath.

"I still do." Molly sighed. "You should see my bedroom closet in my apartment. It's my guilty pleasure. That and all things romance."

"It didn't surprise any of us that you took that job at the bridal magazine," Kara observed.

It was true. The job was a perfect fit. A childhood fantasy come true. For as long as she could remember, she'd loved the idea of weddings: the ball gown, the flowers, the music swelling as the tension built and the bride appeared as people rose, and of course the walk down the aisle. She'd always wanted a long aisle. Long enough to build up the anticipation, to stretch the drama to maximum capacity. And then of course the cake. Who didn't love wedding cakes, often too pretty to want to eat?

She'd planned her wedding at least two dozen times, starting at the age of ten, when she'd wanted everything to be purple, right down to the lilac bridesmaid dresses. The one setback in her fantasy was that her father was no longer with them to walk her down the aisle. She had cried about this when the realization first hit her, but Luke had just given her a quizzical look and told her that was what he was for— if she'd let him.

Molly smiled at the memory, of how eager her brother was to soften her heartache, even though they both knew he could never fill their father's shoes, and didn't intend to, either. Now she suddenly missed her father more than ever, and not just because he wouldn't be here to walk her down the aisle. Something told her that her father would know how to help her through her mixed feelings better than her mother could.

Molly stopped and picked up a scrapbook. It was similar to the ones she'd filled over the years, collecting ideas for her wedding cake, her dress, her shoes, her bouquet... Her visions had gradually changed over the years, but one thing had never wavered. She would get married on Valentine's Day. And now...she was about to do just that.

She put a hand to her stomach. God, she suddenly felt sick.

Doing her best to rearrange her grimace, she managed to smile as Shea O'Riley, the store's owner and an old acquaintance, came to greet them, her pretty blond hair pulled back in a chic chignon.

Molly had already planned on a classic bun for her wedding day, but now she wondered if a chignon might be more elegant. Something to think about, and she was happy for it. It suddenly occurred to her that it might have been easier to distract herself from all these nerves if she was busy planning the wedding instead of more or less executing a fine-tuned plan.

"Merry Christmas!" Shea said, coming over to give Molly a hug. "And congratulations, I see. Go on, show me the bling. Make us single girls green with envy." She tossed a wink at Kara.

Molly felt her smile slip as she pulled her glove from her hand. It was becoming considerably less enjoyable to show the thing off, it seemed. She was grateful it was winter, that she could hide it most of the time under her outerwear. Somehow it felt...wrong to show the ring off so much. Like a...sham.

She stiffened. Nonsense! She'd chosen this ring, and Todd had bought it for her, slipped it on her finger, and made all her dreams come true. Sure, it wasn't exactly the grand, romantic proposal she'd detailed, with some secret planning on his part, but she was a modern girl, and that meant relinquishing some traditional fantasies. If she'd left Todd to pick out the ring himself, there was no telling what he would have come up with. Did she want the perfect proposal or the perfect ring? She settled for the perfect ring and came up with a cute spin on their less-than-swoon-worthy proposal. After all, she'd be wearing this ring forever... technically.

Her stomach knotted again. "Look at that ring!" Shea sighed. "And I bet he picked it out himself, right? Lucky fellow." Turning to Kara, she said sadly, "And then there were two."

"Yep," Kara said, but her cheeks went all red and she struggled to hold Molly's gaze.

Interesting, Molly thought, sliding her glove back on her hand. Her sister hadn't dated much over the years, and Kara hadn't mentioned that there was anyone in her life at the moment; if anything, she'd seemed a bit down about being single during the holidays. But from the flush in her cheeks it might seem she had something to hide.

That made two of them, she thought with sudden dread.

"So, have you decided on a color scheme?" Shea guided them over to a table in the corner of the room where invitation samples were already set up.

Molly picked one up and sighed. She couldn't help it. With the raised lettering and the elegant scroll, she could almost feel her excitement return. "I'm getting married Valentine's weekend, so it will be red, lavender, cream, and a touch of pink." She slid her sister a look. "Just a touch."

"You know, we should probably wait for Mom to be here

to decide on anything," Kara said, and Molly felt her stomach tighten.

It was true that their mother would want to be a part of this. A big part. But their mother had a big personality, and even bigger opinions. And Molly already knew exactly how she wanted to look. She even had her dress picked out—she'd found it two years ago—she was just trying on others to be sure of her choice and to help get her into the spirit of things. She'd waited so long for this event—how could she not be enjoying it more? Finally, she was going to be the bride! She was going to have the dress, the flowers, the veil! All these years of waiting for her moment...and it was only a couple of months away.

"I just want to have an idea of things before I let her in," Molly explained. There would be plenty of time to devote to wedding plans after *The Nutcracker* wrapped up, but she couldn't wait another week to get started on it. She needed to bring it to life, make it real in her mind, embrace the idea until she wasn't able to imagine letting it go. She closed her eyes. She could picture the candlelight, hear the soft sound of piano music, feel the swoosh of her dress...

"I understand," Kara said. "I did the same thing when it came to Sugar and Spice, not that the bakery is the same as a wedding day, of course," she was quick to add. "But it's personal to me, and I needed it to reflect my wishes, not someone else's."

"Well, there's no need to decide today," Shea said, flipping open a binder and turning it to the sisters. "Some brides take months to make a selection."

"That's probably how it would be for me," Kara mused. "I seem to second-guess pretty much every decision I make. But I'm getting better at sticking with my instinct."

She grew quiet, lowering her gaze as she glanced out

the window and onto the town square. The paper store had moved off Main Street when Rosemary and Thyme expanded into its original space, and it was now housed on Chestnut Street, just opposite the green. Molly followed Kara's gaze and looked out onto the winter scene, watching the skaters twirl and spin across the ice. It always made Molly think of their dad and the time they spent with him there as kids.

She knew it was hard this time of year, for all of them, but something in Kara's wistful stare told Molly she wasn't thinking about their father right now. She wondered if there was another man occupying her sister's thoughts instead.

"What are your Christmas plans this year?" she asked Shea as she flipped through the binder, stopping to admire some of the samples. She liked the modern ones best, even though she suspected her mother would want to go for something more traditional, along with something a little more pink for the arrangements. Cream cardstock, embossed lettering. Gold, not silver. She'd know it when she saw it.

Shea swept her ash-brown hair from her shoulders and rested her chin in her hand. "Oh, the usual. Dinner with my parents. Just the three of us. A little sad really."

"Why sad?" Kara asked, frowning.

"Oh, I don't know. I guess I wish I had what you two have. A big family. Lots of siblings. It seems so festive."

"It is," Molly admitted, sliding her sister a smile. She'd spent so much time away from Briar Creek that Boston had begun to feel like her real home, but being here these past few days, she was beginning to feel a little sad about the thought of going back to her apartment...and Todd. Todd, who liked to relax in the evenings with a few hours of boring documentaries and often didn't think to make room for her on the couch. Todd, who didn't like to read. Todd, who left his dirty socks wherever he decided to fling them. Todd, whose eyes drifted ten minutes into her telling him something about her day.

Nonsense, she told herself. It was natural to feel that way. You didn't call off a wedding over something as silly as a man putting an empty bag of chips back into the pantry! Of course she felt more fulfilled with her family. They were all she knew. And Todd was just one person—he could hardly be expected to fill the place of two siblings and a mother and some cousins and an aunt...

Todd was handsome. Damn handsome. The best-looking guy she'd ever dated. And he was now her very handsome fiancé. She should be bursting with pride. And she was. She kept a picture of the two of them on her desk at work, and people always stopped to admire it. Several girls were jealous of her. What they wouldn't give to have a guy like Todd. And she was actually marrying him! The thought of taking it down...

"Of course, I'm sure that Molly would be just as happy having a quiet, romantic Christmas with her fiancé, though," Shea continued.

Molly's smile felt tight.

"Lord knows that's all I've wished for," she added, thinking back on how sad she'd been when they broke up last year. She grinned at Kara, forcing herself back to the present. "I think we need to make some resolutions this year. I'm feeling optimistic, and something tells me that this time next year, you and I will both be in a very different place."

Kara smiled shyly. "I guess it's possible."

"Of course it's possible. Christmas is still a week and a half away. Maybe my wish will come true and I'll be curled up by the tree with a handsome stranger by then. It's Christmas after all. Anything is possible."

Kara nodded. "I wouldn't have agreed with you a few months ago, but I think you're right. Anything is possible. Molly should know."

Molly felt her cheeks heat with guilt, even though she knew there was nothing to be ashamed of. The girls were right— anything was possible. And maybe, just maybe, when she went back to Boston and saw Todd after the holidays she'd realize how much she'd missed him and that she couldn't wait to spend the rest of her life with him. Just the two of them.

So why then did imagining that exact scenario feel nothing short of impossible?

Kara knew she could have mentioned her budding friendship with Nate to Shea and Molly, but something was holding her back. She was still figuring out what was going on with them, if they were rivals or friends or, maybe, something more. She wouldn't mind there being something more—in fact, she was beginning to think she'd like that very much— but did Nate feel the same way? So far he'd given no indication that he saw her as anything other than someone to spend time with while he was in town.

Still, her stomach bubbled with hope as she crunched across the snow to Main Street, the corner of her eye locked on the inn. He was in there somewhere, probably helping out his aunt with some decorations. He was a good nephew. It took a lot of patience to put up with the stronger side of Mrs. Griffin's personality—and she should know. She could still remember the way her heart had pounded for the entire five-minute, pinched-lip inspection of her cookies the first time she'd delivered them for tea. She'd all but broken a sweat by the time Mrs. Griffin had looked up, a gleam in her eyes, and remarked that she was just teasing, and of course they looked beautiful.

It was strange that Nate hadn't come to visit more often,

if ever, Kara mused, but then dismissed the idea before she could give it further thought. Life was busy, and days were easily filled. She of all people could relate to that, lately.

The dance studio was just a few blocks off Main, and Kara and Molly arrived just in time to see the tail end of rehearsal. Their mother stood at the end of the room, wearing a black leotard and long, flowing chiffon skirt. She barely blinked as she watched the routine.

Seeming satisfied with what she saw, she called a break and slipped out of the studio. "A week until opening night, and you'd think we still had a year." She clucked her tongue and shook her head dramatically.

Kara bit her lip, knowing it was better to feign sympathy than to remind her mother that she said this every year and that every year the production surpassed the previous. "How's the food drive coming along?" she asked by way of changing to a less stressful topic. For years, her mother had contributed a donation for the Hope Center in the neighboring town of Forest Ridge, setting up a corner of the lobby for a collection of canned goods and announcing the proceeds during the finale of closing night. Last year, the Hastings family had decided to extend the drive to the weeks before Christmas, thus allowing for more contributions, and this year their cousin Brett, who ran the free clinic at the hospital, had added a coat drive to the mix. He'd seen too many sick kids coming in without proper clothing— and the community had been all too happy to scour through their attics for items that no longer fit.

"We've had a big turnout this year, no doubt thanks to Brett's help at the hospital. He posted signs in the doctors' lounge and in the pharmacy in the lobby. Pulling from a bigger area has certainly helped. If things keep up, we'll be able to give twice as many families a magical Christmas this year."

"That's wonderful!" Kara felt a little tingle of warmth spread through her at the thought. "I'd like to donate a dozen cookies to each family, too." It was an impulsive thing to say, and probably not the best business decision, considering everything else she'd committed to, but she didn't regret her decision for an instant. Rosemary was already providing a turkey to each family from the proceeds of the *Nutcracker* sales, and the nonperishables would make for good sides, but everyone deserved a special treat for the holiday. Kara felt grateful to be able to provide them with one.

"Excellent. Mark and Anna said they'd provide fresh bread and some breakfast rolls, too. It's certainly beginning to feel like Christmas."

That it was, Kara thought, yet a part of her wished the day would never come. When it did, Nate would be gone, and life in Briar Creek would be considerably less interesting.

"Speaking of Christmas, I wanted to tell you in person… I've decided to enter the Holiday House contest." Kara had expected her mother to react with some degree of surprise, but the confusion that knitted her brow instead made Kara's stomach roil.

"Are you sure that's such a good idea, Kara? I mean, I understand wanting to join in the Christmas fun, but a new business takes time and care—"

"I can do it." She smiled a little wider, hoping to portray some of the confidence she felt slipping away from her.

Her mother didn't look convinced. "I just think you need to assess your priorities. Where are you going to find the time to decorate?"

"I'm not actually decorating my apartment," Kara said slowly, bracing herself for what was next. "I'm actually entering a gingerbread house."

"A gingerbread house!" Both Rosemary and Molly stared

at Kara with wide eyes. "Honey, why don't you focus on the gingerbread houses you actually plan to sell? Unless... Are people not buying them anymore?"

Kara felt her defenses prickle. "Of course they're buying them! In fact, I've had to limit how many I sell per day."

"Exactly my point." Her mother shook her head, her ruby-painted lips pinched tight. "Part of running a successful business means staying focused."

"I am focused," Kara began, and then stopped. There was no point defending herself; she wasn't on trial... even if it sometimes felt like she was when she and her mother got into conversations like this one.

"Well, maybe I shouldn't have you make the cookies for the refreshment table," Rosemary said, and Kara felt her jaw slack. "I don't want you taking on too much or finding that you can't fulfill your obligations."

When she had found her voice, Kara said firmly, "I'm not going to have a problem making the cookies in time for *The Nutcracker*, Mom. I already had the varieties all planned, too."

Rosemary sighed. "If you think you can do it."

"I know I can do it," Kara insisted, trying to ignore the pain that was twisting in her chest and showed no hope of going away any time soon.

She'd thought by now that her mother believed in her, knew that she was committed and that she was doing a good job. But her mother still saw her as the flighty girl who got bored with each job after six months and then quit, in search of another.

"This is my business, Mom," she said gently. "I know what I'm doing."

Her mother just raised her eyebrows, but said nothing. Still, her expression spoke a hundred words. Kara turned before her mother could see the pain in her eyes and muttered something about checking on the food drive items. The music for the opening scene of *The Nutcracker* swelled before she'd even made it to her mother's office.

Hot tears prickled the back of her eyes, and she brushed them away quickly before they could fall. She was being ridiculous, letting words hurt so much. She had the bakery under control. She was turning a profit—barely. She had customers.

And she would win that Holiday House contest. For her father. And for herself.

"Nate?"

Nate pushed the last of the swans onto the frozen pond and turned to see his aunt standing in the doorway. "Yes?"

"When you're done with that, I have another favor to ask of you. I just came up with an idea." She rubbed her hands together excitedly and disappeared back into the house.

Nate huffed out a breath and studied the seven swans a-swimming, hoping they passed muster with his aunt. Another idea. She made it sound as if it was a rare occurrence, when, in fact, it was an hourly occurrence. The list she'd started with had grown to several pages, and throughout the day he'd see her eyes pop, and off she'd go, scurrying to scribble down her latest idea.

He could only imagine what this one would be.

He adjusted the red velvet bow on the last swan's neck and walked back into the house. It was dinnertime, and most of the guests were off in town. He'd been hoping to slip out, too, maybe try that restaurant Rosemary and Thyme that Kara's cousin ran. The place looked as good as the options he had in Boston, and the thought of Kara possibly being there added to the appeal.

But it would appear his aunt had other plans for him tonight. And that's why he was here, he reminded himself.

He grinned, hoping to summon some enthusiasm even though he'd kill for a hot shower and a cold beer. "What brilliant idea do you have?"

"The pièce de résistance," his aunt said with a sly smile. She gestured to the hearth in the lobby. "I want a painting above the mantel. A Christmas painting, not just any painting. I want a Nate Griffin exclusive."

Nate blinked, trying to process what she was suggesting. A Nate Griffin exclusive could only mean one thing, though. "No, Aunt Maggie. I'm sorry, but no. I haven't painted in years."

"Why not?" she asked with an air of petulance.

"Because I'm a businessman," he replied evenly, even though his heart was starting to race and he could feel the blood coursing through his veins. "Because I don't have the time. Or the interest."

She waved his excuses away. "Nonsense. I've seen what you've done with this place. You can't tell me you haven't enjoyed yourself."

No, if he was being honest, he couldn't. "I haven't picked up a brush in years," he said instead. "And painting was never my strength." Drawing was. He'd loved to draw, and he'd been good at it. Damn good. Good enough to get into the art school he'd secretly applied to. The one he'd chosen not to attend.

"Still, you'd do a better job at it than I could, and I just think this would be such a dramatic statement. Imagine, right there, above the mantel, when the judges walk in...the twelve days of Christmas. In acrylic. Or oil..." She stared at the rather boring-looking wreath that currently occupied the space, as if she could see something he did not.

"I'm sorry, Maggie, but I don't even have the supplies."

"There's an art store on Main Street!"

He sighed. "I don't have the time."

"You have nothing but time. It doesn't need to be a van Gogh."

He ran a hand through his hair, his temper beginning to bite. "I don't want to, okay?" Damn, his tone had been sharper than he'd expected, and a look of surprise flashed in his aunt's eyes. He hated the hurt that followed, but this was one time he was going to have to turn the other cheek. "I'm sorry, Aunt Maggie. I'm happy to help any way I can, but I do have to put my foot down here."

She nodded her head slowly. "I understand," she said. "I just…thought I'd ask."

Nate released a shaky breath as an awkward silence stretched. "I think I'll go grab a shower," he said, and turned to the stairs without another word.

CHAPTER
11

Hastings was buzzing when Nate pushed through the door the next day, his gaze quickly drifting to the counter, hoping for another glance of Kara. Shame bit at him when he thought of how quick he was to misjudge her—but one thing he wouldn't take back were his suggestions for her bakery. She wanted it to succeed. Needed it to succeed. He'd find a way to mention some of his other ideas without stoking her temper, although with that work ethic and attitude, she might not need his help after all.

He smiled to himself as he slipped into a booth and pulled the menu from behind the napkin dispenser. Not only was she pretty and smart, but she was also almost as driven as he was. After all, Kara was probably hard at work right now, icing cookies and cleaning up after customers, not kicking back for an early lunch and a third cup of coffee.

He turned his mug over as the woman he recognized from last week walked by with the pitcher of coffee. She stopped to fill his cup, leaving room for cream, and smiled at him. "Still in town, I see."

Nate shrugged. "Just through the holidays. I leave the day

after Christmas." Just the thought of going back to his empty apartment left him cold. He silenced that thought with a sip of hot brew. He was on vacation—and no vacation lasted forever. Any town could feel like paradise in a small dose.

"Shame. Corned beef and cabbage happens to be my specialty." Sharon grinned. She took his order and left with the promise to return for refills.

Nate settled back against his seat, sipping his coffee and listening to the Christmas carols that were almost smothered by the din of the customers. He was in no hurry, even though he knew there was a lot more to be done at the inn, and he didn't want his aunt lifting anything heavy while he was away. This morning, she'd simply smiled at him, pretended like nothing was wrong, and busied herself by talking to guests and passing around her peppermint scones.

He knew his aunt meant well, but she'd touched a nerve. Picking up a paintbrush was something he hadn't done since he'd left high school. Doing so now would be like going back, and he didn't want to think about those days.

He pulled out his phone and scrolled through his emails, happy to distance himself from Briar Creek and the strange and overly comfortable bonds he was forming here. His life was in Boston. His job. His friends. His fancy apartment and his fancy car . . . He thinned his lips.

By the time his food arrived, he'd caught up on work, enough to feel clearheaded and capable of facing his aunt with some perspective. She might not understand his choices, but they'd been made for a reason. And he was better for the path he'd chosen. They all were, he thought, thinking of his parents.

After leaving a generous tip and sticking around long enough to give a personal goodbye to Sharon, Nate pushed out onto Main Street. The snow had started again, and the wreaths and garland that covered windows and doors were dusted with white powder. Nate passed the art store his aunt had been sure to mention and kept his eyes straight ahead. Another time, another place. He held his chin high, looking instead at the pink and white striped awning, his pulse picking up speed as he thought of Kara tucked inside, wearing that apron that cinched at the waist and hugged her in the all the right places, greeting customers with a wide smile and bright blue eyes.

He checked his watch. She'd probably be stopping by the inn soon with today's cookie delivery. He'd save her the time by picking them up himself.

Slowing his pace as he approached the storefront, he glanced through the frosted window, his spirits lifting when he saw her standing behind the counter, plating a dessert for an older woman and a little girl. She grinned when he walked in, her cheeks flushing a bit as she turned her attention to the cash register.

"Busy day," he commented when he moved to the front of the line.

"You could say that again." Though her smile was wide, her eyes lacked some of the sparkle he'd seen the day before. She wiped a loose strand of hair from her forehead with her wrist. "Are you by any chance here to pick up the cookies?"

"Thought I'd save you the trouble."

"You're a sweetheart," she said, and then, her eyes widening, began stammering to backtrack.

Amused and flattered, he held up a hand. "Consider the favor all mine. I'm afraid I've had a bit of an argument with my aunt and I'm finding ways to stall my return." He felt his brow pinch when he recalled the hurt in Maggie's eyes. He hated to turn her down, but there were some things he wouldn't back down on, and going back to his high school hobby was one of them.

She slipped him a grin. "She has a strong personality. Believe me, you'll know how much I understand when you meet my mother."

He felt his shoulders relax when he caught the gleam in her eye. "Ah, yes. The famous Rosemary of the *Nutcracker*-themed Holiday House."

Kara sighed as she grabbed a rag and began wiping down the smooth white and gray marble counter. "The very one. Though I don't think she really cares too much about the contest. *The Nutcracker*, however…" She looked up to meet his eye. "You should come see it. I mean, if you want to… Ballet's not everyone's thing." Her cheeks grew pink as she began scrubbing at some spilled coffee.

"When is it?"

She stopped scrubbing for a moment. "The night before Christmas Eve."

If his aunt didn't already have tickets, no doubt she'd love a night out on the town. It might be just the way to make things up to her and overcome their little tiff yesterday. "I'll plan on it."

She looked up at him, seeming a little startled, but her mouth curved into a pleased grin, and Nate felt something within him stir. He had a strange urge to reach over and brush that loose strand of hair from her cheek, to linger a little longer in the shop, and not just because he was avoiding his aunt.

"Great. Tickets are twelve dollars apiece, and this year, half the proceeds are going to families in need. If you're able to donate any nonperishables, we have a food drive set up in the lobby."

Nate grew silent as his good mood immediately vanished. "That's a really noble cause," he managed.

Kara set the rag down and shrugged. "It's the least we can do. If we all work together as a community, then every family can have a special holiday."

He nodded, his jaw set tight. He could still remember the ringing of the doorbell, the sound of a woman's voice, his mother teary with gratitude and well wishes. He'd come running to see what was going on, and there was a lady, dressed in a crimson wool coat with shiny buttons and a black fur collar, a huge basket in her hand, tied with a big gold ribbon. That Christmas they'd had a feast. He knew they were supposed to be happy about it, supposed to be grateful, and they were, but his father had sat at the table in silence. He didn't go to church with them that year, and Nate remembered being confused that his mother hadn't made a fuss. He was out of a job, his mother had explained. But he'd get one, she'd countered brightly. And then...then things would be better, she'd promised.

"I'll be sure to bring something," he said, squaring his shoulders in an attempt to banish the image. "Just food, no toys?"

"Oh..." Kara shook her head. "We do a coat drive. My cousin Brett, Sharon's younger son, runs a clinic as an extension of the emergency room at the Forest Ridge Hospital. He helps with the donations. We'd love to do more, but we're only one family."

Sometimes one family was all it took. "I'd be happy to help with a toy drive," he volunteered, shoving his hands into his pockets. He thought of the toy shop he'd passed on Main Street his first day here, the gifts he would have loved to have received and never did. He felt a spark of something he couldn't quite pinpoint—hope perhaps. Or maybe closure. It would feel good to give back, to make someone else's Christmas one to remember, to take the burden off the parents, give them a holiday to enjoy, too.

Kara blinked at him. "You'd do that?"

"Every kid deserves to wake up to something special under the tree." Nate swallowed hard, determined to keep his memories in the past, where they belonged. "Consider it taken care of. Would it be okay to collect everything at the show?"

"Would it? That would be wonderful!" Kara beamed.

Nate tried to keep his expression neutral, but he was struggling not to match Kara's enthusiasm. "Good. I'm looking forward to it." And as he turned to leave, he realized with a lightness in his step that he was.

Kara could barely keep the smile from taking over her face as she slipped into the kitchen to get the box of snowflake cookies she'd prepared that morning for the inn. A toy drive would be just the thing to round out their Christmas donations. She could just imagine the joy in the children's faces when they came downstairs to find that doll or game they'd been wanting. She loved spoiling her friend Jane's daughter, Sophie, as they all did, but she had a feeling she'd find it just as rewarding, if not more so, to brighten the holiday of a child in need, even if she wasn't there to see them open the gift.

Kara sneezed, managing to quickly snatch a tissue from the box first. That was at least the tenth that morning. Her eyes watered as she rubbed her nose and then washed her hands, pleading silently with herself to pull it together. She couldn't get sick. Who would run the counter? Who would make the Christmas cookies and the gingerbread houses?

She was just run-down. Worn out and exhausted. She'd try to get to bed early tonight, and with any luck she'd wake feeling refreshed and energized.

She sneezed again and released a long whimper into the tissue. Maybe it would be a twenty-four-hour thing. Or maybe it was just dust.

Kara washed her hands and then grabbed the box of cookies from the counter. She took a moment to linger, looking at the progress she'd made so far for her Holiday House. She smiled, feeling her heart tug a little at the memories it stirred up, and then, squaring her shoulders, she pushed through the kitchen door and into the storefront. Instead of giving a little squeeze, her heart began to skip and dance when she caught Nate's eye and he gave her one of his slow, friendly grins.

It was sad to think that in a little over a week he'd be gone. He'd started to feel like a fixture in her day, and one she very much looked forward to.

He's a friend, she reminded herself. *Nothing more.*

"Here you go, sir." She smiled as she handed over the box, feeling the heat of his hand on hers as their fingers grazed each other. His skin was smooth and masculine and the tingle that ripped down her spine and made her stomach tingle told her that he was much more than a friend. Or he could be. If circumstances were a little different.

She sighed and let her hand fall. No use wishing for things that couldn't be.

"These smell delicious." Nate flipped the lid and peeked inside the box. "And they look delicious, too."

"No stealing any," Kara warned. "I don't need your aunt giving me any grief when she doesn't have enough for her guests."

"I've gotten you in enough trouble with Maggie for one visit," Nate replied, winking. "Besides, she's probably too annoyed with me to start trouble with you."

Kara's curiosity piqued, but she decided not to pry. "By this time tomorrow she'll be singing your praises to anyone who will listen," Kara said, laughing.

Nate pulled a face. "I'm not sure whether that's a good thing or not."

"It's a good thing," Kara said firmly. "It's important to have someone in your corner." She frowned a little when she thought of her mother. Rosemary had made great strides when it came to supporting Sugar and Spice, but the little comments were a reminder that she hadn't won her mother over just yet. But she intended to. She intended to win them all over. And it started with winning that Holiday House contest. "How's the Holiday House coming along?"

Nate shrugged. "Fine, but I'm not sure what my aunt will do to me if we don't win." He waggled his eyebrows and Kara laughed. "Dare I ask about your entry?"

"You may." Kara tipped her head, considering how much she wanted to give away. Something about the project was special to her, personal even. It wasn't just a test of her baking and decorating skills; it was also an opportunity to reconnect with memories she sometimes didn't dare to dwell on. "It's going well. I'm feeling…confident."

Confident. She blinked and smiled to herself when she realized how true this was.

Nate lifted an eyebrow. "Well, don't get too sure of yourself. Word is that Kathleen Madison is a force to be reckoned with."

Kara had to laugh. "Stick around Briar Creek much longer and you'll officially be a local."

"That doesn't sound so bad, actually." He held her gaze, his eyes filling with warmth.

Kara felt her insides quiver, and she glanced away, wishing there was something closer by to keep her hands busy and her mind occupied. She needed to stop feeling this way every time their eyes met or he flashed her that grin. He was a handsome man. And sadly, an unavailable one.

"Small-town life is growing on you, then?" She held her breath, daring to hope for the answer she wanted, even though she knew it was probably a lost cause. Christmas was only eight days away—suddenly a holiday she cherished so much was now one she associated with dread. Nate would be gone after Christmas, and given his history, chances were he wouldn't be returning again for a while.

"A bit. But don't tell my aunt Maggie." Nate tipped his head as his gaze drifted over her face. "Are you feeling all right? You seem a bit... pale."

Her hand shot up to her cheek. Not beautiful. Not pretty. But... pale.

"I'm fine," she strained to say through a weak smile. "Just a little tired. There's a lot going on right now."

"Ever think about cutting back?"

She stared at him. "Are you forgetting that I just opened this business?"

"I meant with the other stuff."

"Says the man who challenged me to enter the Holiday House contest," she remarked, wagging a playful finger at him. "I'm afraid I'm just not willing to scale back, not right now. But I have gotten a little better at saying no to people." Even if it made her feel terrible.

"Well, I shouldn't keep you then."

Kara knew she should get back to work, but disappointment swelled. She'd looked forward to this visit all morning, and now she'd have to wait until tomorrow to see him again. There wouldn't be many more tomorrows left.

Brightening, she thought of the toy drive. Perhaps she was wrong; there might be a few extra chances for conversation after all.

She waved as she watched him walk out the door and onto the snowy sidewalk. And then she sneezed four times in a row before scurrying back to the kitchen.

CHAPTER 12

The grandfather clock at the base of the stairs in the inn's lobby chimed one o'clock. Nate frowned and cast another glance out the window. It was a gray day—the sun having never shown its face all morning—and the lights from Main Street and the town square shone brightly across the blanket of snow.

It wasn't like Kara to be late, but then, tea didn't start for another hour. Still, she did look pale yesterday. With newfound purpose in his stride, Nate decided to feel out the situation with his aunt.

He'd been avoiding Maggie since their awkward conversation the other night, and he welcomed the opportunity to change the subject and, hopefully, make a fresh start. He owed her an explanation, but he didn't want to get into details. A tricky balance with the curious nature of her personality.

He found her in the kitchen, pulling some ginger cakes from the oven. She'd baked them in loaf tins in various holiday shapes. One was made to look like a large Christmas tree, complete with a star on top, while the other was of three gingerbread men.

She brightened when he appeared in the doorway and then quickly handed him a strange-looking metal object.

"It's a sifter," she informed him. And then, noticing his blank expression, she said, "For the powdered sugar. Make it look like snow!"

He did a poor job at suppressing his smile but was nevertheless grateful for the task. "Show me how this works. I don't want to mess up your cakes."

With a pinch of her lips, she took the contraption from him, but there was a twinkle in her eye when she handed it back after evenly coating the first cake. He had to admit that the result was pretty.

Carefully, he tried to match her effort. "Not quite as good as yours, I'm afraid," he said, stepping back. He cast a wary eye on the uneven coating of sugar that fell in larger clumps at the middle and all but faded out near the edges.

"Oh, it will do," Maggie replied, wiping her hands on her apron. "Mind passing me that bowl over there?" She motioned to a large ceramic mixing bowl on the center island. "I have to get these cookies in the oven or they won't be ready in time."

Nate handed her the bowl, noticing a heavy lump of disappointment in his chest as he did so. "Doesn't Kara usually make the cookies?" He'd hoped his tone had come out casual, conversational, but the pointed look in his aunt's sharp gaze told him he hadn't succeeded.

"Unfortunately Kara won't be making the delivery today," Maggie told him as she began spooning the batter onto a cookie sheet. She glanced at him sidelong.

Nate pulled in a breath, rolled back on his heels, told himself to fight the urge, to not go there, to not give in. Aw, hell. "Oh? Is something wrong?"

Maggie did a poor job of masking her pleasure. "Oh, she's just a little under the weather."

He knew it. She'd been pale yesterday, with a telltale rim

of pink around her eyes, and she'd looked tired to the bone, too. He kicked himself, silently chastising his challenge for her to enter the contest. Sure, it would be great to win—for any of them—but the chances of that seemed low if Maggie's hand-wringing details of Kathleen's newest ideas said anything. Kara was already spread thin. Too thin to keep that bakery going much longer. And he'd just gone and made it worse.

"That's too bad. Hopefully she'll be back tomorrow." Catching the flash in his aunt's bright green eyes, he added quickly, "So you don't have to go through the trouble of making the cookies yourself. You have enough to take care of around here."

"That I do." His aunt slid the cookie sheet into the oven and set the timer. "But I enjoy it. It will be a sad day when I have to say goodbye to this place."

Nate flashed his eyes on her, his pulse skipping a beat. "What's that supposed to mean?"

"Oh, nothing." She waved away his concern. "Just getting ahead of myself. This place has been in my family for so long. A lot of good memories here." Though she smiled, there was a sudden sadness to her eyes.

Nate frowned and reached out a hand to set on the older woman's shoulder. "I'm sorry for the other night. I was caught off guard, but I reacted too harshly. I want you to know how happy I am to be here."

His aunt's smile turned knowing. "I told you this town would grow on you."

Nate couldn't argue with her there. But it wasn't just the town—someone had gotten under his skin, and he was more than a little disappointed that he wouldn't be seeing her today. He eyed the pot of soup his aunt had simmering on the stove. "I might drop a bowl of this off for Kara, seeing as she's sick and all," he added quickly.

"Seeing as she's sick," his aunt repeated, her eyes shining.

"I'll just drop some off at the bakery..." He shrugged, trying to sound casual, but there was no slipping anything past Maggie.

"She lives above the bakery. You can't miss it. And you'll want to hurry before it cools."

Nate grinned as he accepted a plastic container from his aunt. He'd hurry, all right. In fact, he couldn't wait.

Nate carried the canvas bag containing soup, some fresh bread, and a couple of his aunt's peppermint scones to the bakery, which boasted a CLOSED sign despite the holiday shoppers who strolled down Main Street, sipping coffees and laden with red and green shopping bags.

He scanned the front of the building, searching for the door that would lead to an upstairs unit, and felt his heart tick when he finally spotted it. The black, paned door was set in an alcove, not very noticeable from the street, and a small intercom above the mailbox listed one name: K. Hastings.

Nate pressed it quickly and waited. It rang twice. By the third time, he began to worry that she wasn't home, or wouldn't answer, and the disappointment that landed in his gut confirmed what he already knew. He wanted to see her. Looked forward to seeing her.

And what did that mean for next week, when he went back to Boston?

Nothing, he told himself firmly. Sure, it might take a day to acclimate, to get this town and the people in it out of his system, but he would. His life was busy, and full. And January was going to be busy, just like every year. He was already struggling to keep up with his inbox, and some days here he hadn't even thought to check it. It wasn't like him, but it didn't matter. It was a vacation. One vacation in ten years.

It was easy to get lost in it.

"Hello?" The voice crackled through the speaker, pulling Nate back to the present with a jolt.

He licked his lips and clutched the canvas bag tighter in his grip. "Kara? It's Nate."

The pause was so long, Nate had to press his ear against the intercom to see if he'd lost the connection. The exaggerated sound of a sneeze forced him back.

"Hi. Did you…need something? I don't know if your aunt told you but I'm not making the cookies for tea today."

Nate smiled. "I know. I didn't come here to pick them up. I brought something for you instead." He glanced at the door. "Mind buzzing me in?"

There was another pause, longer this time, and Nate was just beginning to feel that he had overstepped when the door buzzed and clicked. He quickly grabbed the handle and pushed it open. There was a single door visible at the top of the stairs, a simple boxwood wreath gracing its front. And Nate's heart beat a little faster with every step closer to it.

Holy. Crap.

Kara flung the chenille blanket off her lap and dashed into her small bathroom, whimpering at the sight. Her dark hair was as tangled as a rat's nest, flat on one side, sticking up in all directions on the other. Her nose was as red as Rudolph's, and her eyes were watering so much, she looked as if she'd been crying.

Listlessly, she reached for her mascara and then realized there was no point.

She glanced down at her pajamas, the very ones she'd worn last night and never changed out of, and frantically searched for a robe. She found a cashmere turtleneck sweater instead and stuffed it over her head, managing to cover most of the unflattering plaid flannel.

He was already knocking at the door when she reached for a brush, and, unable to even pull it through her hair, she gave up and pulled it back into a haphazard knot.

Hardly her finest moment. The bitter irony that for the first time in God knew how many years a handsome man was knocking on her door and she looked like she had, admittedly, just rolled out of bed was not lost on her.

She stared up at the ceiling. *Why?* She mouthed. *Why?*

Closing her eyes, she counted to three and then slowly undid the locks. The door creaked open and there he stood, looking so darn cute it stole her breath for a moment. He was bundled in a scarf, no doubt of his aunt's choosing from the handmade look of it, but it was the grin he wore that caused her heart to race and her insides to go all mushy.

"I brought you some soup," he said, holding up the bag.

The man had brought her soup. Kara stared at him, then down to the bag he was holding, and then back into the warm, golden eyes that crinkled at the corners when he smiled. He may as well have said he'd brought her a four-carat diamond ring.

"I...I don't know what to say." She blinked as she stepped back to let him in. "I think this is the nicest thing anyone has done for me in a while."

His grin turned slightly bashful. "Well, I can't take all the credit. My aunt made the soup. But..." He held up a playful finger. "I run a mean microwave. How about I heat you up a bowl? It's already gone a bit cold from the walk over here."

Kara hadn't been able to summon an appetite since yesterday morning, but the thought of a warm bowl of broth suddenly made her stomach grumble. "I'll show you the kitchen."

"No. No, you sit, relax, and I'll be right back."

Kara settled on the slipcovered sofa near the front bay

window, but relaxing was the furthest thing from her mind as she watched Nate disappear into her kitchen, followed soon by the sound of opening and closing of her cabinets.

She eyed the hallway, wondering if she could dash into her bedroom, maybe throw on something a little sexier, but knew it was no use. She was sick. And the man had brought her soup. She'd roll with it.

Nate carried the steaming bowl into the living room a few minutes later, balancing it on a tray that told her he'd made himself completely at home, considering she kept that on the bottom shelf of her pantry, and set it on the coffee table. She was touched to see that he'd even folded a napkin and set a spoon on top, along with a few slices of what looked like homemade bread.

"This smells delicious," Kara said, breathing in the rich aroma. "I'm happy to share."

Nate shook his head, and for a moment, Kara was worried he would leave, that perhaps he'd just been running an errand for his aunt, nothing more, but when he settled himself onto an armchair near the fireplace, she felt a little tingle of excitement rip through her. She reached for the bowl. No reason to get carried away now...

"I'm surprised you don't have a tree," Nate remarked, motioning to the completely undecorated living room. "I thought you were just bursting with Christmas spirit."

Kara laughed, almost spilling her soup all over her flannel pajama pants. "I haven't gotten around to it, I'm afraid."

"But Christmas is a week away."

Their eyes met for a beat, and Kara wondered if he was thinking the same thing she was. That Christmas was a week from today, and after that...life went back to reality. Whatever was blossoming between them would be over.

And the contest would be, too, she thought with a start.

She sighed. "I guess I won't get around to it this year. No doubt the good ones have all been picked over by now anyway." She sipped her soup off her spoon and eyed him. "Why? Do you have a tree in your apartment?"

He looked affronted. "Me? God, no." He shuddered. "No time. No desire, either."

She set her bowl down and looked at him properly. "Just what is it that you have against Christmas?" She wanted to know once and for all. "Someone break your heart over the holidays?" She was fishing, but she couldn't help it. The man was a bona fide Grinch, and there had to be a reason. Besides, she couldn't resist a little more insight into his heart while she had the opportunity.

"Bad memories." Nate shrugged, but the way his eyes drifted across the room told her he was hiding something.

Deciding he didn't want to open up just yet, Kara let it drop and resumed eating her soup. It was delicious, with large chunks of carrot and celery and thick noodles. "Well, I love Christmas, even though I do understand the memories part." She paused, thinking of the gingerbread house downstairs, the hours she was losing by sitting up here, sniffling through a box of tissues. The soup was warming her from the inside out, as was Nate. When he left, she'd try to muster up the energy to work on it a bit. Not that she was in any rush to see Nate leave.

"Christmas has a way of doing that," Nate mused. "People make too big a deal out of it, if you ask me. It brings out the worst in people. This Holiday House contest is a prime example."

Kara stared at him. "And here I thought you were starting to enjoy the contest."

"Oh, I'm always up for a good challenge." His eyes were intense as they latched on to hers, and Kara felt her breath catch. "But it's hardly the meaning of Christmas to compete with your neighbors over who has the best decorations."

"I see it a little differently," Kara ventured. "It's a community event, a way to bring people together. Everyone might look like they're at war over this contest, but deep down, there's a real sense of camaraderie. It's fun."

"I'm glad you think so," Nate said, giving her a slow grin that made her stomach roll over. She suddenly felt nervous in his company—in a good way. "I was starting to feel a little bad for suggesting it to you."

She raised an eyebrow. "Suggesting it? From where I stood, you didn't leave me much of a choice. Not that I'm glad you didn't."

"Competitive, are you?"

Kara considered the question as she broke off a piece of the crusty bread. "Not competitive, no. More like...determined. Even though I opened the bakery for myself, part of me feels the need to keep it going to prove the naysayers wrong."

He nodded thoughtfully. "I understand," he said, and something in the distance in his voice told her that he really did. Why he understood was yet to be determined. She hoped to get to the bottom of it—to know him better.

But why? she asked herself, remembering how Christmas would come all too soon. There was no sense in getting to know Nate; she needed to just enjoy his company and leave it at that.

She stole a glance in his direction, her pulse skipping at the sight of his face. Easier said than done, she realized.

"I'd love to see what you've come up with for the contest," Nate said suddenly.

Kara hesitated. It wasn't like she worried he would copy her idea—how could he?—but more that she wasn't sure she was ready to share such a personal part of herself yet. With him. Or with anyone.

"It's nowhere near finished, and after today, who knows if it will be. I'd hoped to do some baking today, to work on the roof. If I feel better later on, I might go downstairs and try." She sneezed and guiltily met Nate's eye. So much for that.

"If you'd rather not share, I understand. My aunt is guarding that house from anyone but paying guests. And beautiful women who deliver mouthwatering cookies in time for high tea," he added with a grin.

Kara's hand stilled midway to the soup bowl, and she felt her cheeks grow warm at the compliment. He'd just called her beautiful—something she hadn't heard in a long time, especially from a man. And it wasn't just the fact that a person of the opposite sex found her attractive. It was that a man she was growing more and more fond of might feel the same.

She let out a small sigh. If only he wasn't leaving in a week.

Not knowing what to do with the compliment, and embarrassed by the heat of her face, she blurted, "I'll show you what I've done so far, but remember it's not finished. I still have to do the roof and the chimney, and most of the decorations, too." She stood, finding she already had more energy than she did before he stopped by, and guided him to the kitchen door, which led to an internal staircase down to the first floor.

She began questioning herself as soon as her foot hit the first step. What was she thinking? This man was the competition! And unlike Kathleen Madison or her mother, or some of the other people in town, Nate had made it clear that he was determined to win, and no doubt Mrs. Griffin was, too. She hardly knew the guy—he wasn't willing to open up much. And here she was about to reveal something that wasn't just her chance at a big break for her bakery but also something that was deeply personal. Where was her judgment?

But that was just the thing, she supposed. When it came to Nate, she hadn't shown much of it. He had a knack for talking her into things.

Minutes later, they were standing in the kitchen of Sugar and Spice, Kara careful not to breathe on anything for fear of spreading germs, and Nate almost deadly quiet as he stared at the giant house she was constructing in the back corner of the room. Kara shifted the weight on her feet, feeling uneasy and full of regret, knowing they should have just stayed upstairs in her apartment. But oh...the thought of sitting there, looking into those eyes, alone in those quiet four walls...It made her want something she probably couldn't have.

"I think this Kathleen person may have met her match," Nate finally said.

Kara blushed and waved away the remark, but her heart was racing with fresh hope. She might actually stand a chance! She might really win!

"It's not finished. See this?" She pointed to the pattern she'd managed to cut the day before, just before the cold hit full force and before the fever started. "I still have to make the roof. It's the last piece I'll add, but it needs to be finished soon so I can focus on the decorations."

Nate nodded and quietly studied the rest of the house. "Is this design modeled on anything?"

Kara hesitated. She didn't often talk about her father; he'd died so long ago. It was sad in many ways, even though he was always in her heart. "It's my childhood home. My mother still lives there. I wanted to re-create the feeling of

Christmas morning. The excitement. The joy. The comfort." She glanced through one of the windows. "See that chair near the fireplace? My dad used to sit there while we all scrambled around, tearing open our gifts. I love that chair."

She swallowed the lump that had welled in her throat and stared at the room as memories sprang to life, almost real enough to touch. When she finally blinked, she realized that Nate was staring at her.

"Sorry," she muttered, tucking a loose strand of hair behind her ear. She suddenly felt vulnerable, exposed. Here she was in her pajamas, with no makeup, getting emotional about her past with a guy who was just passing through town...Only somehow he was beginning to feel like so much more than that.

"No apology needed," Nate said, giving her a kind smile. "It sounds like your Christmas mornings were something to be cherished."

There was something wistful in his eyes that made her think his Christmases weren't ones he wanted to remember.

She nodded, struggling to push back the mix of emotions she felt when she thought of those days. Picture-perfect moments. Hers to keep forever. Just ones not meant to last forever, however much she'd wished they could.

She blinked back the tears that threatened to spill, telling herself firmly she had nothing to be sad over. She should be grateful, really, that she'd had that time. After all, she thought, drifting her gaze to Nate, perhaps not everyone did.

Kara sneezed, managing to turn her back from the gingerbread house just in time.

"You should get some rest," Nate said firmly. He reached out to wipe the strand of hair from her cheek, the pad of his thumb lingering a second longer than probably necessary as his gaze bored into hers.

Kara held her breath. It was the perfect moment to kiss. To just lean forward and...She sneezed again, managing to bring her arm up just in time. Laughing, she said, "You're probably right."

The moment was gone, but something told her she hadn't imagined it. She'd seen the way his eyes had locked with hers, and her cheek still tingled from the memory of his touch. She brought a hand to it, recalling the warmth of his skin.

With great reluctance, she walked over to the door and turned to see him still standing near the gingerbread house. "You coming?"

Nate shook his head. "I'll let myself out. You focus on getting better."

Kara nodded, even though she wished she could press the matter, invite him back upstairs. Disappointment landed heavily in her chest. "Thanks. For today."

"It was my pleasure," Nate said.

Kara rested her hands on the doorjamb and smiled. The pleasure had been all hers.

CHAPTER 13

The next morning, Kara stared at her Holiday House contest entry in disbelief. For a moment she considered the possibility that she was dreaming, but the warm morning sun told her otherwise. She couldn't believe it. She honestly couldn't believe it. Her mind whirred with possibilities, but every question led to the same answer. Nate.

But how?

Gingerly, she reached out and touched the edge of the perfectly assembled roof, created exactly from her pattern and held together with royal icing, expertly piped.

Maybe he'd gotten Anna involved. But he'd only met her briefly at the Christmas party. No, he must have done this himself. There was no other way.

She shook her head as the smile spread over her face. And here she'd thought a bowl of soup was one of the nicest things a man had ever given her. This? This required some kind of payback.

She set to work on the cookies right away, and even though she knew they'd probably be snatched up if she sold them in the shop, she decided against it. Nate had supported her entry yesterday. Today, she would support his.

After she'd made her morning batches of snowflake cookies, iced gingerbread men, chocolate-dipped short-bread, and today's special, cranberry spice biscotti, she got to work decorating the individual sugar cookies and carefully set them in a tin lined with parchment paper.

The sun was back, and shoppers were ticking off the last items on their list as they strolled Main Street. While still not one hundred percent, Kara was feeling much better than yesterday, and she suspected that the soup, and Nate's visit, had something to do with it.

By noon she was able to turn the sign on the door, allowing herself enough of a break to dart over to the inn to deliver the daily order. She was already dreaming of the day when she'd have someone to help in the kitchen, and another to man the counter, thus making these little delivery breaks a little less cumbersome. It could happen, she realized with a flutter in her stomach. And soon. All she needed to do was win the contest and then...

She stopped herself right there. No use getting ahead of herself just yet. As Nate had inadvertently reminded her yesterday, Kathleen Madison was a force to be reckoned with. It would take something really special to compete with the woman who had won the contest every single year she had entered. People had tried, and no one had succeeded thus far. But maybe this was the year...

The paths through the town square had been shoveled, and Kara took the shortcut, knowing she had a lot to make up for since she'd lost all of yesterday. Her gingerbread house orders were behind, thus doubling today's work on them, and if this morning's traffic was any indication, then she'd be busy serving customers through to the close of the day. It was a good thing she'd had the sense to double her batches.

Kara glanced longingly at the skating rink. Once January came, and the contest and Christmas orders were behind her, she hoped to find more time in her week to get out on the ice. Not that it would be the same skating alone, instead of with Nate...

She stopped and looked up at the inn. He'd certainly been busy. In the one day she'd spent holed up in her apartment, the outside had all but sprung to life. Lights were wrapped around every tree branch and shrub, and each window box now boasted beautiful greenery with sheaves of magnolia to match the wreaths on the front door. The house was large, with three windows on each side of the door, a large, dome-shaped window above it, with three paned windows lined with black shutters on either side. In each of the twelve windows, a different item from the song was featured, starting at the top left corner with a gilded partridge.

Kara felt a flicker of panic. Competition was stiff this year. Kathleen Madison might lose her reign, but that didn't mean Kara's gingerbread house would top the list.

She hurried to the inn before her nerves could get the better of her, eager to get back to the bakery. But first... she had to thank Nate.

He was inside the lobby when she pushed through the doors. She held back, stomping the snow off her boots as he helped an older guest carry her luggage down the stairs. Spotting her, he raised his arm in greeting, a signal she took to mean she should wait.

"I've called a cab to take you the airport," he was telling the woman as he led her over to the sitting area. "They should be here in about twenty minutes. In the meantime, why don't you relax by the fire? There's coffee and tea on the console near the hall if you'd like anything."

"You're becoming a pro at this," Kara remarked with a smile as he came to meet her.

"I enjoy it, actually," Nate said. "I'm not really sure how my aunt does it all on her own." He frowned a little at that.

Kara shrugged, hoping to downplay his distress. "She loves it. It keeps her young, fills her days."

"I suppose so. Especially since she's here all alone." Again the little wrinkle between his eyebrows appeared.

"She's not alone," Kara corrected. "She has a whole community of people who know and love her." *And tolerate her*, she thought to herself. "She knows any one of us would roll up our sleeves and pitch in if needed."

Nate grimaced. "That's what family is for, though, right?"

"She understands you're busy in Boston with—"

"My fancy job and my fancy car and my fancy apartment." Nate gave her a long look, his mouth set in a grim line. "I know. But I haven't made the time to visit like I should have."

Kara felt her heart speed up. "Do you intend to change that?" she dared to ask.

"I do," Nate replied, and Kara felt a grin break out over her face. She hoped he kept to his word.

Clearing her throat, she broke his stare and got back to the purpose of her visit. "I have your cookies," she said, handing him the order for tea. "And I brought you a thank-you gift, too," she added, a little more hesitantly.

His expression turned puzzled. "A thank-you gift?"

She gave him a knowing look. "You never told me you could bake."

A slow grin curved his mouth. "You never asked."

So it was true. It had been Nate, all on his own, without help from his aunt or a mysterious guest. The thought of him working on her contest entry, while she lay in bed just one floor above sneezing and coughing, made her feel warm and fuzzy all over. So often she was alone—at work, in the kitchen, and upstairs in her apartment. She liked the image of him there, in her home, in her bakery. It was a feeling she could get used to.

"But gingerbread…it's not the easiest dough to work with. Especially when it involves patterns and precision."

"My mom used to make gingerbread," Nate explained with a casual shrug. "It's actually one of the only fond memories I have of Christmas."

Kara frowned at this. "The *only* fond memory?" Her chest felt a little heavy when she considered the meaning behind his words.

"Pretty much." Nate shrugged again. "Let's just say that Christmas was always a stressful time for my family. Still is for me."

The holidays were stressful for most people, but something in the way his eyes had gone flat told her that Nate wasn't talking about the usual chaos that came with roasting turkeys and getting presents wrapped in time.

"Well, hopefully this Christmas is a little different," she said hopefully. She wanted to think of Nate happy, enjoying the season the way so many others did. The way she did. It would be nice to share that with him, she realized.

"It is," Nate said, giving her a slow grin. "So far, I might even say, it's one of the best Christmases I've ever had."

Kara beamed at him, feeling her panic slip away. "Me too," she said, holding his gaze. His honey-brown eyes were warm and flecked with green, and something unreadable passed through them. Something she almost thought matched her own secret feelings.

A car horn honked, and Kara jumped. It wasn't a sound

you heard often in quiet Briar Creek, but based on Nate's lack of reaction, it was something he was all too used to.

"Mrs. Lancaster's cab is here," he said, his voice laced with regret as he began moving toward the stairs.

"I'll leave you to it, then," Kara said. "I should get back to the bakery anyway." She turned, feeling the same twinge of disappointment that came every time she said goodbye to him. The days to Christmas were dwindling, and today's visit had come and gone far too quickly.

"Wait." His voice was thick and insistent, and with a flicker of her pulse, she looked back at him. "What time do you close for the day?"

She swallowed against the pounding of her heart, not even daring to think of why he might be asking or what he could be suggesting. "Four," she said as casually as she could manage. "Why?"

"I was planning on stopping by the toy store today to buy some gifts for the toy drive. If you're free, maybe you could help me pick out a few things for the girls? I have to admit, my knowledge of children stems solely from my own life experience."

Kara thought of the hundred and ten things she had to do before she went to bed that night and tossed them all aside. "I'd love to," she said.

Nate couldn't remember the last time he'd actually gone shopping. Typically, he limited the experience to online purchases only, something that could be done with a click of a button in between meetings or while he was listening to a conference call. But there was something more personal about picking out a gift in person, and as he reached for the toy car set and set it in his basket, he could almost imagine the child who would receive it.

"Can I ask you a question?" He walked a little closer to Kara, who was studying the back of a board game box with fixed concentration. Hints of sugar and cinnamon and sweetness filled the air as he approached, and he stood as close to her body as he could without it getting awkward. Luckily the toy store was cramped, packed to the ceiling with every kid's delight, making the gesture a little less noticeable than it might have been somewhere else.

"Hmm?" Kara slid her blue eyes to him, distracted.

"How do you structure the donations for the families? Do they pick up their items, or does someone deliver them?"

Kara set the game in her basket. "Each family stops by the Hope Center on Christmas Eve. Why do you ask?"

Nate looked away and tried to focus on some action figure set high on a shelf. "No reason." Eager to shift his thoughts away from the growing dread of memories he'd rather forget, he nudged her with his elbow. "Do girls really like these dolls that eat and drink and—"

She laughed. "They do. At least I did. I had one of those dolls when I was little. I suppose it was good practice for whenever I have kids."

He frowned, imagining her with some guy, a couple kids in tow. He didn't like it. Didn't like the thought of another man in her life. Someone who lived with that soft laugh, eating her delicious treats, living a cozy little life in this cozy little town.

"Hungry?" he asked as they walked to the counter. He reached for his wallet, holding up a hand when she began to protest, and paid for the items in both of their baskets.

"At least let me give you a donation receipt for your taxes," she said.

Nate shrugged. It wouldn't matter. He had enough money to buy the toys. Enough money to buy most things he wanted in life, not just needed. He'd made damn sure of it. And he'd continue to do so, too. It was what he'd come to live for. Not the act of working, not even the business itself, which could be interesting but was hardly his passion. It was the thrill that never tired with each paycheck. The relief that settled in when he checked his bank account.

He'd told himself when he made a certain amount, he could relax. But then he found a way to worry it would run out, so he raised the bar a little higher. Would it ever be enough to undo the worry that plagued him, the knot in his stomach whenever he thought of the dark time in his life, the sad days, the look in his parents' eyes? He wasn't sure. He kept reaching and reaching. Maybe he was reaching for the impossible.

"You didn't answer my question," he said, nudging her arm as the girl set the toys in red paper bags.

"Considering the only thing I've had to eat today were nine cookies and your aunt's peppermint scone, yes. Very hungry."

"Why don't we try your cousin's place, Rosemary and Thyme?" He held his breath, knowing this was more than a friendly dinner invitation. Any question he had that she knew it, too, disappeared when he saw the pink rise in her cheeks.

"That would be nice," she said with a slow smile. "We'll drop these off on our way."

The dance studio was a few blocks off Main Street, disguised in a renovated barn. Inside, the space was fully modernized, with skylights in the lobby and studios through glass doors. A fresh bouquet of pink flowers was centered on the coffee table, where women read magazines while behind the doors music swelled and girls in tutus twirled across the floor.

"Let's leave them back here," Kara instructed, motioning for him to follow her down a hallway and into a crowded storage room. "Mind the glitter…" She smiled over her shoulder as she wove her way through gold and pink and red costumes. Lace and sequins and satin in every color and fabric brushed his coat as he wound his way through the stuffed racks to a clear spot at the back of the room.

"There are already some toys here," he said, setting the bags on a bench.

Kara nodded. "My friend Jane brought some over. She has a little girl, and they went through some of her unused toys. She wanted to teach her that Christmas isn't just a time of receiving presents, but also for giving back."

Nate thinned his lips. "Not every parent bothers with that lesson."

"Sadly, no." Kara sighed. "I think Sophie was excited to think of a little girl she's never met enjoying one of her toys and having a magical Christmas on her account."

"She sounds like a special little girl," Nate observed, thinking of how different she seemed from the kids he'd grown up with. If he closed his eyes, he could still hear the names they'd call him, see their sneers, feel their eyes on his back as they whispered.

"She is. She's Kathleen Madison's granddaughter." She laughed again.

"Ah, Kathleen. I have to admit I'm sort of curious to get a peek in that house. And to meet this elusive woman."

"I think you'll find she is quite normal. Still, she's extremely talented when it comes to her holiday decorations. It's hard to top a professional designer." Her tone turned sad as her brow furrowed on that thought, and Nate realized again how much winning this contest meant to her. Recovering quickly, she grinned at him. "Word is she bought a snow machine. She intends to flock her trees if we don't have a true white Christmas."

"Considering all the snow on the ground, I don't see that happening," Nate remarked.

Kara tipped her head. "Still. She's in it to win it. So am I."

He held her gaze, seeing the fiery determination that flashed through her blue eyes and wondering if the same could be said for himself. For the first time in a long time, there might be one challenge he'd be happy to lose.

CHAPTER 14

Rosemary and Thyme was busier than Nate had anticipated. He'd been inclined to assume that most people in Briar Creek went home for dinner with their families in their quaint homes, a Christmas tree flickering in the bay window for everyone on the street to admire. Instead, every table was booked, and the only thing that saved them from a twenty-minute wait was Kara's relationship with the owners.

"Gotta love nepotism," he joked as they took their seats.

"I do have a lot of relatives in this town," Kara admitted as she unwrapped her scarf and set it on the back of her chair. "But I used to work here, too."

"Oh? In the kitchen?" Nate waited to open his menu, interested in hearing more.

Even in the dim lighting, he sensed a flush in Kara's cheeks as she cracked the spine on her menu and tucked a strand of hair behind her ear. "No. I was the hostess, actually. Then I was promoted to work in the back office, handling the orders, overseeing paperwork, that type of thing."

"I thought you said Anna taught you how to bake," he said, wondering if he'd misunderstood.

Kara nodded as she reached for her water glass. "Oh, she did. But that was before she opened this restaurant. It used to be a café. She ran it alone, and I had a lot more responsibility in the kitchen there." She stole a glance at the hostess stand and shifted her gaze back to him, leaning to lower her voice. "I have to admit that I always feel a little guilty when I come in here."

Her blue eyes were so earnest, he felt a little tug in his chest. He tipped his head. "Why?"

Kara leaned back against her chair, shrugging. "Anna is one of my closest friends. My brother is married to her sister Grace. I grew up with those girls. And Mark...he's my cousin. It didn't feel good to have to hand in my resignation."

Nate grimaced. "Yeah, that would be awkward. But they must have understood. You wanted something for yourself."

Kara's eyes lit up. "Exactly. And they did understand. In fact, they've done nothing but support me. I even supply cookies to the restaurant on occasion. Their menu is seasonal," she explained.

"It sounds like everything worked out then," Nate said.

A shadow fell over Kara's pretty face. "I hope so. I...I don't know what I'll do if it doesn't. It's another reason I feel so worried about my own store's fate, too. I don't want it to all be for nothing."

"Don't think that way," Nate said. He hesitated, wondering if he should risk ruining what was turning out to be a very pleasant evening. He eyed her, deciding he couldn't hold back. "I won't tell you what to do, but I still think you should reconsider raising the prices for the gingerbread houses."

Kara pursed her lips. Finally, she said, "Maybe next year."

"Ah, now see, that's the right attitude." Nate grinned. "There will be another year, and a year after that."

"You sound so sure of it," Kara remarked.

"I speak from experience," Nate considered. "When you want something bad enough, you find a way to make it happen."

Kara smiled. "I think that calls for a drink."

"Should we split a bottle of wine?" Nate asked, turning his attention to the list.

Kara hesitated, but the spark in her eyes as she caught his gaze didn't go unnoticed.

"I'd like that," she said softly.

Nate felt his pulse kick at the slight change in her tone. He'd be happy to linger, enjoy the candlelight, sit in her company. He wasn't ready for the evening to end any time soon.

And maybe it wouldn't have to.

Kara relaxed into her seat after they'd placed their orders and the waitress promptly brought them a bottle of their best Cabernet. The restaurant was dimly lit, and the flame from the single candle at the center of the table flickered against the glass.

"A toast," Nate said, holding up his glass.

"To—" She laughed. "I was going to say the Holiday House contest, but I'm not sure I want to think about that too much tonight."

That made two of them. They were still competing for the same prize, after all. Why add any tension to the mix?

"To new friends," he offered, and then saw the slight pinch of Kara's brow. "And...new possibilities."

Kara's cheeks pinked as she clinked her glass with his, and Nate took a sip, feeling something within him shift.

"So, do you think the kids are going to like the toys we picked out for them?" she asked, lifting the glass to her mouth.

"I should hope so," Nate remarked. "I know I would have."

Kara frowned at this as she set her wineglass down on the table. "Would have?"

Panic flared in his gut. "Oh, you know…if I were one of the kids." He held her gaze, wondering if she'd bought it.

"I suppose there's something to be said for less is more. The children who benefit from the toy drive will probably appreciate their gift more than the kids whose tree is overflowing. Same goes for the Christmas dinner, I suppose. I have to admit, my mother is good at many things, but cooking has never been her strength." Her mouth quirked as she met his eye.

"You have a big Christmas dinner then?"

"Oh, of course!" Kara's look was incredulous. "My mom, my brother and his wife, my sister, me, then my cousins, their fiancées, my aunt…Sometimes friends join, too," she added, then looked away, reddening.

He hadn't considered Christmas yet. Did his aunt have any traditions in place, or had she spent the past few years alone or with her guests? For all he knew he was already on the guest list at the Hastings table. He wouldn't mind it. Bad food and all.

"What about you? I feel like I already know you from your aunt's stories, but do you have any brothers or sisters that you've trumped for favorite nephew?"

Nate laughed. "Only child."

"Ah, spoiled then." Kara grinned.

Nate unfolded his napkin, his heart pulling. "In a way. Every choice my parents made was in my best interest. They…they really sacrificed for me."

Nate's pulse kicked up a notch and he reached for his wine again, wondering what it was about this woman that made him question everything he'd promised for himself, everything he'd built, everything he'd tried to bury in the past and hide. He'd never told anyone the details of his past. Hell, even his parents didn't know the half of it. There was no reason to go back there, to dwell on those times, not when everything was different now. But was it? A part of him was always that kid, the poor kid, the charity case. And damn it if he didn't fear the day would come when he'd be right back where he'd come from.

"My parents...they struggled a bit when I was young," he said. His voice felt hollow, his words unsure, but the kindness he saw in Kara's gaze encouraged him. He cleared his throat. "My parents both came from nothing, and unlike his brother, who ended up here, my father didn't have, well, the charmed life." He gave Kara a wry smile.

"Briar Creek is sort of idyllic," Kara admitted.

"It sure beat the one-bedroom apartment over the deli where I grew up. We lived in a rough part of Boston, but my parents always hoped someday they'd be able to give me more. When I was in middle school, my dad took a job as a janitor at a private school in Beacon Hill. One of the perks was free tuition. You should have seen how proud he was on my first day. It was like he was a new man. A man who was providing for his family the way he'd always wanted to and...couldn't before."

"He wanted the best for you," Kara commented, giving him a sad smile.

"I know it's because of that opportunity that I went on to Harvard. My dad knows it, too. You think my aunt has a bragging problem?" He cocked an eyebrow and Kara laughed. Nate relaxed, feeling the weight of the burden ease off his shoulders. It felt good to unload, to share something about himself he'd never told anyone before. To know it was all right. That he wasn't judged. Wasn't even looked at funny. With his friends back in the city, he kept things light and current. They knew the present-day him, not the whole story.

"Sounds like a great experience, then."

"In some ways," Nate mused. He hesitated. "But the janitor's kid is treated worse than the scholarship kids."

Kara frowned. "You were bullied?"

"Bullied is a strong word," Nate said, but it was probably the accurate one. Did getting your lunch stolen four out of five days a week count as bullying? And that wasn't even the worst of it. "Kids can be cruel, especially to ones they perceive as different or weaker."

"That's terrible," Kara scoffed, shaking her head. "Well, you've shown them. Look at you now!"

Yes, look at him now. He was financially secure, self-made, living in the tony neighborhood his former classmates had taken for granted. But what else did he have to show? He'd buried himself in his work, clung to it, afraid of what would happen if he ever stepped back.

"Can I ask...Is this why you wanted to help with the toy drive? To give back?"

Giving back was something he should have done a long time ago. Oh, he gave to charity, in the form of a check, but he'd never dared to take it to another—more personal— level, to purchase individual gifts for a family that could live just a few miles down the road, a family whose Christmas might depend on the donation. It hit too close.

But being here, seeing Kara's spirit of giving, the lack of shame she attached to those in need...It made him want to do more.

"My parents didn't have a lot of extra money. Holidays were tight. There were some years we didn't even have a tree. My gifts came from secondhand stores, and they were rarely the ones I asked for. I was too young to know not to show my disappointment." He swallowed hard, shaking his head. "I'll never forget the look in my father's eyes."

"You didn't know better," Kara said, reaching out to hold his hand. It was small and a bit cool to the touch, and light on his skin, feminine.

"The year before I started at the private school, we were selected as the sponsor family for our local church. They brought us a Christmas dinner and some coats and boots. New. Nice. But my father wouldn't wear any of them. He stopped going to church after that. When I started at the school the next fall, one of the girls I'd become friendly with recognized my coat, knew we were the needy family. She turned on me faster than you could snap your fingers. The teasing got pretty bad." He frowned.

"What did your parents say?" Kara asked, holding his hand a little tighter.

He shrugged and reached for his wine. "Nothing. They never knew. It would have killed my father. For the first time he was able to give me something really wonderful— an education. A chance for a better life. I couldn't ruin that for him."

"Oh, Nate." Kara shook her head sadly. "I guess you're entitled to be a bit of a Scrooge then."

He grinned. "Hey, you're the one without a Christmas tree." He hesitated, thinking of how much she loved the holiday. It didn't sit right that she shouldn't fully experience it. "What do you say we change that, after dinner tonight?"

"Tonight?" Kara blinked. "Well, I don't even know if there are any trees left."

"We'll find one," he said firmly as the waitress approached with their food.

Kara wagged a finger at him. "Why, Nate, I believe this town is having an effect on you."

Nate picked up his wineglass and let his gaze drift out the window, onto the snow-covered town, lit for the holidays. This was the most relaxed he'd been in years, and the most at peace, too.

He glanced at Kara, her pretty face, the full rosiness of her lips, and felt something in his pulse flicker. "I think you may be right."

Buying a tree from Bob's Christmas Tree Lot was a Hastings family tradition, which had sadly lapsed in recent years. Rosemary went for artificial, claiming it was friendlier on the environment, and Luke opted to cut one from his own sprawling acreage this year. Mark and Anna did the same, and Brett let Ivy pick a small one from the flower market and make it her own.

It just didn't feel the same anymore coming to the lot by herself, and there was something sort of sad about decorating a tree all on her own. It was a reminder of the fact that she didn't have someone special in her life to share such a festive event.

But that was all about to change... thanks to Nate.

Despite the chill in the air, Kara felt warm and snug as they crossed the street to the lot, which was a little sparse but still showed some promising options, at least from a distance. The lot was illuminated by strands of lights, and Bob conducted all of his business out of a trailer he'd decorated to look like Santa's shed—something that had just thrilled Kara and her brother and sister as kids.

"What we wouldn't have done for a glimpse inside that thing growing up," Kara said to Nate as he took in the red-painted trailer with the gift-wrapped front door.

Nate's brown eyes flashed with boyish delight. "Did you ever get a peek?"

Kara gave him a wry smile. "Sadly, we did. Luckily, we were old enough to have stopped believing in Santa, or the entire illusion would have gone bust. A bottle of rum and a carton of cigarettes just never quite fit my mental picture of the jolly old man..."

Nate laughed as they walked through the rows of trees, sizing each one up. It felt intimate to share such a personal experience with him. Made them feel almost like a couple.

She pushed that thought away. She was getting swept up...in Christmas, in fond memories, and in those deep hazel eyes.

"What about this one?" she said, walking over to a small-ish Douglas fir tree.

"Seriously?" Nate stood still on the gravel path. He didn't look impressed. "That's a shrub, not a tree. I was thinking something more along the lines of this one." He gestured to the twelve-foot spruce beside him.

Now it was Kara's turn to laugh. She closed the distance between them under the guise of inspecting the tree, but she felt a little shiver at the proximity, the brush of his wool coat against her own, the subtle heat that came from his body, a contrast against the cold winter night. "You've been in my apartment. That would never fit."

"It would if you got rid of all your furniture." Nate winked, then nudged her playfully. "Hey, I thought you went all-out for Christmas. Don't let me down."

Kara took the opportunity to cozy up next to him, feel the heat of his body next to hers, the reassuring size of him, and lost the battle of her mounting desire. This flutter, this thrill...it was what people talked about, what she'd been waiting to find.

"Cold?" he asked, gesturing to her hands.

Dutifully, she handed them over, and he slipped her

mittens off her hands, tucking them in his pocket along with his gloves. He began kneading her fingers slowly, massaging each one by one, the pressure of his touch gentle but firm, the heat of his skin smooth and persistent. Fire shot through her belly and lower, as his fingers worked magic on her own, her entire body heating from his touch.

"Better?" he asked as he slid her mittens back onto her hands.

She could only nod and swallow back the tingle that was firing low down in her stomach. "Much better."

"Good. Then let's get our tree."

Our tree. She tucked her chin into her scarf, hiding her smile as they wound their way through the rest of the lot. In the end they decided on a seven-foot noble fir and told Bob they'd carry it themselves. Kara suspected it was more like they'd drag it, but she said nothing as Nate confidently said no delivery would be necessary. Normally Kara would have paid for the service, but given Nate's strong hands and wide back, there was no doubt in her mind that Nate could manage the tree himself. The thought of his strength sent a tingle through her.

Ignoring her protests, Nate paid for the tree. "Consider it an early Christmas gift," he said, slipping his wallet back into his pocket. "Besides, this is the first Christmas tree I've ever picked out, so I'm hoping for visitation rights."

Kara's pulse kicked. "I think that can be arranged," she said smoothly, even though inside, her stomach was fluttering with excitement.

His grin flashed. "Good." Sliding his gloves on, he reached down and took hold of the top end of the tree. Kara grabbed the trunk and they began the slow trudge back to her apartment. They walked in silence, their conversation revolving mostly around maneuvering the large item and when to stop to rest, which Kara was a little surprised to realize she needed to do several times along the way.

"I never realized trees could be so heavy!" she explained the fifth time they'd stopped in less than three blocks.

Nate regarded her quizzically. "You're from Briar Creek, right? That's the kind of comment I'm allowed to make, not you."

"I guess I just never...carried the tree before." It really would have been easier to deal with the fake kind. Even if they did look, well, fake.

She started to worry about how she would get it out of her apartment once the holidays were over. She'd have to ask Luke to come over and help, and she hated the thought of it. Maybe she could cut it up, bring it down piece by piece... But then she supposed that would require a chainsaw, and that just felt entirely too crazy to consider. She sighed. She liked to think she didn't need to be married or have a boyfriend to live what she considered a normal life, but the sorry truth was that she doubted Ivy or Grace or Anna had to consider this dilemma.

"It's part of the entire Christmas experience," Nate said. "You pick it out, you carry it home. You decorate it. If I'm going to do Christmas, I'm going to really do Christmas."

"You don't mess around," Kara remarked, suspecting that this attitude extended to other things in Nate's life.

"Nope," Nate said, his dark eyes intensifying their hold on hers. "I don't. Life's too short. If you're going to do something, go all in or don't bother."

Kara nodded, knowing that she hadn't exactly lived by this motto...until recently. She was all in with that bakery, well past knee-deep; she was giving it her heart and soul, everything she had.

Except a small part of her was still waiting, and hoping...

for someone to come along and give her all the other things that were still missing from her life—a strong hand to hold, a person to laugh with, to tease, to bring her soup when she was feeling sick. A man who was starting to feel more and more like the one standing right in front of her.

The tree looked right at home wedged in the corner between her front window and the hearth. Almost as at home as Nate was beginning to feel in her small apartment.

She looked over at him, sitting on her sofa, untangling a string of lights with a frown creasing his brow. "How the heck did you let this happen?" he asked.

Kara just laughed. The timer to the oven dinged, and Kara reluctantly left to run to the kitchen just in time to pull the cookie tray from the oven. She let them cool while she made cocoa from white hot chocolate shavings and steamed milk, and then added some whipped cream and the same crushed candy canes she'd sprinkled on top of her chocolate fudge cookies. In the background, carols played softly, and so far Nate hadn't made a sound of complaint.

Her heart tugged when she thought of what he'd shared with her, but she smiled as she brought the tray into the living room. This man deserved a merry Christmas. And she might be able to give him just that.

Nate stood up and grinned triumphantly. "The lights are ready." He crouched to plug them into the socket, but Kara stopped him.

"No, not yet!" she cried, setting the tray down on the coffee table. "Not until we're finished with the tree. That's all part of the magic."

He looked at her doubtfully, but his mouth curved into a grin as he began stringing the lights over the branches. "You're an expert on this, are you?"

"I have a lot of experience, you might say." Kara picked up a mug of hot chocolate and handed it to him. "It probably seems silly to you, but it's easy for me to get caught up in the holiday."

"It's not silly. You have happy memories. What's not to enjoy?" He looked down at his cocoa. "Is peppermint in everything in this town?"

Kara laughed. "Well, it is Christmas. But I can take it off if you'd like."

"No," he said, taking a sip. "It's growing on me. Like some other things." He held her gaze, and Kara's heart skipped a beat.

She looked away, shaking aside the ripple of excitement that charged through her chest. "I'll get the ornaments."

She left him to finish the lights, hurrying to her bedroom closet, where she stowed most of her personal belongings. The box was small, on the top shelf, and she found it quickly. Pulling it down, she began to walk back into the living room and then hesitated, briefly, to check her reflection in the mirror above her dresser and add a touch more lip gloss.

Ridiculous. So they enjoyed each other's company. The guy was probably passing time. Looking for an excuse to get a break from the inn and his aunt's demands for a few hours.

Except...the look in his eyes when she rounded the corner into the living room told her he might not be looking for an excuse at all. His gaze was direct, hooded and penetrating, and Kara felt a shift between them. Her pulse skittered with anticipation.

"Found them!" she announced, crossing the room to stand next to him. He reached for the box, his hands skimming hers, and locked her eyes for a beat. Kara felt her cheeks flush and swallowed hard.

She glanced at the flames flickering in the fireplace. "My, it's getting warm in here. I think I'll turn down the heat."

Nate gave her a curious look. "Feels fine to me."

"Does it?" Kara asked weakly. "Must be the hot chocolate." And the fact that she couldn't recall ever feeling this way in a man's company. Most of the dates she'd had were polite and a little stiff, but certainly not exciting, and certainly not interesting enough to make her all giddy and nervous.

But then, this wasn't a date. And she'd best remember that.

They hung the ornaments, each taking a turn, their hands brushing the other's as they reached into the box, and Kara scooted past him, feeling her hip brush his thigh as she hung the last of them on the tree. She nearly tripped over the velvet tree skirt, and Nate reflexively reached out and grabbed her by the waist. His hands felt strong and secure wrapped around her body.

"You okay?" he asked, his voice warm and husky.

She nodded and finally managed, "I told you this place is cramped."

His hands lingered on her waist before he finally released her, and she turned to him, seeing the hooded look of his eyes, sensing the possibility of something she was beginning to long for.

She cleared her throat, her nerves getting the better of her, and gestured to the strand of lights. "You may now do the lights," she said gallantly.

He lifted an eyebrow. "Oh, may I? You sure? No more traditions that need to take place? No mistletoe or star—"

"The star!" She'd been so caught up in Nate's company, she'd almost forgotten the most precious part of her holiday. Kara clapped her hand over her mouth and darted back into her bedroom, quickly reemerging with the box holding her Christmas star. She opened the lid and gingerly lifted out the glittery gold star. "I've had this for as long as I can remember."

Nate stepped forward and inspected the object. "Did you make this?"

Kara nodded, feeling her throat knot as hot tears welled. "It doesn't look like much, but it means the world. There was one Christmas where we were snowed in for days, couldn't leave the house, and it was too cold to even go sledding. My dad put us all to work making ornaments for the tree, even though we already had boxes of them in the attic. I made little snowmen from cotton balls, Molly made some felt elves. My dad made this."

She blinked quickly, but it was no use. A single tear trickled down her cheek as she met Nate's gaze. He was frowning at her, but there was softness in his eyes as he reached up and slowly wiped her face with the pad of his thumb.

"Then our tree wouldn't be complete without it."

She smiled. There was that word again. *Our* tree. She could get used to that.

She held the star gently in her hands, wondering what had become of Molly's elves, if any had been saved over the years. Though she knew Molly had fine-tuned her wedding registry long before she was ever actually engaged, Kara wanted to give her something special and sentimental. She made a silent promise to herself to look through the attic next time she was at her mother's house.

Nate took her hand as she climbed onto one of the Windsor chairs from her dining table and then moved his hands down to her legs as she secured the star to its branch. Year after year, a little bit of glitter fell off, and she was careful to preserve as much of it as she could, taking her time with the placement to ensure it wouldn't fall off. It was just made of cardboard, but a dent would be devastating.

"I almost have it," she said.

"No rush," Nate said, his voice low and deep and—dare she say slightly suggestive? She had been so fixated on the star that she hadn't paid attention, but now she noticed the way his hands gripped her legs, the way they moved this way and that, as if exploring her, caressing her even.

"There. All done." She hopped off the chair, landing dangerously close to his body.

"Anything else?" His mouth quirked, and she fixated on it for a moment, wondering what he tasted like, how he felt.

"Just one more thing," she said. "When you turn on the lights, you have to make your Christmas wish."

He chuckled as he bent down and connected the strand to the socket. Immediately the tree sprang to life, lighting up the room in a warm glow, reflecting off the ornaments that now shone and glistened, her father's star glittering at the very top.

"Beautiful," she sighed, taking it all in.

"It is."

Kara had been so lost in the magnificence of the tree that she hadn't even realized Nate was watching her. Now the hair on the back of her neck prickled, and she looked over to him, her breath catching at the look in his eyes.

"Did you make your Christmas wish?" she asked.

She assumed he'd laugh it off, but instead he nodded once. "I did. And how about you? What's your Christmas wish?"

She swallowed hard, steeling herself from that unreadable expression, from the jumping jacks in her stomach. "Oh, for my bakery to succeed," Kara said. But that wasn't true. Not entirely, at least. What she really wished for was for this—what she had right here, right now—to continue, just a little longer, past Christmas. "And yours?"

He leaned forward, closing the distance between their

bodies, as his hand came around her waist. Kara inhaled sharply and felt the pull of his strength as she set a hand on his chest, feeling the steady drum under his sweater.

"This," he whispered, slowly bringing his mouth to hers. His kiss was light, gentle, and heat pooled deep between her thighs as his mouth opened to hers. His tongue laced with hers, exploring her, bringing her deeper as he pulled her tight. Kara reached up and wrapped her arms around his neck, letting their bodies fuse together, pressing the length of herself against the hard plane of his chest.

He pulled back slowly, looking into her eyes as a lopsided smile tugged at his mouth.

"And we didn't even need the mistletoe," she whispered.

"What can I say?" Nate said. "This is shaping up to be the best Christmas yet."

"I couldn't agree more," Kara said through a smile as her lips found his once more.

CHAPTER 15

Molly opened the oven door and set a tray of sugar cookies in the oven. She carefully set the timer—something she'd forgotten to do with the last batch—and then turned to her sister. "What else can I help with?"

Kara gave her a tired smile. "I feel guilty. I should really be the one helping you!"

"With what?" Molly asked, frowning.

Her sister stared at her in disbelief. "Your wedding, of course!"

Oh. That. Molly brought a wooden spoon to her mouth and licked the sticky and sweet batter from it. "It's okay," she said. "You know I've had it planned for years anyway. Besides, I feel like we made a lot of progress and it's only been a week. I took Mom over to the stationery store to the see the invitations. She liked the same ones we did, but I let her think she persuaded me."

Kara laughed. "Any more luck with her present this year?"

Molly set the spoon back in the bowl and brought them both to the sink. "Nope. Have you given it any more thought?"

Kara expertly piped some royal icing on the roof of a gingerbread house she was making for the school librarian. "Oh, I was thinking a candle. Maybe a picture frame..." She met Molly's gaze, and both girls winced. "It should be the thought that counts, right?"

"It should," Molly agreed. "But Mom can sometimes be hard to please."

"Tell me about it." Kara sighed, and her brow pinched as she concentrated on her task. "Has she...said anything to you about the bakery?"

"This place?" Molly thought back. Most of her conversations with her mom had been about *The Nutcracker* or the wedding. The wedding. Just the thought of it made her stomach knot. She set a hand to it, trying to settle herself. "Not really. Why?"

"Oh, no reason," Kara said, but her voice was abnormally high, and Molly wasn't buying that fake nonchalance.

"You're doing a great job," she said, coming to set a hand on Kara's shoulder. She watched as her sister's hands worked, swiftly and expertly, until the last piece of the house was complete. She stared at the finished creation, marveling in the details, a flicker of pride mixing with those same old doubts. "I'm really impressed. You have a lot more going for you than I do."

She looked away from the house, wondering what she had to show for herself. Certainly not a beautiful bakery, or a happy customer, or a gorgeous gingerbread house.

She glanced down at her finger. She had a diamond ring. And a gift registry. And a perpetually upset stomach.

"Me?" Kara set the piping bag down and stared at her sister. "You're the one who's getting married."

Molly sighed. "I suppose I'm just anxious about taking time off work," she fibbed. "Thanks for letting me help out today. It keeps me busy. And it's a nice break from decorating the house. Speaking of which..." She walked over to the corner of the room where she knew Kara was keeping her entry, but her sister darted to stop her, using her arms to barricade her.

"Nope. Sorry, not until it's finished."

"Top secret, huh?" Molly just smiled. "You're really not going to let anyone see it until then?"

"Well..." Kara's cheeks flushed, and she pushed past Molly, not meeting her eye, as she began wrapping the gingerbread house in cellophane.

Molly turned, watching her sister in suspicion. "Well... well, what? Don't tell me you let someone else see your creation and not your favorite sister!"

"You're my only sister," Kara commented, giving a rueful smile. "Besides, I didn't do it on purpose. It just happened. Nate stopped by and—"

"Nate?" Molly cocked an eyebrow as she leaned a hip against the counter. "Mrs. Griffin's nephew?"

Kara took her time cinching the plastic wrap and securing it with a bright green bow. A stall tactic, Molly surmised.

Finally, Kara turned to her. "That's right. We've been... spending some time together. He's... very nice."

Molly was nodding her head, eyeing the nervous twitch in her sister's gaze. "Nice..."

Kara wiped her hands on her apron and huffed out a breath. "That's right. He's very nice. He brought me soup—"

Molly felt her eyes widen. "He brought you soup."

"I was sick," Kara explained hurriedly.

"He brought you soup when you were sick," Molly said slowly. She couldn't hide her smile any longer. For as long as she could remember, she was the one always falling too hard and too fast for every guy who gave her a second glance, and

Kara...well, Kara didn't fall hard at all. Until, perhaps, now. She felt a sting of something sharp. Jealousy, she realized. And happiness, too, of course. Kara deserved to find someone special. They both did. "He certainly does sound nice. Cute, too." She remembered the thick brown hair and warm eyes from Anna and Mark's party.

Kara just gave a casual shrug. "You think so? Maybe. I never really noticed."

Molly stared at her sister, watched as she washed a dish, then set it to dry, her back purposefully to the room, her cheeks still on fire.

"You kissed him!" she cried in delight.

Kara whipped around, but the look in her eyes said it all. "What? What are you talking about?"

Molly waved a playful finger at her. "Kara Hastings, you can't lie to me. I know you too well. Besides, don't you want to dish the dirt?"

"Dish the *dirt*?" Kara scoffed.

"You know, tell me how it was. Was it good? I bet it was good." Molly blinked rapidly as she chewed her thumbnail.

Kara gave her a long, hard look, her hands on her hips, but Molly wasn't backing down. Finally, Kara's mouth curved into a small, knowing smile. "It *was* good," she whispered, and then laughed.

Molly giggled and clapped her hands. "I knew it! When did this happen? What's going on? Are you going to see him again?"

Kara dropped onto one of the stools clustered around the kitchen island. "You're asking every question I'm thinking. The guy lives in Boston..."

"So? So do I! You can visit me more often."

Kara pulled a face. "I have this bakery. You see how much

time it takes. I'm in no position to be leaving town for weekends, and I don't even know if that's what Nate is looking for. It was just a kiss. A nice kiss. Who knows if it will even happen again."

"Do you want it to happen again?" Molly asked, reaching for one of the cookies she'd slightly burned earlier.

Kara gave her a slow grin. "Do I ever."

The oven timer buzzed, and Molly snatched an oven mitt. She smiled as she pulled the cookies from the oven, but her heart felt a little heavy. She was happy for her sister, of course she was. After all, she'd had how many boyfriends over the years while Kara...Kara never seemed to find anyone that sent her heart aflutter.

And now, well, now the situation was a little reversed. And could you really marry someone who didn't make your pulse skip a beat at least every once in a while?

Molly didn't think so. And that...that was a problem.

Kara stopped and counted to three in an effort to steady her racing heart before she turned the door of the Main Street B&B. It was a busy day at the bakery, but Molly had offered to handle the counter so that Kara wouldn't be in any rush from her errand. In fact, Molly had encouraged her to take all the time she needed, with a suggestive grin.

Kara glanced around the lobby, which had slowly transformed day by day, holding her breath as she swept her gaze for a hint of nut-brown hair and a smile that could thaw the snow right off her boots.

But all she saw were a few guests and, to her slight dismay, Mrs. Griffin.

"Well, there you are!" the innkeeper said, pushing past a box of decorations to greet Kara near the door. "It's hard to believe the holidays are already nearing an end. I've gotten used to having you pop by each day."

"I've looked forward to it quite a bit," Kara said, even if her motives might have been more centered on Mrs. Griffin's handsome nephew. Her chest squeezed when she realized just how quickly the time was passing. Christmas was now just around the corner, coming to an end right when she was finally starting to enjoy the holidays.

"I have to say, these snowflake cookies have been quite a hit for my holiday tea."

Kara smiled, grateful for the compliment. "I suppose Christmas Eve will be your last holiday tea?" It had been a steady gig, one she had benefited from greatly, and another reminder that the holiday rush was almost behind her and that business would surely slow when it did.

Valentine's Day would be popular, she knew. She already had some ideas for her menu then. But she had to brace herself for a slow January. And possibly a few other months throughout the year, too.

She thought about Nate's comments on her pricing. She probably could have charged a bit more for those gingerbread houses—she hadn't really assessed what was fair or what people were willing to pay. She didn't want to take advantage, but they did consume a fair bit of time. She'd definitely raise the price a bit next year. If she was still in business by then.

"Yes, Christmas Eve is the last tea of the season," Maggie sighed. "Makes me a little sad, honestly." Her eyes turned a bit misty for a moment, but as Kara's frown grew, Mrs. Griffin straightened her shoulders and gave a quick smile. "Well, I shouldn't take up too much of your time. This must be a busy time of year for you."

"It is," Kara agreed. "And I still have the Holiday House contest entry to finish."

Mrs. Griffin's expression turned quizzical. "The entry? Are you decorating your apartment?"

"No, I..." Kara hesitated, wondering why Nate hadn't mentioned his challenge to his aunt before. "I'm entering a gingerbread house, actually."

"A gingerbread house!" Maggie's green eyes were wide in astonishment. "How perfectly clever." She gathered her hands into fists near her chest, her eyes darting to the left.

"It was Nate's idea, actually," Kara said, wanting to give fair credit where it was due.

Mrs. Griffin's snapped to hers. "Nate? My nephew Nate?"

Kara nodded. "That's right. I teased him about helping out with your entry, and he sort of dared me to do it. I'm glad he did," she added, smiling to herself. She planned to work on her project tonight, considering she'd be busy with her friends at the Winter Festival tomorrow. It was a big event in Briar Creek, and one she hadn't missed in all her life. One of many traditions that made her love this town so much.

"Nate is the best person to be helping me out with the decorations," Maggie said, and Kara bit back a smile. Didn't Nate's aunt love any opportunity to brag about him? She listened patiently, enjoying a little insight into this increasingly irresistible man. "He's quite an artist, actually. Won the school art prize every year. Even had a few pieces in a magazine."

Kara blinked. This wasn't a side of him she'd ever seen. "Really? Then why didn't he go on to pursue it?"

Maggie shrugged. "I don't know. I tried to commission a painting from him the other day and he told me in no uncertain terms that he wouldn't do it. Oh, if you saw some of his creations. He has a gift, I tell you. A raw talent."

Kara mulled this over, remembering what Nate had said about his aunt being upset with him. She could only assume the two were related. It wasn't like Nate to say no to his aunt—from what she had seen, he patiently put up with the somewhat demanding woman, feeding into her whims, doting on her every wish, and helping out around the inn.

"Ah, there's my little Nate now!" Mrs. Griffin cried, swooping her hands together as she beamed at the staircase.

Sure enough, Nate was already at the bottom, his hand on the banister, his smile suspicious. He was anything but little, though, with his broad shoulders and thick biceps that pushed against the camel sweater he wore. A little jolt zipped down her spine, and Kara wondered if the thrill of seeing him would ever fade.

"Why, Nate, we were just talking about you!" his aunt crooned.

Nate met Kara's eye as he came over to join them, and she wondered if he was thinking about last night nearly as much as she had since he'd eventually left her apartment. "All good things I hope." He cocked an eyebrow.

"Of course!" his aunt said, and Kara sensed a secret smile pass between herself and Nate.

"Your aunt was telling me that you're quite the artist," she said, lest there be any confusion she'd been talking about the kiss they'd shared instead.

Nate's eyes lost their gleam. His jaw pulsed as he pulled in a breath. "I see."

Kara opened her mouth to say something but stuttered on her words. Whatever the reason, this was most definitely a sore subject. "I was just bringing over the cookies for the tea," she said quickly, happy for a reason, however painfully obvious, to change the subject. Turning to Mrs. Griffin, she added, "I'll be bringing tomorrow's order over early, since I'm closed due to the festival."

"Oh, the festival. I hate to miss it myself, but duty calls.

I might pop in for a bit where I can, and Nate will be there, won't you?" She gave her nephew a smile that said there was no room for argument.

Nate smiled patiently at his aunt. "Wouldn't miss it."

Satisfied, Mrs. Griffin took the box of snowflake cookies and turned to talk to a guest.

Alone, Kara felt her pulse begin to race with anticipation, wondering if something would be said about the kiss, or if she should apologize for mentioning something that was clearly so sensitive to Nate. Curiosity built, but it wasn't her business, and in a town like Briar Creek, where everyone found a way of having an opinion on everything, she valued privacy.

"So what's this festival I've inadvertently agreed to attend?" Nate asked in a low voice, so soft and smooth that it made Kara stiffen with pleasure. He was standing close to her, close enough for her to take in his soft hazel eyes and drop her gaze to his lips, the very ones that had touched her own just a mere matter of hours earlier...

Remembering where she was, she quickly looked back up at him and cleared her throat.

"It's the annual Winter Festival," she told him. "It's one of my favorite days of the year. The town square is transformed with games, contests, and vendors." She smiled fondly at the memories of many happy days spent with friends and family, a cup of hot chocolate in her hand and the feeling of Christmas seemingly everywhere.

"Are you selling cookies?" he asked. His gaze lazily roamed her face, and Kara almost forgot his question for a moment.

"What? Oh, no. No, you have to register for a stand in August, and I wasn't sure of where I'd be with the business yet. Next year," she added hopefully.

"Now that's the kind of optimism I like to see," he said.

"Says the man who is full of unsolicited advice," she added, feeling her defenses prickle, but only a little, especially once she caught the curve of his grin. She gave a shy smile in return, wondering what was going through that head.

She skirted her gaze across the lobby, hoping she might be free to say something more meaningful, some reference to last night, but Mrs. Griffin was standing at the base of the stairs, her green eyes wide and alert as she pretended to fluff the garland that wrapped the banister.

"I only offer up suggestions because I want you to succeed," he said, and her breath heaved. "Besides, I can't help myself. It's what I do. Ignore me."

Easier said than done, she thought, sweeping her eyes over his rugged frame. Nate was hardly a man she was quick to overlook.

"It's fine that I have the day off, though. Leaves more time for fun," she said.

"Do I take it to mean you'll be at the festival?" he asked, giving her a slow grin that made her knees go a little weak.

Kara swallowed. "Wouldn't miss it."

"Good," Nate said, pulling back. "In that case, it should be a good time."

Kara met his eye. "I couldn't agree more."

They were far from alone, and Nate could tell by his aunt's less-than-subtle glances from the other end of the lobby that she was watching their every move under the pretense of fiddling with the decorations. He took hold of Kara's elbow, edging her into the corner of the room, wishing he could move his hand lower, reach through her thick coat, and properly feel her—the way he'd done last night. He hoped to have another chance to explore things between them, but for now, he'd just have to wait.

"Do you need to get back to the bakery right away?"

"My sister's helping me out today, so I can spare a few extra minutes." When she looked up at him, her blue eyes were bright. "Why do you ask?"

His gaze dropped to her mouth, her soft, pink lips, recalling the way they'd felt against his just a mere matter of hours ago. He cleared his throat and rolled back on his heels. "I bought a few more gifts for the toy drive." He started to explain and then stopped. Some things couldn't be described, and he was eager for her opinion. "Here, I'll show you."

After stomping the remaining snow from her boots, Kara followed him into a storage room off the kitchen, her gasp audible when he flicked on the light. He couldn't help but smile at her reaction as she ventured into the room, her eyes full of awe.

"You said a few more gifts!" she cried, walking over to a bright pink bike with matching training wheels and sparkling streamers. "More like you bought out the entire store!"

Nate gave a modest shrug, but he couldn't deny the swell of pride he felt at her reaction. With any luck, the kids would feel just as excited as she did. "What can I say? I couldn't stop. Every time I thought I had enough, I saw something else a kid might enjoy." He eyed the model plane building set in the corner—it was just like one he'd had on his list one year. Back when he still made lists.

He swept his hair back from his forehead, pushing at those memories. There was no room for them here. Not when so many children would be able to have a better Christmas than he'd ever had.

"Oh, Nate." Kara smiled warmly, coming over to set

a hand on his arm. For a brief moment something passed between their exchange, and he thought she might lean in and kiss him, but just as quickly she pulled back. No doubt she knew his aunt well enough to know that if she caught them, she'd all but put a wedding announcement in tomorrow's newspaper. "You know, you aren't the Scrooge you say you are."

Nate held her gaze, which was alive and sparkling. Her smile was contagious, all at once removing him from the bad mood that had threatened to encroach. He supposed something in him had started to thaw, that a new outlook on the holiday was forming, but that didn't mean he was as crazy for Christmas as the rest of this town. He just wasn't as opposed to it anymore. "I'm tolerating the holiday," he said, catching the playful purse of her mouth. "But buying the gifts for these kids…it feels good. I just hope they enjoy them."

"Of course they will!" Kara picked up a video game system and whistled under her breath. "You certainly spared no expense. The kids will be grateful. And…I'm grateful." Her hand brushed his just long enough to send a rush of heat to his groin, to remind him of the passion in their kiss last night, of the connection that was forming between them.

"Should I bring these by the dance studio or store them here?" he asked. He resisted the urge to set a hand on her hip, to wrap his arms around her waist and pull her close. His aunt was getting curious—more so than usual—and he didn't want to break the spell that Kara had started to cast over him.

"It might be better if you keep them here for a few days," Kara said, and then rolled her eyes. "*The Nutcracker* is in peak panic mode, with the curtain call just a few days away. Believe me, you don't want to step foot in there unless you plan on getting trapped in a few hundred yards' worth of tulle."

Nate laughed. "Thanks for the warning."

Kara looked at him wistfully, seeming to hesitate for a moment. Eventually she said, "Well, I should probably go relieve Molly. She doesn't have much retail experience, and every time I turn around she's eating another one of my cookies. If I leave her alone much longer, I might not have any left to sell."

Nate dropped his gaze to her mouth and finally pulled away. "I suppose I should get back to some Holiday House decorating myself," he said begrudgingly. "My aunt has given me a last-minute to-do list that should carry me straight through to midnight."

"Good luck with that," Kara said, laughing softly.

"May the best man win," Nate replied lightly, but he frowned a little when he thought of their original bet. It was that bet that had broken the ice with them, given them a common bond, but would it also be the factor that would end this little flirtation they were forming?

Kara patted his arm fondly and slipped him a smile. "More like the best woman." She winked and turned from the room, leaving Nate to watch her go, her silky ponytail bouncing against her shoulders, her laugh merry and light, and her hips...Oh, those hips.

He flicked off the light to the storage room and went back to the lobby, eager to get a start on his aunt's list so that nothing would be left over until tomorrow.

Tomorrow he intended to spend the day enjoying Kara's company, even if it was at a Christmas festival, of all things. And as for the Holiday House contest outcome...He'd cross that bridge when the time came.

CHAPTER
16

Briar Creek's annual Winter Festival was everything Nate would have expected it to be and more. He'd caught a glimpse of it from the inn's front windows shortly after waking up, wondering who had transformed the town square overnight, as if by magic. The previously empty, snow-covered park space was now filled with stands with bright red awnings, and pine garland roped off various events, which even extended to an igloo-building competition. It was only ten, but already the inn had cleared out, and it seemed that every resident of the small town was gathered together to share in the festivities.

Aunt Maggie wore a bright red coat and matching hat and kept pressing that ridiculous knotted cap into his hand, the same one he'd obligingly worn when he'd gone skating with Kara.

His pulse skipped a beat when he thought of her, and he darted his eyes over to the rink, hoping to steal a glance of her long dark hair, her twinkling blue eyes, and the smile that was warmer than the sun on a cold day. It seemed there was some kind of event taking place on the slick surface today, though. No spins, jumps, or figure eights to be seen.

Deflated, he took his aunt's arm as they pushed through the crowds. It would be hard to find Kara in this mix of people, but he wasn't giving up just yet. It wasn't in his nature to give up.

"You'll catch a cold without a hat," his aunt fretted, thrusting a cap at him once more.

There was no way in hell Nate was wearing this thing around the festival, but he tucked it into his pocket nonetheless, hoping he would calm his aunt's nerves when he told her he'd keep it in case he needed it.

"Oh, look. Warm chestnuts. I hadn't intended to stay long, but I might just be convinced to set housework aside for a bit longer." His aunt smiled as she motioned to a stand, and, catching the hint, Nate bought her a bag. They were flavored with cinnamon, and the aroma was rich and heavy, a sharp contrast to the cold snow that crunched under their feet. Looking around, Nate felt a moment of guilt when he thought of his parents, on a sunny cruise, no overt reminder of Christmas to be seen on the vast Mediterranean Sea, and wondered if they might have enjoyed a few days of Briar Creek instead.

Or if it would have made them think of how Christmas could have been for them, had circumstances been different. He knew his mom would have loved the festival and the Holiday House contest. She'd always tried to make the most of their small apartment, with the few decorations they had, often calling on Nate to create something homemade, since he was so good at it...

He squared his jaw and reached into the bag, bringing a warm chestnut to his mouth as his aunt did the same. He was getting caught up, in the carols blasting through the air from speakers, in the decorations and the laughter and the twinkling lights. No doubt his parents were having a wonderful time. It was a luxury vacation, after all. What more could they ask for?

Nate frowned. No doubt indeed...

Shifting back to a topic he was more comfortable with, he said to his aunt, "I suppose this event is good for your business."

"Oh, absolutely. This weekend is always booked months in advance, and there's a waiting list, too. I hate having to turn people away, but there's only so much room..."

Nate considered the suite he was occupying, no doubt one of the best in the inn, and said, "I'd like to pay you for the accommodations."

His aunt looked at him in surprise. "What? No."

"But you could have filled my room with a paying guest," he pointed out.

"My dear boy, do you think I do this for the money?" She laughed away his concern.

He'd never stopped to consider there could be any other reason. You worked to pay the bills. To put food on the table. You didn't work to indulge your interests. Hobbies didn't keep the lights on.

"I had that room reserved for your parents, and then when you sent them away, well...Of course I could have rented it out to a guest, but I held out hope that you'd come, and here you are!" She beamed.

Nate frowned. "I didn't send them away. I gave them a vacation."

"Ah, well. Same thing, really. I would have set two rooms aside if all three of you could have come. Besides," Maggie continued, "you've earned your keep. I think we have a real chance of winning that contest this year."

He muttered something noncommittal. His aunt had a cozy home, a comfortable inn, and she'd just admitted she wasn't doing this for the money. While Kara...she had freely voiced that she was entering the contest for the money. He could appreciate that.

"Can I ask you a question?" Nate stopped walking as they neared a clearing. "If you aren't running the inn for the money, then what are you doing it for?"

He needed to know how much effort to sink into this contest, decide where his loyalties lay, who deserved to take home the prize. His aunt loved a little neighborly drama, no doubt it kept things interesting around here, but if the only reason she was entering was to toot her horn to the likes of Kathleen Madison, then he could think of someone whose efforts were considerably more heartfelt.

"That house has been in my family since before I was born. I was raised there. I lived with your uncle there. Even though he's not with me anymore, and neither are my parents, they're in the fabric of that place—every room, every corner...It has a memory. I love that house, and it's important for me to give back the love that house has brought to me by giving my guests a good experience. I'm proud of it. I can't run it forever. I just want to make the most of it while I still can." She gave him a watery smile. "Does that make sense?"

Nate swallowed hard and nodded silently. That inn was her legacy; it was all that she'd known. In many ways, all that she had left.

It made sense, all right. And it also put him in a damn near impossible situation.

Kara sipped her hot cocoa and skirted her eyes over the festival again, feeling a twinge of disappointment that Nate might not have showed after all. Christmas was hardly his thing, after all, and the Winter Festival was about as Christmassy as things got around Briar Creek.

"Looking for something?" Molly asked as she handed over a few bills for her own hot chocolate.

"Oh, just looking for Grace and Anna," Kara said.

Molly pursed her lips knowingly. "And I'm looking for Santa Claus." She elbowed her sister and leaned in close. "You're looking for Nate. It's okay to admit it. I'm your sister, after all."

Kara sighed, but she couldn't fight her smile. "Okay, fine. You caught me. Satisfied?"

"Immensely," Molly said, slanting her a glance. "But for someone who has a night of hot passion on her mind, you look a little down."

"It wasn't a night of hot passion. It was just a kiss." A very nice kiss, but still, just a kiss. "And I'm not low. I was just... Well, Nate said he was coming, and I was starting to wonder if he'd changed his mind. He's not really into Christmas."

"Who doesn't like Christmas?" Molly remarked. "Besides, it looks to me like he likes Christmas quite a bit." She lifted her chin, motioning to a stand a few yards away from where they stood, where sure enough, Nate stood among the crowd.

Kara felt her heart begin to flutter, and a ripple of excitement danced through her stomach. She suddenly felt nervous, like she couldn't go over to him, couldn't tap him on the shoulder, watch as he turned to give her one of those broad grins, and feel the surge of hope swell within her.

The man was leaving town in a matter of days. She needed to put her feelings in check and remember that, or else... But the thought of not enjoying this time, not acting on the feelings that were making her think a little less than clearly, not enjoying the magic that only Christmas could bring, well... that was darn near impossible.

"Are you going to go over and say hello?" Molly pressed.

"Oh…I don't want to come on too strong." Kara took a sip of her cocoa, feeling it warm her blood, even though she was already so stifled and overheated in her down parka and wool hat that she had a sudden desire to strip down to her cashmere sweater, or maybe sit down in the snow…The man was under her skin. Making her pulse race. Her palms sweat. Her mind run with fantasies of another taste of those lips.

It was exciting. But it was also a little scary. She'd never felt this way before. Would she ever again, once he was gone?

"Well, you don't need to worry about that. Here he comes." Molly tossed her a wink and, before Kara could protest, turned on her heel and walked off, waving to Jane and Anna Madison, who had just arrived with their fiancés.

Fiancés. Everyone was engaged now. Everyone except her.

She eyed Nate steadily as he walked over to her, his grin mischievous, his gaze a little jaded. No doubt all this country flair was far from his idea of fun, especially given the theme. What made her think he had any long-term plans for Briar Creek? Or her for that matter?

She probably would have been better off listening to her mother. Letting one of the eligible bachelors in town take her on a date. But then, those guys didn't make her insides go all mushy or her knees go all weak or make her smile herself to sleep with the possibility of tomorrow.

Wow. She had it bad.

"I was beginning to think you wouldn't show up," Nate said conspiratorially, coming to stand close to her.

Kara felt a bubble of satisfaction swell in her belly. "I've been walking around with my sister," she said.

"Ah, yes, I met her at the party. At least I think I did." He frowned a bit. "There were a lot of new faces that night, and it was a bit of a blur."

As much as she wanted to be alone with Nate, she knew now wasn't the time. Everyone in town was gathered on the square, and besides, she couldn't resist the opportunity to show him off. Just a little.

"Come on," she said, slipping her arm through his. "I'll introduce you properly. But first you need a proper tour of the festival." She grinned up at him as she walked in the direction opposite her friends and family, taking him on the long path through the various stalls offering everything from hand-knitted stockings to beautiful glass ornaments. The wind was picking up, but between the heat lamps and the comfort of Nate's body so close to hers, she didn't even seem to care. She buried her chin a little deeper in her scarf as they rounded a bend to stop for hot cider.

Kara accepted the steaming cup from Nate with a smile and leaned back against a tree trunk to watch a sledding race in the distance.

"Do you ever enter?" Nate asked, his voice low and deep in her ear, causing her to shiver into her coat.

Kara took a sip of her drink. "I did when I was a kid, but my brother always beat me."

Nate grinned, but there was a shadow in his gaze she couldn't quite decipher. "Something tells me you gave it your all, though."

"Of course." Kara gave him a strange look. "Is there any other way?"

"There isn't," Nate said, his jaw pulsing as he brought the paper cup to his mouth. His eyes shifted from hers to the hill again, just in time for the next race to start.

"I was just thinking…" He stopped talking, and Kara turned to look up at him, frowning when he lapsed into silence.

"Just thinking?" she pressed, feeling herself tense.

He looked down at her, his gaze soft again in a way that made her insides go all warm and mushy. She could have kissed him right here and now, leaning against the bark of an old maple tree, in front of half the town. Instead she blinked, straightened up, told herself to stop thinking like a teenager for five minutes.

"I was just thinking it's sort of a shame two people can't win the Holiday House contest," he said a little hopefully.

Her grin was wry. "Kathleen Madison is going to win that contest. Not that I won't give it my best shot and all, and not that I don't really want to win, but if I were you, I'd prepare your aunt for a disappointment. She can be…"

He raised an eyebrow so dramatically, she burst out laughing. "Oh, I know how she can be. And believe me, I'm scared of what will happen if she doesn't win the prize." He pulled in a breath and looked down at his cup. "Anyway, enough talk of this contest."

Kara knew she couldn't keep him to herself all day, and with a bit of a sigh, she led him over to where her friends were gathered near the line for the snowman-building contest—a tradition in their group since they were kids. Luke and Grace always gave it their all, but she knew that Jane, Henry, and little Sophie were determined to win this year.

"I see Anna has persuaded you to enter this year," she said to her cousin Mark.

"Hey, I wasn't about to let my brother beat me," Mark said, giving his brother, Brett, a long look.

Brett smiled knowingly and put his arm around Ivy's shoulder, pulling her close. "With this one on my team, I don't see any way we can lose." He looked down fondly at Ivy's face and gave her a single kiss.

Kara felt Nate looking at her and realized with a jolt that

he was waiting to be introduced. "Everyone, this is Maggie Griffin's nephew, Nate. Some of you probably met him at Mark's house."

The Madison sisters looked him up and down with unabashed interest before shifting their wide-eyed gazes to Kara. Kara felt her cheeks flush from the weight of their scrutiny, and she swallowed hard, wondering what they thought, what Nate thought, and what was really going on between them.

"Are you two entering the snowman-building contest?" Sophie asked, coming forward. Her knitted hat was lopsided, covering one of her eyes, and Kara laughed as she bent down to straighten it on the little girl's head.

Nate shrugged, checked with her. "I'm game if you are. What do you say?"

"Whoopee!" Sophie cried before Kara had a chance to reply. "Now Kara doesn't have to enter alone again like last year." Her look of joy was promptly replaced with bewilderment as she remembered Molly. "But who will you enter with?"

"Oh, I can't enter. I have to help my mom with something at the dance studio for a little bit. *Nutcracker* emergency," Molly groaned by explanation, quickly taking over while Kara all but melted with embarrassment. She stole a glance at Nate, but other than the mirth in his eyes, he showed no reaction to the six-year-old's summary of Kara's lackluster dating life.

"Just so you know," she whispered, "I might have entered alone last year, but I did come in third place."

"Oh, I have no doubt in your abilities," Nate replied evenly as he set his hand on the small of her back and led her onto the patch of snow reserved for the contest.

"Do we have a particular theme in mind?" Kara asked,

eyeing the timer. She knew from past experience they had half an hour, and noticing that other teams had already worked out their strategy and were beginning construction, she was eager to get started.

"Now you sound like my aunt." Nate snorted. He bent down and began packing the snow into a ball. "Let's figure it out as we go along."

Kara followed his lead, but she watched him quizzically. "Somehow I never took you for the laid-back type."

"You can't plan creativity. Takes all the fun out of things."

Kara patted the large ball they had quickly formed into place. "Fair enough." She waited until they were finished with the middle layer to broach the topic again. "You like working with your hands; I can tell."

"It's therapeutic," Nate agreed. "You should know."

"Oh, I do," Kara remarked. "I'm lucky to love what I do."

A line formed between Nate's brow, but he just lifted the snowball into place and motioned her closer. "Come on, last one. Let's show them all what we can do."

"Oh." Kara looked over at Jane, Henry, and Sophie, who were hard at work on a rather sad-looking snowman, given that Sophie was doing most of the work, laughing in delight through most of it. "We don't really need to win; it's just for fun."

Nate stopped rolling. "That's no fun at all. What's the point?"

"The experience," Kara said, feeling uneasy. "It's something to do. Something...festive."

"So is sitting around drinking eggnog. Why bother entering the contest if you aren't going to give it your all?"

Kara held back as Nate set the snowman's head on top of the two larger balls and began carving what he said would be a top hat made of snow. It was an original idea, and one

Kara was impressed by as she watched him work, but she couldn't stop glancing at Jane and her daughter, thinking of how much it would mean for Sophie to take home that blue ribbon and how terrible she would feel to rob a child of that experience.

"I just think... it might mean more to other people..." She gave a pointed glance in Sophie's direction, but Nate just shifted his gaze, looked at her, and shrugged.

"She has two adults helping. No doubt they're in it to win it. What's wrong with a little healthy competition?"

"But it's a child," Kara replied, feeling her temper rise.

"But then why bother entering?" Nate retorted. Though his tone was good-natured and his grin was friendly, there was something in his eyes that told her he wasn't going to come around to her view on this.

Kara shifted on her feet, uncomfortable with the shift in their exchange. She'd thought it would be fun, maybe even a little romantic to build a snowman together, laugh at their efforts. But Nate was a fighter. He put his all into everything. Even a silly contest.

Her gut churned when she thought of the Holiday House contest. Entrants made a big effort, but if Nate was this determined, there really might not be a chance for her at all.

"Look," Nate said, softening his tone. "I don't need to do the top hat. It was just an idea, and I thought it might give us an edge. But you make a point." He glanced around at the other entrants. "Let's just shoot for second place."

Kara nodded, but her heart felt heavy as they finished the contest. Even though they toned down their efforts, there was no denying they'd made the best snowman of the group, even though Jane and Henry had stepped in and helped Sophie out quite a bit. Ivy and Brett's was given a hat made from flowers and a beautiful scarf from pine garland, while

Grace—usually a competitor—was too busy laughing with Luke to try so hard this year.

And Anna and Mark's...well, they should probably stick with cooking.

"What the heck happened?" Brett laughed, coming over to pick up the broken branch that was supposed to be their snowman's arm.

Mark raised an eyebrow at his brother, unimpressed. "Snow was never my medium."

"We make a pretty good team," Nate whispered in Kara's ear as he came to stand close to her.

Team. That they did, Kara thought, looking at their perfectly symmetrical snowman, the classic, jolly expression it wore. Nate was a good person to have on your team, but when it came to being a competitor, she wasn't so sure.

Sophie's royal princess snowgirl (a yearly tradition that she never seemed to tire of) was awarded first place, and sure enough, Kara and Nate's was given a second-place finish.

"What do you say we have some mulled wine to celebrate?" Nate asked, grinning down at her as the group dispersed.

Kara shoved her hands in her pockets and watched her feet sink deeper into the snow with each step. A part of her wanted to say yes, of course, that she couldn't think of a more perfect way to spend the rest of the day. She hesitated, thinking of the kiss, of how his mouth had felt on hers, and a tingle ripped down her spine at the thought of his arms around her again. Their time together was fleeting; she should be making the most of it. Or maybe she should be making the most of her opportunity to secure a better future for herself and her bakery. After all, in a week Nate would be gone, but life would continue on.

She looked up at his eyes, feeling torn. Kathleen Madison

might win the contest every year, but from what she'd seen and heard today, Nate wasn't going to make it easy for her. Or for Kara.

"I should probably get back to the bakery," Kara said wearily, pulling in a long breath. There, it was out. She'd made her choice.

"But I thought you were closed for the day?"

Kara chewed on her lip, watching her feet leave imprints in the snow, a trail right beside Nate's own footprints. Still, she stayed firm, thinking of January, of the unknown, of how much she wanted to do right by her father and all he'd ever done for her. She owed him that much, no matter how easy it would have been to procrastinate, to spend the day with Nate... "I am, but I still have a lot of custom orders to take care of. Christmas week and all, and tomorrow night's *The Nutcracker*."

"Oh, yes. *The Nutcracker*. I'll see you there, then? If not before?" She knew he was referring to the cookies for high tea, but the quirk of his mouth suggested something more.

Kara nodded mutely, taking another step away from him. She needed air. She needed to clear her head. She needed to stop looking into those warm, deep eyes long enough to remember what was at stake and what she stood to lose. Her heart. And so much more.

CHAPTER
17

Nate heard the shuffle of his aunt's footsteps outside his door, only this time he didn't need to hurry up and put on a robe. He'd been up for over an hour, since before the light had peeked over the Green Mountains, when his aunt was no doubt busy warming her peppermint scones and grinding coffee. He'd finally charged his phone, only to listen to it ping from daybreak on. Work emails had begun to pile up, and if he didn't start clearing out his inbox, he'd be in for a mess next week.

Next week. Briar Creek felt like a different world than the life he lived in Boston. A more idyllic, peaceful, even happier life.

He brushed that thought away as he clicked on the next email, skimming it while mentally composing his reply. No doubt he'd be saying the same thing if he'd joined his parents on their cruise. He'd taken a break from his responsibilities. It couldn't last forever.

Even if a little part of him sort of wished it could.

This time his aunt knocked before trying the knob. "Are you decent?" she called out.

"And if I wasn't?" He couldn't hide the amusement in his expression when his aunt's head poked around the frame and gave him a mock menacing stare.

"Oh, what am I going to do without you? You've certainly brightened my Christmas, Nate. I hope you're having a bit of fun on your stay." She closed the door behind herself and settled in at the empty armchair opposite his own.

Nate closed his laptop and set it on the end table. "I have had fun. I can see why you love this town so much."

Maggie's face lit up. "Can you? Oh, Nate, I was hoping you would feel this way!"

Taken aback by the joy in her reaction, Nate frowned. "I think I'll plan another visit for the summer," he said, hoping that would curb the guilt he felt for not having visited sooner. "And who knows, maybe next Christmas we'll all come. Me and my parents. I think they'd like that a lot," he added pensively. His dad always got a little quiet around Christmas, even now, and he struggled with his emotions when Nate gave them gifts—always one special thing, never so much that it looked like charity. But his mother...Nate knew that his mother had always loved Christmas. Always tried to make it special, even when it wasn't. It meant so much to her...

He thought of Kara, of how her eyes danced and then welled when she spoke of Christmases past. Bittersweet, he thought, wondering if he'd ever be able to get to the same place with the holiday.

"Next summer. I see." His aunt nodded slowly and stared at her hands in her lap. "Here I thought..."

Nate leaned forward. "Thought what?"

His aunt brushed a hand through the air, but she wouldn't meet his eye. "It's nothing. You'll visit in the summer. I'd like that."

Something was wrong, and Nate wasn't going to back down until she told him what. "Aunt Maggie. I can tell that something's wrong. What is it?"

"It's silly," she said, twisting the wedding ring she still wore.

"Try me," he said gently.

"Yesterday at the festival, you were asking about the contest and why it meant so much. You know how much this inn means to me."

"It's your legacy," he commented.

Her green eyes were clear when they lifted to his. "Exactly. And who do I have to leave it to?"

Nate squared his jaw, considering her words and hating the truth he heard in them. She'd never had children. He was her only nephew.

"Wait. Were you—"

"I just thought, if you helped with the contest, if you really got into the spirit of things, and if you saw what a wonderful place Briar Creek was, that you might…" She gave a watery smile. "I can't run this place forever. And I can't bear to give it up."

"Oh, Aunt Maggie." Nate sighed.

"I told you I was being silly." She leaned over and patted him on the cheek. "You sure did give an old lady a Christmas to remember. And we did have fun with the contest, didn't we?"

He nodded once. "We did."

"And who knows, we might win. You know I'll split the earnings."

Nate rolled his eyes. "You certainly will not. It was fun, you're right. And Briar Creek is a charming town. It's just—"

"Your life is in Boston," she finished for him. "I know." She huffed out a breath and folded her hands in her lap. "I've asked enough of you." She glanced at her watch, her brows shooting up. "My, I should hurry. I just came in to give you a wake-up call and look at me, getting all emotional at this time of day!"

She stood to leave, all at once the cheery innkeeper, boasting about her Christmas blend of coffee topped with cinnamon whipped cream and those peppermint scones he really must try. Nate watched her go with the promise of being down in a few minutes, but it took him several more than that to decide how to process what he'd just learned.

He would have loved to have given her the one thing she wanted more than anything this Christmas, but for now, he'd do what he could.

Kara knocked on Kathleen Madison's door at exactly five o'clock, and she couldn't resist a peek through the windows that framed it as she waited for this evening's hostess to let her in from the cold. As she'd been told, the walls of the Victorian were now a beautiful shade of ivory, and the banister was wrapped in a frosted white noble fir garland, frocked with white. Fairy lights were wrapped around it, as well as the garland that framed every archway.

She'd thought the exterior to be impressive enough, with the twinkling lights and pristine wreaths that hung from every window by a thick ivory velvet ribbon, but as the door swung open and her friends' mother greeted her with a warm smile, Kara felt her breath fade away.

"Kathleen," she muttered, looking this way and that. "This is . . . stunning."

She couldn't decide where to look first. The entire house seemed to glow.

"Oh, just a little makeover. Keeps me busy." Kathleen helped Kara to shrug her coat from her shoulders. "I heard you were entering the Holiday House contest yourself."

Kara grimaced, her entry suddenly feeling amateur compared to this professional effort. "Oh, I'm just making a gingerbread house."

"Just a gingerbread house?" Kathleen shook her head. "Sounds impressive to me, dear. Most people couldn't bake something that stands straight enough to hold a roof, much less something on a scale large enough to enter a contest."

Kara had to agree. Her gingerbread houses had been a success, and her entry was by far her finest effort yet. "I'm proud of it."

"As you should be. I can't wait to see what you've created."

Kara clutched her paper bags of cookie boxes, feeling excited again about her entry, until she turned the corner into the dining room, where her eyes all but dismissed the cookie table set up for tonight's cookie swap and went straight to the hearth, the mirror, the ivory satin curtains that extended from ceiling to floor. And . . . was that a new couch in the living room?

Sensing her thought, Kathleen said, "Reupholstered. It needed freshening up."

Kara struggled to find words as she dipped her hand into her paper shopping bag to pull out her first cookie box. As soon as she popped the lid to plate them, she saw they were her snowflake cookies, and all at once her thoughts went from worries about the Holiday House contest to worries about Nate. The one who had gotten her into this mess in the first place.

He hadn't been at the inn when she'd stopped by today—his aunt had said he'd gone out on an errand. Kara had been a bit relieved, but a bit disappointed, too. Without the chance to see him today, that left only tomorrow, and the day after was already Christmas Eve.

"Are those the cookies you make for tea at the inn?" Grace said, coming to admire them.

"The very same," Kara said. "How did you know?"

"I had tea there today with my mother and Anna. Anna couldn't stop praising them. I think she's hoping for the recipe...if you're wondering what to get her for Christmas." Grace winked.

At the mention of gifts, Kara felt her stomach knot. "Do you know if Molly has gotten my mother anything yet?"

Grace blanched. "I was hoping the three of you would have figured that out. I told Luke he had to ask her directly this year, but do you know what she told him she wanted? Other than a grandchild, of course." She rolled her eyes.

"What?" Kara asked so eagerly that several women turned to stare.

Grace gave her a pointed look. "Dish towels."

Kara felt her expression fall along with her hope. "Please tell me you're joking."

"Nope. Burnt-orange dish towels to match the flecks in her granite counters. Do you know how hard it is to find that color at Christmastime? Why couldn't she have told us back in the fall, before everything turned red and green?"

"And white." Kara looked around the beautiful room once more. "I think your mother's going to win again this year." Though she smiled, her heart felt more than a little heavy.

Grace looked nonplussed. "Well, she's outdone herself. Again." She reached over to take a cookie, but Anna appeared, slapping it away.

"You can't eat them just yet. They're for the swap."

"Well, I didn't know there wouldn't be any food at this party. It's a cookie party!"

Kara laughed. "I see the plates of food on the coffee

table," she said, motioning to the equally stunning adjacent living room. "And there's even some cookies."

"Oh good." Grace grinned and went off to join Molly and Jane, who were already deep in conversation with Ivy. No doubt discussing wedding plans, Kara thought a little sadly.

"So," Anna said with interest. "Business seems to be going well!"

Despite the warmth in her friend's smile, Kara felt herself wilt with unease. "It is," she said a little hesitantly. Anna and Mark had a well-oiled machine thanks to the hard work and hours they put in. Had they ever struggled as she did, or slipped up and forgot to offer things like…beverages to customers? Probably not.

"Give it time," Anna encouraged. "When I first opened the café, I didn't sleep for an entire year. But when something means a lot to you, you find a way to make it work." Her smile turned a little shy.

"Like you and Mark?" Kara asked.

"That's one example," Anna said, laughing. "Now tell me, what's up with you and Mrs. Griffin's nephew?"

Kara stiffened. "Nate? Oh, nothing. We're just…friends."

Anna shrugged and helped Kara to plate another box of cookies. "Well, he asked about you today when I stopped by for high tea."

"He did?" Despite her reservations, Kara felt her pulse begin to race.

Anna's expression was deadpan, but her blue eyes twinkled. "I thought you two were just friends?"

Kara swatted at her friend. "It doesn't matter what we are." She sighed. Or what they might have been. "He lives in Boston."

"So?" Anna took the empty bags from her hands. "As I said, if something means a lot, you find a way to make it work."

Truer words had never been spoken, Kara knew, but that was easy for Anna to say. She and Mark had a history, a shared goal of opening a restaurant, and they both lived in Briar Creek. Kara didn't have half those things on her side. Besides, Nate had proven that when he wanted something, he didn't back down—and his job, and the life he'd earned for himself back in Boston, clearly meant a lot to him. How could she compete with that?

Helping herself to a glass of sparkling wine, Kara followed Anna into the living room, where she greeted Ivy and Jane. As expected, Ivy and Molly were deeply engrossed in a conversation about their wedding plans, and Molly was offering up some back issues of her magazine for new ideas. Kara tried to smile politely, but as the conversation went on, and then Anna joined in, followed by Jane and Grace, who spoke from experience, she felt her heart begin to sink.

She'd always prided herself on standing on her own, not needing someone, just hoping to find someone, but the longer this conversation went on, just like the more time that passed, she felt more and more left out. Wouldn't it be fun to join in, talk about centerpieces and party favors and the perfect song for the first dance?

"I actually have something to tell you girls," Anna said, smiling mysteriously as she glanced at her sisters, Grace and Jane.

"Sounds like big news!" Ivy leaned in eagerly.

"It is. Mark and I finally set a date." Anna's smile was so broad, Kara couldn't help but put aside her own self-pity and get swept up in the excitement.

"That's wonderful!" she cried. "When?"

"New Year's Eve," Anna said.

"Oh, good choice. And you'll have a whole year to plan," Ivy said knowingly.

"No, not next year, this year," Anna corrected.

Kara glanced at Ivy, whose look of bewilderment matched her own. "But...that's only a week and a half away!"

"I know," Anna said happily.

"But...how long have you been planning this?" Ivy pressed. Ivy had been planning her wedding since the fall, and Kara knew she still had several details to iron out.

"Since yesterday," Anna said, laughing. "We've put it off long enough, and it's the holidays. Seemed like the perfect time to do it."

"Are you going on a honeymoon?" Kara's voice felt strained. When she'd finally worked up the courage to leave her job at the restaurant, she'd worried what impact it would have on her cousin and friend. Mark and Anna put endless hours into Rosemary and Thyme—they were hardly in a position to take a step away, especially without a full staff.

Kara felt the familiar weight of guilt take hold again, and she pressed a hand to her stomach to settle herself. Now, with the bakery, she understood more than ever just what kind of pressure Anna must be under with the restaurant, especially given its success.

She should have waited. Given her notice after they'd gotten married. Made sure they had a proper honeymoon. But then...they still hadn't set a date. And her dreams had been on hold for so long.

"We're going on a short honeymoon, yes," Anna said, to Kara's relief. "We're going up to Cedar Valley Resort for a few days. It was where we reunited and...it holds special meaning."

"But a wedding!" Ivy said in alarm.

"It can be done on short notice. Look at Molly."

At this, all eyes turned to Molly, who seemed uncomfortable at the sudden shift in attention. "Yes, but I'm sort of an expert at wedding planning. I already had my checklist ready to go."

"Mark and I don't want something elaborate," Anna said, sighing. "We're getting married here, in this house. I can't think of a venue that could top this," she said, opening her arms to the glittering room.

No, Kara thought, she couldn't either. It was like a page out of a magazine. A very expensive, very professional magazine.

"Will you all be able to make it?" Anna asked worriedly.

"Of course," Kara reassured her. "Where else would we be?"

"I'll come back for the weekend," Molly assured her.

"Then a toast," Grace said, raising her glass. "To the soon-to-be Mrs. Mark Hastings!"

Kara raised her glass, overwhelmed at the thought of Anna joining her extended family, but a little part of her began to sink when she realized that yet again, she'd be attending a wedding on her own.

The past few days with Nate had been enough to make her see what she'd been missing. And what would be gone again, and all too soon.

CHAPTER
18

For the third time since she'd arrived at Sugar and Spice that morning, Kara was grateful that the shop was closed on Mondays. Already her mother had called four times, in a tizzy about something with *The Nutcracker*, and Kara knew that Luke was already over at the auditorium, helping with the scenery.

Molly was scheduled to go over two hours before curtain call, to help with hair and makeup, and technically all Kara needed to worry about were the cookies and the food and toy drive, but twice she'd been asked to pick up last-minute necessities, like some silk ribbon for Clara's sash, and some bobby pins, just in case...

In between the calls and the baking, she put the finishing details on her Holiday House entry, more driven than ever after seeing Kathleen's effort the night before. Hurrying to finish some piping around the chimney, her hand slipped, and some royal icing dribbled onto the roof. Kara cursed under her breath and grabbed a paper towel to wipe it away before it set.

"Calm down," Molly ordered through a mouthful of

cookie. "You'll do a better job if you aren't rushing. I still wish you'd stop standing in front of the thing and let me see it already. Are you really going to make me wait? What's the mystery?"

Kara managed to sop up the mess before disaster occurred, then took a step back. She brushed the hair from her forehead with the back of her hand and sighed. She felt hot and agitated and entirely too overwhelmed. "I don't know why I'm even bothering with this. Everyone knows Kathleen Madison is going to win. She always wins."

"So? Maybe this isn't her year." Molly plucked another coconut macaroon from the tray and broke it in half before cramming one piece into her mouth.

Kara eyed her steadily over her shoulder while shielding the bulk of the gingerbread house with her body. She wondered if it was worth her time to have a conversation about those being for tonight's *Nutcracker* bake sale and decided it wasn't. She could always make more, and who knew how many would sell anyway.

"You saw Kathleen's house last night," Kara said, giving her sister a pointed look.

Molly polished off the second half of the cookie and winced. "Yeah. I did."

Kara shut her eyes, but only for a moment. She still had to decorate the last batch of snowflake cookies for the inn and then get back in time to shower and prepare for tonight. She eyed the gingerbread house, feeling almost as sad for it as she did for herself. It was everything she'd hoped it would be, exactly as she'd pictured it, but it wouldn't be enough. How could it? She couldn't make it glow or sparkle. It was edible. An edible house. What made her ever think she could compete with the real thing?

Nate, she thought, smiling a little sadly to herself. Nate

had challenged her, but he'd always made her almost believe she could win.

Huffing out a breath, she picked up her piping bag and began working on the cookies for tea. She hadn't seen Nate since the Winter Festival, and she didn't really know what she'd say when she saw him again. He'd been asking about her, and that excited her. More than it probably should. Already that kiss was fading away. That was probably for the best, too.

When the cookies were ready, Molly arranged them in a box while Kara grabbed her hat and coat from the hook on the back of her office door.

"Don't you need to get over to the dance studio to help Mom soon?" she asked.

"I told her you needed me," Molly said, her expression turning pleading. "I'll go over after lunch, but...I just want to put it off as long as possible."

Kara laughed under her breath. Molly should be helping their mother; they both knew that. But they also knew just how tense things were at the studio right now. She didn't blame her sister for hiding out for a bit.

"I'll be back in a few minutes," she said, hoping that wouldn't exactly be the case. "And *no* peeking at the gingerbread house! Feel free to help yourself to whatever else you'd like."

Molly lit up as she reached for a piece of candy cane fudge. "Don't mind if I do."

Kara shook her head as she pushed through the kitchen door and into the empty storefront. Molly had never been one to indulge in sweets—she was always too worried about her weight. And with a wedding just around the corner, she'd expected her sister to announce some crazy fad diet instead of a sugar bender.

She smiled to herself. Molly was probably just getting caught up in the magic of the holidays. It was an easy thing to do in Briar Creek.

Nate set down the paintbrush and sighed. He knew his aunt had requested a painting to go along with the theme of her contest entry, but he hoped she would like what he created more than that. It had been too long since he'd last picked up a brush—years, maybe even a decade—but once he'd started, he'd found he couldn't stop. The hours went by and he'd barely even noticed. And now it was almost time for Kara's daily visit, he realized with a jolt.

After tucking the canvas into the bathroom, where he hoped his aunt wouldn't be inclined to go, he closed the door to his suite and jogged down the stairs to the lobby. He paused at the bottom, admiring the way the room looked, so festive and warm and alive and cheerful, the way his aunt's face shone as she talked to the guests, offering up suggestions, pride in her voice, and...passion.

Would she really give this all up? Retire, close it down, or worse—move out and sell to a stranger? She was right; no one could love this place as much as she did. No one could appreciate its history, its value, on an emotional level.

He'd spent so much time assessing businesses for their extrinsic worth, not their intrinsic value, and this old house was overflowing with it...much like Kara's bakery, he thought, as she stepped through the front door.

He raised his hand to meet her, noticing the shy smile she gave him as she stomped the snow from her boots. His gut tightened at the pretty way her lips curved, the way her eyelashes fluttered for a moment before she looked down at the doormat.

He hadn't seen her yesterday, and that had disappointed

him. A lot. And that disappointment had caught him by surprise, made him realize just how hard he was falling for her. Concern over how Kara might feel if he beat her in the contest reared sharp, and he shifted his gaze to his aunt, tightening a fist against his jeans with conflicted loyalty.

"Hello," she said brightly as he came to greet her.

"Hello," he said, letting his gaze rove over her pretty face. Her cheeks were pink, as was the tip of her nose, and her hands were like ice when his thumb grazed her skin as she passed him the box of cookies. "You're freezing."

"People can thaw," she said, cocking an eyebrow at him.

He caught the meaning at once, took it for what it was: the truth. He had thawed in the brief time he'd been in this cozy little town. The walls he'd built without even knowing were starting to come down piece by piece, and for the first time in years, he felt free. Free of the demons of his past. Free to be himself. Free to look forward to the simple pleasures again.

"I missed seeing you yesterday," he admitted.

Her expression was pleased. "I heard you ran into the Madisons," she said.

"Ah, yes," he said, recalling the group of attractive women who had come for holiday tea. "At long last, I can finally say I have met the famous Kathleen Madison."

"And?"

Nate rolled back on his heels, remembering the way his aunt had tensed, her eyes darting this way and that, the way she'd set a hand on his arm, her grip surprisingly tight, and assessed the decorations they'd worked so hard on this past week.

"And she seemed like a very nice woman. She handled my aunt's questioning like a pro," Nate said.

Kara laughed. "Well, she has a lot of experience. What was it that your aunt was fishing for?"

Nate lifted an eyebrow. "Let's just say her questions were all answered at last night's cookie swap. My aunt came home last night talking of nothing but how beautiful Kathleen's house was."

Kara cringed. "It was...exquisite."

"Aw, come on. It's a house. How great could it be?"

"So great that someone who couldn't find time to squeeze in a wedding was suddenly inspired enough to tie the knot next week. On the premises." Kara shrugged. "Granted it's Kathleen's daughter, and a New Year's Eve wedding does sound romantic."

Nate frowned. By New Year's Eve he'll have been back in Boston for a week, and Kara would still be here, in this cute little town, dressed in something sexy that showed off her smooth skin and pretty face, and quite possibly, on the arm of another man. He shook away the thought, not wanting to dwell on it. His life was in Boston, his job, his parents...And those were things he couldn't give up.

"So, are you, uh, taking a date?"

Kara blinked, sputtered on a laugh. "What? No. No." A blush crept up her neck. Aw, damn. She was cute. It was taking everything in him not to kiss right here and now. "Unless..."

He stiffened. "I'll be back in Boston by then, unfortunately."

"Unfortunately?" She eyed him.

Nate ran a hand through his tousled hair, suddenly feeling agitated. "The thought of going back to that office on Monday suddenly leaves me cold."

"I thought you loved your job," Kara remarked.

Nate frowned and held her stare. "I did, too. But being away...It's easy to get lazy," he joked. More like it was easy to forget. His past. His future. His promise to himself.

Kara's eyes drifted to the clock, and her expression tightened. "I should get back to the shop. Molly's helping out today, and I'm afraid if I don't get back soon she'll have eaten all the cookies I've made for tonight's show."

"I plan on bringing the toys over ahead of time. Does five o'clock work?"

"Five sounds perfect. My mom is there all afternoon, but I should be there by then to help."

"I'm looking forward to it," Nate said, grinning.

"Well." She huffed out a breath and turned to go, but Nate's hand was light on her wrist and discreet enough that prying eyes might not notice.

"I'll walk you out," he said. He turned over his shoulder and called to his aunt, "I'll salt the path again, Maggie."

Maggie's eyes lit up as she beamed at her nephew. "Don't forget a hat, now. Or something for your hands. Those mittens I found for you are so warm. I do wish you'd wear them."

Kara giggled into her scarf as she pushed out onto the front stoop. "Mittens?"

Nate nailed her with a look. "At least they're not pink."

Kara laughed. "She adores you."

"And she forgets that I'm not eleven." Nate shook his head, suddenly looking a little sad. "But you're right. She does adore me. Why, I don't know. I hardly deserve it."

"Oh, now here's where I disagree. Not every nephew would spend his Christmas holiday decorating an old inn. It's one of the things I like about you. Even if you have turned out to be stiff competition."

"You're giving me too much credit," he said. "And you don't give yourself enough."

She blushed, and he reached out and stroked her cheek with his thumb. She was an accomplished girl, and not just because of her bakery. He saw the way she treated people, the way they responded to her. She was a catch. And he wasn't ready to let her go just yet.

Nate leaned in, wanting to finish what they'd started the other night. He could anticipate her taste just before his lips grazed hers, but the feel of her mouth on his was even better than he remembered, sending heat coursing through his veins as she opened her mouth wider to his, letting him in.

He pulled back, stopping himself before he got too carried away. It was too easy to get lost in the moment, to forget that they were standing outside the inn, where his aunt could be peeking through the lace curtains, no doubt suppressing a squeal.

"I'll see you in a few hours then," he said.

Kara nodded. "Don't remind me. There is always so much buildup to this day, and then it goes by too quickly. There's still so much to get done."

"Sounds like a wedding day," Nate mused. Then, seeing the question in her eye, he said, "Not that I speak from experience."

"Me neither," Kara said. "But let's just say that I hope when I do get married, my mother is considerably calmer than she is in the final hours before the show."

He grinned as she walked down the path, which he now kept salted every day. "Aw, it can't be that bad," he said.

She turned at the sidewalk and arched an eyebrow. "Can't it? You'll see. Bet you can't wait to come now, huh?"

Bet you I can't, Nate thought, watching her go.

CHAPTER 19

Kara could recall in vivid detail at least fifteen major disasters that had threatened to ruin the local production of *The Nutcracker* over the years—power outages due to inclement weather, fruit punch spilled down the front of a white costume, and of course, sound system issues—but tonight's was perhaps the worst yet.

"What do you mean Mom lost her voice?" she asked Molly, who had officially bitten off all her nails by the time Kara arrived on the scene.

Molly stared at her with big blue eyes, not blinking. "It was a little scratchy last night, but this morning she was out of the house before I even woke up, so I thought nothing of it."

"But she always introduces the show," Kara said.

"Well, that's hardly the problem. She's been running through the dress rehearsal today using big hand movements and trying to pantomime her instructions. She finally resorted to a whiteboard, but she's gotten herself so worked up that no one can even read her writing anymore."

"Oh dear," Kara said, biting her lip. Regardless that the

show always went off without a hitch from the audience's perspective, Kara knew all too well how chaotic things often were backstage. Last year she'd had to talk a twelve-year-old girl through the disaster of breaking a barrette before the girl cried off all her makeup less than forty-five seconds before she was scheduled to pirouette onto the stage. "Well, I guess it's a good thing you're here."

"Me?" cried Molly. "What about you? I've been dealing with this all day."

"I have to oversee the refreshment stand at intermission. And the charity drives," Kara pointed out. She looked at the clock. It was ten past five. Meaning...

Turning, Kara pushed out of the costume room, where Molly had apparently taken shelter for the last twenty-five minutes, and marched out into the lobby of the auditorium, where, among the six-foot-tall nutcracker statues and endless garland and fairy lights, stood Nate, surrounded by piles and piles of toys.

"If you were a little heavier and a little older, I'd say you look like Santa," she said warmly.

Nate shrugged. "I think I've officially bought out Main Street Toys and Trains," he said, laughing. "I hope the little tykes enjoy it."

Kara admired the loot. "How can they not?" She gestured to the beautifully decorated tree that Molly had been in charge of that afternoon. "Why don't we set them around the tree for tonight, and everyone who brings a gift can add to it? Tomorrow I'll be bringing everything over to the Forest Ridge Hope Center."

"I brought some nonperishable items, too," Nate said, gesturing to the half dozen bulging bags at his feet. "Does the back corner work for those?"

"Perfect," Kara breathed. This was exactly what she

needed right now, someone who could make some helpful suggestions and take over one of the tasks on her list. With each passing second, her own anxiety was growing, just as she knew her mother's was. People started to mill around out front a solid half hour before the show, some even earlier, and she knew from past experience that the hour leading up to the doors opening passed by with lightning speed.

"Are you okay? You look a little…frazzled." Nate reached over and tucked a stray hair behind her ear.

"Do I?" Kara frowned, looking down at the new outfit she'd bought for the occasion.

"I stand corrected," Nate said, stepping forward. "You *look* beautiful." He gave an appreciative sweep down her body that made her tingle with pleasure. "You *seem* frazzled."

"Is it the feverish glint in my eyes or the hysteria in my voice?" Kara joked.

"Both," Nate said, grinning.

"If you think I'm frazzled, you should see my mother. And my sister. We're always a little stressed before the show, but by the end, we're always pleased with the outcome."

"Maybe we could have a drink after the show?"

Kara couldn't contain her excitement at the invitation. "I'd like that," she said, stepping back to begin setting up her cookies for the refreshment stand.

The front door burst open, carrying a blast of icy wind with it, and Luke marched through, Grace close at his heels. "I've been told there is an emergency," he said, giving Kara a conspiratorial wink.

"How'd you know if Mom can't even talk?" Kara asked.

Luke waved his phone. "Text. I must have received a hundred of them today. I was ready to throw the damn thing away."

Kara tipped her chin in the direction of the hall leading backstage. "Tell me you brought some extra dry erase markers. Apparently she's already gone through a pack."

"I believe that one of her texts asked me to raid the school supply closet," Luke said wanly, "but yes, I have them."

Kara and Grace exchanged a knowing glance as Luke left them in the lobby to deliver the goods. "Is Jane backstage?"

Kara nodded at Grace. "I only saw her briefly. She's helping with costumes. A few girls already ripped their tights—"

Grace gasped. This had been an issue in the past, one that kept Rosemary awake at night in the weeks leading up to the show, usually resulting in dozens of extra pairs on hand, even if they weren't needed.

"Luckily, Jane managed to handle the situation before my mother found out. At least the sound system's working this year." Kara knocked on the refreshment table and heard Nate snort in laughter from under the tree.

Grace slid her gaze to the man crouched under the large fir with interest, and with a teasing smile, gave Kara a less-than-subtle wink before hurrying off to find Luke.

Kara smoothed her red skirt over her hips and began quickly setting up her stand. She didn't look up again until the doors opened and Mrs. Griffin entered, her winter-white scarf wrapped around her neck, with Ivy and Brett close behind.

"Look at all those toys!" Ivy remarked, standing before the tree in awe.

"We can thank Nate for his generosity," Kara chimed in, but when she saw Nate's bashful grin, she wondered if he'd have preferred not to have the attention on him.

"That's my nephew for you!" Mrs. Griffin remarked, and the look that passed between Nate and Kara eased whatever tension might have arisen.

"This is wonderful," Brett said, coming to stand next to Ivy. "I've done my best at the hospital, but this surpasses my own efforts."

"It was nothing," Nate said, shrugging.

Anna and Mark arrived next, looking more giddy than Kara could ever recall, no doubt already looking forward to their big day next week.

"You've really put us on the spot for a bachelor party," Brett told his brother, giving their cousin Luke a look of chagrin. "But we're pulling something together. This Saturday night, if that works."

"It works," Anna spoke for him, adding, "You're taking the night off. Boss's orders."

"Well, then consider Sunday morning ours for the shower," Grace said. "Kara, will you bring some cookies for the dessert?"

Kara brightened at the request. "My pleasure!"

"Then it's settled," Grace said. She turned, eyeing the thickening crowd, some of whom were already gathering around the refreshment stand. "And speaking of cookies, it looks like you're in for a busy night."

Kara gave her friend a nervous smile. "I suppose I am."

Soon the lobby was filled with all the familiar faces she'd known and loved for as long as she could remember. More than half her cookies were sold before the patrons had even taken their seats for the first act, but somewhere in the whirlwind of it all, she managed to catch Nate's eye, watching her from the side.

She would have loved to have gone into the audience with him, taken a seat by his side, and enjoyed the show, but her attention was needed behind the scenes. It was a family affair, after all. And besides, she had the entire evening ahead to look forward to.

And oh, was she looking forward to it.

• • •

Kara chattered excitedly the entire walk back to her apartment, and even though ballet was hardly his thing, Nate found himself getting caught up in her energy. The show had come and gone in a blur, and he'd been paying more attention to the audience than the dancers onstage. There was an energy in the room, a feeling of togetherness in the packed house that made him feel something close to depressed. More than once he'd thought of his mother, how much she would have enjoyed seeing the performance, how delighted she would have been when the music swelled, how she would have talked for hours about the sparkling costumes, the scenery, the talent.

She would have loved everything about Christmas in Briar Creek. Almost more than he was himself.

"I don't know about you, but I could use a drink," Kara said, opening the fridge. For a moment, he thought she was going to reach for the eggnog, but instead, she plucked a bottle of white wine from the inside door and handed it to him.

"I'll hang up our coats, if you'll do the honors," she said, giving him the corkscrew.

Nate found two glasses and allowed them each a generous pour. From the living room, he could hear Kara humming under her breath, a song he recognized from tonight's show.

She was just shutting the closet door when he joined her, two glasses in hand, and he allowed himself a sweep of her curves, his gut stirring at the way her hips flared under the soft red fabric of her skirt.

"Thanks," she said, taking the wine from him.

"I think a toast is in order," Nate said, raising his glass. "To . . . a successful night."

Kara clinked her glass with his and took a long sip,

raising her eyebrow over the rim. "Let's see if tomorrow night is as successful."

When he looked at her blankly, she said, "The Holiday House judging is tomorrow night! You didn't forget, did you?"

Nate managed a tight smile. "Of course not. How could I?" He laughed uneasily as they settled onto the couch. "The days are just slipping away from me."

"Time flies when you're having fun," Kara said. She looked away, her smile turning a little sad.

"Well, I don't know about you, but I'll be happy when this contest is behind us," Nate remarked. With any luck, Kathleen Madison would just win the whole thing. Chances were high that would happen, and it would save him having to feel like he'd somehow let Kara or his aunt down.

"Oh my God, I can't believe I forgot to tell you!" Kara said, setting her drink excitedly on the table.

"What?" Nate searched her face, looking for a clue.

"With Anna's wedding being next week, Kathleen decided to devote all her attention to getting ready for the wedding, and she's taken herself out of the contest. Grace told me tonight at the intermission. I was so busy with the refreshment stand that I almost didn't even have time to properly digest it." She grabbed his wrists with two hands and squeezed. "Do you know what this means?"

Nate swallowed hard. He knew what it meant, all right. It meant their chances of winning had increased. But there could only be one winner. And both were so deserving. For so many reasons.

"Are you going to be disappointed if you don't win?" he asked, bracing himself.

"More than I thought I would be," Kara admitted on a sigh, and Nate brought the glass to his lips once more. "I can't help thinking of how much the money would help the bakery. I really do need some help. I'm on to something, but I'm still in that gray area…"

Nate nodded. Most of his clients were in the gray area, that fine line between sinking and succeeding. "Could you apply for a loan?" he suggested, thinking that might cover the cost of some part-time help.

"I'm not sure I'd qualify," Kara said. "I don't have much income."

Nate briefly closed his eyes. She had a point there.

"I have to admit, I was really worried about tonight," Kara said.

"Worried that someone would fall off the stage?" Nate asked, and Kara burst out laughing.

"Now, that's never happened. Yet." She played with her bracelet. "No, I was worried about the cookies, I guess. Worried that no one would buy them. That my mom would regret asking me to sell them."

"But she's your mother," Nate said, confused.

"Yes, but she has high standards, and even though I'm an adult, I still seek her approval. I can't help it."

"I understand," Nate said, pulling in a breath. He took a sip of his drink, feeling it chase the heat down his throat. "You want to please her. You don't want to feel like you've let her down."

"Exactly," she said.

"Well, you haven't. From the look on her face just before we left, I'd say she was nothing short of impressed." He looked down into his glass. "I'm afraid I'm the one who's let my parents down recently."

"You? How?"

"I ruined their Christmas," Nate said.

"What?" Kara swatted his arm. "Please. You sent them on a Mediterranean cruise!"

"Exactly. I sent them away. At Christmastime. I didn't do it for them. I did it for me." The bitter taste of guilt filled his mouth. "My mother loves nothing more than taking evening walks in the snow, just to look at the lights. Or making gingerbread, just so the apartment is full of the smells of the holiday. I used to think it was sad, too simple. But now I see that it was enough."

"It sounds lovely," Kara said, "but I'm sure the Mediterranean is, too."

Despite the heaviness in his chest, Nate managed to smile. "Last year I claimed I had scheduled a big meeting for the day after Christmas. I managed to fly out early, claiming precautionary action due to weather conditions."

"So dodging Christmas is sort of your holiday tradition," Kara surmised.

"It used to be," Nate said. "Now...I don't think Christmas will ever be the same again."

"You know you're welcome to come with me tomorrow, to drop off the toys," Kara said. "Given how generous you've been, I thought you might like to see it through."

Nate shifted against the cushion, hating the part of himself that wanted to say no, that he didn't need to stare into the eyes of a kid who only knew Christmas like he once had, who relied on the kindness of others to make it something better. But he knew Kara had a point, too. Besides, she probably just needed his help for the heavy lifting.

"I'll think about it," he said. "My aunt might have other plans for me," he added, hoping the joke would lighten the mood.

If Kara was offended, she didn't show it. "Fair enough," she said. "I'm leaving right after I deliver the cookies for tea. Sad to think it's my last cookie drop-off of the year."

Nate finished his wine and set the glass down. "I've

gotten used to those visits," he said as he leaned closer to brush a strand of hair from her cheek. Desire burned within him as he felt the heat of her skin against his fingertips. He *had* gotten used to those visits. And he wasn't ready yet to think of how he would feel when they were gone.

Kara hissed in a small breath as he reached out a hand and traced it down the back of her ear and down the length of her smooth neck. His other hand grazed her fingers as he slowly took her wineglass from her hand and set it down on the table. Kara held her breath, knowing he was going to kiss her again, feeling how much she wanted it as her stomach tightened. Anticipation bubbled within her as his face neared hers, his lips slightly parted until their mouths were joined. His kiss was light, but far from tentative, and she responded eagerly, letting herself enjoy the comfort of his touch, the thrill it sent within her as he wrapped an arm around her waist and pulled her close. The kiss was familiar, as if no time had passed since the last, and he pressed her to his chest now, wasting no time in finishing where they'd left off. She could feel the pounding of his heart against her breast as their mouths explored each other, barely stopping for breath.

Heat radiated somewhere deep inside her belly as their kiss intensified, breaking only long enough for her to feel his warm breath on her face as his mouth moved to her neck and that little spot behind her ear that always made her shiver. His arms loosened their hold on her waist, and his hand came to slide up her stomach and over her breast, and she craned her neck as his mouth continued its trail, lower, the touch so light but effective, she could only close her eyes and sigh with pleasure.

Needing that close, breath-stopping connection again, she opened her eyes and traced a finger over the stubble of his jaw, and laced her hands through the hair that curled at the nape of his neck as he brought his mouth to hers once more. He nibbled her bottom lip, teasing her with his light touch, and then opened his mouth to hers once more, deepening their connection.

Kara sighed into his mouth as he moved his hand down around her hips, exploring the lengths of her thighs, moving his hands down and around, until shots of fire sparked in her belly as he brought his hands up the inside of her thighs, pulling away just before she thought the anticipation would break her. With the heat of the flames in the fireplace, her body heated under the soft wool of her cashmere sweater, but she shivered as he slid a hand under the hem of her shirt, his fingers soft on her stomach as he slowly traced his way up until his hands cupped her breasts over the lace of her bra, pulling it back to press his warm palm to her skin.

Breaking their kiss, Kara pulled back and let him push the sweater over her head. He flung it to the side, his eyes fixed on her body as his hands slowly unhooked her bra. She gasped as he leaned forward, bringing her nipple to his mouth, teasing it with his teeth as she ran her fingers through his hair.

Sliding his hands down to her hips, Nate gently pushed her from his lap onto the floor, tilting her back against the rug. Kara reached up, tugging at the sweater Nate wore, eager to feel the heat of his skin against hers, run her fingers over the smooth plane of his chest.

He leaned into her, his kiss hungry and intensifying with each second as they pressed against each other. She felt him hard between her legs, felt the strength of his desire in bursts as his body rubbed against hers, her fingers digging into his back.

They could go to the bedroom, she knew, but somehow

she couldn't be bothered to suggest it. The light from the tree continued to twinkle long after the last of the logs was snuffed out, and Kara leaned into Nate, wrapping her arms tighter against his bare skin under the thick chenille blanket they'd covered themselves with, and waited for morning to come. Even though she never wanted it to come at all.

CHAPTER
20

Kara was already gone by the time Nate awoke, and the little note she'd scribbled and placed on the throw pillow next to his said, "You know where to find me."

He smiled as he pushed himself onto his elbows, orienting himself with his surroundings. There was something nice about the thought of Kara just one floor below him, rolling out dough and baking cookies, serving them with a smile. He pulled his sweater on quickly, eager to get dressed and downstairs, until he saw the flashing light on his phone and the fifteen missed calls. From his aunt.

Nate cursed under his breath and clicked on the first message. It was casual enough, a simple inquiry into what time he might be coming back that night. By the last of the messages, she was threatening to report him missing, unless, as she all but cooed into the phone, he was lucky enough to still be in Kara Hastings's company?

Nate closed his eyes and shook his head. He'd deal with his aunt later. Right now, he needed a good, strong cup of coffee. And a cookie.

Remembering the back stairs to the kitchen that Kara had

used the first time he'd been to her apartment, Nate tidied up the living room, grinning ruefully at the mess they'd made in their passion last night, and hurried down the back stairs. The bakery's kitchen was empty; no doubt Kara was attending to a line of customers, and he couldn't help but let his gaze linger on the gingerbread house for just a moment. It was a work of art—perfectly designed and scaled, with thoughtful and colorful decoration. Kara might have her doubts, but it would be a tough entry to beat.

He wasn't sure whether that was a good thing or not anymore.

Eager to get away from the entry and all thoughts of the contest and its ramifications, Nate pushed on the door to the storefront, hoping to casually join the rest of the morning crowd, when he was instead greeted by alert and all too familiar green eyes.

"Well, there you are!" Maggie exclaimed, pressing her lips together with a look of mock scolding.

"Aunt Maggie." Nate chuckled under his breath and glanced over at Kara, who winced and offered only a helpless shrug before turning to the next customer. "Shouldn't you be at the inn?"

"It's not a jail," she quipped. "I do get out and about, you know. Once the breakfast plates are cleared, I come and go freely until high tea."

Nate scratched his forehead. Oh boy. "I just... I've never seen you here before."

Now that was a stupid thing to say. The look his aunt gave him underscored her surprise, no doubt cementing what she'd secretly known to be true all along or had at least hoped. "I see," she said. He waited for her to blink. She didn't. "I didn't realize you'd become a regular at Sugar and Spice."

"Oh, well, I like the cookies. I try not to eat the ones for the tea, but…" She wasn't buying it, and he decided to stop there.

"You like the cookies or you like the company?" she asked pertly.

Nate looked over at Kara again. Her dark hair was pulled back in a ponytail that bounced at her shoulders, and even from across the room he could catch the tinkle of her laugh, the sound as sweet as bells. "Both, you could say," he told his aunt.

"Oh!" She clasped her hands to her chest, where he noticed a giant Santa face grinning back at him in various textures of yarn. "Oh, I was hoping this would happen! I knew it. I just knew it. I told Kara over and over that I knew just the man for her, but oh, would she listen? No. You young people have to learn everything the hard way."

"Is there any other way?" Nate asked wryly.

"Oh…" Maggie narrowed her eyes in frustration as she reached out and gave him a good shaking by the shoulders. "So…does this mean you'll stay?"

Nate blinked at his aunt. "Stay in Briar Creek?"

"Well, where else?" she trilled. "What reason do you have to leave now?"

He wasn't amused. "My job, for starters," he said.

"*Pfft.* I told you…you have a job here," she said gaily.

Nate studied her in dismay. "Aunt Maggie," he said softly.

He hated the look of hurt that dimmed her eyes. "Don't mind me. I'm just getting carried away. Of course you have to go back to Boston. You have an important job there. You have responsibilities."

"I do." He sighed. Big responsibilities, and not just professionally speaking. He'd worked hard to give himself financial security, to provide a good life for himself, for his parents. He eyed his aunt. "But you're important, too, Aunt Maggie. I'll visit more often, I promise."

"You say that, but..."

"But I mean it," he said firmly, squaring his jaw. "I mean it."

His aunt patted his arm and leaned in closely, her green eyes misty. "I know your parents struggled at times, and I know your father was too proud to admit it. But money isn't everything, my boy. A wise old woman told you that. Remember it." She winked and turned to join the queue that was now wrapped around the store, all leading up to Kara, who was frantically punching numbers into the cash register and bagging cookies as quickly as her arms would let her.

His aunt was right. Money wasn't everything. But that was easy for her to say.

Nate seemed quieter than usual as they drove down the snow-covered road into Forest Ridge. He'd bought so many toys for the Hope Center that they wouldn't all fit in the back of his car, but luckily Ivy offered up the use of her shiny new flower-delivery van. Clearly, business was going well for her, and it inspired Kara with the hope that she could someday say the same for herself.

"Christmas Eve was always my favorite day of the year," Kara mused, and then silently motioned Nate to turn right at the next stop sign. "There was so much anticipation, so much excitement waiting for the next morning."

Catching his stony expression, she stopped herself. "I'm sorry. That was thoughtless of me."

Nate's brow pinched as he gripped the steering wheel, following the course she'd instructed. "It's fine. I don't need protecting."

Kara frowned. "Everything okay?"

Nate slid her a lazy smile and her heart rolled over. "Just thinking about work. Getting back into that mindset. I'm not used to taking much time off. I've got to hit the ground running, as they say."

"When do you go, then?"

"The day after tomorrow," he said.

Kara nodded, hating the disappointment that landed squarely in her chest, even though she'd known all along their time together couldn't last forever. Much as she had started hoping it could.

"Do you think you'll visit again?" she asked.

"I plan on it. My aunt seems a little lonely. It makes me sad."

Kara had never thought of Mrs. Griffin as lonely. She was surrounded by guests, her friends, and she was always in the thick of activities on Main Street. Now she wondered if it was all a brave ruse, meant to disguise a broken heart. "Everyone loved your uncle," Kara offered.

"He was a good man, not that I knew him well. My father didn't keep in touch much. I think it was easier for him that way."

Kara stared out the window at the snow-capped trees, the suggestion of a deer darting in the woods somewhere in the distance. After this bend, they'd be in downtown Forest Ridge, and the Hope Center was just at the edge of town.

"I can't wait to see the look on the kids' faces when they see all this," she said, feeling her heart warm at the image.

"I thought you said there weren't going to be any kids there. That it was an anonymous gift. I thought this was a drop-off." Nate looked at her sharply, and Kara opened her mouth and then closed it again.

"There's a special event for some of the kids today. A party, if you will. They've been looking forward to it. I thought—"

"I wish you'd told me." Nate sighed as he pulled into the parking lot at the back of the brick building.

Kara sat perfectly still in the car even after he'd turned the ignition. He looked so unhappy, she wanted to reach out, hold his hand, but she wasn't sure if he'd push it away. "You don't have to come in," she said softly.

"No," he said. "Some of that stuff is heavy, and this parking lot is a sheet of ice." He muttered to himself as he unlocked his seat belt and flung open the door.

They didn't exchange words as they carried the toys into the back room, where a volunteer would itemize everything and assign it to a child's name on the list. From behind a half-closed door, they could make out sounds of Christmas carols and children laughing.

Kara slanted a glance at Nate, who looked tense, trying to focus on making sure every item was accounted for.

"Well," said Bridget, the volunteer coordinator, as she wrote the last toy down on the list. "Looks like these children have someone watching over them this year."

Kara lifted her eyes to Nate, but he didn't meet her gaze. His jaw was squared as he stared down at his feet, his shoulders hunched.

"Well, we should probably get going," Kara hedged. It wasn't what she had planned, but seeing how uncomfortable Nate was being here, she thought it was best under the circumstances to make a polite excuse for them both.

"Wait." Bridget sized up Nate, her lips pursing as she did some internal calculations. "You're a little thinner than I would have liked. A little handsomer, too," she giggled, and patted her gray hair. "But the man who was scheduled to play Santa called in sick today, and there's about fifty kids out there who are waiting for him to walk through that door."

Kara stared at Nate in horror, her mind racing as she

thought of an excuse, somewhere they should be. She shouldn't have brought him here. He'd been so generous, so selfless, and she'd touched a nerve.

"We wouldn't want to let the kids down at Christmas," he said, managing a tight smile.

"Excellent!" Bridget clasped her hands together and flung open a closet, where she pulled a Santa suit off the rack. Turning to Kara she said, "And do I have a Mrs. Claus?"

Kara blushed and looked at Nate for a reaction, and for a moment she saw a hint of that man she'd come to cherish. His brown eyes glinted with amusement and his mouth quirked as he struggled to hide a smile. "Only if she has to wear a wig," he said.

Nate had to admit Kara looked more than a little cute in that wig, but it was the dress that really made him look twice. Short and red with striped tights that resembled candy canes; he itched to rub his hands up the length of her thighs and have a repeat of last night's bliss.

It had felt so right, under the tree, with the lights twinkling and the fire crackling, warm against their bare skin. He'd been caught up in the moment, in her taste, the softness of her skin, the comfort of her touch. But getting close to Kara like this was no different than getting swept up in the magic of Christmas. He lived hours away. They both knew it. It was a picture-perfect fantasy, just like the idyllic town of Briar Creek itself. But it wasn't reality. Not his, anyway.

Kara hooked a basket of candy canes over her wrist and grinned up at him. "Let's hope half the kids left their glasses at home," she said.

"Ah, but he's Santa's helper then," Bridget stressed, giving them both a push toward the door. "You know, for the ones who express doubt."

Nate winked down at Kara. Oh, there would be doubt all right. He barely filled out the suit, even with a few extra pillows thrown in at the waistline, and the beard was a step above a string of cotton balls. Surely some perceptive youngster would notice his eyebrows were still brown...

But there was no time to worry about any of that now. The doors opened, and, as instructed, Nate waved his bells. A roar of excitement went up from the children, some of whom were jumping up and down, their faces brightened with such pure joy, he felt a ball of shame at his hesitation.

Such a simple thing. Santa. He remembered when he believed, himself. And he remembered when he stopped believing, too. When that wonder he saw shining in the eyes he passed on the way to the chair at the end of the church hall vanished from his world.

He settled himself onto the chair, remembering at the last minute to throw out a few "Ho, ho, hos" as he did so, and glanced up at Kara, whose cheeks were pink from trying not to laugh.

The first few kids were easy. So easy, it made him a little sad. A doll for a little girl with brown hair and big blue eyes and a baseball glove for a boy whose hair looked like it hadn't met a brush in days. Would they receive it? No doubt their classmates were asking for so much more.

Kara handed each child a candy cane, greeting them warmly with a promise of a merry Christmas, and told them to go to the back of the room, where milk and cookies would soon be served. It was only then that Nate realized she'd made the cookies, and looking across the room, there had to be dozens. Shame bit at him when he thought of how much she'd invested in this, how much time, spirit, kindness... while he...he'd just thrown money at it. Bought out a toy store. Tried to drop them off and slip out. But Kara...she was what made the event special.

He swallowed hard when she looked at him, her smile so wide and genuine, he felt a little bit of his chest begin to hurt. No one he knew smiled like that back in Boston, at least not in his circle. They were too busy looking for the next big client, focusing on the bottom line, not the meaning behind it.

"Santa...Santa..."

Nate wasn't even registering Kara's words until he suddenly realized that for this moment, he was Santa. He startled just in time to see a chubby little boy hurtling toward him at full speed, and he grunted loudly when the kid landed firmly on his lap.

Grimacing against the pain rushing down the length of his thighbone, he put on his best Santa smile and said, "Ho, ho, ho."

The boy blinked at him, not buying any of it. "That's not a real beard," he said matter-of-factly.

Nate thought quickly. "I had to shave this morning. Once a year. Mrs. Claus insists. Says it tickles." He gave Kara a wry grin, and she shook her head, a pleased smile teasing her lips.

"But your hair isn't white," the boy continued. "Your eyebrows are brown. You're wearing a wig."

Aw, darn. It was bound to happen. Nate leaned in close to the boy's ear and whispered, "Now between you and me, you're right. I'm not the real Santa. It's Christmas Eve, and Santa is busy loading his sleigh."

The boy pulled back, frowning at him. "Then who are you?"

"I'm Santa's...son," he said, deciding to shortcut what he anticipated as yet another long explanation about how helpers worked.

"His son?" The little boy's mouth formed a big circle. "Then you're the real deal!"

Nate heard Kara's sweet laugh over the raucous kids who were still waiting their turn and gave his leg a little jostle. "That's right. Now tell me, what do you want for Christmas this year?"

At this, the little boy looked sad. "It doesn't matter. You can't get it."

Nate's gut stirred with unease. Who was he to make false promises to these kids? To offer them a dream that might never come true? To disappoint them on Christmas morning, all for a few moments of fun right now?

He gritted his teeth as heat coated his body, the velour suit suddenly suffocating.

He thought of everything he'd bought, what the kid might like. That train set, maybe. Or the bike. "What about a bike?"

The little boy just shook his head and picked at a hole in the knee of his jeans. "I just want a job for my dad," he said. "That's all."

Nate swallowed hard, unable to say anything, to make a promise he couldn't keep, or worse, to let the kid down, to take away his Christmas wish and his belief in Santa in one fell swoop. It was cold. Cruel.

He couldn't do this.

"I can't do this," he said to Kara when the boy had gone off to get his cookies and milk.

Kara's blue eyes turned round. "But you're a natural! The kids love you!"

"But I'm lying to them," he hissed, hoping to not be heard. "These kids are asking for things I can't promise them."

"But they want to see Santa," she pleaded. "They love seeing Santa."

She didn't get it. She didn't understand. How could she? They came from two different worlds.

"You don't understand," he said. "These kids...they think Santa can turn their life around. They think Christmas is some magical day."

"It can be," she said hopefully.

"Not for everyone," Nate said simply. "Not for kids like me. Not for these kids."

Kara's expression crumbled as she looked in dismay over at the kids waiting in line. "But what are we supposed to do?"

Nate shook his head. "Ask Bridget for the list. Make sure each kid gets one toy today—something they really want. We can make today special at least."

Kara nodded. "Okay. I'll be right back."

Nate sat back in the chair, smiling sadly at all the children who stared at him with hope, but all he saw looking back was the little boy who would wake up tomorrow and realize his father still didn't have a job, that life hadn't turned around, and that Christmas was just a holiday for the lucky ones.

CHAPTER 21

It had started to snow while they were at the Hope Center, and Kara tried to attribute Nate's silence to the slick roads on the drive back to Briar Creek. He was perfectly pleasant as he handed the keys back over to Ivy and thanked her for the use of the car. He even managed to laugh with them when Kara told her friend about her itchy gray wig and the kid who had all but broken Nate's femur when he ran for him.

But Kara saw something in Nate, a shift in his demeanor, a faraway look in his eyes that made her heart sink a little. She'd messed up. Stirred things up. She'd pushed him too far.

"I'm sorry if today upset you," she said as they walked down Main Street toward the bakery, where she was eager to relieve Molly of her counter service responsibility. "I saw that you wanted to help, and I thought..."

"It's fine," Nate said, but she could tell by the set of his jaw that it wasn't.

"No, it wasn't. Christmas is hard for you. I should have remembered that."

Nate stopped walking and stared at her properly for the first time since they'd left the children's party. In the cool winter light, his eyes were clear, and she could see the flecks of green around his pupils. "It's my fault. I let myself get carried away with the magic of the holiday, with the energy of this town. It's idyllic here, but it's not reality. Not for everyone."

Kara frowned. She didn't like the way he was talking, generalizing this town, lumping her in with it. Setting himself apart. They'd made a connection, and somehow, so quickly, it felt like it was coming undone.

"Everyone has struggles," she pointed out. "My life has been far from perfect."

"But you haven't experienced what those kids do. I have. It sticks with you. It shapes you. And this…" He swept his arms up and over the street. Kara followed his gaze, allowing herself to see Briar Creek through his eyes, from the garland that wrapped every lamppost to the wreaths that hung on every shop window, to the pristine snow and the shoppers with their bright red bags and the twinkling lights that had already flicked on in anticipation of sunset. It was like something off a postcard.

A far cry from the Christmases those children today knew.

Her brow pinched into a frown when she considered her efforts, what she'd tried to accomplish, and her temper began to stir in her defense. "I think those children had fun today. What would you have preferred, that they didn't have a party? That they didn't get to see Santa and just be like every other kid for a few hours?"

"But they're not like every other kid," Nate insisted. "Tomorrow morning they're going to wake up and realize that. And when they go back to school, and the other boys are bragging about their new bike, they're going to remember again. They're always going to remember."

She nodded. "Just like you're always going to remember."

"There are some things you don't forget."

She blinked, waiting for him to say something more, wondering what there even was to say. "So I guess that means you won't be sticking around Briar Creek much longer?"

"I have to get back to Boston, Kara," he said, his tone firm, determined, and without an ounce of emotion or regret. "That's my life. That's my reality. This…this was just a little glimpse of how life might have been."

She set her hand on his arm, not ready to give up just yet. "How it *could* be. I've seen the change in you since you arrived. In a matter of two short weeks, you've changed."

"No, I got swept up. There's a difference."

"But—" She felt her eyes sting with tears, not because he was going back to Boston, but because he didn't seem to care.

"We come from two different worlds, Kara," he said tightly. "I should have remembered that."

"So you're just going to let the past determine your future?" she cried. Even though it was snowing, even though the ice crunched below her feet, she felt hot and agitated and at a complete loss. "You're not that same person anymore."

"Yes, I am," he said quickly. "And shame on me for forgetting that."

Kara opened her mouth to say something, but it didn't matter. Nate was backing away, muttering an apology, his hands sinking into the pockets of his coat as he turned on his heel and walked away. She watched him walk down Main Street, hunched against the cold, his tread determined. She waited for him to stop, to turn around, to look at her one more time, but his pace never slowed.

To an outsider, he looked just like the man he'd tried to become, in his expensive wool coat and leather shoes, but only she knew the lost soul hiding beneath and the demons that wouldn't go away, and today had gotten the best of him.

She watched, with a heaviness in her heart, until the distance between them grew longer, and soon she couldn't see him at all.

Nate closed his suite door with a click and, for good measure, turned the lock, even though he knew it had little effect if his aunt was set on seeing him.

His duffel bags were in the closet, where he'd set them nearly two weeks ago, and he pulled them out now, quickly pulling his clothes from the hangers and drawers, not bothering to fold anything.

It was time to leave. Time to get back to Boston. Back to his routine. Back to his life.

And soon…soon all this would be a memory of the sweeter side of life, of the way things were for some, but not for him. As much as he wished he could say differently.

He hesitated, thinking of the look in Kara's eyes before he'd turned and left her standing on the sidewalk. His jaw pulsed, and he realized he was clenching his teeth, fighting back the emotions he couldn't indulge in, not when his parents were still relying on him, not when going back to Boston, doing what he'd set out to do, was the only life he knew, the only true path.

His inbox was piled with unopened emails from the office, and even though he knew that no one was looking for him to respond today, he wanted to engross himself, get back in the mindset, remember his responsibilities. Where he came from. Where he'd never be again.

He sat down at his laptop and got to work, happy for the distraction, hoping to numb the heaviness in his chest, the image of Kara's face, still so pretty, despite her bewilderment. He'd seen the confusion in her eyes as she'd searched his face, looking for an explanation she could understand—but how could she understand?

He'd been one of those kids from the center today. And just because he drove an expensive car and sent his parents on vacations didn't mean he still wasn't one of them. He'd changed his circumstances through hard work and perseverance. Loafing around Briar Creek and getting swept up in some silly holiday traditions undermined that struggle and denied the essence of who he really was. She could never understand that, and a part of him envied her for it.

He was so engrossed that he didn't even realize his aunt had let herself into his room by use of her house key.

"My, you are smart," she crooned in his ear, making him jump so hard he almost dropped his laptop. "All those big words and all that advice. It looked like that email went out to at least ten people, too. I bet they were important."

Nate closed the computer and waited for his pulse to resume a normal speed. "Was there something you wanted?" Something worth breaking into his room for, he thought to himself.

"It's Christmas Eve," his aunt announced, standing to clasp her hands together with excitement. "It's my last holiday tea of the year, and I'd like you to come and enjoy it."

Nate closed his eyes. The last thing he wanted was to partake in yet another Christmas tradition. He'd had about enough of that for today. "Aunt Maggie—"

"I have a table waiting for you," she informed him in a tone that told him she wasn't going to back down, at least not easily.

He looked up into her expectant gaze with dread. "Is it really important to you that I come down? I have all these emails to reply to and—"

"And you'll have plenty of time to work once you're back in Boston," she quipped. She rattled her keys, which hung from a giant brass ring, and moved to the door. "Come along. You wouldn't want your Earl Grey getting cold."

So she hadn't been exaggerating when she said it was all ready for him. Nate smothered a groan and pushed himself up from the chair. He followed his aunt silently out of the room and down the stairs. In the dining room, right near the big bay window, a tea tray and pot were waiting at an empty table. The best table, he realized. The one with the unobstructed views of the town square and Main Street.

Shame nipped at him as he took his seat. "Aren't you going to join me?" he asked his aunt as she watched from a few feet away.

"Heavens no! Someone has to serve the guests!" She smiled at him fondly. "This is for you. Relax. Enjoy. And be sure to try those snowflake cookies. They really are delicious."

Nate looked at the tray, where, on the top racks, among the peppermint scones and lemon tarts, was the same kind of snowflake cookie he had seen every day for nearly two weeks and never tasted. His mouth felt dry, and he tightened a fist in his lap, his appetite lost. He thought of Kara making the cookie fresh that morning, while he was still asleep on her floor, her scent still on him, reminders of her... everywhere.

It felt just as wrong to eat it as it did to ignore it.

He poured himself a cup of tea instead, wishing it was coffee and black. Despite his aunt's warnings, it was still too hot to drink. At the surrounding tables, guests laughed and chatted, some catching his eye before turning back to their spouses. Nate thought of Kara and what she'd said about this inn, how she'd always admired it and had been sad to miss the tea this year. Instead she was probably putting the finishing touches on her gingerbread house for the contest judging tonight or frantically dealing with the holiday rush.

He wished it had been her sitting here, enjoying this moment. He wished she was here with him.

Nonsense. He sipped the tea, almost scalding his tongue, and set it back on the saucer. The porcelain rattled, adding to his anxiety, the anger that was building within him at what he'd seen today and how it made him feel.

It would have been nice to have stayed in this town. Hell, it would have been nice to have grown up here.

But this had never been in the cards for him.

He stayed in his seat until the tea service was over and the other guests began reluctantly leaving their chairs. He ate the lemon tart and even that damn peppermint scone, which, admittedly, was sort of good. He ate the salmon and arugula sandwiches and the mandatory cucumber sandwiches, even though he hated cucumber, always had. But he didn't eat the snowflake cookie.

He looked out the window, onto the skating rink where he and Kara had first held hands, and to the square where they'd built a snowman. His gaze traveled over to Main Street, where neat little shops lined the cobblestone sidewalks. If he squinted hard enough, he could almost see the bakery, glowing in the fading sunlight.

And he could almost see Kara looking back at him.

CHAPTER 22

If you keep staring out that window like that, the glass will fog up and you won't be able to see a thing," Molly remarked from the back of the bakery, where she was polishing off the last of today's leftovers. There hadn't been many. Several customers had revealed to Kara that they had opted to buy her cookies instead of making any of their own this year.

Kara was pleased to hear it, but it did remind her that the holidays were nearly over. They'd ended even sooner than she'd expected.

She brushed away a hot tear that slipped from the corner of her eye, hoping her face wasn't as red and blotchy as it felt. She didn't need her mother and sister asking questions right now, not when she didn't want to relive or explain the events of the day. Not when the judges for the Holiday House contest would be here any minute.

The contest. She sighed. Every time she looked at that gingerbread house in the hours since Nate had so abruptly left her on the sidewalk, she thought of him. She couldn't help it. If he hadn't come into her life, she never would have thought to enter it. She probably wouldn't have believed she had the chops. But she did. She knew that now. The house was everything she had envisioned it to be, and all the hours, all the effort, had been worth it.

She supposed she had Nate to thank for that. Even if he had broken her heart.

"Are you going to show us the final product yet?" Molly asked with impatience.

From the back of the storefront, Kara made out the murmur of an exchange between her mother and sister.

"Not until it's been judged," she said. The last thing she needed was to lose her confidence or see her mother's pinch of silent criticism when she pointed out something that was of course too late to change now.

"Well, we won't have to wait long now," Rosemary remarked. "They should be here soon."

Kara still couldn't bring herself to turn from the window, but she wasn't looking for the judges, not like her family thought. Her gaze was on the distance, past the town square and over to the Main Street B&B, which was all lit up now, twinkling in the twilight. It had always been a charming sight, a view she enjoyed, one she could linger on, but now . . . now it felt different, personal. Now it represented the first time she'd felt that spark—the kind that others seemed to find so easily.

She'd hoped when she finally felt it that it would be for the right man. But you couldn't make someone believe in something they didn't. And you couldn't make someone feel something they didn't.

Her throat felt raw and scratchy when she swallowed. Her mother was right: The judges would be here any minute. They were making the rounds, though she didn't yet know in what order. She did know, however, that her mother's house had been judged twenty minutes ago. "A thrilling experience," Rosemary had announced when she flew into the shop shortly thereafter.

Tearing herself from the window, Kara plastered a smile on her face, even though her heart felt like it was breaking. It wasn't a feeling she was experienced with, at least not recently. It was something she hadn't known in a long time, not since she was a child, and her dad... a feeling of loss, not just of a person, but of hope of ever filling that empty space in her chest again. She squeezed her eyes shut for a moment. She couldn't cry now. Later, yes, but now, no.

She still had to think of her business. Of winning this contest. She owed that much to her father. His hard work had financed this place, after all. She couldn't throw it all away.

At the edge of the room, Molly was helping herself to another cookie. Rosemary was all but biting her tongue as she eyed her youngest daughter, but as her cheeks pinked and her hands wrung in her lap, her inner restraint snapped. "Now don't take this the wrong way, Molly, but do you think you should perhaps lay off the cookies for a bit? What about your wedding gown?"

Kara winced, hoping she wouldn't be called on to intervene, and watched the exchange from behind the shelter of the glass display case, under the guise of some last-minute touches on her gingerbread house.

Molly gave her mother a long look, crammed the last of the cookie into her mouth, and took her time chewing. Once she'd finished, she tipped her head and calmly said, "It doesn't matter, because I'm not getting married."

"Not getting married?" Kara almost knocked over the gingerbread house as she sprung up to look at her sister properly, her expression no doubt matching the frozen shock on her mother's face. "But... but..."

Molly just shrugged. "But what? I'm not getting married."

Kara looked down at Molly's hands. Sure enough, the beautiful diamond ring was gone. "Did you and Todd have another fight?" she asked. It was nothing new, and if history proved anything, they'd be back together tomorrow, all forgotten and forgiven.

"Yes. No. It doesn't matter. We're not getting married. The wedding is off."

Their mother turned to Kara with desperation, her eyes silently communicating that Kara should somehow say something, fix this. But how? Molly's announcement had come about as quickly and unexpectedly as her engagement. Whatever was going on with her sister, she couldn't figure it out.

"Are you...okay?" she asked worriedly, recalling how badly Molly had taken the last breakup with Todd. Maybe they could cry together tonight, she thought, but it was little consolation.

"Never better." Molly grinned, daintily wiping the corners of her mouth with a napkin.

"I just..." Kara shook her head, at a loss for words, but Molly all but shot up from the table, her finger jabbing at the window. From the reaction, Kara almost thought it was Santa Claus himself.

Jolting, Kara turned, her heart racing as she saw the judging panel crossing in front of her store. "Oh my goodness," she breathed. "This is it."

"Good luck, honey!" Rosemary said, crossing both sets of fingers in support.

Kara tittered nervously. "Thanks, I think I'll need it."

Slowly, she walked to the door, plastering a smile on her face as she held it open for the judges. They stared in confusion for a moment at the giant house that was set up on the table Kara had moved to the center of the room, and then began chatting among themselves in voices too low to hear, bending down to peer in windows, seeming to like what they saw.

They couldn't have been there for more than five minutes, but the seconds passed by so slowly, it felt like an hour until they said their polite goodbyes and slipped out the front door. Kara let out a long breath, not even realizing she'd been holding it in all this time, and sank into a chair.

"I can't believe I did it," she said.

"I can," said Rosemary, coming to sit down next to her. "Oh, Kara. The house...It's beautiful. Molly, come look, look at what your sister's done!"

Molly hurried across the room to stand next to their mother, gasping as she crouched to look through the windows of the house. "That's our living room! You even put the photos on the mantel just how they're arranged."

"And the tree." Rosemary paused to collect herself. "There's your father's star on top."

"And my elf ornaments!" Molly cried. She shook her head in wonder. "I almost forgot about those. Remember how Dad helped us make them that one year? We got glitter all over the kitchen and for once Mom didn't even care."

"How could I care? Those are priceless decorations!" Rosemary set an arm around Molly and wiped at her eyes.

"You like it?" Kara asked, searching her mother's face.

Rosemary blinked back the tears that shone bright in her blue eyes. "I *love* it."

Kara set a hand to her stomach, still waiting for the butterflies to leave it. She'd put so much time and energy into this one moment, and it was already over. "I just hope it was enough."

"To win the contest? Why shouldn't it be?" Her mother smiled. "Besides, even if it doesn't win, look what you've created! It reminds me of so many wonderful Christmases we've all shared together. You've brought a glimpse of that time back to us."

"Are those Daddy's slippers next to the chair?" Molly looked up, startled, but Kara also thought a little pleased at what she saw.

Kara nodded. "He loved those things, even though they were all worn out."

Rosemary pulled Kara in for a long, hard hug. "I don't think I've said it enough lately, but I'm proud of you, Kara, and I know your father would be, too."

Kara's eyes burned with tears that threatened to spill. But she knew from the looks on her mother's and sister's faces that if she started crying, none of them would be able to stop, and it was Christmas Eve. Now wasn't the time for sadness. Now was the time to look back on what they had and the memories that would always be with them.

She knew now more than ever just how lucky she was to have had those moments. Even if they didn't last a lifetime, for a while, things had been perfect. That was more than she could say for some people. Including, she thought sadly, Nate.

"I just..." She gritted her teeth. She rarely opened up to her mother about her worries and fears. She was too concerned they would only be confirmed. But something in her mother's eyes, in the connection they all had looking at a replica of a moment frozen in time, made it somehow feel all right. "I worry I'm going to let him down somehow."

Let you down, too, she thought to herself.

"But how? Look at all you've done, Kara. As a business owner myself, I know how much hard work it takes."

"Yes, but... what if someday it doesn't pan out and the doors shut? And the gift Dad left me, the inheritance..."

"It was put to a good use, Kara. You followed your heart. You've worked hard. That's all either of us expected from you."

"Thanks, Mom." Kara smiled, leaning in to give her mother another squeeze.

"Group hug!" Molly announced, maneuvering herself under their arms until she was part of the fold, and the awkward tangle of hair, arms, and limbs made Rosemary laugh, and soon, they were all joining in.

Definitely not a day for tears, Kara thought, her heart warming at everything she had this Christmas, even if the one person she'd wanted to share it with had made it clear that he didn't care to do any such thing.

Nate watched his aunt's expression as the judges walked from room to room, pausing every now and again to study a decoration or write something down on the clipboards they carried. Each time they lifted their pens, Maggie flinched, causing him to do so in turn. He hadn't expected to be this nervous, or this invested, but he was. He saw the look in his aunt's eyes, the approval she sought, the validation, and he couldn't help it—he wanted this for her.

About as much as he wanted it for Kara.

"Make sure they see the ten lords a-leaping," she whispered to him as the group moved into the dining room.

Nate nodded quickly. They'd decorated every inch of this old house, with the exception of the attic, and he wanted to be sure every detail was accounted for.

He moved to the back of the house just in time to see them move out onto the back patio, where they reacted with overt surprise to the swans a-swimming in the frozen pond.

"I think they've seen everything," he reported to his aunt as he came back into the lobby.

She was pale, her eyes brighter than usual as she stared at him. "Do you think they liked what they saw?" she asked anxiously.

"I think so," he said confidently. Even if they didn't win, they had to be a strong contender. He'd never seen anything like it. Again he was filled with a twinge of sadness when he thought of how much his mother would have liked to have seen all the decorations.

The judges came back through the main room and bid their goodbyes without a hint of insight into their innermost opinions. Nate whistled under his breath as the door closed behind the last of them. "They're a tough group," he said. "I've never seen so many poker faces!"

"It must be a tight decision this year, then," his aunt replied. She dropped into one of the armchairs near the hearth, her gaze turning pensive.

"You okay, Aunt Maggie?" he asked, coming to join her.

She briefly met his gaze. "I was just thinking, this might be my last Christmas in this house or running this inn."

"Please don't talk that way," he said. "You've got a lot of years ahead of you."

"I know, but I'm tired. I don't show it, but…it's a lot of work."

Nate pulled in a sigh. "Would you consider hiring someone—"

"I'd rather not," she replied quickly. "This is a family business." She eyed him carefully.

Nate nodded, knowing there was nothing he could say that would tell her what she wanted to hear. She was holding out hope that he'd change his mind, give in and move to Briar Creek, take over the inn, but he couldn't do that. Not to himself. Not to his parents.

He eyed the base of the tree, covered in a red velvet cloth.

He'd bought a few gifts for his aunt, ones he intended to give to her in the morning, but now he wondered just how many Christmases had passed where nothing sat under the branches. And he thought of all the kids he'd seen today at the Hope Center who would go to sleep tonight dreaming of things that would never come true and wake up tomorrow morning to find that all that magic, and all that hope, had been for nothing. That some children were lucky and others weren't.

He couldn't go back to that place. He wouldn't. He'd come too far. Worked too hard. Made it his mission to never be poor again, to never wonder where the next meal was coming from, how the next bill would be paid. It was because of him that his parents were living a comfortable life now. Because of him that they were on a cruise, enjoying the good life.

Because of him that they weren't having a Christmas at all.

His jaw tensed. "Aunt Maggie, I'm sorry I can't give you what you want."

She waved away his concern, but he could still make out the sadness in her eyes. "Nonsense. You stayed with me for Christmas. That's more than I could have asked for. Did you enjoy yourself?"

Nate didn't know how to answer that question. He leaned forward in his chair, balancing his elbows on his knees, and watched the flames flicker and crackle in the hearth. "It was a nice escape," he finally settled on.

"Well, it's a nice town. Nice people." She stared at him until he finally gave in and met her gaze. "You weren't here long, but it felt like you really fit into the community."

No thanks to her gentle persuasion. "I became friendly with some people, if that's what you're referring to."

"Your donation to the Hope Center was impressive," Maggie continued. "Don't think I didn't notice the merchandise being stored in my back closet. You're a generous man. Most successful men don't bother to give back."

"And some don't remember where they've come from. I didn't grow up with much; you know that."

She lowered her eyes. "I know. It was a sensitive subject, so we never let on, never offered overt help, even though we wanted to. Your father was a proud man, and the few times we suggested anything, he seemed to take offense."

Nate frowned. "I wonder if that's why we didn't visit very often."

"Oh, that, and your parents were both busy working. They weren't in a position to take time away. Neither were we, unfortunately. The inn never closes."

"My father worked hard. And you're right, he did take offense."

"It's a shame, really, that he saw it that way. All we wanted to do was show that we cared about him. That we were a circle of support. That's what our community is founded on. It's why I love Briar Creek so much."

Nate grew quiet, considering his father's attitude, mirroring it to his own. He was proud. Proud of what he'd accomplished, proud of the security he could now provide. But he wasn't proud of where he'd come from, was he? He was too worried about being judged. Just like his father had been. Too worried people would see him a little differently.

Even when they didn't.

Nate thought of the desperation in Kara's eyes when he told her about the little boy's Christmas wish for a new job for his father. She wanted to help. Like his aunt, like the people at his church growing up. And what was he doing to help? Tossing money or toys or food at a worthy cause wasn't going to change the lives of those children. They needed hope. Real hope. A path toward a future.

He was one of the lucky ones, he thought, thinking back to the school he'd gone to, the grades he'd worked for, the scholarships that were awarded. But not every kid had that drive. Or opportunity.

He turned to his aunt. "Do you think it's too early to give gifts?"

Her expression turned tickled as a hand flew to her chest. "A gift? I wonder what it could be!"

Nate didn't say a word as he walked to the staircase and up to his guest room. The painting was tucked in the back of the closet, where he'd last left it, the acrylic paint now dry. He hadn't wrapped it, but instead held it behind his back as he reentered the lobby.

"I know you wanted a painting above the hearth for the contest entry," he explained. "And I started to do that for you, but then…" He huffed out a breath. Some things just didn't need explaining. "I thought this made more sense," he said, bringing the painting out from behind his back and propping it against the coffee table.

His aunt let out a small gasp and then brought one hand to her mouth. She blinked rapidly, and Nate knew she was struggling to hold back tears as she looked at the painting of the inn, not as it had been decorated for the contest, but as it was the first night he'd arrived. Fresh snow fell in mounds along the shrubs, and two wreaths hung from the front doors. Across the way, there was a hint of Main Street, the town square, and the skating rink, where a couple was gliding, hand in hand.

It was a beautiful painting, one he was proud of, but it was a beautiful house, too. That couldn't be overlooked. Or forgotten.

"Can I ask you a question?" his aunt asked when she finally met his eyes, her own glistening. "What made you stop painting?"

"Time." He shrugged. "I had to keep up my grades to maintain my scholarship. I didn't have time for hobbies."

"Yes, but you had won so many awards for your art in high school. Why didn't you pursue that?"

Nate looked at her quizzically. "Art isn't exactly a lucrative profession, at least not for most people."

"So that's what mattered? You followed the money instead of your heart?"

"It's just a reality," Nate said evenly, but he felt his temper begin to stir. He'd have had to have been callous to enter into a risky or potentially low-paying profession when his dad was working himself to the bone for minimum wage.

"Perhaps," his aunt said sadly. "But sometimes, following your heart leads to the biggest reward of all." She smiled at the painting, lost in it for a moment. "Thank you for this, Nate. This inn is my home, my heart, and I can see from this painting that you really understood that."

They sat in silence until the flames began to die down in the fireplace, both admiring the painting that his aunt placed proudly over the mantel. Nate stared at the picture of the inn, of the life his aunt had lived, and he wondered just what might have happened if he'd followed his heart.

And what would happen if he suddenly did.

CHAPTER 23

It had snowed overnight. Kara knew before she'd even gotten out from under the warm duvet. There was a stillness in the air, a crispness in the light that poked through the curtains on her bedroom window. Growing up, she'd always found that a fresh dusting of snow on Christmas morning made things extra magical.

But right now, she wasn't feeling it. She wasn't feeling much, other than a heaviness in her chest and a sudden yearning to just have the entire holiday over with.

She'd hoped Molly would have spent the night with her, but her sister felt she should really be at home with their mother, and Kara understood. She supposed she could have stayed in her childhood home as well, but she'd felt the need to come back to her apartment last night and wake up in her own bed.

Oh, who was she kidding? A little part of her had hoped that she might run into Nate or that he might stop by. But Christmas Eve had come and gone without a word. And by this time tomorrow, he'd be gone. She supposed in some ways, he already was.

A ringing of a buzzer jolted her from her pillow, and she sat upright in bed, blinking into the empty room. She must have imagined it.

But no—there it was again. Her heart began to pound as she considered the possibility. Nate, standing downstairs, waiting to be let in. To talk. To...

She grabbed the clock on her nightstand and closed her eyes. It wasn't Nate. Of course it wasn't. What was there to even say, to salvage? It was her sister. Molly had said she'd pop by around ten, and here it was, ten sharp. Kara hadn't slept a wink past five in ages, and fatigue had finally caught up with her.

She slipped her feet into slippers, grabbed her robe, and padded to the front door to buzz her sister in. Peering through the peephole, she held her breath, just in case...But no. There was Molly, bounding up the stairs, all fresh faced and merry-looking.

"You look awfully happy this morning, considering..." Kara gave her younger sister the once-over. Her hair was brushed and neat, her eyes showed no sign of crying, and she was wearing red earmuffs to match her sweater.

"Well, merry Christmas to you, too," Molly said.

"Sorry." Kara sighed, stepping back. She rubbed her forehead. She felt strangely like she could go back to bed, sleep for another few hours. So much for breaking routine. "I just woke up, actually."

"Hmm." Molly pursed her lips, giving her a look of disapproval as she unbuttoned her coat and tossed it over the back of a chair. "You sure that's all? Your eyes look a little red."

Kara brought a hand to her cheek. She'd cried last night. She couldn't help it. It was silly, she realized now. So she'd felt a spark. It was just a nuance. Something others felt all the time. It didn't mean anything.

Except, why did it feel like it had?

"I told you," she said hastily. "I'm tired. This is the first day I've felt like I could breathe in a long time. Besides, you're the one everyone is worried about."

"Me? Why?" Molly wandered into the kitchen and, without being asked, began making coffee. Kara leaned against the counter and let her, already anticipating the first cup. It would clear her head, erase all these murky, heavy-hearted feelings that still plagued her. And after that, she'd shower, wash away the pain of yesterday, and get on with her day. The new year was almost here. No use dwelling on the past couple of weeks.

"I'm perfectly fine," Molly continued after she'd set the machine to brew. "I don't know why everyone thinks I should be falling apart."

Kara's chin dropped as she stared at her sister, who had the audacity to look all wide-eyed and innocent. "Molly, you and Todd broke up."

Her sister shrugged. "So?"

"So, last time that happened, you could barely get out of bed to shower," Kara reminded her.

"Well, it was different then. I was still in love with Todd then." She opened a cabinet and pulled out two mugs. Kara struggled to find words for her response.

"And...you're not now? But you were engaged. You accepted his proposal!"

Molly set the mugs down on the counter and sighed heavily. "I know I did, but...I shouldn't have."

Kara closed her eyes for a brief moment. "Oh, Molly."

"After Todd broke up with me, well, you saw how upset I was. I thought I would die without him. Dramatic, I know, but...I ached for him," she said, shaking her head sadly. "I got swept up, I lost sight of the fact that we had broken up in the first place for a reason. He's not the man for me."

Kara didn't say anything. She understood. Sort of. At least if the little tug in her chest since her conversation with Nate yesterday meant anything. It hurt. Badly.

The coffee had finished percolating, and Molly filled their mugs. She added a heaping spoonful of sugar to hers, and Kara added a splash of milk, before they brought their mugs into the living room and settled on the sofa.

"I thought, if he really wants me, he needs to make a commitment this time. And then he did! And then we were engaged, I guess. And then I was bringing him to the jewelry store where I'd picked out my ring."

Kara lifted an eyebrow pointedly. "When had you picked out this one?" Molly had been clipping photos of engagement rings for nearly as long as she'd been snipping photos of cake toppers.

"About a month earlier when the magazine ran a cover shoot of the newest collections." Molly grimaced. "If it had happened last year, I would have been stuck with a square shape. I know, I'm terrible."

"You're a romantic," Kara said. "And you love weddings."

"And I thought I loved Todd. I really thought so." She took a sip of her coffee and sighed. "It didn't feel right anymore. Maybe it was because he'd broken up with me, or maybe it was because I'd gotten over him. But I didn't feel it anymore. That spark. It was gone."

That spark. The one she'd finally felt...for the wrong man. "I'm not the one to talk to about sparks," Kara said tightly.

"Oh, but I think you are," Molly insisted. "I've seen the way you light up around Nate. That's how it should be."

"I was just caught up in the holidays. In his cute face. In..." In his kindness to his aunt, and to others. In his sense of humor, his easy wit, and his loyalty. "It doesn't matter now," she said, shaking away those thoughts.

"But it *does* matter," Molly said. "I almost sold out for a satin ball gown and a three-carat diamond."

"Was it really that big?" Kara asked, stricken.

"It was," Molly said, sighing. She flexed her bare ring finger. "But seeing the way you lit up these past couple of weeks, it made me realize I'd trade it all for half of what you felt."

"Oh, Molly," Kara said, feeling her eyes well with tears. She looked up at the tree in the corner of the room, thinking of the day she and Nate had set it up. Their first kiss. "It wasn't meant to be," she said, her voice feeling thick. She took another sip of her coffee. It was doing little to clear her head in the way she'd hoped. She supposed some things just took time.

"You never know," Molly encouraged. "But I'm glad you met him all the same. Now you know how it's supposed to feel. And I do, too."

Kara could only nod. "So much for a merry Christmas," she said wryly.

"Oh, I wouldn't give up that easily," Molly said, a sly smile curving the corners of her mouth. She set her mug down and crossed the room to her coat and handbag, where she produced this morning's newspaper, all rolled up and tucked into a plastic bag.

"Oh my goodness," Kara breathed. The Holiday House contest. She'd completely forgotten that the winner would be announced on the front page. She set her mug down before she spilled coffee all over her white sofa and pressed a hand to her stomach. "I feel like I might get sick."

But Molly wasn't backing down. Her arm was extended, the paper so close, Kara couldn't stall her much longer.

"Open it already," Molly pressed. "Aren't you curious?"

"More like terrified," Kara admitted, staring at the rolled-up paper. It was such a simple object, so plain, really, but in this moment, it was the worst thing she'd ever looked at. She held her hands up and brought the paper to her lap. Slowly, she pulled it free of the plastic bag, her breath stagnant as her heart beat double time in her chest.

"Oh, for God's sake!" Molly exclaimed, and leaned forward to yank the paper from Kara's hands. She opened it faster than Kara could process what was happening, and triumphantly held it up in the air.

Kara stared at the image, trying to process what she was seeing, what it meant. There, on the front page of the *Briar Creek Gazette*, was a picture of her childhood home…in gingerbread.

"Oh my God!" she cried, jumping to her feet to snatch the paper back. "Does this mean…does this mean…"

"You won, Kara! You did it!" Molly was laughing and shaking her by the shoulders as she jumped up and down.

Kara stared at her sister and then narrowed her eyes. "You knew all along!" she cried, giving Molly a playful swat with the paper.

"Well, I was going to tell you right away, but then you had to go and be in such a grumpy mood," Molly said, laughing.

"I can't believe this," Kara said, staring at the picture in wonder, the image blurring from her tears of happiness.

"I can," Molly said proudly.

"And I can, too," a voice in the doorway said.

Startled, Kara looked up to see her mother standing at the edge of the living room, beaming at her with shiny eyes.

So much for not crying on Christmas, Kara thought as she crossed the room to give her mother a hug. And when she looked over her shoulder to pull Molly in, too, she could have sworn her dad's star on top of the tree twinkled just a little more than usual.

• • •

It was a slow morning at the inn. Aunt Maggie had pre-pared a feast in honor of the holiday, opting for a sit-down hot meal instead of her usual buffet, and the few guests that had remained in town were now off in their rooms or wan-dering through the snow-covered town.

Nate busied himself by helping his aunt, but it did little to lessen the guilt he felt at leaving her tomorrow morning.

"Have you heard any news of the Holiday House con-test?" he asked conversationally as he dried the last of the dishes. He'd been putting it off all day, but he knew there was no denying it. Today the winner would be announced. He wasn't so sure how he felt about that.

Maggie took the plate from his hand and set it back on the stack in the cabinet. The dishwasher was already full and running, and Nate couldn't help but wonder how long it would have taken her to clean everything herself had he not been there to help.

"Found out first thing this morning," she announced.

He shot her a look in surprise. "What? But why didn't you tell me?" He searched her face, looking for a clue, but she just gave him a mysterious smile and tipped her head toward the door. "The paper's on the coffee table in the lobby. Go see for yourself."

Nate set the towel down on the counter and left the room, wondering why his aunt hadn't just come out and said it. She liked a bit of drama, he decided as he rounded his way through the dining room. No doubt she'd won but wanted to see the look on his face when he picked up the paper and saw—

He saw the cover before he was halfway into the lobby. There it was, the whole front page, just like he'd been hear-ing about since he'd arrived in town. Kara's gingerbread house. She'd actually won.

"It's a beautiful gingerbread house," Maggie said from somewhere behind him.

Nate picked up the paper and stared at the image. It was a beautiful house. Well done. Meaningful. A picture-perfect moment made of sugar and spice. He'd had a couple of those picture-perfect moments himself recently, thanks to her.

He set the paper down and turned to his aunt, resting his hands on his hips. "I feel like this is my fault," he admitted, giving her a long look. "I challenged Kara to the contest. She wouldn't have entered if it wasn't for me."

"There's nothing to apologize for!" his aunt proclaimed. "That girl deserved to win fair and square. Did you see that thing? She's certainly more talented than I gave her credit for."

"More talented than most gave her credit for," Nate added, thinking of what Kara had said about the passing comments, the people who had judged her on her past. They'd thought less of her, didn't believe in her.

But he had. Maybe it was because he saw through to her. Or maybe it was because he knew how she felt.

"But the money," he said, remembering everything his aunt had lost by not winning this contest.

She waved a hand through the air, dismissing his concern. "I told you, money isn't important to me." She picked up the paper and tapped the front page. "I came in second place. Did you see that?"

"So close," he said, frowning. He scanned the paragraph she was pointing to. Sure enough, runner-up.

"That's all I needed," she said, folding the paper carefully and tucking it under her arm. "A little recognition that this place is something special. As if my guests don't already remind me of that every day."

Nate smiled at her sadly. It pained him to think of this

place someday shutting its doors or being put up for sale. He could only imagine it pained his aunt even more.

He swallowed hard, the idea he'd come up with during his sleepless night still nagging him. He eyed his aunt, wondering if he should broach it, if it even made sense or was what she wanted. She hadn't suggested it. Was it even his place?

He blew out a breath. He decided to try.

"I know that my parents have been a bit distant over the years," he said. "But they care. They were going to come visit you this holiday."

"Your mother finally talked your father into it," Maggie replied. "I know."

Nate hesitated. "This may not be my place, but when I see an opportunity, I like to bring it to attention. This inn, it's your family home, you've said so yourself. And my parents...Well, what would you think about them helping out, taking over, eventually? They're quite a bit younger and—"

"And I can see now why you're the successful business genius you are!" she whooped, clapping her hands. Sobering, she looked up at him worriedly. "But do you think they'd go for it?"

"My mother would be in her glory," Nate said truthfully. He could see her now, living in this beautiful house, doting on guests, baking her gingerbread every Christmas. "And my dad, well, he wouldn't want to admit it, but he'd love it. And...I'd love it. And if I knew that they were going to be okay, that they had something...Well, you'd be doing me the favor, Aunt Maggie. Is it too much to ask?"

"More like it's the perfect solution," she replied. "And don't you worry about your father. I know how to get what I want when it comes to men," she said, winking.

Nate blushed. He realized she was right. She'd gotten him

right where she wanted him, hadn't she? And she'd probably been planning it all along.

He looked at the clock, then skirted his gaze around the empty lobby. It was quiet and still and he hated to ask his aunt for any more favors, but this was one time he had to be selfish.

"Can I ask you one more thing?" he hedged. "The tea. I know it's finished for the season but do you think you might be willing to set up a table in the dining room, the one near the window?"

"Christmas high tea. My pleasure. One serving?" she asked knowingly.

"Two," Nate replied. "With any luck."

CHAPTER 24

Kara was still pinching herself as she followed Molly down the stairs of her building to Main Street. Her step was quick, her heart a little lighter than it was before, and the smile hadn't left her face until—

"Oh no," she all but screeched as she ground to a halt on the snowy curb. She grabbed Molly's arm in horror and stared into her sister's deep blue eyes. "Mom's present! I completely forgot!"

She put a hand to her head, trying not to panic, but a cold sweat was sending chills down her body as she chastised herself for overlooking something so important. She looked frantically down the street, but she knew it was no use. The shops were closed. The only place open was the diner, and even that would be closing soon.

She thought of anything she might have, what she could give. She'd gotten Molly a bracelet. But her mother hated bracelets.

"Relax," Molly said calmly. "I bought her a necklace. It can be from both of us. I even kept the receipt, too."

"Oh, thank you," Kara gushed, and waited for her pulse to resume a normal speed.

"But between you and me, I think that gingerbread house was the real gift. Even if you hadn't won the contest, you still created something precious for our family. Thank you for that." Molly's eyes glistened for a moment, but she sniffed and gave a knowing grin. "Besides, you know what Mom really wants for Christmas."

Kara rolled her eyes. They all knew.

"I know that Luke has put her off, but did you see Grace at that cookie exchange?" Molly raised an eyebrow. "The girl must have eaten half the buffet. She made me look like I was on a diet."

Kara blinked. "You don't mean..."

Molly shrugged. "I can't be sure, but I have a feeling that by this evening, everyone will have gotten what they want for Christmas."

"I hope so," Kara said, but she wasn't so sure she had. Yes, she'd won the contest, but Nate was still gone, still convinced they were a mismatch, that she could never understand him. Maybe she couldn't. But she'd have liked to have tried.

Kara's car was parked around the back of the bakery in its usual spot, and Rosemary was at the diner, fetching Sharon, who insisted on serving Christmas breakfast each year to all the old widowers in town, who counted on her for it. Kara tried not to look across the town square at the inn as they cut around to the back of the building. Soon they'd all be piled in the car, on the way to her childhood home at the edge of town, and the celebration would begin. And she had a lot to celebrate this year.

And it was all thanks to Nate.

It saddened her, and she wondered again what he might be doing today, how he'd be spending his Christmas, if he was back to living in the past.

Guess she'd never know.

Her phone rang. "That's probably Mom saying Sharon needs a few minutes," Kara said, reaching into her bag. Only it wasn't her mother's number. Or her aunt Sharon's. It was Mrs. Griffin's.

"Hello?" she answered warily. No doubt the woman was calling to congratulate her, and Kara felt a little awkward, knowing the effort the innkeeper had put into winning the contest. But as she listened to Mrs. Griffin's request, she stopped walking.

"A cookie delivery?" she repeated. Beside her, Molly's expression was incredulous. "I'm sorry, Mrs. Griffin, but I'm closed for Christmas Day. I'd gladly make you some for tomorrow."

"But my guests!" the woman cried. "They need a dessert, and oh, my oven has gone out, today of all days. They'll have nothing to go with their afternoon cocoa after they come back from skating!"

Kara closed her eyes. There weren't many guests at the inn for the holiday, and a dozen cookies wouldn't take very long. She could probably have them baked, decorated, and delivered in about an hour, especially without any other pressing orders demanding her attention. And the poor woman had lost the contest. It seemed like the least she could do for her.

Still, the thought of seeing Nate made her tense. But then, Nate didn't seem to want to see her. He'd probably steer clear.

"All right," she sighed, swatting away Molly's indignant cry. "I'll be there in an hour or so."

She disconnected the call and dropped her phone into her bag. "It's Christmas," she told Molly.

But a slow smile had appeared on her sister's face. "So I've noticed."

• • •

An hour later, Kara was trudging across the town square, a box of snowflake cookies in her hands. She hadn't minded making them—if anything, she'd felt a bit nostalgic. Christmas would be over as of midnight tonight, and with it, her holiday offerings. She'd done it. Made it through the season and the rush of those first few months with a new business. She'd survived with little sleep but next to no major setbacks, at least not professionally speaking.

She stopped walking and eyed the inn. The entire town seemed to have fallen hush, and despite the lack of activity outside, she could only imagine what was going on behind the set of double doors, beyond the windows where lights shone brightly and almost, she dare say, invitingly.

For all she knew, Nate had already left town. He'd seemed eager enough to be on his way. He hadn't even bothered to congratulate her on winning. Much less stopped by for any other reason.

Kara squared her shoulders and lifted her chin as she crossed the street and approached the inn. She had nothing to be ashamed of. She'd opened her heart—for the first time ever, really—and it hadn't been accepted. Maybe Nate was right. Maybe they did come from two different worlds. In her world, you didn't judge someone for where they came from or what they'd been through. You saw them for what they were now. And Nate had made it clear that money, and the bottom line, trumped everything.

The door was unlocked, of course, and Kara hesitantly pushed it open, her eyes darting this way and that until she blew out a breath, happy to see no sign of Nate or that handsome grin that made her a little weak in the knees and, now, a little heavy in the heart. It was Christmas, and she wanted to focus on the good news the morning had brought, the hope she had for the future, not the disappointment of the past.

"Mrs. Griffin?" she called out in a stage whisper, lest she attract the attention of the man she was hoping to avoid.

She waited, listening for a sound of life, but the inn was quiet, so quiet she could make out the crackling of the embers falling off the logs burning in the fireplace. She waited a little longer, then checked her watch. Still nothing. She hated to just leave the cookies on the dining room buffet and leave—it was Christmas and that felt a bit rude. But she'd already delayed getting to her mother's house by an hour to make the cookies, and she didn't want to keep them waiting much longer.

Sighing, she finally gave up and decided to leave them on the buffet stand, where they wouldn't go unnoticed. She walked into the dining room, still hoping to catch the innkeeper herself, when she felt her breath catch.

There, standing at the dining room window, was Nate.

"Oh." She skirted her eyes to the door and then back to him. "Hello."

"Hi." His smile was hesitant and almost warm. Damn him. She didn't have time for his soft side. Didn't want to see it either. Tomorrow he'd be gone. Back to work. Back to his fancy job, his fancy apartment, and all the fancy things that all his money could buy him.

While she...She supposed she'd be doing what she loved, surrounded by those that mattered.

She wondered for the first time if Nate felt proud of himself. He should, she thought. But only partly.

Kara crossed the room and set the box of cookies on the buffet table. "Your aunt asked me to bring these over," she said as she turned to leave. "I'm sorry I can't stay and wish her a merry Christmas, but I'm afraid I'm already late as it is."

"Can it wait? Just a little while longer?" Nate added quickly.

Kara stopped walking toward the doorway and looked up at him. His eyes were clear and hopeful, but his jaw was tight. Tense. "I'm sorry, but I really should be going," she said, willing herself to be strong.

No good would come from lingering. There was nothing between them. Maybe there never had been.

"You won the contest," Nate said abruptly. "I saw it in the paper this morning. I'm really happy for you," he said, his voice a little scratchy.

Kara softened. But only a bit. "Thanks," she said.

"Your father is smiling down on you," Nate said, locking her eyes as he gave her a smile.

Kara swallowed the emotion that was building in her chest. Right. Time to leave.

"Don't think I've forgotten our bet," Nate said as Kara turned to go once more. "You won, fair and square." He held up a hand, motioning to the table near the window, where Kara noticed the flickering votive candles, the tea tray, the two wingback chairs cozily pulled together for a view of the snow-covered town square, glowing with fairy lights.

"What is this?" she asked warily.

"You won the contest," Nate said. "If memory serves me correctly, I owe you dinner. But seeing as it's Christmas, I thought this might be a little more festive."

Suddenly everything became clear. "Your aunt set this up, didn't she? That's why she called about the cookies." She tsked under her breath. She should have known.

"Actually, I asked my aunt to call you." His jaw tensed as his eyes bored steadily through hers, and Kara felt herself waver. But only for a second.

"This was all your idea? So, the cookies...?"

"I'm sorry to make you do the extra work," he said. "It was that or knock on your door. I wasn't so sure you would answer. And at the very least, I owe you a meal. I'm a man of my word."

"Are you?" She wasn't so sure anymore, but seeing the table, the candles, the effort he'd put into it, she dared to believe he was.

Except he'd had several other choice words the other day, too. Did he still mean everything he'd said?

"Nate." She shook her head. "It's too late. The things you said. I think you were right. We really are from two different worlds. And besides, you're leaving tomorrow anyway."

"And what if I said I wasn't?" he asked.

Kara felt her jaw slip. When her mind had stopped spinning, she leveled him with a long look and asked, "What do you mean?"

"I mean, what if I stayed?"

"After everything you said the other day?" She shook her head. "Why are you changing your mind now? Nothing has happened."

He took a step toward her. "But something has happened, Kara. I've felt differently since coming here. I started to feel like my life could be so much more than it is. More than it was," he added softly. He swallowed hard, shaking his head. "I was upset. Seeing those kids…It got under my skin. But you did, too."

He was telling her everything she wanted to hear, but she wasn't so sure it was enough. "You meant what you said. I know you did. About our differences and about your priorities. You belong in Boston."

"I belong here," he said so firmly that her breath caught. His stare was deep and long, and even though she wanted to look away, she couldn't. "You opened my eyes, made me see that it doesn't matter where I came from. Until you, I never thought a girl like you would really do anything other than misjudge me."

"A girl like me." She snorted. "Seems to me that you're the one judging people."

"Maybe," he said, shrugging. "Maybe so. And for that I'm sorry. You're...special, Kara. For a lot of reasons. And I couldn't let you go without a fight. Without you, I don't see much reason to stay."

Kara eyed him, trying to keep her eyes from shifting to the beautiful table set up behind him. "Oh, I'm sure your aunt would be happy to keep you here."

"She has what she needs now," he said quietly.

"And you? Do you have what you need?"

He jammed his hands into his pockets and shrugged. "I have my answer, I suppose. But not the one I had hoped for." His eyes had gone flat, and Kara's pulse flickered for a moment. He was giving up, taking her word for what it was, but she wasn't so sure if she wanted to stop fighting, either. If she was ready to end it here and now, in this room, next to the table he'd set up just for her. On Christmas.

She sighed, feeling her shoulders relax a bit. "You broke my trust, Nate," Kara said. *And my heart*, she said to herself. "I wasn't trying to upset you the other day—"

He held up a hand, cutting her off. "I know. It's my problem, my issue to resolve, and I've been going about it all the wrong way. But seeing you, how you were with those kids, how you gave not just money, but time and, well, love. I haven't forgotten it, Kara."

Kara swallowed the lump that had wedged in her throat, willing the tears that were prickling the backs of her eyes not to spill. He was a good man. She knew it before, and she knew it still. But was it enough?

"I just did what I could. As you said, it wouldn't change their circumstances."

"No, but it changed their day. And a few magical days like that can mean an awful lot to a kid." He took a step forward, and her breath stilled. A part of her wanted to move back, to run from the room, and the other part of her wanted to run right into his arms.

She didn't move. She needed to think.

Or maybe she just needed to follow her heart and, for the first time in her life, let herself fall. And believe.

"I want to give those kids another magical day," Nate said. "I want to give those kids the hope to see that their life can be so much more than it is right now. And I want those kids to know that it doesn't matter where they live or what they wear. It matters who they are."

"What are you saying?" Kara asked, searching his face.

"I'm leaving my job," Nate replied. "I have more than enough socked away, and who knows, maybe I'll still do a little consulting on the side. I like helping struggling companies succeed." He grinned, and despite herself, she did, too. "But for now, I want to do something else. I was thinking of starting a new youth program at the center."

"Oh, Nate." Kara blinked, and a tear slipped down her cheek.

"But I can't imagine doing any of those things without you. You're the reason, Kara. You opened my eyes. You made me rethink my future."

Kara closed her eyes as Nate reached up and brushed a tear from her cheek with the pad of his thumb. "You made me rethink my future, too."

"What do you say we start with today, then?" Nate's hand dropped from her cheek to grip her hand. His fingers were warm and smooth and solid, and she clasped his hand tightly, never wanting to let it go again.

"It is Christmas, after all," she said, smiling through her tears. "I can't think of a better day to start."

"Me neither," Nate said, wrapping his arm around her waist and pulling her in for a long, slow kiss. No mistletoe needed.

EPILOGUE

Okay, I have to say, your gingerbread house was amazing, but this..." Nate whistled under his breath as he scanned the living room of Kathleen Madison's house, where it seemed half the town had gathered to see Anna and Mark tie the knot.

"I know," Kara said, laughing. Either Kathleen had added more details since Anna made her big announcement or Kara had managed to overlook some of the beauty in her last visit, but now she couldn't stop staring at the heavy ivory velvet curtains that draped the floor-to-ceiling windows or the way the oversized silver candle holders on the mantel perfectly reflected the light. "I suppose we all came out on top this Christmas," she said, reaching over to take his hand.

A little tingle of excitement ripped through her stomach. Maybe she was getting ahead of herself, or maybe she had finally discovered what all the hype was about, but she couldn't help it: Being here, in this beautiful house, with the dozens of flowers filling the air with soft fragrance and the gentle sounds of piano wafting over the crowd, she could almost dare to imagine her own wedding day. But for now, she was looking forward to dancing with Nate later during the reception and then sharing a nice quiet evening together.

"Isn't this exquisite?" Molly said, coming to take the chair next to Kara. "I just told Kathleen the good news. The magazine wants to run a piece on the wedding. So few couples are getting married in their childhood homes these days, and this... Well, this is very inspiring."

"It is," Kara agreed, thinking that she would opt for a small, sentimental event over a big country club extravaganza any day. But then, she and Molly had always been different when it came to those things.

She eyed her sister, who seemed swept up in the details of the planning, the candlelight and flowers that lined the ivory carpet rolled out for the aisle. Maybe she and her sister weren't so different anymore, after all.

Molly elbowed her sharply, but her eyes never left the front of the room. Kara had to smile to herself. Her sister may have changed a bit, but some things stayed the same. The girl loved a good wedding. And so, Kara thought, did she.

"It must be starting soon. Here comes Mark."

Sure enough, Mark was striding to the front of the room, looking nervous and excited in his black tux, her brother Luke right beside him. Brett, she knew, would be walking their mother, Sharon, up the aisle. Since Mr. Madison was no longer with them, Henry had stepped in to escort Kathleen, who had done a fine job of hiding her nerves when Kara checked in on the girls before taking her seat, but she could see the tears in the woman's blue eyes, just waiting to spill.

The last of the Madison girls was getting married today, and next it would be Ivy and Brett's turn. And then... Kara eyed her sister. A few weeks ago, she might have said next it would be Molly's turn, but now, now she almost dared to think it could be her next.

Nate looked down and smiled at her as the music swelled and the procession began, and he squeezed her hand tightly, giving no sign of letting go. Kara watched with a knot in her throat as her aunt and cousin walked down the aisle, followed by Kathleen and Henry, and then Grace and Jane, both looking beautiful in soft gold-colored dresses, followed by sweet little Sophie, who was thrilled to be a flower girl. Again.

And then Anna. Her friend. Her mentor. The woman who had taught her how to bake, motivated her to follow her passion, and today, walking down the aisle of her childhood home to the only man she had ever loved, who inspired her to follow her heart.

"All my girls are married," Kathleen said, fanning her eyes as she stood near the cake. Though Kara had offered to make one for the couple, Anna had insisted on doing it herself. Kara had to laugh: Her friend was a hard worker; that much couldn't be denied.

"And now the next chapter begins," Rosemary said, clasping her hands together in excitement.

It was true. Grace and Luke were expecting a baby, and that meant that Rosemary and Kathleen would soon have a grandbaby to spoil terribly. Kara looked over at Jane, who shook her head to the waiter passing Champagne, and raised an eyebrow. Who knew, maybe there was more in store for the upcoming year than any of them knew just yet.

But looking around the room, at Anna in her simple but elegant ivory satin strapless A-line dress, and Mark, looking so proud, and Ivy and Brett huddled on one of the sofas, whispering into each other's ears, she couldn't help but think that all of their futures looked very bright indeed.

But none, perhaps, more than her own.

Across the room, Nate was making his way back to her, two Champagne flutes in hand. When he caught her eye, he winked. A subtle but intimate gesture that reminded her that even in this room of people, they were somehow connected, and that to him, she was set apart and special.

"Did your parents make it in safely?" she asked, thinking of the roads. It had snowed last night. Not much, but enough to give Anna's winter wedding a truly magical feeling.

"They did," Nate confirmed. "My mom was over-whelmed by the decorations. I think she's going to be very happy here."

"And your dad?" Kara almost hesitated to ask, but she had hope for the man, and she knew Nate did, too.

"He won't say it, but he's happy with the change. In typi-cal form, he went right to work, chopping wood for the fire, inspecting the house for potential repairs. It's important to him that he feels needed. It was Maggie who figured that out. I think it's the only way she got him up here at all."

"So that hernia she said she had was all a ruse then?" Kara pursed her lips and shook her head as she brought the Champagne glass to her mouth.

"Oh, completely. She had this all planned for months, I guess. It was all a ploy to get one of us up here for the Christ-mas holidays, sell us on taking over the house."

Kara slipped her arm around his waist. "Well, lucky for me then that you came along first."

He looked down at her, brushed a loose strand of hair from his forehead. "I'm the lucky one."

He bent down to kiss her, but at that moment there was a clapping of hands, and everyone was asked to quiet down for the toast. Kara leaned back against Nate's chest as Luke and Brett each took turns poking jabs at Mark, once the town's biggest catch and self-confirmed bachelor, and Grace and

Jane gave more sentimental, somewhat teary speeches sprinkled with fond childhood stories.

"So let me get this straight," Nate said as Anna and Mark took the center of the room for their first dance as husband and wife. "Anna is married to your cousin and her sister is married to your brother."

"That's right," Kara said, nodding.

Nate laughed lowly, giving her a quizzical glance. "Tell me, is everyone in this town related to everyone else somehow?"

"No, but we're still like one big, happy family." She looked up at the newest addition, giving him a soft kiss on the mouth as she set one hand on his chest. Pulling back, she looked into his eyes and smiled. "Welcome to Briar Creek."

As the wedding planner and maid of honor at her best friend's wedding, there's nothing Kate Daniels won't do to make her friend's dreams come true. So when Alec Montgomery, the infuriating—and sexy—best man threatens to derail everything, Kate is ready for battle. But as the electricity crackles between them, could planning the perfect wedding help Kate find her perfect match?

Please turn the page for
an excerpt from

One Week to the Wedding

the first book in Olivia Miles's new
Misty Point series!

CHAPTER 1

If there was one part of her job that wedding planner Kate Daniels struggled with most these days, it was the dress fitting. She used to enjoy these appointments, finding it a true perk to sit in a beautiful, sun-filled boutique, surrounded by breathtaking gowns made of satin, lace, or tulle. What wasn't to love other than the occasional meltdown of a bride who hadn't had much success with that crash diet, or the long, patience-testing afternoon spent with a bride who tried on every dress in the store—twice—and still couldn't make a decision? The wedding dress was the focal point of the entire ceremony, the object that flowers and lighting and even color schemes were built around, a symbol of hope and happiness and dreams that had finally come true.

Except not all dreams came true, Kate thought as she wrestled with the overstuffed silk pillow wedged behind her back. Her stomach roiled with bad memories, and she tried to stay focused on the reason she was here at all. Her best friend was getting married. She could have a good cry when she went home, and if recent history proved anything, she probably would. But right now she would hold herself together, show her support, and not let her own recent set-back taint what was a very special moment.

"Do you need any help?" she called out. It would be easier to make herself useful, help with a zipper or buttons or a train. Anything would be better than sitting on this too-stiff velvet love seat, trying not to let her gaze drift too far to the left, where another bride was trying on the very dress Kate had chosen for herself not so long ago, her girlfriends fawning over her selection.

"I'm fine. I just…Well, let's see what you think." Elizabeth stepped out from behind the dusty pink curtain of the dressing room wearing the classic ivory lace strapless ball gown she'd chosen months back when William first popped the question and she'd blissfully accepted, and despite the ache in her chest, Kate couldn't help but smile.

"You look stunning," she whispered. She had known Elizabeth since they were five years old and had been there every step of the way that had led to this day. How many summer afternoons had been spent twirling in their mothers' lingerie, clutching dandelion bouquets, Elizabeth's reluctant brother Simon bribed into playing the groom, even though he always took off across the lawn before the vows were complete?

Elizabeth turned uncertainly in the gilded three-way mirror that anchored the small store. "I was planning on wearing my grandmother's pearls, but now I think a necklace might be too much."

Kate nodded her head in agreement. "They're too formal for a beach ceremony. Besides, the gown speaks for itself." And it did. Some lace gowns could be heavy or overly formal, but this one gave just enough of a nod to the bride's classic style while still feeling summery and light.

"I think you're right." Elizabeth scrutinized herself in the mirror and released a nervous breath. "I just want everything to be perfect."

Kate smiled tightly. Every bride said the same thing. She'd said it herself at one time.

"It *will* be perfect," Kate said, standing up to fluff the back of the dress. "I'm seeing to it myself."

"You know why I'm so nervous, don't you?" Elizabeth turned to face her properly, her eyes clouding over as her mouth thinned. "William's brother."

Kate did her best to hide her smile. Every wedding she planned had some element of familial tension, and in this case, the source was rooted with the best man. Oh, she'd dealt with her share of unruly wedding party members—groomsmen who hit the bar a little too hard during the cocktail hour, bridesmaids throwing hissy fits over their ugly dresses, mothers-in-law showing up in white—and Alec Montgomery was no different, really. Though she hadn't met him, she knew enough about him to know that he'd show up and play the role as dutiful brother. He and William were close, after all. And society weddings didn't leave room for public outbursts or noticeable drama.

No, that was usually left behind the scenes, she thought, chuckling to herself when she considered all she heard and saw.

She checked the row of satin-covered buttons on the back of the dress, making sure none were loose. "You'll be so caught up in the excitement of the day, you won't even notice he's there," Kate assured her, knowing this was true. People claimed they barely remembered their wedding day, that it was all a blur. That it was too surreal to capture. Too overwhelming in its emotion.

Kate released a soft sigh. Not that she would know.

"I'm still amazed he even agreed to come to town early

for all the festivities, what with how glued to that office he is." Elizabeth tutted as she took her veil from the sales associate and set it on her head. "At least I'll be so busy this week, I won't have to spend much time with him. But given how little he approves of William marrying me, or should I say, marrying into my average American family, I wouldn't put anything past him."

If it were any other bride, she'd chalk it up to high emotions, but Elizabeth was levelheaded and not prone to exaggeration. Kate laughed nervously, wishing she could better disguise her growing alarm. There was no way that anything or anyone could upset this wedding. If that happened, Elizabeth wouldn't be the only one in tears on Saturday. Kate would be crying all the way to the unemployment line.

"Oh, he won't," she said with a dismissive wave of her hand. "It will be the happiest day of your life. I promise."

Elizabeth looked unconvinced. "If you say so."

"I do say so." If she had any control in it, at least one of them would have the wedding day that they deserved. Kate turned her friend's shoulders to face the mirror, admiring their reflection. "I still can't believe you're getting married," she said, feeling that tug in her chest again.

"Me neither," Elizabeth said, her tone laced with wonder. Kate recognized the sound of it—the disbelief that all your dreams could actually be coming true. That years of hoping and waiting were over. That you could be so lucky. That your entire future was decided, and bright.

It echoed the emotion Kate had felt once. She blinked quickly, then smoothed Elizabeth's veil, trying to not think about everything that had happened instead.

An hour later, Kate triumphantly scratched the final dress fitting from her to-do list and said goodbye to Elizabeth, waving cheerfully from her perch on the cobblestone steps outside the bridal salon. She held her smile until her friend was safely out of sight and then fell back against the wrought-iron railing with a frown. For months she had obsessed over every detail of this wedding—right down to spending an excruciating amount of time holding various invitation samples to the light to determine the closest shade of pink to the bridesmaid's gowns—but not everything, she knew, could be controlled. An inebriated guest, she could handle. A sniffling flower girl, sure. But a stubborn man who didn't support the wedding? He'd require a tight leash.

And that was why she, as best friend, maid of honor, and wedding planner extraordinaire, was going to personally greet him upon his arrival.

It was a warm June day, and the downtown streets of Misty Point were filled with tourists mingling around, browsing boutiques and antique shops and lining up at the ice cream parlor. Kate made a mental note to pick up a fresh paperback at the bookstore before heading home. These days they filled her spare time just fine—plenty of excitement but all the drama neatly resolved by the last page.

A wave of salty sea air accompanied her as she tapped along the cobblestone to the Beacon Inn. She'd personally seen to the out-of-town guest room reservations, and she knew the arrival times of the entire wedding party. She couldn't fight the satisfied smile that played at her lips when she reflected on her diligence. It was because of her attention to detail that she knew the best man was arriving from Boston this afternoon. *Take that, Alice*, she thought with a shiver of glee.

She knew what her boss thought of her these days. Incompetent. Frazzled. Alice Fielding had a comment for everything Kate did wrong lately, but never anything she did correctly. Not long ago, Kate was a rising star at Bride by

Design, and she was determined to remind herself and her boss that she still had what it took to succeed in this business.

Everything was riding on this wedding being perfect.

The Beacon Inn was an icon in Misty Point and the perfect introduction to their quaint Rhode Island beach town. Kate was confident that guests traveling from all over the country would be impressed with the panoramic Atlantic views and the sweeping front porch dotted with white rocking chairs. Hotel guests relaxed on deck chairs and played croquet on lush green grass that stretched to the sea, where the waves silently lapped at the white sand. Seeing it now, Kate felt her heart swell with hope in place of nerves. This was going to be the most beautiful wedding she had ever planned. There was absolutely nothing to worry about.

Still…better safe than sorry. She pushed through the large front door and stepped into the expansive lobby, helping herself to a piece of saltwater taffy at the front desk. A quick conversation confirmed that Alec Montgomery had not yet checked in, and with a lingering glance around the room, Kate marched back out onto the veranda and settled into a rocking chair. It creaked beneath her on the sand-worn floorboards.

"Lemonade, miss?" a young waiter in crisp white inquired. Kate shook her head quickly. She wasn't here to enjoy the scenery or hotel perks. She was here to make sure everything was going to plan.

Kate checked her watch and bit down on her lip. She hadn't the faintest clue what Alec even looked like, only going off his brother's dark looks and the less-than-flattering stories she'd heard over time from Elizabeth. Still, she was sure she would recognize him when she saw him. She prided herself on her razor-sharp instinct, which rarely failed her.

Except that one time.

Determined to stay focused, she scanned the new faces as they strolled up the stairs to the grand entrance. Bellhops carrying heavy luggage followed close behind. Frowning, she knit her brow and ruffled in her bag for her notebook. In large, loopy scroll she wrote Alec's name and propped it against her bare knees, feeling all at once silly and paranoid. What would she even say to him when he appeared? She laughed softly, realizing just how touchy she was being these days. She was probably overreacting. And so was Elizabeth. The man might not be the bride's greatest admirer, but the groom was his only brother, after all, and it wasn't like he was skipping the event.

"Excuse me?"

Kate jumped in her chair and lifted her chin to face the owner of the smooth, deep voice. Her pulse began a slow and steady drum as she stared at the man before her. With rich brown hair that curled ever so slightly, Alec was a good two inches taller than his brother, but there was little doubt to their relation.

"Alec Montgomery?" she asked quickly as she stood to meet him.

Alec's dark eyes crinkled with confusion as he scanned her face. The corners of his mouth curved upward into a surprisingly friendly smile that made Kate feel nothing short of ridiculous for being so wary of his motives. "I'm afraid you have me at an advantage. You are?"

Kate shook her head in apology and flashed an equally bright smile. Even with her in heels, he towered over her. "I'm Kate Daniels," she said, realizing that probably wasn't enough explanation. "The wedding planner."

"Ah yes. We exchanged a few emails about the bachelor party, if I recall."

He gave her hand a firm, well-practiced shake. His palm

was smooth but strong and Kate let the warmth of his touch spread through her fingertips. It was hot outside, and even the sea breeze did little to break the heat. She had the unnerving sensation that her hand was a little slick.

"So you're the wedding planner." His gaze roved over her until she shifted on her feet uneasily. Elizabeth had said many things about this man, but never had she mentioned how cute he was...

"I didn't see you come in," she said, feeling her cheeks flush as she tried to stay professional. Was it always this hard to keep eye contact with someone? He probably had a girlfriend. There was no reason a man like Alec would be single. So really, she was being silly.

"I didn't know someone would be waiting for me." He pointed to the sign. "It's nice to know someone is thinking of me." He winked as his lips curved into a broad smile.

Kate felt her defenses prickle. Was he *flirting* with her?

She cleared her throat, eager to get back to the reason for her visit. "I was passing by the hotel and I thought I'd stop by and see if you'd arrived. If the room suited you..." She trailed off with her excuse as she awkwardly thrust the makeshift sign into her tote. Really, she should have just bided her time, checked in occasionally at the front desk, and called up to his room. And she would have, if she didn't have another hundred things to accomplish in the span of a matter of days.

The paper crumpled under her awkward movement, and Kate had the uneasy feeling that Alec was watching it all. She pressed her lips together and forced herself to look up at him. Yep. There was a decided gleam in those deep-set eyes. She broke his stare, her eyes roaming over the black canvas backpack thrown over Alec's shoulder and down to the bulging briefcase at his feet. It was time to remember why she was here. "Have they already taken your luggage to your room?" she asked, tilting her head.

"Got everything I need right here." Alec smiled as he patted his backpack, and Kate felt that little pinch between her eyebrows deepen.

"That's all?" She blinked rapidly.

Alec shrugged. "I travel light."

"Hmm," Kate murmured, trying to understand the implications of this scenario. There was no way he could have stuffed a suit into that bag. Much less a pair of shoes. The wedding attire would be taken care of, but what was he planning on wearing for the rehearsal dinner?

Her mind raced with the implications of this problem as her eyes latched on to the briefcase sitting quietly at his feet. She could take him shopping or direct him to a few appropriate stores . . . but if a man were this helpless when it came to proper clothing, chances were she'd have to guide him through it. If she switched around a few appointments the day after next, she could squeeze it in. Or they might find something suitable at the best man fitting. She chewed on her thumbnail, trying to think through the tight schedule.

"I'm kidding!" His voice boomed and Kate lifted her eyes to see Alec laughing and shaking his head. His smile was wide, his teeth perfect, and his eyes glimmered with pure mischief. "The bellhop is taking my luggage upstairs. I checked in a couple minutes ago and thought I'd stroll the grounds." He gestured to his briefcase. "This is just full of files. Business stuff."

"*Business*?" This week was supposed to be about the bride and groom. Her pulse began a slow and steady drum as her inner alarm bells tolled. "What do you mean, *business*?"

Alec shrugged. "I can't be expected to put my life on hold simply because my brother's getting hitched, can I?"

"It's only for a few days," Kate said archly. She was starting to see what Elizabeth meant about this man.

"A few days too many," he continued with a sigh. "I'm a busy man. And all this little wedding planning stuff is an inconvenience I really can't afford right now."

An inconvenience. Little wedding planning stuff.

Narrowing her gaze, she stared at him with sudden contempt, disgusted with herself for even briefly falling for his earlier charm. Honestly, one would think she would know better by now!

"This wedding may not be important to you, but I can assure you it is very important to your brother and Elizabeth." *And to me*, she thought. "If you have a few minutes, I thought we could quickly go over the plans for the rehearsal dinner."

Alec looked at her in surprise. "Right now? I thought my father was taking care of this."

"He hasn't arrived yet and I need some last-minute input. Since your family is hosting, I thought you might have a few personal things to contribute."

Alec glanced at his watch with a look of impatience. "What time is the bachelor party tonight?"

"Eight," she replied, pleased to have been able to answer so quickly. She'd memorized the entire week's schedule of events, but she still carried a hard copy with her, just in case.

"Who the heck plans a bachelor party for a weeknight, anyway? Isn't this usually a weekend activity?"

"It was the only way all the guests would be able to attend," she said. "Most are from out of town."

Alec shrugged, seeming to accept this. "Well, I don't have time to go over plans for the rehearsal dinner right now."

Kate took the opportunity to flash her biggest grin. Guilt was always a last resort, but one she fell back on all too often in heated situations like this. "I know it means *so* much to William that your family is hosting the rehearsal dinner." She didn't bother to add that it was also, typically, tradition.

Alec frowned at her. "And how do you know that? You're just—"

Kate interrupted before he could say something that would cement her displeasure with him. "Elizabeth's best friend," she said warningly, her eyes wide with meaning.

Alec's brow creased and he clamped his mouth shut as he studied her. "I thought you were just the wedding planner."

Just the wedding planner. "I am. And I'm also Elizabeth's best friend. And the maid of honor," she added with a smile. "So as best man, you should expect to be seeing a lot of me for the next few days."

And that, she realized, was something she didn't know what to make of anymore. That this man was about to cause her an inexplicable amount of grief, she was certain. But in just how many ways, she was yet to find out.

Fall in Love with Forever Romance

MERRY CHRISTMAS COWBOY
By Carolyn Brown

No one tells a cowboy story like *New York Times* bestselling author Carolyn Brown. So grab your hot chocolate and settle in because this Christmas, Santa's wearing a Stetson. Fiona Logan is everything Jud Dawson thought he'd never find. But with wild weather, nosy neighbors, and a new baby in the family, getting her to admit that she's falling in love might just take a Christmas miracle.

Fall in Love with Forever Romance

A CHRISTMAS BRIDE
By Hope Ramsay

USA Today bestselling author Hope Ramsay's new contemporary romance series is perfect for fans of Debbie Macomber, Robyn Carr, and Sherryl Woods. Haunted by regrets and grief, widower David Lyndon has a bah-humbug approach to the holidays—until he's shown the spirit of the season by his daughter and her godmother Willow. Paired up to plan a Christmas wedding for friends, David and Willow will discover that the best gift is the promise of a future spent together...

Fall in Love with Forever Romance

CHRISTMAS COMES TO MAIN STREET
By Olivia Miles

It's beginning to taste a lot like Christmas...or so Kara Hasting hopes. Her new cookie business is off to a promising start, until a sexy stranger makes her doubt herself. Fans of Jill Shalvis, RaeAnne Thayne, and Susan Mallery will love this sweet holiday read.

Fall in Love with Forever Romance

A HIGHLANDER'S CHRISTMAS KISS
By Paula Quinn

In the tradition of Karen Hawkins and Monica McCarty comes
the next in Paula Quinn's sinfully sexy MacGregor family series.
Temperance Menzie is starting to fall for the mysterious, wounded
highlander she's been nursing back to health. But Cailean Grant
has a dark secret, and only a Christmas miracle can keep them
together.

VISIT US ONLINE AT

WWW.HACHETTEBOOKGROUP.COM

FEATURES:

**OPENBOOK BROWSE AND
SEARCH EXCERPTS**

•

AUDIOBOOK EXCERPTS AND PODCASTS

•

AUTHOR ARTICLES AND INTERVIEWS

•

**BESTSELLER AND PUBLISHING
GROUP NEWS**

•

SIGN UP FOR E-NEWSLETTERS

•

**AUTHOR APPEARANCES AND TOUR
INFORMATION**

•

SOCIAL MEDIA FEEDS AND WIDGETS

•

DOWNLOAD FREE APPS

Bookmark Hachette Book Group
@ www.HachetteBookGroup.com